LIE STILL

WILLIAM MORROW

AN IMPRINT OF HARPERCOLLINS*PUBLISHERS*

LIE STILL

A Novel of Suspense

DAVID FARRIS

HarperCollins books may be purchased for educational,
business, or sales promotional use. For information please write:
Special Markets Department, HarperCollins Publishers Inc.,
10 East 53rd Street, New York, NY 10022.

FIRST EDITION

Designed by Gretchen Achilles

Printed on acid-free paper

Library of Congress Cataloging-in-Publication Data
Farris, David, 1954–
Lie still : a novel of suspense / David Farris.—1st ed.
p. cm.
ISBN 0-06-050554-0
1. Emergency physicians—Fiction. 2. Hospital patients—Fiction. I. Title.

PS3606.A74L5 2003
813'.6—dc21   2002044899

03   04   05   06   07   JTC/BVG   10   9   8   7   6   5   4   3   2   1

For Kendra
MY ROCK, MY OXYGEN

ACKNOWLEDGMENTS

The better parts of this work owe much of their existence to many godparents, critics, coaches, cheerleaders, and midwives. My courageous early readers were Nancy Reichley, Teresa Dooling, Andrea "Radar" Tworek, Tudy Brody, John Paul Blodgett, Janet Smith, and Heidi Goetz. My steadfast consultants were Detective Shirley McLaughlin, Dr. Monica Wehby, and Richard Dooling. Marianne Merola and Theron Raines gave generous professional critiques. Trish Grader found me a home at William Morrow.

Any effort to adequately acknowledge the roles of Sarah Durand, editor, and Henry Dunow, agent, etc., would likely create an embarrassing mess. Here I'll say only that without you I'd have been four-plus DOA.

Kendra, Brian, and Nicko—you kept me *stable*.

Finally, many dozen doctors, nurses, technologists, and patients at Maricopa County Hospital in Phoenix, a lot of years ago, made me— kicking and screaming—into a doctor. Along the way, I've learned from hundreds more. The clinicians and their charges at Portland's Emanuel Hospital inspire me daily. Witnessing the sweating, tireless commitment of talented professionals and the painful, quiet dignity of the aggrieved is a constant reminder of what it's all about.

LIE STILL

1

HENRY ROJELIO, DAY ONE

All she said was, "Doctor, he's turning blue." She spoke the words softly, quickly into my ear. I turned to look, expecting a grin. All I got, though, was backside, hurrying away to the exam bay, like a game of tag.

I've relived it a million times. It wasn't a game, it was a play. A stage whisper blurted by a vanishing actress. She knew her audience. She told me the patient was cyanotic—cyan-colored, like ice—but the delivery had its own message: *I may be new here, but I'm not panicked. I've done this before; I'll do it again.* On TV she would have stood up straight and tall in the center of the ER and ceremonially announced just short of a shout, "Doctor! The patient is *acro-cyanotic*. Come *stat!*" Writers love the word *stat*. Clinicians only use it when they're pissed off. *Stat* is Latin for "hurry the fuck up."

Anyway, that's how it started. *Henry, Day One.*

She got exactly the response she wanted. On cue, I thought, *Bullshit.* I probably snorted. Robin Benoit was a nurse. I knew well the common doctorly chauvinisms about nurses as diagnosticians.

In all the retelling, the reliving of the opening—for the other doctors, the family, my closest friends, my parents, the police, the lawyers, and over and over for myself—I have always admitted that I hesitated, though only for a few seconds.

Don't misunderstand me. I would never let a patient lie there starving for oxygen for even a millisecond, no matter whose ego is on the line. But I did not believe thirteen-year-old Henry Rojelio really could have been blue. Not ten minutes earlier he and I had been talking about baseball and his crooked penis. He was not that physically sick.

Nor did my hesitation make one whit of difference. The record will support that. Five seconds was not long enough to have mattered. But the issue has never laid down and died.

Professional machismo looks lousy in the hindsight of self-recrimination.

I was on the phone. I ended the call, abruptly, then sat there with a vacuum-tube stare long enough to show that I wasn't impressed and certainly wasn't panicked either. This from the rules I'd learned early on: Never run. For punctuation I took a last gulp from my can of Squirt and made a point of finding my stethoscope. "Where's my fucking stethoscope?" I remember saying out loud. I was annoyed. Whether the patient's cyanosis is real or imaginary, it's a pain in the ass for all concerned. I patted all my pockets, then found it looped over my shoulders. All this may have added five seconds to the downtime. That could not have been critical. I sauntered after Robin. I didn't—I wouldn't—believe her. Five seconds.

Though new to me, Henry had been a regular in the Glory ER. His chart—which I had dutifully read over—was into its fourth volume. At his worst he was only a moderately bad asthmatic. When I listened to his chest on admission he was not all that tight, and he was getting over-aggressive treatment as it was. True "blue" was not possible.

I pushed open the door, smiling, stupidly optimistic that a doctorly presence would right the misdiagnosis and end the scurrilous rumors. It had worked before.

He was, however, lying oddly flat and straight, unconscious and limp, and by-God blue all right. And starting to turn a mottled gray, which is worse than blue, because it's what comes next.

I thought to turn around, not to run away, but to find the Resident-Who-Knew-What-to-Do. For almost all of my time tending patients, there had been somebody at least one year further along in training standing behind me, sheltering both the patient and me. Certainly I'd signed on in little Glory to be The Doctor, but I had hoped to avoid conflagration at least until the locals had come to trust me. I knew I was a good doctor despite anything they might have heard. They'd told me it was a quiet little ER in a quiet little town, and no one would bother me. Turns out, though, sickness is pervasive.

I was, I confess, paralyzed. Though not as long as they tried to imply. A second can seem so long. Panic, however ephemeral, looks bad. All my brain parts were going off at once, chattering and bickering. "Hurry, think, hurry, think, hurry, think." Robin, bless her heart, spoke, coaching me. "Is he breathing?"

I put the back of my hand an inch under the boy's nose, hoping for a tiny current or hint of warmth. Nothing was moving. Of course he wasn't breathing; that's why he was so goddamn blue. He was, though, a known malingerer. It said so in his chart. Maybe he was holding his breath. I'd heard mothers swear their children would hold their breath long enough to turn blue, but I'd never seen it. I didn't really believe it possible, but at that moment I was willing to believe in the Tooth Fairy if she could help. I dug a knuckle into his sternum, hard, and twisted it. It's one of the accepted bits of medical sadism we use to weed out fakers and wake up drunks. Henry, however, lay still.

He was dying or maybe already dead. He needed me to breathe for him. I looked for the bag. Every ER room in the world is supposed to have a breathing bag and mask in plain sight, ready to go, no glass to break in case of emergency. It's usually hanging on the wall by the oxygen outlet. In Henry's room there was only a stripe of yellowed adhesive tape, loose at one end, no bag. The breathing bag had not been replaced from the last disaster, which, in this backwater, may have been years earlier.

I imagine there are times in every profession when you feel as though you are the last fledgling hawk or hawklet high up the rock wall in a canyon and it's time to see if your upper extremities are functional or merely decorative. You sit on your ledge and look down and all around for as long as you can. Then you jump.

Just as I'd done on vinyl dummies, only faintly fearful I'd ever have to do it on flesh and mucus, I tilted his head back, pinched his nostrils, sealed my mouth over his, and blew in. I think his chest rose like it was supposed to, but it wasn't as if I knew what a good chest rise looked like. This was my first time. I muttered an inanity, "Holy shit," then the obvious: "Get the crash cart."

"It's here," Robin said.

I gave Henry another breath. I did indeed know what to do.

Henry's chest rose, I was sure, but only a little, then fell. A gurgling sound came from his lips. I stuck my thumb into his mouth, under the tongue. I wrapped my other four fingers over the chin, closing a circle around the jaw, and pulled up. I held it there with my other hand and tried a third breath. It moved a bit more air.

The next step seems odd. It's peaceful. You check for a pulse. You lay two fingers on the throat, just to the side of the trachea, and try to dig them gently under the muscles and feel the carotid artery. Even with only a very weak pulse, say a blood pressure of 40, they say you can feel it there. It's peaceful because you stand perfectly still. You can't have anybody jerking the patient's clothes off, sticking in IVs, or doing CPR. In fact, you really want it quiet. You get a glazed-over stare. Your eyes aren't focusing on anything. All your focus is in your fingertips.

Until you've done it, you think it's an easy call. That's what they blithely teach in CPR: "Check for pulse." Either there's a pulse or there isn't. But in a real live or maybe dead person, when there isn't, you keep thinking it's your fault. You're missing it. "It's weak but it's there." "Try a little farther over that way; no, back the other way." "Surely there's a pulse." "There ought to be a pulse there."

Robin was rummaging in the crash cart. She was hurrying to uncoil a length of green plastic oxygen tubing. She jerked on it violently to straighten a tangle, then slammed the cart drawer shut. I said, "Could you be quiet for just a second?"

Immediately she was as still as the other two of us, staring at me. Her I'm-not-panicked bit was gone: She looked terrified.

As much as I wanted there to be a pulse in that boy's neck, I couldn't find it.

I had already waited too long in Fantasyland. That's always how it is. Time slips by as you try to find a way around admitting that the heart really isn't beating and by God you need to do chest compressions, and by God, now that you think of it, you should have been doing them for some time now. You don't want to admit, on the hospital overhead speakers, The Reaper is winning. But you have no choice: I called a code.

"Launch" is probably the better verb. It's a rocket with a very short fuse. You strike the match and make sure you can get the hell out of the way because a million things are about to happen, and the process, unless you and someone from Hospital Security physically block the door, will run its course. "Get help" is all I said. That's all it takes. I closed my eyes for half a second and when I opened them Robin was gone. I heard her shout just outside the door, then someone running, then another voice shouting.

I felt Henry's breastbone and walked my fingers down to its end. I backtracked an inch and squared the heel of my left hand in the center of his chest. I put my right hand on top of my left, locked the fingers together, then rose up on the balls of my feet, directly over him. The gurney was too high for me to lock my elbows, but I could still bear my weight into his chest, feeling for what I guessed was just enough "give" to squeeze the heart between the spine and the ribcage and pump blood downstream.

I wondered what a small-town code team would look like. I don't often pray but I remember thinking of God, and for a couple of milliseconds I might have asked for mercy for Henry, and just as much for me.

Even alone and scared I was thankful to be doing something physical. Just like everyone else doing CPR for the first time, I didn't know if I was doing it right. I imagined his heart being squeezed under my palms, then passively refilling. Once as a med student I watched an intern do chest compressions on a pulmonary cripple who had a line in the artery in his wrist. We could see on the monitor the blood pressure waves she was generating, and she adjusted her stroke to the best wave. In him at least, the best flow came with a sharp and frighteningly deep squeeze. His ribs cracked. The intern winced. The resident said, "It's better than staying dead." He did that also.

I bore down on Henry's chest, trying to do the same kind of stroke. I counted to fifteen, because that's what I'd learned in CPR class. I gave him two more breaths, then started over. The eternity of pumping and breathing alone probably measured less than ninety seconds by the clock.

He was an awful color. I stopped once and again laid my fingers on his throat. Some patients bounce right back. If my desire counted, his carotid would have been booming. I tried to invoke all my years of study and training and a fiercely wrought want and strength of will. As if it might help.

The exam room door jumped open, shattering our silent supplication. It hit the wall behind it and shook with a deep bass vibrato. Patty Kucera, RN, one of the ER regulars and a sizeable woman of around six feet and 280 pounds, was first of the motley cavalry of backwater medicine to charge in. On her heels were two other women, a tall man in hospital scrubs, and Robin.

I had run codes as an intern, but when you're the intern giving orders to an experienced code team, it's like being a little kid telling Mom what goes next in the cookie dough. She'll do what you say as long as you say the right thing. If you say the wrong thing, Mom will do the right thing and smile at you. You'll learn. I knew the approved protocols for a standard code, but sometimes that's not enough.

The best spot at a code is the one standing over the patient's heart, bobbing up and down. The job is at once the most mindless and the most critical. You can look around, talk to people, smile sometimes. It is like sex: You can do it with empathy and passion or you can do it with your head in the next county—if your mechanics are adequate the immediate outcome likely will be identical. It is not, however, the place for the person who's supposed to be making decisions, so I tagged Patty to take over the chest compressions.

It's a sea change to go from the physical simplicity of one-rescuer CPR to the role of the Guy-in-Charge-of-the-Code. I stood there for a second knowing I was forgetting something. I mouthed to myself, "ABC. Airway, breathing, circulation." I asked, "Where's Respiratory?"

"Right here, Doc." It was the lone male in the crew, a respiratory therapist—RT—named Roger. He had somehow materialized a breathing bag and mask and was jamming the mask onto the boy's face, squeezing in oxygen. He gave me a little sideways grin. He was straining to hold the mask tight to Henry's face with one hand. The mask was too big and half the oxygen was being expelled over the eye sockets with a farting noise. Even so, the chest was definitely moving.

Vickie Rhoades, the evening shift charge nurse out on the wards, slit Henry's sleeves and pant legs with long gliding scissors strokes. In

seconds he was naked
around his neck and co
tucked the free parts of t
flop around and get pulle

Vickie wrapped a wide
left biceps area and slip-kn
vein over the elbow, wiped
She finessed the catheter ot
on the vein with the other
tourniquet, connected the lin
spilling a drop of blood. The

"Got an IV," she said. "D
now. Atropine and epi going in

I was blank. There was no ı _____ gıve sugar. I mumbled, "No.
Hypoglycemia this isn't."

"It's protocol," she said.

"Well, okay, I guess it won't hurt. We'll try everything."

"Narcan?" Vickie asked.

Again a blank. Narcotic reversal? "He a user?" I asked.

"No. Protocol."

I said, "Sure. Wouldn't want to buck protocol." She smiled and
nodded.

Patty was breaking a sweat over Henry's chest. "You need a break?"
I asked her.

"Naw, I'm fine."

Two more women had come in, but there was nothing immediate
for them to do. They stood waiting for a job, adding their worry. One
said, "Oh my God, it's Henry."

Half the hospital's evening personnel were in the room. "Who's
tending shop?" I asked.

"Beulah," Patty answered with a grunt.

"Who's she?"

"Ward secretary. She'll call us if somebody needs something important." In a thirty-bed hospital even the secretary will know who's in
trouble.

Robin was bent over the EKG, staring, running out foot after foot

one hand like toilet paper. With a
the kid's chest the print needle was all
it meant a thing. You could have seen that
t's the rhythm?" I asked, making conversation.
the pained expression of someone awaiting her ex-

of artifact but there's nothing underneath it," she said.
Hold your compressions a sec," I said. Nurse Kucera wiped her
row. Robin stopped bunching up the EKG printout and slowly stretched out her left arm as the strip got longer and longer. The needle lazily drifted back and forth like it was dreaming about something pleasant, then spiked an irregular plateau wave. Maybe somebody was popping popcorn in a microwave in the next building. "Looks pretty flat," she said.

"Resume compressions," I said. "Let's draw up another round of epinephrine and atropine and get an intubation tray ready. Can somebody get a blood gas?" I felt better giving real orders, even if they were obvious. "I'd say he's about forty kilos. Give another half milligram of epi and o-point-five of the atropine."

Once the drugs are emptied into the IV port and chased into the vein with a flush of IV fluid, you stand there hoping somehow something will change. It's a lull in the action.

"What happened to Henry?" Vickie asked Robin.

Robin jerked more upright like a puppet coming to life. She was pretty, slim, stylish, and in her mid-twenties, all of which set her apart in Glory's hospital. She jerked her head a bit, swinging brown hair over her mouth. "How well do you all know him?" she said.

"We all know Henry," Patty said. "Frequent flyer. Asthma. Seizures. Well, real seizures maybe—fake seizures for sure. Big-time loser."

We stared at Robin. "I wish I knew what happened," she said. "He told us his asthma was bad. Pollen or something. Wanted his epi shot." She shrugged. "We gave it to him," she said, nodding toward me.

They looked at me. There was a moment of silence, either sympathetic or accusatory, I wasn't sure. "He didn't bounce around on the stretcher for you?" Patty asked, screwing up one side of her face and jerking her arms like fishhooks.

"No," I said.

"Did he insist on showing you his crooked penis?"

"Well, yeah, that did come up."

"Did you feel honored?"

"I had a feeling I wasn't the first."

"His asthma must have been way worse than we thought," Robin said.

"Maybe," Vickie said. "Maybe he was so tight he couldn't even wheeze. I've heard that happens."

"He's never been even close to that bad before," Patty said.

"Did Daniel come in with him?" Vickie asked.

"Daniel? His dad? Is Daniel his dad?" Robin asked.

"Yeah. Pompous little greaseball. Dark goatee," Patty said. "Bigger loser."

"Yes. But he kind of disappeared," Robin said. "I thought it was weird."

"He's like that," Patty said.

Roger, the RT, interrupted. "Doc, I don't think I'm ventilating him too good. What do you think about maybe intubating him?"

"Stop compressions. Check for a rhythm," I said.

Patty stepped straight back and slowly raised her locked hands and elbows over her head. The room was silent. Vickie poked in the neck for a pulse. The EKG was still flat.

I mumbled, "Resume compressions," and looked at Roger. I said, "Sure, Roger." We both knew he probably had done a hundred more intubations than I had.

I ripped open the plastic wrap around the intubation tray and unfolded the sterile wraps to check the equipment. The blade fit the handle and the light worked. I slid the fat soft aluminum wire stylet inside the tube and bent it into a banana curve, just as the anesthesiologists always did.

I stepped under the IV line, over the EKG cable, under the oxygen tubing and slithered up to the head end of the gurney. I would need leverage. I leaned into the gurney. It began to roll away. "Lock the fucking gurney, please," I said. Patty stepped back from the CPR. She kicked down the wheel-lock lever then leaned back into Henry's chest.

I said quietly to Roger, "Okay." He looked at me. I repeated it, making a small waving motion with the laryngoscope in my left hand, staring at the boy's mouth. Roger moved the mask aside and stepped back.

Henry's mouth was full of regurgitated food. "Oh shit. We got chunks. Suction." I was nearly yelling now, which of course adds nothing of use. Vickie handed me the suction tubing. Attached was a tip the size and stiffness of wet spaghetti. I wrenched it off and flung it backward against the wall behind me, cutting the back of my hand on a metal bracket. "Fuck. Who put this sucker on here?" I asked— shouted. I tried to scour out Henry's mouth with the open end of the main tubing. "Those are for getting secretions out of bronchi, not for getting peas and carrots out of the trachea."

"I'm sorry, Doctor," Robin blurted. Though she had spoken to me she was staring straight ahead, apparently focused on Henry's spirit leaving the room. I was surprised anybody had answered my rhetorical question. It reminded me, though, whose ER it was. The staff was not here to be subversive. They were here to help sick people and I was a guest on a reluctant invitation. I'd best not bite at them.

The stream of what had been stomach contents looked like vegetable beef soup. Once I got the mouth cleared I said to Roger, "Let's give him some of the good air." After eight or ten breaths of oxygen I again said only, "Okay," cueing Roger to step back. I guided the tip of the laryngoscope blade down the boy's tongue and lifted.

I prayed for the anatomy to be clear, just this once. It wasn't. All I could see was a muddle of mucus secretions and pink, puffy soft tissues shaking in jerky synchrony with the chest compressions. The only thing I recognized with certainty was a single pea stuck to a tonsil. "It never looks like the goddamn pictures," I said. "Stop compressions a second." I used the suction tip to clear the secretions and then as a probe to gently part the tissues. Suddenly the cavity seemed to pop open and there lay the target, the inside of Henry's voice box. Then, just as suddenly, the tongue flopped around the blade and all I could see was a fat gray wad of blubber covered with taste buds. "Fuck," I mumbled. I pulled out and motioned Roger to give Henry some breaths.

While the oxygen went in I sighed and looked around at the

nurses. Robin spelled Patty at the chest compressions, diving into Henry's chest like she was pushing the Devil himself back to hell. After a dozen breaths Roger stepped away again. I put the blade down Henry's throat again, concentrating on keeping the tongue to the left where it belonged. The view opened up again. The target was clear. I passed the endotracheal tube to what I was certain was the trachea.

"In," I said.

A flurry of concerted activity began, like a string quartet, all moving in different ways but creating a single result: I inflated the cuff at the tip of the tube, Roger connected the breathing bag, Patty laid her stethoscope into the boy's right armpit, and Robin resumed bouncing on Henry's sternum. Roger squeezed the bag. The stomach rose. A gurgle came from the mouth. I groaned. Patty listened to both sides of the chest, then the stomach, as Roger repeatedly squeezed the bag. She told me, practically shouting because her ears were full of stethoscope, what I already knew: "It's in the esophagus."

Angry with myself, I jerked the tube out too fast. "Ventilate, please," I said. Roger reattached the mask and pumped oxygen, probably pushing chunks of dinner farther down the respiratory tree.

I grabbed at the laryngoscope and knocked it to the floor, where the blade and handle separated with a mocking clang. "Keep breathing, please," I said, bending to get my tools off the floor. I reunited blade and handle and looked at the ceiling, biting my lip.

I sucked out Henry's mouth one more time and slid the blade in so deep I knew my first view would be esophagus. I slowly backed out the blade until the voice box suddenly fell into view. I finessed it open with the tip of the blade and saw the by-God vocal cords. They're distinct when they show up. "Well, hot damn," I mumbled. I slid in the tracheal tube. Again the string quartet routine. This time the chest rose instead of the stomach.

Though Patty was listening to the chest again, the Doctor's Rule is to disbelieve until you hear it yourself. "Where's my stethoscope?" I asked, scanning the growing clutter of syringes and wrappers and alcohol pads surrounding the boy.

"Around your neck, Doc," Roger said, smiling. "That's always where they are."

Henry had definite wheezes and new gurgling noises that made the picture ominous. Roger taped the tube to Henry's face while Patty did the breathing.

"More epi, please," I said.

"Do you want another dose of atropine?" someone asked.

"No. He's blocked out for the next four hours at least."

I asked Vickie to stick the big artery in his groin for a blood gas. Shock plays hell with acid-base balance. She managed to find a vessel on the first pass. It was darker than spoiled claret, but at least it wasn't black.

An elfen blonde making notes on a clipboard, leaning back on the counter, blurted, "It's been twenty-three minutes." It's about now in a code when the team begins to back down, hoping the Guy-in-Charge isn't one of those who thinks he can cheat death if he works everyone to exhaustion. I'm usually one of the first to pronounce the dead dead, but they usually hit the door dead, not sassy like Henry had been.

"You want to try shocking him?" Patty asked.

Vickie said, "Live better electrically."

"He's in asystole," I said. "No point."

"Maybe it's fine v-fib," Patty said. That's the excuse for getting out the electricity when there's nothing else to do.

"Well, if you want to, we can," I said.

"I just thought it was the only thing we hadn't tried." Subtext: *Nothing's working means he's dead. We got work to do elsewhere.*

I checked his pupils with a light—both were dilated open and paralyzed. In this setting it didn't mean anything definite, but it looked bad. Robin paused her chest compressions two beats' worth and looked at me with what I took to be a plea. Like everyone else, she and I were exasperated, but we had, by virtue of Henry having shown up on our watch with an apparently functional heart, the most at stake in his resuscitation. Our eyes locked for a second before she went back to staring into the ether.

I said, "There's no reason for this kid to be dying."

I knew they were all thinking, *Even if heart starts, brain still dead.* The books say even the best chest compressions achieve only 20 percent of normal blood flow. However, I had seen a patient open his eyes and look at me during CPR. He nodded to a question. Ten minutes later he died. You don't forget that.

"Anybody got any ideas?" I said. "Am I missing anything?" Before you let go it's always best to be sure no one on your team is silently thinking you've forgotten something. "Anyone object to stopping?" There was verbal silence.

Robin spoke. "Maybe one more round of drugs."

"Sure," I said. "Epi. And give some bicarb." I nodded at Vickie and Patty.

One of the gallery spoke: "American Heart Association doesn't recommend bicarb."

I nodded. "Yeah, I know. And I know why. And I want it anyway."

"Want to try high-dose epi?" Patty asked.

"High dose?" I said, obviously seeking guidance.

"It's kind of new. One of the other docs told me about it. I guess it's still controversial, but apparently sometimes it works when nothing else does."

"Okay," I said. "How much?"

"Well, like six or eight milligrams at a time in an adult."

"Okay. Give him four," I said. "And two amps of the bicarb. Sometimes it helps the epi work."

The nurses injected the drugs. The chest was bellowed up with the breathing bag and compressed down by Robin's weight in alternating synchrony. We all stared silently at the EKG monitor. At first nothing happened. In fact, it probably took a full minute, but the needle made a sudden jump up in the middle of its regular CPR-induced bounces. We all saw it, but all knew it could as likely have been from sunspots as Henry's heart. Then it did it again. And again. "Hold compressions," I said.

Robin wiped the hair from her eyes and leaned over to join us watching the EKG. The needle jerked upward, then retreated back to midline with a lazy floating motion. In the next fifteen seconds, the jerks upward began to come more rapidly and the floaty motions downward began to sharpen, to look more like the inverse of the twitches upward, and these "beats" sped up to about one per second.

"Jesus Christ, I think it's beating," I said quietly. Louder: "Stop compressions a sec."

The waveforms, at first only an evil approximation of an EKG, lost, beat by beat, their aberrant slopes and plateaus. An army of upright and familiar-looking spikes marched across the screen like soldiers to the rescue. Just as slowly I began to smile. In the next few minutes the stagnant venous blood, with its overload of epinephrine, was accelerated back into action. Henry's pulse hit 180, and he developed a real blood pressure.

The faces of the staff showed a mix of relief and surprise. While they set up drug infusions Patty made a speech out of a medical cliché: "Geez, it's good to have the heart of a thirteen-year-old."

Vickie said, "Yeah, but Henry will find a way to make us pay for this. You know he will," she laughed.

Sometimes after a full arrest you get a honeymoon recovery; the heart will beat like crazy for twenty minutes, then rapidly degenerate and finally quit forever—the last cardiac gasp. I hovered over Henry's monitor, expecting the worst.

Watching the hypnotic march of the EKG, I mentally replayed the first half of my encounter with Henry, looking for clues. When he'd been checked into the ER, Robin had written on his clipboard only "asthma" in big quotes. She'd found normal temperature and blood pressure, though his heart rate and breathing were both a little fast.

When I'd gone in to talk to him, he was alone, sitting on a gurney, bare to the waist. "Hi, Henry, I'm Dr. Malcolm." I squatted a bit to get to his eye level.

He squinted at me. "You're new here," he said.

"Well, I've been here off and on for a couple of months," I said. "How's your breathing?"

"Like always." His voice was low and croaking—froglike.

"Like always when you come in here, you mean?"

"Uh-huh. I don't come in unless it's bad. Or I'm having a seizure."

"No, of course you wouldn't." I warmed the business end of my stethoscope between my palms. "Who's your favorite Diamondback?" I gently laid it on his back.

"My what?"

"Your favorite baseball player. The D-Backs? You don't like base-ball?"

"No. It's boring."

His heart was fast, and he was wheezing and struggling a bit to move air. But for scrawniness, the rest of the exam—the belly, the throat, and reflexes—was all normal. "What sports do you like?"

He said, "None."

"Okay, Henry, let me see about getting you some medicine."

"Wanna see my penis?" he asked, reaching for his pants. I am not often speechless, but that did it. "It's crooked."

A good doctor would never ignore a symptom. Though I figured I would probably regret it, I went along. "Is it bothering you?" I said. Maybe it was infected or something. Infections can set off asthmatics.

"Here," he grunted, pushing his pants and briefs off his bony little hips. "Look at it."

I was indeed regretting this. I found some gloves and began an or-derly genital exam. He had very scant early pubic hair. His testicles were normal, but there was a mildly contracted surgical scar on the un-derside of the shaft.

"Looks like you had a hypospadias repair," I said, suddenly re-membering I should have had a nurse "chaperone" present for any genital exam.

"Is that where—that thing you said—does that mean the piss comes out the bottom?" He was pointing to his scar.

"Yes, if you mean the bottom side of the penis," I said. "The open-ing of the urethra—the hole the pee comes out—is on the underside of your penis when you're born. It was probably fixed when you were a baby."

"It was," he said. "Now it's crooked."

"Well, not too much," I said, straightening it and letting it fall back. Time to change the subject. "It looks like you're working pretty hard to breathe, Henry. I think we better get you a respiratory treat-ment."

"A 'neb'?"

"Yes, Henry, a 'neb.' "

"I don't like those," he said.

"Well, I'm sorry about that, but the alternative is a shot, and my guess is you'd like that less."

He grunted and said, "I get those all the time."

"Let's try the easier thing first, shall we?"

He grunted again.

Awaiting me at the doctor's desk were the three and a half volumes of old charts from his dozens of prior visits and admissions. I ordered his inhalation treatment and began reading the highlights from The Book of Henry.

In addition to his hypospadias repair and asthma, he now clearly had "pseudo-seizures." More of his prior ER visits were for feigned seizures than for asthma. Most of the seizures had been easily debunked by the usual bedside tests. Someone having a generalized seizure—a real one—is incapable of doing anything purposeful, yet Henry would routinely make small movements to help the nurses get him into a protected position. One time, on hearing that he needed a bite block between his teeth, he opened his mouth.

"Pseudo-seizures syndrome" is a diagnosis both ugly and complex. I pulled a text. What I remember now are things like "complex disorder of behavior," and "commonly dead of suicide before age thirty." These patients learn to use fake seizures to get maximal attention. The psychiatric progression is both predictable and extremely refractory to treatment. A few cases had responded to the most intensive psychotherapy—on the order of two to four hours with a therapist every day. No health insurance in the world would pay for that, nor would the State of Arizona or Maricopa County.

His prior caretakers believed he had been abused as a toddler by his biological father. I mentally laid the psychiatric disorder on an abusive father, despite the lack of any evidence of a connection between the two pathologies. I went to the hallway vending machines for a can of Squirt. When the neb was finished I listened again. His wheezing was better but not much. Robin told me he asked her for his shot. He told her that was what he always got. I checked his chart. As he said, he had been given sub-Q epi at each of his last two visits for asthma and responded well. I wrote the order. Minutes later the dam broke.

Henry's cardiac honeymoon was holding up without any more heroics from us. He stayed pink. His pupils stayed big, though, and he wasn't waking up. Brain in limbo.

Convinced he was going to live at least the next half hour, I decided I could afford to attend to the mundane. I sat at the desk to write my report, but the cut on the back of my hand was bleeding on the page. I found two sterile cotton balls and taped them over the gash. Thus made safe for paperwork, I wrote a two-page chart note headed "Code—MD Report." I put down every clinical detail I could remember, from the moment Henry first arrived in the ER until we declared our standoff with death. It lacked only an explanation of the cause.

Henry needed to be in a pediatric ICU. From our faux-oasis outside Phoenix, I had two choices. St. Elizabeth's was closer, more pleasant, more "moneyed." But like any fledgling doctor, I chose what I knew, the one on my old turf, University of Arizona, Maricopa Branch. "The 'Copa." While Patty called an ambulance for transport, I phoned the Maricopa operator and asked for the Pediatric ICU.

"Who's the resident 'on'?" I asked the charge nurse.

"Intern is Michelle Rosenbaum," she said. "Senior is Mary Ellen Montgomery." Dr. Montgomery was my housemate and closest friend.

"Is either one there?"

She found Dr. Rosenbaum. The intern said "Sure" as formal acceptance of transfer. I told her everything I knew about Henry and asked her to have Dr. Montgomery call me back.

My next job was one of the particularly hellish moments of doctoring—facing the family. I would need to tell people I had not previously met that their son had nearly died at my hands and might yet finish the job. Despite my natural desire to hurry through any such discussion, I have learned it is best to go slowly and give information by implication, nursing along the aggrieved until they get it. I leaned on my elbows at the desk for a good three minutes of silence, rubbing my face and rehearsing my words. I remembered the troubled boy I had spoken to—their son. I stood up straight enough to make my mother proud and marched into the waiting room as if I did this every day.

All for naught: The waiting room was empty.

I asked Patty to call Henry's home. She left a vague message.

So we entered the many stages of waiting. Waiting for the ambulance, waiting for a callback from the family, waiting for Henry to wake up, waiting for an answer. The hardest part of medicine.

Wandering about the ER, I passed in front of the motion detectors over the ambulance-entrance doors. They slid open, offering an automated invitation outside. I stepped into the sun, warm and pleasant in the late-winter afternoon, for a time to think. The view across the parking lot was a golf course. I heard a *thwack* and a curse. Beyond the artificial greenery were low red mountains shielding Glory golfers from the snarl of Phoenix.

Had I known what caused Henry's arrest, I would have written it down in big letters. When you don't know, you enter the many stages of analysis and reconstruction, an unscientific process of untestable theorizing and conjecture by dozens of doctors and nurses who were not involved.

This I knew: His arrest made no sense. Though I could not have claimed great experience with the nuances of asthma, I certainly knew how to treat it, a disease so common it's boring to most pediatricians. Nor was I an expert in pseudo-seizures, but there was no link in pathophysiology connecting pseudo-seizures to cardiac arrest.

I went back in. If there was going to be reconstructing done, I wanted to have copies of whatever data there were. Even scanty evidence might be useful. I made photocopies of the code sheet, the nurses' notes, and my own chart notes, then went back to Henry's room to see if I could think of anything else.

But for the tubes and wires he would have looked pink and healthy, just asleep. Roger had brought in a ventilator to breathe for him. One of the nurses had wrapped him in a thick cotton blanket to keep him warm on his ride into town.

The room was cluttered with torn paper and plastic wrappings, a few bloody gauzes, partly emptied syringes, and long strands of EKG printout. On the counter by the sink was a scattering of syringes and needles. I gingerly poked through them and found the one Robin had used for the sub-Q injection just before the code. It was the smallest; the only one-cc tuberculin syringe in the detritus, still full to the eight-tenths mark, with a brown glass ampule, minus its top and its contents, taped to the side of the syringe. The ampule said, "EPINEPHRINE (adrenaline) 1 mg/cc."

As I was reading it Robin came in. I thought she saw me staring at the syringe. I looked up at her, but she had turned to fuss with Henry's IV drips.

The ambulance people came in. "We're ready to go, aren't we, Doc?" Roger said from the head of the bed.

"Sure," I said. I smiled wanly at the paramedics.

I didn't really think about why I was doing it, but I went around the corner and out of sight to the med room, found a small Baggie marked "Specimen," and put the syringe in it. At the desk I found a big brown interdepartmental envelope, put the Baggie in it, rolled it up, taped it, wrote my name on it, and put the package in the drug refrigerator back in the med room. It was pure reflex.

As the gurney was being wheeled past—Vickie steering it from the foot end, Roger squeezing the breathing bag—Robin set on top of Henry's legs a big plastic bag, like a discount store shopping bag. It had in it the shreds of Henry's clothes. It said on it, "Thank you for choosing Providence of Glory Medical Center, Glory, Arizona."

2

That was almost seven years ago.

Now I am "home." In Hooker, Nebraska, my point of origin.

I practice medicine in the Hooker ER and places like it. I work the hours the other doctors don't want.

Hooker, population 9,858, is the only town in an eighty-mile radius with a hospital. There's a one-doctor clinic over in Othello, but that's a really tiny town, twenty-seven miles from Hooker, and they lock down on nights and weekends. From 7 P.M. on any Friday until 7 A.M. on the following Monday, the only doctor the ill or injured can see is me, or somebody like me.

My Henry Troubles in Arizona left me practicing medicine as an itinerant physician. I camp on weekends in ERs like Hooker's, scattered across the plains, for sixty hours at a stretch, for an hourly wage, currently forty-three dollars. I am, or so it says on my papers, only partly trained.

The hospital in Hooker has the kind of noncommittal name they seem to like in generic small towns—Hooker County Community Memorial Medical Center. HCCMMC. A medical center, not just a hospital mind you, that commemorates the community. My guess is it had the least chance of being controversial when the Board of Trustees had to pick.

I grew up in Hooker, an age ago. It seems it is my home again. Relocation by default.

Through college in Boston and medical school in San Diego, I told friends Nebraska was a great place to be from, emphasizing the "from." There was mild dishonesty in participating in the clichéd bashing of a place I loved, but it helped shut off the stupid jokes from people at the edges of the continent about how backward everyone knew us Midlanders to be.

Luckily I had a Nebraska medical license before the Troubles began. Licensure requires medical school, internship, and the National Board Exam, not a residency. Near the end of my internship in Arizona my father harangued me into doing the paperwork to get my Nebraska medical license. Dad was planning on my taking over his practice when I finished residency, and he was getting impatient. When he started the practice thirty-odd years before my internship, he was the only doctor in an eighty-mile radius. It was catching up with him.

I made it clear I had little interest in either a generalist's practice or a life on the prairie, but for the cost of a license fee I figured I would be able to get him off my back for at least the duration of the residency.

Getting a license, however, was a happy event. Pre-Henry I was a jauntier soul; the future was boundless. While home for a week vacation I made rounds with Dad every morning. With my shiny new License to Practice the hospital was willing to give me "courtesy" privileges, and I got to scrub an appendectomy with him. He actually let me do the operation, though my deliberate manner, under the eyes of thirty years of proficiency, must have seemed plodding. It created palpable impatience at the operating table. Nonetheless I count it as a trophy memory.

Though he didn't entirely approve of my choosing to be a full-time surgeon, he did understand that no one, these days, could do it all, the way he had. He was a throwback to the days before every doctor did a residency; a living, breathing General Practitioner. He still did routine operations and delivered babies. In those days of hubris I told him he was a living fossil. I also pointed out that a fully trained surgeon, should he be so inclined for some silly reason, could take over the majority of Dad's practice, whereas a fully trained internist or family practitioner could not. He nodded and smiled, believing I would still find just such a silly inclination.

My next visit—after my failed residency, after Glory, after Henry—was the antithesis of the Proud Homecoming. Tail between my legs, unable to explain in sufficient detail, Nebraska was a hideout, my sanctuary. Jauntier days looked quaint.

For gainful employment I checked on the hometown ER, hoping

to pick up some hours. They said to call Western Acute Health, Inc.; they "had the contract." Western Acute was the cash-flow brainchild of Mel Steele, an ER doc in Cheyenne. Mel figured out he could develop an income stream by holding contracts to supply doctors for ER coverage at tucked-away little towns few doctors would otherwise find. Western gets paid by hospitals like Hooker County to keep a licensed doctor available in the ER for the entire weekend every weekend. So the local family docs don't have to cover all the hours of the day and night. So they don't get too fried and pack away like moths to the lights of the city.

It started out as a way to pay my bills while I waited out my appeals and applications. I would work weekends but get the uncrowded weekdays to be skiing in Colorado or fishing or hunting in Wyoming. It became a habit.

The work can be good.

The waiting can be brutal.

The hospital in Hooker is at the western edge of town. Sometimes I stare out the window of my second-floor call room—"The Penthouse"—watching, just across a gravel road, beef cattle graze. Hooker has no golf course, and no low mountains. But then, there's nothing that needs to be hidden.

Watching the sky is the best. Clouds of hospital cotton float overhead on sunny summer days, and the blackest, most malevolent thunderheads roll across grassy dunes just before sunset. The better ones kick up all kinds of flotsam with their opening salvos, then pelt it back to earth with fishing-sinker raindrops or, on a good evening, hail that sounds like glass slowly shattering.

Recreation inside a hospital is cramped. Sixty-hour shifts, mostly spent in the on-call quarters, reading, watching some game-of-the-week on the tube, sleeping, eating cafeteria fried foods. Since Henry and my time in Glory, flirting with nurses has lost much of its allure. But the time is not all a waste. I do study my area of medicine. I mix literature into my often-pedestrian reading list, and for at least part of every weekend I get paid forty-three dollars per hour for sleeping.

When things fell apart I told Dad the final outcome and a smattering of the details. Naturally, he was angry with all concerned. He wanted to bring legal action. Afraid the law might have something to say to me, too, I silently demurred. I told him about certain clauses in Arizona employment contracts that would make a suit pointless. These gnawed at him, too.

Two months ago I was back in Arizona. Though I am persona non grata there to the medical establishment, they have not yet set up border barricades.

Mary Ellen Montgomery, my former housemate and the doctor who took Henry Rojelio off my hands that night in Glory, called, via my parents, saying she had something for me. I made it to Phoenix in thirty-six hours.

While there I called a criminal attorney, Gerry deLee, and made an appointment. A cop I know recommended him. His office was in a bank tower in central Phoenix. It smelled of cigarettes and sweat. The view from the lone window was of a city block across the street, sandy and completely vacant but for three broken-off palm trees and an equally topless concrete foundation.

Mr. deLee's face had redundant folds of the upper eyelids that made him look half asleep most of the time. From the questions he interposed, though, it was obvious he was listening, acutely. I retold Henry's story. I rambled. It ran to two hours. He rendered professional judgment: The statute of limitations was running out on minor things, and for major things the situation was too murky and the time too long ago for any DA with an ounce of sense to want to pursue it.

Apropos the events, there can be no certainty.

Also apropos the events, I am going to act on the knowledge I possess: I have a certain freedom to speak.

My would-be career as a surgeon was castrated so long ago it is irrecoverable, and to me, through the years, a vanishing concern. Still, these events were real. They redefined my life.

I will tell two stories: Neither means a thing without the other. They are separated in time by ten months. Though they are nearly seven years old they are clearer to me than my last weekend ER shift. Both happened in the Phoenix area. They call it "Valley of the Sun."

Some may see crimes or insufficiencies in my manifest acts. Certain omissions trouble me more. Major parts are played by individuals believed by most to have known better. Most of the cast is still about, playing their parts, greasepaint intact.

Ergo, my story.

THE BOOK OF MIMI

3

THE BOOK OF MIMI, CHAPTER ONE

My having crawled into Glory, Arizona, where I met Henry on Day One, was a consequence of having known, slightly too long and unquestionably too well, Miriam M. Lyle, MD, Associate Professor of Surgery, Division of Neurosurgery, University of Arizona, Maricopa Medical Branch, Phoenix, Arizona. She was a brain surgeon. What I eventually tripped over was that Mimi Lyle, professionally speaking, was, if not actually incompetent, less than sterling at the operating table, despite being well regarded at the academic level.

Such a conclusion comes, however, only through pain and suffering; all the early impressions were far more favorable. We cub residents were given to believe she had a reputation as a bright young academic tigress in the stultified world of professors of neurosurgery. It was said this was based on some esoteric research she had published prior to moving to the desert. The move itself was poorly understood. It was said she left a plum fellowship without finishing the course. No one expected a rising Eastern or even Midwestern star to relocate to the land of golf courses and tennis courts. That usually happened as a prelude to retirement. The rumors around Professor Lyle generally invoked themes of sexual intrigues or inordinate salary offers. Neither was true.

No one had to tell us she was tall, classically beautiful, and, from my testosterone-hardened viewpoint, undeniably sexy. I had seen her in the hospital, striding down the long corridors of linoleum and buzzing, garish lights. In silk blouses, all types of skirts, open white coat, and pumps, she was—visually at least—the lone Rose amidst the bands of wandering and grubby Gypsy doctors.

She eschewed the low-maintenance short-cropped hair considered mandatory for any woman in a surgical specialty. Hers was long and a deep auburn. It didn't flounce and bounce like a TV model's; she generally had it braided and wound up on top of her head, but with her perfectly sculpted neck it looked elegant. She had a long thin nose, thinly arched eyebrows, and pale blue eyes. She usually wore fitted clothes, so there was ample evidence to believe that her body was everything a woman's body, in the tightly closed eyes of a twenty-seven-year-old, often lonely male, should be. Despite her being at least a dozen years older, my Y chromosome went on alert whenever she was near. Call it a schoolboy crush.

My distinctly mixed fortunes with *la Profesora* began in the spring of my second year of general surgical residency. I drew a rotation on Neurosurgery while she was the Attending assigned to the teaching service—my immediate boss. Though no one would expect a general surgeon, even one, say, stranded in the Nebraska Outback, to operate on brains and spinal cords, we were expected to have at least a rudimentary understanding of the field.

I'd been warned of her operating room deficits, sort of. Among medical underlings the right kind of story about our superiors easily becomes mythic, retold often enough that senior residents will correct details in their juniors' versions of the story just as they would an incorrect medication order. Oral history is a healthy tradition in teaching hospitals.

The neo-campfire for us Maricopans was The Longhorn, a Tex-Mex restaurant a block from the hospital. A maze of sprawling cinderblock rooms growing like mushrooms from a decrepit old adobe house, it had been the residents' bad habit for as long as anyone could remember, loved and hated in equal parts: The meals were cheap, yet big enough to fuel the average mortal for days. The secret of their success was grease.

The center of the action was a certain large, oval table—forever ennobled among the brethren as "The Oval Table: Where Everyone's More Equal Than an Intern." There, I got my first Tales of Mimi, over chips, salsa, and *cerveza*. Maybe when the crunch came I was carrying along the opinions and judgments of my residency peers instead of forming my own based on firsthand observation. Not very doctorlike.

But the stories were scary.

A talkative resident two years my senior had told me she was once scrubbed in with Mimi for six hours to do a one-level laminectomy, an extraordinarily long time for a routine operation on a herniated spinal disc. Reason: They couldn't find the offending piece of disc. "No wonder," I was told. "She was two levels off."

"But couldn't that happen to anyone?" I asked.

"One level, maybe. Two? Rarely. Anyway, you're supposed to get films."

"Films. Looking for . . . ?" A pause. I was obviously not in on this.

"X-ray comes in and shoots a cross-table lateral, after the surgeon has marked the level she's at with something that will show up on the film, like a twenty-two-gauge spinal needle. It's standard. Then anybody who can count backwards from five can see that the needle is at L Two-Three, not L Four-Five, and you move down."

"She never got films," I said.

"Refused to. The nurse asked twice if she should call X-ray. Dreamy Mimi was humming to herself and didn't answer the first time. So the nurse repeated it. She had the needle up on the field, ready to go. Like I said, it's considered standard.

"Meems didn't like it," she went on. "She said, 'Listen, honey'— kinda singsongy, like it was supposed to be a joke—'at the Mayo Clinic only wimps need radiologists looking over their shoulders. Do you know what they charge to review an intra-op film, two days after we've finished the surgery?'

"The nurses here have a lot of guts," my resident went on, "I guess they have to. This nurse is about older than God and *big*. She says to Mimi, 'I've heard Dr. Hebert ask what the three most overrated things in America are.' "

Dr. Hebert was the Chair of General Surgery at Maricopa, my ultimate boss.

She went on: "There's a real painful silence because everyone there—probably Mimi included—has heard Dickie Hebert's pat line about the Mayo Clinic. She finishes, 'Home cooking, home fucking, and the Mayo Clinic.' There's a longer silence, except from the anesthesiologist, who's doing a very bad job of trying not to laugh—he must have heard that line twenty times. My guess is he's just enjoying seeing someone throw it in Mimi's face. She's so full of herself and that Mayo Clinic shit."

"And . . ." I prompted.

She leaned slightly toward me. "I've heard Mimi Lyle has a pretty good vindictive streak. They say she does target practice at a shooting range every few months. Like a cop. I wish I knew this nurse's name. She might die a mysterious death someday. Say a thirty-eight to the thalamus or scalpel to the medulla oblongata. Mimi hasn't said a thing, so the nurse says, 'I don't know about the home fuckin' part. I never really thought of it as being that highly rated to begin with.'

"Mimi is, I guess, not up for this repartee. She can only drop names. 'Ian McWhorten is one of the finest neurosurgeons on the planet, and he could operate circles around anybody in Phoenix,' and blahbedy blahbedy."

"Who's Ian McWhorten?" I asked.

"Her mentor at Mayo's. Supposedly a great neurosurgeon, so he probably could operate circles around anybody in Phoenix, but he apparently didn't let Dr. Lyle in on any of his secrets." She paused. "Like I said, she was two vertebrae off. Spent two hours inside that guy's L-spine before she'd get a film."

"And when she did?"

"Spent a long time looking at the CT and then the film, then the CT, then the film. Finally she extended the incision, did the lam, pulled out a chunk of disc the size of a goddamn almond, closed up, and went home. "

"Never said a word," I guessed.

"Said, 'These things happen,' to me. Never said a word to the nurses."

"Anything happen after that?"

"Are you on drugs? What would happen? The nurses *maybe* write up an incident report, which goes into a confidential file and rots. I imagine Joe Kellogg, the Chief of Neurosurgery, heard about it all, eventually, though it's not like an official report. I was the only other doctor scrubbed and I'm not writing it up. I suppose the anesthesiologist or nurses dropped a few hints around the OR for Kellogg. But face it, the only thing Dr. Kellogg is going to do is tell her to get a film. It's not like she's the first neurosurgeon to open at the wrong level."

"What about when she opens the wrong side of the skull?" I asked. This wasn't the first story I'd heard about Dr. Lyle.

"I wasn't there for that one," she said. "In fact I don't know anyone who was. I heard the story, though: car-wreck-coma, CT shows a big clot on the brain, rush to the OR at midnight, turn a really neat flap, but it's on the *wrong side*. Close up, turn the head, do it again. This time find a big ugly clot, suck it out, close up, go home. Patient dies. Probably would have died anyway. Most do."

"I heard he ended up in long-term care."

"Well, same thing."

"And nothing came of that."

"Sheesh. You don't get it. She's hot shit around here. She was the first female neurosurgeon west of St. Louis and not in California, and Joe Kellogg landed her here. She was considered a hot little go-getter and something of a plum for a shithole like this. She's smart—she knows the science. And she gets grant money. She does a little research and goes to all the meetings and flounces around like a princess among the good-old-boy brain surgeons. They like her. They publish her papers. She gets more grant money."

"But she can't operate."

"Say what you will, Doctor"—she opened her hands up like a crocus—"I'd call that operating."

"Does she get films now during lams?"

"I try not to be around when she's in surgery."

As a "PGY-2" (Post-Graduate Year-2) resident, my standing on the clinical totem pole was just on top of the interns ("PGY-1's"), who were only on top of the medical students (baggage.) In this continuous initiation process one is regularly moved from place to place and service to service, and therefore continuously ignorant. Ignorance is vulnerability, and rather than worrying over her operative skills I was more interested in the stories of her occasional meanness and caprice. She was said to have thrown an intern out of the operating room for

not knowing some fact of neuroanatomy that she thought was supposed to be basic knowledge. About all I remembered of neuroanatomy, beyond the names of the big lobes, was that studying it was
like trying to memorize a huge computer circuit board you couldn't
see and none of it seemed like basic knowledge.

She was known to have stationed interns with her post-op patients
for forty-eight straight hours in the ICUs, calling in at odd hours, supposedly a little tipsy after late-night trysts, more to see that the hapless
trainees were there and awake than how the patient was doing. The
patients often as not did poorly, but that wasn't unusual in neurosurgery. The problem, I was told, was that she would have mucked
around in their brains for eight or ten or twelve hours, pressing retractors on their memories or motor abilities or coordination until
they disappeared into oblivion as the underlying brain slowly turned to
yogurt. Another surgeon might have taken a fourth that long, and the
parts of the patient's brain that were in the way would have seen less
physical abuse and more blood flow and had a better chance of hanging around.

The Book of Mimi has its genesis, appropriately, in an intensive care
unit.

Just as I did to start every rotation, I showed up on the designated
patient unit—this time it was the Surgical ICU—at 6:30 A.M. on the
appointed Monday to see the patients with the interns in preparation
for rounds with the professor. That day, though, I was alone. Maricopa
Medical Branch is the junior varsity of the UA Centers for Health; the
smaller specialty services like neurosurgery often don't get both an intern and a resident. Though a resident is usually better off sans intern
in terms of efficiency, it meant I was alone in the gunsights. On top of
that, my particular "Month with Meems," through a quirk in the academic calendar, was to be six weeks. Six weeks at the foot of the mistress, seeing patients only in her clinic, rounding just with her, reading
up on literature germane to her research projects, sharing the meals on
the fly, and, in my case at least, getting highly personal.

With the stories I had collected around the Medical Center of
Mimi the Witch, no one had told me she was charming. Nor would
our introduction suggest it.

That first morning I asked the ICU charge nurse, a woman who had sheltered me a few times during the storms of internship, if Dr. Lyle had any patients there. She smiled wryly and nodded. "Mrs. Gottshok. Bed five." I turned but she went on. "You and Mimi, huh?

"Yes."

"This'll be good."

I shot her a look. I assumed she meant I was going to be another case of medical-training mincemeat. She was smiling. I said, "You'll be sure I get a decent burial, won't you?"

"Whatever you need, Doctor."

I gave her back a look of surrender.

I found the patient's chart. She was a seventy-one-year-old woman with a leaky mitral valve, prone to congestive heart failure. The Friday prior, Dr. Lyle had taken an irritating rub off a major nerve to her left arm by fusing two of the woman's cervical vertebrae. They put the woman in the Unit supposedly for overnight monitoring only, but she became short of breath post-op. The resident on the cardiology team put a catheter in her pulmonary artery to diagnose what he already knew, namely that water was backed up in her lungs. He gave her diuretics and her heart failure resolved. She was still in the ICU because, in poking the huge needle under her collar bone to get the catheter in, he had also punctured her lung, giving her a small pneumothorax—a collapsed lung. The morning chest film had already been done, so I compared it to the ones from the days before; the lung was again up and working.

Mrs. Gottshok was sitting up flicking through the television channels with the old-fashioned hardwired remote control unique to hospitals. I introduced myself and asked how she was feeling.

"Bored," she said, nearly shouting. "I want to go home. You people are all boring."

I smiled. "You're an astute observer," I said. "How's your breathing this morning?"

"I'm here, aren't I? My breathing is just peachy. Now are you going to let me out of here?"

"I sure hope so. Your chest X-ray looks like you're headed in that direction. But better let me have a listen, first."

I had the bell of my stethoscope on the woman's back when Dr. Lyle came into the room. I nodded a hello. Dr. Lyle asked Mrs. Gottshok something like, "How are you this morning?" With my ears full of stethoscope, trying to sort out normal wind tunnel sounds from a few stray whistles and a whooshing heart murmur, all I heard was mumbo jumbo. Mrs. Gottshok began a long answer at high-decibel volumes, nearly deafening me. I held up my hand to cut her off, and again asked her to just take a nice deep breath. It never occurred to me that I was cutting off Dr. Lyle's interview of the patient, only that I could not complete my physical exam if they were going to talk. Auscultation of the patient's chest is relatively sacrosanct, even when done by a trainee.

After we left the bedside, Dr. Lyle asked me what I thought. "Her lung's back up. She's surgically stable. We should get her out of the Unit today, maybe even home tomorrow." Mimi nodded, her arms folded. I said, "I'll write for it. When do you want to see her in clinic?"

"Seven to ten days. Resident clinic."

"Sure."

"Your name Malcolm?" She was reading my nametag.

"Yes, it is. Malcolm Ishmail."

"Dr. Ishmail, please don't ever again cut me off as I'm talking to a patient."

I tensed. "I'm—oh, uh—sorry, Dr. Lyle." Twenty minutes into the rotation and I was already a bumbling nincompoop. "I guess it was just, you know, a reflex. I was concentrating on her breath sounds. You know, trying to—"

"You can do that on your time. Not when I'm making rounds."

"Yes. I'm sorry." I knew the paramilitary drill: Short answers invite the least reprisal.

I spent the next few days being brief and to the point, and trying to do what a good medical resident is supposed to do: Know at any given instant precisely what the professor is thinking despite the absence of discernible clues. I saw all the patients in clinic and in the hospital ahead of her and then presented the history and physical findings with my own speculative assessment and treatment plan. She would nod or frown, prod, ask leading guess-what-I'm-thinking kinds of questions, and correct or sometimes completely ignore, probably out of sympathy, my diagnoses and plans. Sometimes she was curt and sometimes generous, offering impromptu explanations of the pertinent physiology, pathology, or pharmacology involved in the particular case. Her didactic base was as advertised—extensive. She asked for daily lectures from me—schoolboy-style—on various neurosurgical topics, to be certain I was reading my texts at night. Things like, "Tomorrow give me five minutes on the choice of diuretics for cerebral edema."

In the second week, though, our rigid professionalism cracked.

In afternoon clinic I got an urgent page from the operator. She had on hold a patient I had known almost a year, Karen Booker. The operator told me she sounded "bad." I took the call alone in Mimi's office.

Karen was a good-looking blonde, nineteen and round as a beach ball when she showed up on Labor and Delivery with contractions every three minutes. As the intern on Obstetrics, I delivered the baby. Her boyfriend, Enrico, the child's father, was a thick and surly Hispanic who, I came to find out, regularly beat Karen. He also kept her away from any money—even her own—and from talking to her family. This came out during a postpartum encounter when I asked her about some bruises and refused to accept the usual lies.

Before letting her take the baby home I made sure the hospital social worker had Karen in touch with the police in her neighborhood and a shelter. The social worker and I had a long talk with her. Very pragmatic stuff like accumulating a few dollars in change, memorizing phone numbers and the bus route to the shelter.

Eight weeks after going home with Enrico, in the face of a fresh assault, she put the plan into effect, slipping away as he slept off a drunk. She phoned me two days later to share her moment of pride.

True to the course of the disease, she eventually went back to Enrico. And got beaten. She called me in tears one night, speech impaired by her thick lips. I called the police. Enrico, no virgin to the county jail, went away for a while on a parole violation.

Karen's call that afternoon was a kindly warning: Enrico was out. He had roared over to her mother's house, where she was staying, to tell her he would be coming for her when he got an apartment and not to bother to call me, he was going to "dust" me soon. He said he knew my car and where I lived. She was going to take a bus to her sister's in Reno. She thought I would do well to leave town, too. She assured me he meant it.

Mimi came into her office as I was telling Hospital Security that there was a faint possibility of a row on campus and would they mind keeping an eye on my Datsun. Naturally she asked what that was all about. After hearing my tale she gave me an odd smile and said, "Does she call you often?"

"Oh, maybe once every three months. It's no big deal. I give her pep talks. She sent me a picture of the kid she had done at Sears. He's really cute."

"Are you afraid of this Enrico?"

"I don't think so. He just wants her to believe he's her only re-source. Keep his place as sole source of everything. If he can make her think I'm as good as dead, that's all he needs."

"He could be genuinely angry with you."

"Maybe. But I imagine I'm not worth a lot of jail time to him."

"You hope so."

"Yeah, I guess that's it."

She stared at me, smiled and nodded. "How did you know what to do? Most doctors are in the dark about domestic abuse."

"We studied it in a criminal psych course in college. I guess it car-ried over."

"Well, you should be proud of yourself. Seriously. I know a bit about it."

"What do you mean?"

She looked at me. "I mean I've been there. My husband—I was very young—seventeen—I wanted away from my father. I'd dated Tony off and on for three years. He was a sailor, home on leave. The whole thing struck me as awfully romantic. I could live away from my father's obsessive control and have a love 'lost at sea.' Then every few months a week of passion."

"But it didn't work out," I said.

"Well, partly. I got away from Daddy. But the first week home on leave the passion went wrong. On the fourth night together we quarreled. He started hitting me."

"Oh God."

"I was frightened enough to just take it. I knew if I fought back it would only be worse. So I got him more whiskey. When he passed out I took all the money from his wallet and drove to my brother's. I was half hoping he would come after me. My brother would have made him regret ever having met me."

"But he didn't come?"

"No."

"Well, Karen doesn't have a brother. She needed a little help. It was the right thing to do." She was looking at me. I shrugged. "Maybe the guy just pissed me off. The worm."

"Still, you watch yourself."

"Yeah." I got a wry grin. "I'll know if he's behind me. She said he's driving his cousin's big silver pickup. It rides low but it's real loud."

She nodded a smile.

The next morning, our rounds had us crossing paths with Doug Goodbout, one of the general surgery professors. He was a perverse legend among us underlings for always using the longest possible phrase for anything medical and an amusing breathiness in his voice. He was often imitated, though we were definitely laughing at him, not with him.

As we passed in a hallway he suddenly stopped to ask Dr. Lyle to see a patient of his who might have a nerve entrapment. As he waxed aerobic about this "septuagenarian female with abdominal distension and pain," the possibility of "an incompletely obstructing colonic carcinoma," and his plans for "radionuclide scintillography, and a chest roentgenogram," Mimi caught me rolling my eyes behind Dr. Goodbout.

When he had gone she asked, "You find Dr. Goodbout amusing?"

"I'm sorry, Dr. Lyle."

"No. That's normal, I'm sure. Many of us find him amusing."

"Well, you *could* call a roentgenogram an X-ray." I was suddenly feeling less cowed. "Once, after Dr. Goodbout gave a Grand Rounds last year, one of the students on my team started imitating him on rounds: 'Um, Dr. Ishmail, did you happen to notice on that last gentleman the particularly noteworthy examples of the dermatologic manifestations of the stigmata of hepatic degeneration resulting from excessive ethanol intake?' I broke up. The resident thought we were laughing at the poor alcoholic and just about busted our heads."

She laughed. I smiled at her. She said, "I saw on the surgery schedule once a case booked as '*difficult* repair of *large*, recurrent, *incisional*, *ventral* hernia with Marlex mesh.'"

"Isn't that kind of redundant?"

"It positively defines redundancy! I didn't have to look to know who the surgeon was."

Now I was laughing. "Were you at the Grand Rounds last year? When he spoke?" She shook her head. "He was lecturing in his normal style, about something esoteric like vasoactive peptide of the gut, using a lot of"—I again imitated his breathiness—"*excess verbiage*, when, right in the middle some guy near me in one of the back rows, maybe about seventy-five himself, well dressed, I'd guess a retired surgeon, stands up to leave, clattering chairs, and says to no one in particular but loud enough for half the audience to hear,"—I deepened my voice and slowed it way down—" 'I've always said he was a pompous son of a bitch! Can't say what's on his mind. Has to use a bunch of half-dollar words!' and climbs out of the lecture hall. Everyone in the back was busting up, giggling but trying to be quiet."

She was laughing. "Burt Lorenzen," she said. "Gravelly voice. Thick silver hair?"

"Yeah, I think so."

"He's a great man, one of my favorites. Never shy about what's on his mind. He's nearly deaf, though, so he tends to be loud. Not retired either. Keeps busy with general surgery out in Sun City. He's sent me a couple of patients. He's a dear man."

"Well, we figured he had nailed Dr. Goodbout."

She was still laughing. "Don't the students call him Grand-Uncle Doug?"

"Uh-huh."

"Where did that come from?"

"I've never heard."

"Probably Dickens. Or just one of those names that gets passed down from class to class until its roots are lost," she said.

"It just fits because you can't take him a hundred percent seriously."

"And what do you call me these days?" Her eyes were dancing.

"You?" I was caught off guard.

"Dreamy Mimi?"

I grinned. "Well, I have heard that one."

"Any new ones? That one's from junior high."

" 'Fraid not."

"No 'Grand-Aunt Meems'? No 'Wicked Witch of the East'? 'Mimi Lyle the Crocodile'?"

" 'Fraid not."

"When I was in medical school," she said, "our Chief of Medicine, Hanna Johnston, was a very large woman, maybe five foot ten, two-twenty, but not so much fat as just big—big shoulders, big bones—who lived with a very strange little person. Not her husband, it was said. In fact there was some speculation about the person's gender. Everyone said Dr. Johnston smoked cigars, though no one could ever claim to have seen her in the act.

"Anyway, she terrorized the students. She would have sit-down rounds in a conference room once a week with all the third years on Medicine and grill them endlessly on obscure diseases. So, the story goes, one day she was puffing down the corridor in her long white coat, with a white blouse underneath. She passed a bunch of students and housestaff and one of the third years said, 'Who was that?' The resident said grandly, '*That* was Hanna Johnston,' and the student said, 'That was Hanna Johnston? I thought it was a refrigerator.' "

I was laughing again. She went on.

"Supposedly Dr. Johnston heard the comment, because she stopped suddenly, but never turned around. She just started up again and never said anything. Naturally the story spread and Hanna Johnston has forever been 'The Refrigerator' to the otherwise terrified junior students."

"It's their only defense," I said.

"Well I've always been afraid of acquiring a name like 'The Refrigerator.' One might as well be 'The She-Bitch from Hell.' The medical sense of humor can be cruel." We smiled at each other. She looked at her watch. "Let's get some lunch, " she said.

Against a back wall in the Doctors' Dining Room, over some soupy lasagna, she went on reminiscing with a story from her class skit at the end of medical school. "Will you be involved in your resident-class graduation skit?"

"Is there one?" I answered. "Over three years away."

"Well, I'll give you a song you might find useful. But you have to promise to keep my name out of the skit. Can you do that?"

"I guess I could try, but I don't even know if we'll have one, much less who'll be writing it."

"Oh, of course you'll have one. Every surgical residency class does. And you'll have to be involved. You're quicker than most and, it seems, much funnier, too. Anyway, I'll take that as a promise. The song is to the tune of 'Love Is Blue.' Do you know it?"

"Sure."

"We started to write it for our skit but never found a place to use it, so it just hangs out there, waiting." She sang, "Blue, blue, the baby's blue. One ventricle, there should have been two . . ."

I broke up laughing. She smiled at me, all of her scariness gone, vanished with a smile. I smiled back.

During afternoon clinic I asked her what the rest of the song was. She said that was all they'd written.

An hour later I passed her in the hallway, each of us nose down in a patient's chart, and I softly whistled the melody to "Love Is Blue." She grinned over her shoulder and disappeared into an examining room.

Around four-thirty I had just finished helping our last patient—a paraplegic in an electric wheelchair souped up with motorcycle accessories—down the hall to the waiting room. When I turned back Mimi was staring at me from her office door. She turned slowly inside. I went in and was about to say "Goodbye, see you at morning rounds," when she again made me bumble. Very quickly and without looking up, she asked, "Would you consider having dinner with me?"

I'm sure I stopped breathing. She may not have been scary anymore as an Attending but she was still very much in charge, still the boss, still Teacher, now dangerous at a whole new level.

I might have said no, if I'd wanted to, but I didn't.

"What time? I mean, yes. Um, what time?"

"Any time, really. Nothing formal. Do you have evening plans?"

"Well, a basketball game. A bunch of us have a team in a city league. For any game, about half of us can get there. It's a five-thirty game, though, if that wouldn't be too late."

"In my younger days I would have come to the game to watch a bunch of hulking, hormonally overloaded young men sweat all over themselves and each other. And enjoyed it quite a bit. In my situation these days I'll just have to enjoy it in my mind. But, I will wait for your game. Give me your address and I'll pick you up at, say, seven o'clock?" I nodded. "You live alone, don't you? I have to be fastidiously discreet. You understand."

"My housemate is on call tonight. Neonatal ICU service. I won't actually see her during daylight for six weeks."

"Her?"

"Lab partner and best friend from medical school. Purely platonic."

She eyed me.

"We keep secrets from each other," I lied.

"Seven o'clock then."

At the end of the game I declined the usual "Let's go get a beer" invitations with no explanation to my friends. The game ran long, but my house was near the gym so I was home right at seven. A Mercedes convertible was in my driveway, and Mimi was waiting on the porch.

"Uh, Dr. Lyle," I said, "I'm sorry. Still have to shower."

"Don't be sorry," she said. "I came early on purpose. I told you I like sweating young men." Judging from the way she smiled I guess my face flushed. She had on a sleeveless satin blouse, a long skirt of something light and filmy, and sandals. The evening was warm, even for Phoenix in spring. The light was fading and the western sky looked like a rainbow ribbon on fire. The town house I rented was in a typically nondescript development patch with streets that curve around nothing in particular. The grounds were post-bulldozer chic: clumps of boulders and pampas grasses with a lot of cheap little cacti and one stunted or mangled saguaro per acre. The town-house units were staggered along a curve so the adjacent patios were offset from one another. Each unit had a peekaboo view of the big red dog-turd rocks that pass for mountains there, but the back patios were invisible to the neighbors.

There was enough breeze that it would be cool on the patio, so I led her there and brought her a glass of wine for the wait while I showered. When I stepped away to go inside she turned and grabbed my wrist, staring into my eyes.

"Stay a minute," she said.

I felt my heart detonate in my throat. I could only stare, thinking of nothing to say. Apparently this was going to be educational.

She changed her expression to something like a gentle knowing smile and pulled herself closer to me. She took a long slow sip of the wine and gave it to me. I gulped a longer one. She turned and set it on the armrest of my garage-sale wooden chaise. She turned back and ran both hands up my chest. Her perfume was an expensive-smelling cross between rose petals and come-fuck-me musk.

"I told you I like sweaty men," she said and pulled my shirt out of my gym shorts, then up over my head. Keeping her hands on my pecs, she moved her head back to kiss me. Her lips were like water after a mountain hike: cool, wet, delicious, and not altogether satisfying. It was a slow, relaxed nibbling. I didn't know what the protocol response was, so I stood there like an eighth grader, hard as rock in my jockstrap, which I'm sure she felt, pressed against her belly. She teased her tongue into my mouth and ran her hands lightly all around my hips and groin. She slid her fingers inside the waistband of my gym shorts and peeled them down, exposing my arousal poking above the elastic of the jock. Still in my high-tops and two pairs of socks, I tried to think of high school gym class to slow the flutter in my groin.

"It seems you like older women," she said, eyeing the tumescence, and began unbuttoning her blouse. When she was bare to the waist she stopped to fix me with her stare, then lifted her neck very straight to hold her breasts at their most perfect posture and took another slow sip of the wine. My mouth was dry. I took a drink, too, but missed the armrest, shattering the glass on a rock among the cacti.

I fell to my knees and she pulled my head to her breasts. They looked slightly deflated, like those of a woman who had once nursed, but she was sighing and lightly glowing with perspiration. I found her beautifully perfect.

She sat and pushed herself backward up the chaise, drew up her skirt, and shimmied out of her panties. She pulled me out of the jock and squeezed me into her. She locked her legs around mine, scrunched her eyes closed, and rocked. I may have been on top but there was no doubt who was laying whom. Embarrassed, I came.

Obviously she had not participated in that particular climactic moment. Though it was tempting to verbally gush inquiries, apologies, and puppy-dog prattle, I was awed into a better choice—keeping my mouth shut. I think she got exactly what she wanted: proof that despite my relative youth and strength I was absolutely susceptible to her. After about three minutes of nothing but mutual heavy breathing, I pulled out and off of her. "Shower," I grunted.

Her reply was only, "Bring me a towel."

We went to a barbecue restaurant far away on the west side of Phoenix, away from the money side of town. She said it had great food and was sure to have no one in it who would recognize us. There wasn't much talk over dinner, but she did warn me not to get too full because I would need to show some energy before the night was over.

When we left she handed me the keys to her Mercedes and went to the passenger side. As I started the car she leaned onto my shoulder and began whispering into my ear wonderfully explicit observations about my anatomy, what she especially liked about it, her own post-coital state and how much she enjoyed a certain reminder issuing from her during dinner. Perhaps the single most remarkable thing about my time with Professor Lyle was that I did not crash the car during that excruciating drive to her Scottsdale condo. Naturally her anticipatory pillow talk had the desired effect, and by the time we got there I was a juvenile ball of testosterone, painfully erect but otherwise completely malleable to her whims.

Our encore session was unquestionably more satisfying for her, in the usual sense, and for that matter, for me. She conducted us through an extensive repertoire of postures and points of contact, punctuated by two rather vocal peaks from her, followed by brief rest periods and finally a grunting orgasm from me. I ended it with the sleep of the dead.

Her clock radio at 5 A.M. seemed as painful as any hangover I'd ever had. She called a cab for me and gave me a twenty to pay for it. Mimi was explicit: I was to try my very goddamnedest to get to rounds at a normal hour and make not the slightest comment nor facial expression nor untimely erection for that matter to let any of the hospital snoops have even a faint glimmering of a hint of what had happened and, if I had a poker face and any luck at all, would happen again very soon indeed.

I replied softly, "Yes, ma'am."

4

Here on the plains my work hours come to me via a mother-substitute named Adrienne Salter. Technically my "Liaison" at Western Acute, Adrienne is virtually my manager. Though we've never met, she has become a friend. We speak often on Western Acute's WATS line.

Adrienne's job at Western is to find work for me and her stable of semi-retired and quasi-reliable doctors like me. Though it is actually the other way around. Her job is to find a semireliable doctor able and willing to fulfill Western's contractual commitment to these small-town hospitals.

And if the doctor she has available has an impediment—say, a lack of a license in the state—Adrienne's job is to fix it. She is The Mistress of the License. Thanks to her I am officially a Kansas doctor, a Colorado doctor, and, recently, a South Dakota doctor, too. I got a license there thanks to the hard work of Adrienne and a willingness by the director of the South Dakota licensing board to overlook some checkering in my record. Doctors aren't lining up to work in the Little Towns on the Prairie, so the director had a certain motivation to be broad-minded. I am forever to be beholden, professionally, to the kindnesses of others.

Western Acute's usual line, when they want you to sign up for a weekend commitment, is to tell you it's a quiet little ER where nothing ever happens. That was more or less the same thing they told me when I went to work in the ER in Glory, Arizona, where Henry Rojelio provided the quick education still ringing in my ears today. If it's an ER open for business, something bizarre will show up. Certainly not every shift, maybe not even every month, but it's going to happen. So "Quiet Little ER Where Nothing Ever Happens" has long been a joking cliché between Adrienne and me.

A case in point: my first patient in South Dakota. A ninety-one-year-old woman, all ninety-seven pounds of her, was pulled down her own porch steps by her dog, an elkhound, for crissakes, who apparently thought they should chase, together, the squirrel on her fence. Initially I could find only soreness and bruises and a wrist broken in the typical way—cocked backwards to break the fall. Interestingly, though, according to the X-rays I ordered out of sheer compulsivity, she had broken her neck, too. The first vertebra was sitting a good three quarters of an inch forward on the second. Looking only at the film, I would have guessed her to have been dead. She should have cut off all nerve flow below her chin, including breathing signals.

After gingerly getting her into a medieval-looking neck brace and arranging ambulance transfer to a serious hospital where her neck bones could be pulled back into line, then plated, screwed, and wired to keep them there, I asked her for a second time about any nerve-related symptoms. With enough leading and prodding questions, she was willing to allow that there might be, yes, if she thought about it, a little tingling in her fingers. But that was it. And she insisted it would not bother her, she would just like to go back home. Before being wheeled away she insisted on access to the phone so she could contact her neighbor to review the elkhound's feeding and exercise regimen.

Maybe the nine-plus decades of life on the prairie had baked her spinal cord into sinew along with her skin and muscles.

THE BOOK OF MIMI, CHAPTER TWO

In the weeks following my initiation night with Madame Lyle, she took me on an extended tour of the Land of the Erotic, complete with side trips into pseudo-domesticity. We regularly cooked dinners at her condo: elaborate salads or pasta with a quick sauce. And wine.

I was careful to avoid any sense of occupying her private space unbidden. Inevitably, though, I became at home in her home. It began with my asking if it was okay that I leave a toothbrush and razor there. She laughingly approved.

Her style shunned the trite colors and motifs common in Southwestern homes. She favored the austere: blacks, whites, and grays, with small accents of reds and rusts. In her bedroom, though, was an anomaly: an antique glass and walnut bookcase with a fascinating array of artifacts—a small trophy with a figure of a girl in a cap and baggy pants hefting a softball bat, antique glass figurines and metal toys, some of them rusty, and two rows of very old illustrated children's books. One night before bed she found me staring into it. I gave her an inquiring look but she shook her head and turned out the lights.

Though it seemed absurd to think that either Mimi or I could be playing for keeps, we did come to know things about each other beyond the anatomic. I believe I could accurately put to rest the gossip among my fellow heathens about why Dr. Lyle left The Mayos of Minnesota.

Her mother died of leukemia when Mimi was eleven, leaving her with a controlling father and the only female in a family of cops. Her grandfather, father, and eventually all three brothers bore the badge. Family outings involved great noise, smoke, and piles of empty casings as they each tried to outshoot her father at the pistol range. When her academic talents became obvious, Daddy began picking for her a college appropriate for entrée to the FBI or CIA.

Mimi, though, from the time of her mother's illness, found any direction from her father unbearable. She referred to him as The Python.

For her, rebellion became a creative outlet. She took up with older males while barely pubescent and developed a taste for stopping traffic with her sartorial choices. Her favorite high school ensemble was— imagine it from the ground up—knee-high black patent high-heel boots, shiny white tights, black leather hot pants, a skin-tight and low-cut white leotard, and a studded black patent choker. For variety she sometimes wore a black-and-white-checked leotard instead of the pure white. Mimi had the physical attributes to stop traffic in a housedress and hair curlers, so the vision she painted in detailing that costume was nearly more than I could stand. I asked her to re-create it for me in private but she declined. "It's all gone to charity except the boots," she said.

Her brief marriage began with elopement the summer after high school. Her only contact with Tony the Sailor after the one beating was through lawyers.

She said, "Daddy would have taken me back—the Prodigal Daughter—but there was no use in that. Just more suffocation."

47

She went instead to a small liberal arts college in Maine on a scholarship. Her father dismissed it as "snooty" and "pinko." When she majored in English instead of something "useful," the rift between them widened. She graduated in three and a half years, with honors, and then, to be certain her father understood her escape from his shadow, she applied to medical schools, something pioneering in the Lyle clan.

She ended up in neurological surgery, she said, "Because there were no other women there. That was reason enough." After a five-year residency in Pennsylvania she landed a two-year fellowship at the Mayo Clinic. While there she developed, alongside Ian McWhorten, one of the Grand Old Men of the discipline, a reliable animal model of the breakdown in part of the brain's self-protective mechanisms that occurs in certain inflammatory conditions. Such work would have been a springboard to a remarkable career.

Trouble arose, though, over a database she set up—with a very primitive computer—detailing the situations and outcomes of every case of head trauma from child abuse known to have occurred in the three counties around the clinic in the previous twenty years. Naturally this was a large ongoing project that would never be truly finished, but it was certainly a valuable effort. The trouble came when she saw her own data one day in a neurosurgery journal. Without her name. An associate professor whom she would have thought completely unaware of the project, much less entitled to any ownership, had written a paper based on the findings and submitted it for publication under only his name.

Miriam Lyle, MD, daughter of law enforcement, naturally went to war with a righteous vengeance. Letters were sent to first one, then another rung on the ladder. There were heated encounters. The data thief invoked as a defense the notion that she had created the database as a department asset. He, as a member, was entitled to make use of it. Was it his worry that she had not seen the good that would come from publishing the findings?

No one doubted that she saw well the good and only wanted more data before writing the paper. Everyone knew the pirate's motivation—his written output had dwindled to nil in the last few years along with his speaker's stipends. But he routinely took night call in the chairman's place in the rotation, and he had a defense, however mealy-mouthed. Nothing happened. Mimi's only honorable choice was to resign. From there she ended up with a nice job in an academic backwater, reputation marred by an unfinished fellowship.

By the end of the tale Mimi's hands were shaking. I went to pour the last of our dinnertime bottle of wine into her glass. She stared at me and said very quietly, "There is nothing worse than powerlessness."

Maricopa days and nights obviously acquired a dramatically different flavor. Extraordinary things became the norm. Some of them actually involved patient care.

It is said that every case is a teaching case; that is, there is something to be learned. On that rotation two extraordinary cases—one bad, one good—showed me how an individual surgeon might make a difference. I called them the Cases of Extraordinary Teaching.

The first came in my third week on Neurosurgery. It was superficially starting out the same as any other week of residency: I was up way too early in the morning, bleary eyed, and tired after a too-short weekend. The only difference was the secret source of my weariness.

The neurosurgeons at the Maricopa Medical Branch rotate on and off call at 9:00 A.M.: If a case hits the ER at 8:30 on a Monday morning, it belongs to the guy who had the weekend duty. Unless he can pass it to someone else, sometimes by pleading the recipient's greater expertise is needed, sometimes by begging, sometimes by just a sleazy exit out of town. The costs to the giver's reputation are predictable if not meaningful; repercussions are generally only dealt downward on the totem pole.

Keith Coles was a truly unfortunate person at least twice over. During a morning jog along one of the city's many irrigation canals, he collapsed. At the age of thirty-nine. Another runner found him, help was called, and he ended up in the UAMMB emergency room. The ER doc recognized the signs of stroke, got him some IV fluids, got him intubated, pharmacologically paralyzed, and mildly hyperventilated—state-of-the-art treatment then. The CAT scan showed a grape-sized blood clot in the deep substance of the brain in front of the thalamus and free blood in the fluid around the brain. Mr. Coles had blown an aneurysm.

Mimi and I were rounding at seven forty-five or so, struggling to muster the energy needed to appear as if we had spent the weekend in our respective homes reading medical journals, when Dr. Leonard Babcock, one of the more aged neurosurgeons on the faculty, paged her. I heard only a couple of polite conversation fillers and then some nonspecific grunts from Madame Lyle. After hanging up she said, "He said the ER called him with an aneurysm, and would I like the case. Lazy prick."

"Dr. Lyle, you are a diversely skilled individual," I chided her.

"This morning I can barely walk," she said and closed her eyes and formed her lips into a kissing posture.

"You're bad," I mumbled.

We found Mr. Coles in the ER just as the nurse was packing up his belongings to get him shipped off to the ICU. He had two big plastic tubes sticking out of his nose, one on each side. The ventilator was breathing for him through one; his stomach was being drained through the other. Each had blood drying around it. IV fluids were running in both arms; clearish urine was draining from his bladder catheter.

His wife was there, propped up on an ER stool, draped uncomfortably over the chrome side rail of the gurney, holding one of his hands and brushing back his hair while talking to him quietly. She dabbed a bloody washcloth at his nose. Mimi introduced herself and me. Though the woman's eyes looked like they had been on fire, she stood and shook both our hands, then rubbed her eyes with the heels of her palms.

Mimi looked at the man's wristband, then said to the woman, "Is it Mrs. Coles?"

"Roberts. Abbie Roberts, but I am his wife." I lowered the side rail so his wife could get closer to him. He obviously wasn't going to be thrashing around.

"Ms. Roberts, I don't know how much the Emergency physician has told you . . ."

She broke in, "That he might have had a stroke . . ." and began a stuttering sniffle.

"Technically I suppose that's true, Mrs. Roberts. Has he been in good health before today?"

"Yes. Jogged almost every day." I found her a new tissue.

"Never in the hospital before?"

"Not since we've . . . not since I've known him. Thirteen years."

"Has he been on any medications?"

"No. Well, sometimes aspirin."

"How much?"

"Maybe a couple, a few times a week. Could that be what . . ."

"No, no. Very unlikely."

"Because I told him he should be using Tylenol. He said it didn't work as well."

As she spoke Mimi was doing her physical exam. The man was paralyzed with drugs, so there wasn't much to examine. Even if he had been awake in there, he couldn't have responded. "Had he been complaining of headaches? In the last few days?"

"No. He took the aspirin for his knee. He said men were supposed to take aspirin every day anyway. Isn't that so?"

Mimi was looking at his pupils with her penlight. "Mrs. Roberts, I think we can cut to the chase a bit. It appears, from the presentation, the sudden onset, the location of the bleed, his age, and all, that most likely your husband has ruptured a berry aneurysm, probably at the junction of the internal carotid artery and the anterior communicating artery. That's the usual spot. We will get a cerebral angiogram, of course . . ."

"What is that?"

". . . to delineate the exact spot of the bleed and try to see the aneurysm."

"I'm sorry. What is that?"

"What?"

"The cerebral something. A test, I guess." Mimi was silent. Ms. Roberts repeated herself, "A cerebral angie-something."

There was a pause. "Angiogram," Mimi said, patronizing.

"I'm sorry, Doctor. I don't know all these terms. But if you could . . ."

"No, of course you don't. You wouldn't. You let us worry about these technical things."

51

"But I'll need to know . . ."

"Well, we'll see. We'll need to get the angio today. This morning actually. It's a dye study—X-rays of the head. With these things it's best to let the brain recover somewhat. Cool off a couple of days. Stabilize. But there's also the risk of re-bleeds. We can't wait too long. We generally go in at about day two or three to clip the aneurysm. It can be very touchy surgery but our success rate is pretty good."

It was obvious to me Ms. Roberts had not processed much of that. I was used to imperious professors but Abbie had not done the time. Mimi's peremptory attitude would turn Abbie's emotional shock into a turtlelike disappearance.

I said, "The angiogram is a dye study. They inject an iodine contrast—people call it a dye—into the arteries so the X-rays can show what they look like, and frequently it will show if there's leaking—bleeding—too."

Ms. Roberts nodded, but Mimi shot me a withering You're-wasting-my-time-again look.

The thought flashed through my mind, *Fuck it. Maybe I don't want to be a surgeon.* I gave Abbie another tissue.

She asked Mimi, "But what do you think his chances are? I mean . . ."

"He should make it."

"But will he be . . . He wouldn't want to be . . ." She was sobbing too hard to finish. Mimi motioned to me we would leave.

Ms. Roberts said, "But he's never even been sick."

Mimi said, "We'll talk more later."

At the nurse's station she rattled off some orders for me to write: Admit to ICU. Neuro protocol vital signs. Nothing by mouth. Consent for cerebral angiography. Consent for a pressure-monitoring bolt in the skull. Stop the hyperventilation. She seemed agitated but said only, "I'll be in my office," and left.

I found the forms for the consents and wrote for the new ventilator settings. I caught up with Mr. Coles and his wife as the ER nurse was pushing the stretcher out the automatic doors. The nurse was saying, "This is her specialty . . . ," but stopped when I came in.

I offered Ms. Roberts an apologetic smile. "Maybe I can fill in a few of the blank spots," I said. She mustered a small smile in return.

As I helped the nurse negotiate the gurney over the yellowed carpet, up the ramp between buildings, and into the elevator, I explained to Ms. Roberts the procedure involved for an angiogram and what we expected to find. I said Dr. Lyle also wanted her consent for us to put into Keith's head what we call a bolt—a device that screws into a small hole in the skull, through which we thread a thin catheter to measure the intracranial pressure, or ICP. "Because the brain is within a closed space," I said, "any swelling—edema—of injured brain would raise the pressure inside the skull. If the pressure gets too high it can interfere with or even stop the blood flow to the brain." I looked over my shoulder to see her face. She was staring. I wasn't certain she had heard me.

"And then what do you do?" she asked.

"Then?"

"If the pressure gets too high and there's no blood flow."

"The plan, what we try to do, is know how the pressure is going. We can lower it, usually, with certain drugs or hyperventilation, for brief periods. Hyperventilation lowers the carbon dioxide in the blood, and the blood vessels in the brain constrict down. That lowers the pressure in the head. Blood can actually flow in better. Protects the perfusion pressure."

"Perfusion pressure. Blood pressure to the brain?"

"Pretty much. Yeah."

"So the blood pressure can't be too low?"

"That's part of it. The blood pressure has to be a certain amount greater than the pressure inside the skull or the blood flow will be too low. Or stop."

"So you're looking at the pressure difference."

"Uh-huh."

"And drugs can control it."

"Usually."

"And if they can't?"

"The injury to the brain extends."

She blinked. "More brain cells die."

"Uh-huh." I was not being medically eloquent but we had resumed communicating.

"Could the whole brain die?"

"Not really. I mean it can, in the most extreme cases, usually through herniation, where the lower parts of the brain get squeezed down into the hole at the base of the skull, the foramen magnum, and all the blood flow around there stops."

"And then he would be brain dead?"

"Yeah, that can happen. Or even just . . . dead." "Expired" came to mind but we were beyond the usual euphemistic niceties. "That part of the brain controls the heart to a certain extent. But that's not what will happen here. That usually only happens in the severe injuries, the really bad head traumas."

"So what's going to happen in Keith's case?" I offered a sympathetic frown. She went on, "I mean, the most likely things. What could happen."

"The cortex, the outer layer"—I was gesturing over the top of my head—"is the most vulnerable, the most sensitive."

"But that's the most important, isn't it?"

"Well, the deeper parts control basic life functions. They keep us alive."

"But the cortex, the outer . . . the vulnerable part, that's where we think and feel, right?"

"Well, right."

"So if Keith loses his cortex, what would he want with basic life functions?"

I nodded. "Well, I guess most people would see it that way."

There was a pause. She said, "He would see it that way. If his cortex is dead I want him off the machines."

"We think we can avoid that," I said. It was all I could say, though I was not sure it was true.

In the ICU she read over the consents and looked up at me, tearful. "Of course I'll sign them. You've been kind to explain, but, really, how would I know?"

After a silence I looked her in the eye and said, "We're going to be doing everything that can be done. We'll give him the best chances. He's in the best of hands."

I meant it. I did not know better.

Mimi was scribbling furiously on a yellow legal pad when I got to her office. I sat silently on the couch there and went through my note cards on the various patients admitted over the weekend: A pair of three-hundred-pound Hawaiians who had been drunk, sharing a large motorcycle, and turned in front of an even larger truck. A three-year-old admitted with an infection of her ventriculo-peritoneal shunt.

Mimi said from out of nowhere, "You know, if she wants to assume the care of her husband it's fucking fine with me. Four years of college, four years of medical school. Six years of residency, two years of fellowship. You'd think just once someone would be willing to take my word for something."

After a deep breath I ventured, "Well, I went through some of the stuff in detail with Mrs. Coles—Roberts, I mean. She's really pretty sharp. And scared, of course."

"Don't let her run you around. You're the doctor."

I bit my lip—the proper response of a junior resident. Maybe she was showing me what it took to be a surgeon. Maybe I wouldn't make it.

In those days ICP bolts were done in the OR, not the ICU. This meant someone—someone low on the totem pole—had to move Mr. Coles's bed, monitors, IV pumps, ventilator, drainage bags, and body, as a unit, down some halls, around some corners, through some doors, into and out of an elevator, and dock them softly against an OR table. Hallways, corners, and elevators have a surprising ability to reach out and disconnect the critically ill from their life-support devices.

I was in the ICU when the OR team came for Mr. Coles. A tall, quiet OR nurse and an anesthesiologist I thought I recognized, an elfin man with spindly fingers and a naso-whiny Brooklyn accent, unusual in the desert. He was grumbling to the nurse something about ". . . the loser's gonna code in the elevator." She barely nodded.

I asked, "Ruining your day, Dr. Levov?"

"It's 'LeFleur,' Ishmail. Levov is the heart surgeon, and anybody who's been through the three divorces he has wouldn't let a little thing like a code in an elevator ruin his day."

I smiled. "You know, Doctor, I've always wondered, what is that little plastic thing you guys wear around your necks?" The nurse was now smiling.

"Actually, it's a stethoscope—custom molded." He put the blue glop of plastic at the end of his piece of tubing into his left ear. "It's becoming an antique," he went on, "what with all our electronics going beep, beep, beep, we hardly need to listen to the patient anymore. But I'd still rather listen to a steady lub-dub than to a putz surgeon."

"Gee, thanks."

"Not you, Ishmail, you're still a human being. But just wait till you're out. Busy practice, wife, three or four kids, couple of mortgages. Office full of whiny old ladies and your nurse's period is two weeks late. Then we'll see how nice and respectful you are to your copilots of the OR."

I said, "Yes, Doctor," using the very official sounding tone of voice that all the nurses use to mean "Fuck you, Doctor."

Everyone smiled, even Dr. LeFleur.

With a collective grunt we began the parade of stop and go with only a little whining from the anesthesiologist. Halfway there two of the infusion pumps began to emit piercing alarm tones for no apparent reason. Dr. LeFleur cursed them but urged the procession onward, vowing to pitch them off the roof after the case.

Mr. Coles's ICP was about 16 with occasional bumps up to 30. Not good, but not awful. Living in the borderlands.

I helped with the return parade, safely tucking in Keith back in the ICU. I found Ms. Roberts on the pay phone in the hallway outside the ICU waiting room. She was crying.

"... I know you do ... I know you do ... Daddy loves you too. ..." She looked up only long enough to acknowledge me waiting for her. "Daddy's going to be fine, Daddy's going to be fine. I love you, punkin'. Now let me talk to Ma ..." She covered the phone and looked at me. "What was the pressure?" Then immediately back to the mouthpiece, "Helen, one of the doctors is here, just hold for a second. . . . That's what I need to find out," then back to me, a pleading look.

"The pressure was okay; not normal, but not terrible." I patted her arm. "If it bumps up we should be able to get it back down. Just knowing what it is, we'll know better where to keep his blood pressure, too."

"So what now?"

"Wait."

"I hate waiting."

"Yes, we all do."

"But if that's what's best for Keith . . ."

"Yeah, that's what's best for Keith. You finish your call. I'll come find you if anything changes."

Keith Coles's ICP and blood pressure bounced around for two days. He got morphine and sodium thiopental to keep his nervous system barely idling, he got mannitol to carry water and salt out via the kidneys, and he got intermittently hyperventilated when his ICP shot up. He did not wake up, though. I hoped that was from the thiopental and morphine and not the brain injury.

No one liked the waiting. Mimi was noticeably surly and snappish. Not completely antisocial toward me, but decidedly asocial. Which was convenient anyway; her bedside nastiness toward the afflicted had well chilled my ardor. A few nights of sleeping at home was entirely welcome at that point.

On Keith's own Day Three we took him back to the OR.

Clipping an aneurysm deep in the brain is, I am told, probably the most nerve-wracking operation in all of medicine. The exposure is lousy, the room to maneuver nonexistent, the margin for error exactly zero. You're trying to get a titanium clip across the base of a sack growing from the arteries that feed the brain. The usual mental image is that of a berry hanging on a stalk, but in reality the base of the beast is almost never that discrete; the aneurysm is just a bulge, frequently lying between two perfectly good arteries that the patient is going to need. Worst of all, the aneurysm walls are incredibly weak—the arterial tissue was not meant to stretch that far. That's why they bleed in the first place.

Sometimes the damn thing bursts open just by being exposed. It can explode when touched during the dissection or clip application. If it does, you're all completely fucked: Surgeons must try to get the clip deep in a hole, perfectly applied to something they can't see, while counting down the seconds until all the patient's blood is on the floor. Anesthesiologists jump around yelling for blood to transfuse while trying to decide if they should raise the blood pressure to feed the brain or lower it so the surgeon has a chance to see. The nurses are trying to do twelve things at once while wondering if the whole thing is their fault. Of course the patient—well, the patient. If control can be regained somehow, he might still be okay. If there is no quick control, the surgeon might have to clip off the arteries feeding the aneurysm and hope the backup blood supply to the brain is adequate. If the backup supply is weak, the patient has the biggest stroke imaginable and will be either dead or nearly so.

When the case started, Mimi was already mildly pissed off. We were listed as an 11:00 A.M. start, which was not a bad time considering we had only booked the case two days before, but the first case in the room, a hysterectomy, had gone long because of some screwup that should have been minor but apparently, in their hands, wasn't. We didn't even get Mr. Coles into the OR until 1:15. I'd paged Mimi at 10:30 to let her know about the delay. All she said was, "Goddamn gynecologists," using the soft "g" in the word. She probably learned it from Ian McWhorten at Mayo's.

Things started off okay. From what I could tell, the anesthetic induction and the arterial line and all the anesthesia futzing around went fine. Mimi had me shave the guy's head, and I did the sterile prep under minor but continual criticisms from the circulating nurse. We then put his head in the Mayfield head holder. A big stainless steel C-clamp, with two opposable halves, it reaches up and around the middle of the head. It grabs the head via three stainless steel "points" about the size and shape of the end of a pencil, but much sharper. These are pressed into the scalp, two from one side and one from the other. The clamp is then tightened like a vise until the points are firmly into the skull. The whole assembly is then attached with large hand-bolts to the surgical table to provide absolute stability to the head for as long as needed.

Just as we were about to press the things into the skin, Charlie Ryan, the anesthesiologist, said, "Wait a sec, sorry," and pushed some drug into the IV. "Gotta be a little deeper for this," he added. We ratcheted together the two halves of the C-clamp and the points sank home. Blood trickled from each. The beep-beep of Keith's pulse quickened. The anesthesiologist stared at the blood pressure trace on the monitor. It went from 105 over 60 to 155 over 100. He turned a dial on the anesthesia machine. We tightened all the clamps between the Mayfield and the table, and Mimi gave the thing a gentle but firm rock. The whole table bounced slightly. Mr. Coles's head was effectively bolted to the table. We went to scrub.

As we washed our hands and arms she did not seem nervous. She was humming softly to herself. Neither of us said anything until nearly the entire five minutes of scrubbing had gone by. Finally she turned and whispered, "You really have a great cock," hit the water switch with her knee, and headed into the OR with her poker face intact.

She pressed two fingers into the bony nubs at the ends of the skull, then drew a sickle-shaped purple line across his naked scalp with a sterile felt-tip pen. She laid the scalpel onto the far end of the line, took a long breath, pressed the blade through the skin, and drew it sharply along the prescribed arc cleanly to the other end. The two skin edges fell slightly open and then, after an odd pause, began to ooze purplish-red blood.

"Clips," she said. The scrub nurse laid into her opened palm a stainless steel pliers-like clamp with a blue plastic clip loaded on the end. These clips are like barrels missing a few staves. The clamp holds them open so they can be fitted over open skin edges, then released. The clips contract down and press shut the bleeding points, stopping the ooze.

She peeled the skin back from the skull and its lining layers, buzzed a few bleeding points with the cautery, and called for the drill. She bored, with a brace and bit little different from the ones in my grandfather's workshop, five one-eighth-inch holes around the perimeter of the open space.

"Can you do dot-to-dots?" she asked me.

I'm sure I looked stupid.

She handed me the saw. "This is an ultrafast rotary saw. It goes through bone like a hot knife through butter. If you can control yourself, you can connect the dots." She put the tip through the nearest hole. "This deep."

I reached for the handle. The saw had a long, thick, cumbersome power cord. It was driven by high-pressure nitrogen and controlled by a foot pedal. I plowed from A to B to C to D to E. My lines between dots wavered a bit, but I realized the defect would have zero functional importance and would exist only under the skin, where it would never be seen.

With the saucer-shaped segment of skull passed off to the nurse, we were looking at the dura, a tough, fibrous sheath with the appearance and feel of the cover of a well-used baseball. Mimi incised it with a scalpel, then cut a smaller version of her earlier sickle curve with a small scissors and pealed it back to expose the brain.

She stripped away thin filmy sheets of membrane and electrically obliterated the tiny blood vessels belonging to them. This freed up the underlying brain lobes to be eased out of her way.

That's where I came in. My job in an operation like this was to hold retractors, though only temporarily. Once into the brain, she would bend thin strips of stainless steel like long spatulas to conform to certain curves, gently lay them under lobes, and lift. I then held them there until she could get the rod on the other end of the retractor clamped into the support frame, this latter being far more reliable than a resident.

When she handed me the first retractor she made her expectation clear: "Hold this. Like a rock." I believe residents have a "freeze" reflex. I could not have moved if I had wanted to.

Having filled the available space with retractors, we began to advance them. She would lock my hands onto one, loosen its clamp, take it from me, give it another incremental lift, nod for me to grasp and hold, then reattach it. By alternating between the table clamp and the resident, she was able to slowly advance her retractors and open up a view into a deep recess under the brain.

Once the primary exposure was accomplished and secured, the nurses swung in an operating microscope the size of small backhoe. The working end of the thing is cantilevered out from a heavy base. Once it was in approximate position a huge sterile plastic bag was put over it from the business end toward the base unit. Through it we could work the knobs and turn the dials, all the time staying sterile. Rubberized rings in the bag fit over the lenses of the scope so the bag wouldn't interfere with the light transmission.

"Oh hell," she said. "I'm contaminated!" Apparently she had accidentally brushed her hand against the scope; she was holding out her left hand for the nurse to pull off the glove. I had not seen her touch anything outside the invisible boundary of sterility. "Let's change the bag, too," she said.

The nurse said, "You didn't contaminate the bag, though, if you just touched the lens."

"I just want it changed."

"These are expensive."

"Less than wound sepsis."

The nurse was rolling the bag off the microscope. "Waste," she mumbled.

After the false start, Mimi got the scope the way she wanted it, and we sat down again, her eyes pressed to the main scope with me at the teaching head, 90 degrees to her right.

Brain, under binocular 4X magnification, looks like nothing else. The lobules of neurons, for all the power and holiness we imagine they contain, are smooth wet bumps; yellowish pink, cheesy, slightly dirty. Every groove between lobules has two tiny blood vessels snaking through, the vein somber, purple, thin-walled, fragile; the artery smaller but more muscled and a cheerier red. With each heartbeat the artery and even the brain substance itself pulsate and expand, giving the view in the lens a surging rhythm. The first time I sat in on brain surgery I found it unsettling. Very soon, though, like the rocking motion of a boat, you get accustomed to it. You only become aware of your new sense when you are totally unnerved as it slows or stops.

Twenty-four hours later Keith Coles was effectively dead.

5

Since Henry, since escaping Arizona with my hide and little else, my personal life, for all the reasons I am here to tell, has been static, at best. I live in a rented two-bedroom house in the town where I grew up, within walking distance of my parents. My mother cooks me dinner more often than I cook my own, though hospital cafeterias and roadhouse diners outnumber the two combined.

If I have a unique talent it is driving. Driving for distance. During the extended dependency of college, medical school, internship, and residency, one is always short on money. Early in college I learned from a fellow Nebraska-to-Boston vagabond how to compensate with youthful exuberance. He and I would drive nonstop tag-team from Cambridge to Lincoln—his home—and back again, all to spend a few break days with family.

When he was in Europe one quarter I did the trek alone, grabbing a few hours sleep in the cramped backseat of my car. It became my routine mode of travel. Sure, I'm a little bleary-eyed and zombielike when I arrive, having spent fifteen to thirty hours at seventy-plus miles per hour, but being able and willing to put my head down and get someplace far away has proven a useful skill, especially since returning West, where the deserts are vast between the oases.

I sometimes wonder if I've forgotten how to breathe. I have not had a significant romance since leaving Phoenix. Instead I have "friends." Most senior among them is Cheryl, an intensive care nurse, now living in Flagstaff, whom I have known since internship. She is soft-spoken, has a cute nose and slightly wide hips under a small waist, extraordinarily round breasts, and a short, boyish haircut. We use each other shamelessly, guiltlessly, expertly. When one of us can make the full day's journey to the other, we couple to exhaustion. She calls it aerobic intercourse. When months go by without union, we sometimes lie in our distant beds naked, phone held in only one hand.

I like her. She's funny. I find her conversation interesting. And that seems to be enough for her. I wonder why it has been enough for me. It occurred to me the other day, in retelling my history, that Mimi Lyle and her cohort may have made me paranoid about women, though I think of myself as smarter than that.

I fear I am growing middle-aged, though Cheryl and I differ on the threshold for that distinction. Friends and family think I should give up my desperado lifestyle. I say to them, "What? Take up working on weekdays like most of the rest of the world? Ski when the lift lines are longest?"

On my last head-down sprint across the sands, I noticed I needed to stop and sleep more often and I cramped more easily. Conceivably it is time to start getting motel rooms along the way. The horror.

THE BOOK OF MIMI, CHAPTER THREE

In my six-week-month with Meems, my progress in the art and science of brain surgery seemed forgotten at times next to my growing experience in matters sexual and my extracurricular knowledge of the female body. As a trained clinician I could tell early on that hers had, at least once, carried and delivered a baby. There are physical signs produced by nothing else. But we never once spoke a word about it. Things like that don't come up in conversation, particularly between a pair joined only physically. What would I have said? "Hey, Mimi, what became of the kid?" Like a lover's silicone implants, it's safest to pretend you don't notice.

As if regular sex—I suppose we could have called it "dating" for a laugh—between a junior resident and his professor/Attending weren't far enough out of bounds, she took our trysts to places I had only read about, or, ironically, heard about in the best-attended lectures in medical school, "Sexual Variations." She introduced me to penetration *in ano*, which seemed to be something new, even to her. She told me she had tried it before but her other half at the time was a klutz, it hurt, she had panicked, and aborted it. Under her direction, we moved very slowly. She bit her lip through the painful bits but nodded encouragement. She eventually got a faraway look and sound to her, very regressionary on the scale of evolution. I was feeling animalistic myself. After extensive mutual heaving and grunting and sweating, we climaxed within seconds of each other and collapsed in a jumble. I was instantly lost in a reverie, half sleep, half intoxication. When I came around she was lying beside me, a tear drying on her temple, still as a corpse. For a moment I thought she had died, and there I'd be, bare-assed in my professor's bed, my semen in her rectum, doing one-rescuer CPR while awaiting the ambulance and sheriff.

I brushed her cheek. She slowly opened her eyes. She was reassuring without saying a word: She just shook her head slightly and laid her index finger on my lips. She wouldn't talk to me. She just squeezed my chest and sobbed softly. Before rising she said, "It was the intensity, the vulnerability," and would say no more about it.

Two nights later she wanted to do it again. Same sequence, roughly speaking. It became a recurring theme. I found it simultaneously the pinnacle of naughtiness, intimacy, and thrillingness, an internally contradictory and mysterious trinity of simultaneous being, vaguely reminiscent, as I sat and thought about it during an otherwise boring lecture on surgical repair of vascular trauma, of fourth-grade catechism. But this wondrous bit of creation you couldn't even talk about to your friends, much less get raked over by nuns.

As I said, Keith Coles was effectively dead within twenty-four hours of his operation. The final declaration and physiologic passage, though, took many hours longer. Death, I believe, is never a thing of grace and beauty, at least not to those left behind, but when the affected are a young family, hours are eras.

Even as we made rounds the morning after his operation, data were accumulating that he might have been pushed over some invisible line. First, he was not waking up. Waking up after such an operation is highly variable and always slower than we want it to be, but he was making no moves at all in that direction.

Then, about mid-afternoon, his blood pressure shot up. The nurses paged me and I ordered a continuous drip of the preferred "knock-it-down" drug.

An hour later they called to say we had hit the other extreme, they had already hung their favorite "prop-it-up" drug and would I please write the order to make it legal. I let Mimi know we were in trouble and went over to the Unit. Given her antipathy toward the patient's wife, I was happy to handle it alone.

By the time I got there he had started pouring out pints of water-like urine, a sure sign that a deep part of the brain that is supposed to regulate the kidneys had checked out.

We ran him over to X-ray for a repeat CAT scan. This confirmed everyone's suspicion: massive brain swelling, suggesting that we had, in our attempts to find the aneurysm, cut off blood flow to big parts of the brain. It was now looking like a fatal event.

Back in the ICU, I did the bedside tests for brain function. The answer for each was negative.

I told Ms. Roberts things looked grim. She wanted to call together the family to hear the details. Late that evening she, Keith's mother, a brother, and a sister sat with me while I gave them the news. I laid out the facts, as tactfully as I could. They all cried, though most verbalized nothing. They asked that we support him until the next day.

The next morning I steered Mimi away. Ms. Roberts brought in the two daughters. She and her mother tearfully told them their father was not coming home. My eyes welled up, too.

We shuffled everyone in for hugs, kisses, and tears. Abbie Roberts stayed when the others filed out. The nurse and I pulled all the curtains. She got into bed with him and held him as tightly as I have imagined anyone ever held. She sobbed until the bed was bouncing. I turned off the ventilator, slid out his breathing tube, wiped off his face, and without looking back quietly went into the nearest bathroom to bawl alone.

Fifteen minutes later, hiding my sniffling, I sat on a low stool filling out the death certificate and signing his body over to the nameless and invisible people of the basement who clean up our messes. The chief surgery resident, a truly graceless and cynical man, who apparently witnessed parts of the end, leaned over me and whispered, "She going for it, you know, one final time?"

He was my superior and I knew he was trying to be funny or distracting. Still, I said, "Fuck you."

Within a week the rumor went around that the new Chairman of Anesthesiology, some hothead with a Stanford Phi Beta Kappa, decided he should be the arbiter of quality of care and got anal and agitated over the case. He fired off a letter to the Chairman of Neurosurgery seeking some sort of an investigation on competency issues.

Incompetence in doctors is like pain in patients. We know it's real, we know it's a serious problem, and we know people have a right to expect meaningful solutions, but it's still absurdly hard to pin down. Doctors are trained to be scientists and we don't trust things we can't measure.

It is always relative, never gross or obvious. Were there a surgeon who was regularly cutting into the wrong organs or failing to control major bleeding, I suppose he would get gang-tackled in a big hurry. But in a highly specialized field like brain surgery, where the differences between surgeons are all but invisible even to the other doctors in the room, who can say? Only other specialists in that field. Problem is they're all wondering when their next case will go way far south on them. And who will be looking over their shoulders when it does.

When I heard there was a high-level stink it didn't occur to me that the slime would get on us all the way down at the bottom of the totem pole. Nonetheless, not even ten days after Mr. Coles's operation I got a page from the Residency Secretary, Cynthia Blachly.

We house staff all lived and died according to Cynthia. She ran our schedules, handed out the monthly allotment of meal tickets, and was the immediate source of our paychecks. We were all nicer to her than we were to our own mothers.

"Were you scrubbed on the Coles aneurysm case?" she asked.

I hesitated. "Not if I can help it."

"You can't. The nurses' notes say you were scrubbed."

"It could have been a different Dr. Ishmail."

"Sorry, Charlie. There's only one of you. When can you meet with Dr. Kellogg?"

"The Chairman of Neurosurgery?"

"Yes, that Dr. Kellogg. Though actually he's a sub-chair, or I guess vice-chair, in charge here at The 'Copa. He answers to Marshall Bullock in Tucson, chair for all the UA affiliates."

"What does he want me for?"

"Your good looks."

"See, you do have the wrong guy."

"He needs a little information on the Coles operation from those who were there, darling. He's put aside a few hours each of the next three days to get this going. He wants to get it done with. I do too."

We set up a time, then I asked, "Any clues on your end as to how a simple country boy from Nebraska could play this and come out still in possession of his testicles?"

After a second she said, "Leave them at home."

If Joe Kellogg had the kind of simmering intensity just under the skin that one normally expects in a brain surgeon, he apparently had the burner turned down for my visit. What I had feared would be a quarter hour with my fingers in a light socket turned out to be more like a paternal chat about a fishing trip.

For a hotshot professor Joe Kellogg didn't have much of an office. Maybe twelve by twelve feet. A battered oak schoolteacher's desk, metal bookshelves packed with journals and texts, the aroma of coffee spilled long ago, manila folders of assorted thicknesses sprouting among the books, many of these sprouting pages torn from medical journals. The only art was a trite motivational poster in a dime-store frame.

Dr. Kellogg was gray-haired, I guessed prematurely, and had a bony neck and face. His white dress shirt had a collar cut for a neck thicker than his and frayed corners. His tie was crooked. Before I could even sit he asked what I thought of "all this codswallop." He had some residual accent. I guessed New Hampshire.

"You mean . . . this case?"

"Yes. All this fuss."

I did what any good resident knew to do with a loaded question— I ducked. "Well, sir, I don't know what to make of it."

"In Dr. Miekle's letter he referred to it as 'excruciating,' 'Mr. Coles and his excruciating operation.' What did you make of it?" He had on the desk Keith's patient chart, laid open to the graphic anesthesia record. He winced slightly as he motioned to it. "Four pages. Fourteen hours, all told," he said.

Caution lights were flashing before my eyes. "Um, what I remember," I began stupidly, "was basically that it took a really long time because there was bleeding and Dr. Lyle couldn't get a good view of the aneurysm. She was really frustrated. I mean, who wouldn't have been. This guy was seriously stroked and she's torquing on his frontal lobes and can't see the aneurysm."

"Yes, that's what they've already told me," he said, "but what I'm trying to get at was why she couldn't see it, or why she couldn't get a better view. This seems to be the great damned mystery."

I'm sure I looked pained. "I don't really know the different techniques of exposure, you know. I'm just a general surgery resident. . . ."

"Yes, of course. Nobody's expecting you to comment on her technique of getting exposure." He hesitated. "Did she say anything?"

"It was pretty quiet after about the first hour inside the head. Up until then she had been explaining what we were doing, kind of a running narrative, and seemed pretty into the whole thing, but when we got in to a certain depth, well, I guess she expected to see the aneurysm at a certain angle and it wasn't there."

"What did she do then?"

"Well, she kept trying."

"But how?"

"Well, she'd move the retractor a little one way and then suck out the blood, and reposition the microscope and look and then move the retractor a little the other way."

"Again, did she say anything?"

I knew I was walking through a minefield. "I guess not much. After a while she maybe was cussing a little, just quietly."

"Did she try another approach?" he asked.

"I remember once, she looked up from the scope, kind of stretched her neck and took a really deep breath, then closed her eyes for a second. She mumbled something about her stockbroker once saying, 'If you're losing money, try thinking differently.' Then she went to the viewbox." He waited.

I continued: "Actually, she stepped away several times. She would go look at the CT pictures on the wall. Study them and turn her head and all. Then she'd come back and sit down again and say, 'It's right there. I know it's right there. Why can't I see it?' Maybe halfway through the whole thing she said, 'Okay, it's just left of center. You go look at the scans,' she said to me, 'You go look at the scans and tell me which side of the artery the damn thing is on.'

"I went and studied the scans just like she had done, turned my head a little this way and so . . ." Dr. Kellogg smiled.

"Then I came and sat down at the teaching head again. She said, 'Now look at the patient. Which side am I approaching from?'

"I looked and looked, and I must say that once the drapes are over the guy and the skull is open you really can't tell front from back or left from right. Damnedest feeling. Like being lost in the woods. I got up again and went around to the anesthesia side of the drapes. Dr. Ryan lifted up the drapes a little, and I could just see the guy's chin. He had a short beard, and I mentally pictured the rest of the head and how it had to be lying and yeah, we were coming in from the left, just above and in front of the ear. I told her, 'We're coming in from the left.' She said, 'And this is the head?' We all kind of laughed."

"Nervously," he suggested.

"Yeah. Nervously."

"Whose idea was it to call in Dr. Adams?"

Mines everywhere. I had to think a second. "I guess it was hers—Dr. Lyle's. I didn't really pay that much attention to it. I remember Mimi—Dr. Lyle—saying, 'Oh, okay, call him!' Kind of exasperated."

" 'Call *him*'? Not 'call Dr. Adams'?"

"Yeah. Just 'call him.' "

"How did they know who to call?"

"I don't know."

"Dr. Adams's name hadn't been mentioned?"

"Well, it must have been, I guess. I guess I just didn't hear it. But I'm sure she just said 'call him.' "

"It wasn't at the insistence, or the suggestion, of Dr. Ryan?"

"I don't remember that as such. There was some grumbling going back and forth across the ether screen between the anesthesiologist and the scrub nurse. Nobody was too happy by then. Anesthesiologists must hate slow surgeons as much as surgeons hate slow anesthesiologists." Dr. Kellogg nodded. "This case was dragging on forever and people were getting pretty stressed. I remember another anesthesiologist came in to give Dr. Ryan a break, and they were whispering and shaking their heads. Then Dr. Ryan said something to his partner—louder—about 'needing help again.' "

"Did you think Dr. Lyle noticed any of that going on?"

"It was all really tense. I figured she at least heard the comment about help, but she didn't show it."

"Who was the other anesthesiologist?"

"I don't really remember. I think it might have been Dr. Koehler." I leaned over to look at the anesthesia record.

"There's no mention of a break," he said, waving his hand over the chart.

"It was probably Dr. Koehler," I said. "Whoever it was wasn't there but about twenty minutes."

"I'll look into it. One of the other people present during the case reported to me that Dr. Lyle finally asked for help from Dr. Adams only at the insistence of Charlie Ryan."

I just looked blank. "I don't remember it that way."

"You understand what I'm being asked to decide," he continued.

I nodded. "I think so."

"Part of a surgeon's skill set is knowing his—or her—limitations. None of us is as good an aneurysm surgeon as we'd like to be. Each case is different and there aren't enough cases—thank the good Lord—for anybody to get what you would call a whole lot of practice. I'm supposed to get some idea of Dr. Lyle's level of insight into her own abilities. Somebody must think I can do miracles. You and Dr. Ryan were the only other doctors present for the majority of the case."

"But . . . what I don't get, is, this was one case. As I understand aneurysm operations, they can go from bad to awful at any time. The way it's been explained to me, the things lie about dead center in the head. The exposure is never good. They burst if you, you know, disturb their invisible force fields, or whatever. When they do burst you're totaled."

"Well, not always," he said. "There are things one does. Sometimes they work. This aneurysm didn't burst, though. Correct?"

"No. I mean, yes, it did not burst."

"Did not . . . spring a big leak at any point?"

"No. And wouldn't that be in the Op Report?"

"It should be, if it happened."

"Well, it didn't happen. Unless I was asleep on my stool when it did."

He nodded. "If it did, the screaming—well, actually it's not screaming, it's the, I don't know, the lightning flashing around the room. Crisis management. It certainly would have awakened you and half the OR staff in the lounge."

I smiled. "But, sir, if the outcomes are rarely as good as you'd like, and, like you said, each one is different, how does this case mean so much?"

"Well, Malcolm, you hit the nail on the head. Dr. Lyle is a fine surgeon. I am proud to have her here at Maricopa. So I will tell you the party line, same as I'm telling Dr. Lyle: We take any peri-operative death seriously."

"Well, of course," I said.

"And this one generated a formal complaint from Dr. Miekle, Head of Anesthesia, to both Marshall Bullock and me. Which we will answer."

I nodded.

"Marshall has asked me to do all the legwork. We go asking a lot of questions, wasting a lot of time, it seems to me, to find out all over again that aneurysms do poorly."

"Yes, sir."

"It is a bit baffling how it could have gone on so long," he said to himself. "One thing noted on the anesthesia record," he went on, "was '0020: Dr. E. Adams called to help!' There's an exclamation point." He looked up at me. "Plaintiffs' attorneys adore little things like exclamation points around some problem. Then: '0105: Dr. Adams here.' Then '0155: Clip on.' Surgery end time is given as 0240. Patient in the ICU at 0310. Seem right to you?"

"Yeah. I guess so. I don't watch the clock."

"Could you tell me what happened? When Dr. Adams arrived, I mean. What was said?"

"Well, like I said, Dr. Lyle said, 'Oh, all right, call him!' She was exasperated. When she said that, it felt like everybody relaxed, the nurses and the anesthesiologist anyway. Mimi was pretty wound up, but seemed sort of resigned by then.

"So we're kind of sitting on our hands, you know, waiting for Dr. Adams to get there, once in a while sucking the blood out of the wound but mostly just keeping it covered and waiting. So about a half hour later he kind of slowly ambles in, holding a mask over his nose and mouth with one hand"—I slowed my speech way down—"sets his briefcase on the floor,"—Dr. Kellogg was smiling at this—"and looks over the scans on the viewbox while tying up his mask. Doesn't say much, except he drawls out, 'Howdy, everybody.' I'm wondering if this guy's for real."

"He's very real. Seen him do it," he said. "Defusing bombs."

"What?"

"Defusing bombs. Nobody feels like yelling anymore when he's sauntering around saying 'Howdy.' "

"Well, he kind of shuffles over to the table and peeks through my side of the microscope for a minute, nods to me, mumbles, 'Howdy,' shuffles back to the viewbox and studies the scans, then looks at the scrub nurse. I swear she was grinning behind her mask. She says, 'Eight browns?' He says, 'Yyyepp, like always,' and shuffles out to the scrub sink.

"When he came back I got up. Dr. Lyle took my seat and he moved to her seat. I was pretty beat, so I didn't exactly follow what he did, but he loosened and refixed the retractors a few times, looked through the scope, moved the retractor again, moved the scope. He just went in and found it. Clipped it. Took about thirty, forty minutes, I guess."

"Did he say anything?"

"He said, after the clip was on, something about it being in a tough spot, easy to miss. Maybe he was just being nice, though."

"He's like that."

"Then he got up and left. Said, 'Thanks for callin' me.' It was really kind of incredible. I even looked over at Dr. Ryan. He was kind of nodding. I said to him real quietly, 'Who was that masked man?'"

"Indeed." Dr. Kellogg rubbed his eyes. "Did you . . . Have you talked with any of the people who were there since the operation? Dr. Ryan? Any of the nurses?"

"You mean about the case?"

"Yes."

"No. I guess not. I mean, I've run into them. One of the nurses asked me how the guy was doing. That sort of thing. After he died one of the other residents asked me what happened. I said, 'Hey. Some patients die.' Bad disease—bad outcome."

"It is a bad disease."

"I read in the text that something like seventy percent die. Is that right?"

"It may be. About half don't even make it to the hospital. But of those who do, most survive."

"But all gorked out?"

"No. Some, for sure. Nursing homes and bedsores. But most survivors are more or less functional. One of our cardiologists here is an aneurysm survivor."

"Practicing?"

"Came back after rehab. Took most of a year, but now he's bright and busy as ever. It can be done."

"Well, like I said, there's been some head shaking among the residents and nurses and folks, but I haven't hashed through any details with any of them."

"Well, if you could, don't bring it up for a week or so. I'd like to complete my round of questions first. In fact, please don't discuss this case with anyone, other than the usual sorts of things you've already mentioned."

"I think I understand."

He looked at me. "I imagine you do. They tell me you're one of the better surgery residents," he said. "Real talent."

"I don't know about that. It's kind of you to say so, though."

"Going to stick it out in general surgery?"

"Planning to."

"Surgery of the stool-forming organs?" I just smiled. It was an old joke. "Thought of a subspecialty fellowship? Cardiac? Vascular?"

"I've kind of thought about cardiac, but I don't know if I'll be able to swallow another two years. Plus, my dad is expecting me to take over his practice back in Nebraska."

"Well, from what I hear you'll do very well."

"Thank you."

"One last thing."

"Yes, sir."

"I was in Tucson in meetings last Thursday. Was there a Morbidity and Mortality—M & M—presentation?"

"Yes, sir. I presented it."

"What was the gist of the discussion?"

"I presented it as an acute aneurysm, obvious high risk going in, difficult exposure, protracted surgery, Dr. Lyle got Dr. Adams to help. They got it clipped. Unfortunate outcome."

"What was given as the ultimate cause of death?"

"Diffuse cerebral infarction, massive reperfusion edema, brain swelling leading to herniation and ultimately no blood flow."

"The usual final pathway. Was there an autopsy?"

"No, sir, but the CT scan twenty-four hours post-op pretty strongly suggested the picture. The whole brain was massively congested."

"What about the discussion from the faculty, the other surgeons there?"

"Really not much. One asked how long the dura was open."

"What did you say?"

"I told him I thought it was about six hours. I hadn't checked the times. There were a couple of murmurs from the back."

"It was ten and three quarters."

"Yeah. I should have checked, I guess. Anyway there was very little discussion."

"Was Dr. Adams there?"

"I think so, yeah."

"Dr. Miekle?"

"I didn't see him."

He rose and shook my hand. "Thank you, Malcolm. I don't expect we'll have to bother you any more about this."

In the receptionist's room sat Dr. Ryan, apparently awaiting his turn to meet with Dr. Kellogg. I was momentarily frozen, standing in front of him. He cocked his head back, slapped shut the magazine he'd been reading, and said, "Time of your life, eh, kid?" He was smiling from only one side of his mouth.

"Isn't that from a movie?"

"Yeah, I suppose."

"Why do I have the feeling I'm stepping into a tar pit or something?"

"You're already in it up to your nuts, son. And the party's just beginning—I'm coming in after you." He stepped past me, into the inner office.

My enthusiasm for spending nights with Miriam Lyle had been considerably deflated, first by her nastiness toward Abbie Roberts, then by an instinctual sense that I'd aided and abetted a crime of some kind. When we weren't working at the hospital all night, I slept at home.

After my session with Dr. Kellogg, though, Mimi, naturally, was dying to know every word of the encounter. She maintained an air of unworried detachment, though. This, of course, made me want to recite the whole thing in detail, to get her responses, but I, too, restrained myself. As a result, it hung in the air like fog until the end of morning clinic, when we could reconstruct over lunch, one piece at a time, the details of the conversation. She acknowledged that I had no choice but to respond to the questions as I had and told me flat out that the whole thing would blow over, that there was no "meat in the burger." She said, "I don't know what they would expect. Outcomes are lousy in aneurysms."

"That's what I said. I mean, I said that was what I understood to be true."

"It is!" She was going to vent a bit.

"I don't know," I said, "how they make all this stink over a single case."

"Charlie Ryan."

"The anesthesiologist?"

"Yes."

"I thought it was the chairman. I thought he sent some nasty-gram that started this shit."

"That may have been, but I promise you it started with Charlie Ryan. He's such a prick." I smiled—ever the dutiful audience. "He's a card-carrying misogynist."

"What's he got against women?"

"Who knows. Probably thinks we all should be home doing the laundry and folding his underwear."

"Barefoot and pregnant."

"And grateful," she said. "I've heard, also, that he's a bit of a closet racist."

I raised one eyebrow. The resident's job is to be the shill.

"Goddamn gas-passers. Sit on their fat asses reading *The Wall Street Journal* while we struggle with patients' problems so we can serve them their cases on a fucking silver platter." She was starting to roll. "We make decisions, do the tests, plan the operations. They do a simple anesthetic, collect a fat fee. Some of them do their best to make it look hard, take all fucking day to get a case going, take all fucking night to wake somebody up. Can't get lines in. Patients bucking, puking, disoriented. Blood pressures all over the map. Then they have the out-and-out gall to launch this attack on me. And over an aneurysm! Like God himself could make an aneurysm come out clean."

I bought back in: My boss, my *Captain*, was being unfairly persecuted, at least in part, it seemed, because of her gender. That pissed me off. When she again suggested we have dinner together, I had no trouble accepting: The intrigues of my superiors were even more hypnotic than any thought of bedtime escapades.

We picked up as if we'd not missed any beats. Good food, good wine, a late hour, and the aura of a beautiful woman in distress made it easy to emotionally re-up. My self-awareness was numb. Once figuratively in bed together against a common enemy, making the metaphor real, translating one type of ardor into another, brought firework results.

As I said, I'd heard tales of Mimi's mistakes. But I knew the beast Reputation to be an odd and capricious companion. Anyone doing cases runs into problems. The old saw in surgery is "If you don't get complications you aren't doing enough cases." The surrounding people make assumptions about causes and frequency, never having the full picture. The cases that go well don't register in memory.

I'd heard of an ENT surgeon whose very first case in private practice, the eight-year-old daughter of a firefighter, died after a routine tonsillectomy. She had, what I have since learned, is the classic story: Uneventful operation, goes home, eats her ice cream, getting back to normal and—boom—eight days out the healing tonsillar bed breaks open and starts, literally, *pumping* out blood. She bleeds to death in the back of an ambulance. Everybody medical knows this happens with one in a gazillion tonsils, and probably, just on a karmic basis, will never happen again to this surgeon, but at that point his average is lousy. Who wants to send him his next case? What parents, if they heard the horror story, would show up for the appointment?

So I could not judge Mimi. Objectivity? I had no criteria, no experience, no rules, and only one bad outcome. Besides, my potential judgment, like that of many a poor boy before me, was addled by the animal logic of erection.

Having re-upped for the team, I naturally thought to defend the leader. I got mentally up in arms about Dr. Ryan. He seemed, from what I could see, to be a reasonable person, but we were well past the time one could spout demeaning or discriminatory epithets over surgical drapes. He might have been a true regressionary who just hated accomplished women. That sort is not yet extinct, even in medicine, which is as close to a true meritocracy as one can find.

The next day, when Mimi had left me alone to finish up the skin closure and paperwork for a routine laminectomy, I quietly asked the nurse who had scrubbed the case what she knew about Dr. Ryan. I got: "Charlie? He's a sweetie."

"Doesn't hate women?"

"Oh, God no!" This from a young, pretty, and moderately buxom, blonde woman with a faint Texas accent. Not even a fanged Neanderthal would have shown her his misogyny.

"Never any hint of racism?" I asked.

"No. Why would you think that?"

"Oh, I don't think it. I just heard something that made me wonder, is all."

"Well, that's pretty ugly."

"Yeah. That's why I asked. I figured it just didn't fit."

"Well, Charlie is one of our favorites. He's a great doctor and a gentleman, too."

I finished my charting. A full frontal approach to my questions was only going to get me into my own tar pit.

That night I phoned a senior anesthesiology resident, Dawn Stelfox. When I was an intern on the trauma service, she had twice saved my butt by leaning over the ether screen to whisper clues to me about what I might want to be paying attention to instead of whatever it was I was paying attention to. These made me look good to my Attending at the time. I already owed her, but I figured a phone call wouldn't put me too much further into debt.

"I need a woman's opinion," I began.

"Qualified," she said.

"The Anesthesia Department. Everybody treated pretty fair?"

"Hmmm. Pretty much. We all get the same amount of call. We all get the same rotations. We all have to work with Goldin the same amount."

"Who's he?"

"She. An Attending at the VA. Not really bad, not dangerous or anything, but she has this idea that any drug drawn up in a syringe should be in the patient. She'll come in your room and start pushing stuff into the IV while she's telling you some story from her days back in England. She talks all the time. Yammer, yammer, yammer."

"Isn't that a little dangerous?"

"Naw. The senior residents clue you in. You learn before you go to the VA to draw up exactly what you want the patient to get. The other stuff you keep in the drawer. She never goes into drawers."

"I knew you guys were high scientists," I said.

"Yeah," she laughed. "Cause and effect. We're on it."

"But, in your department, do women get a fair shake?"

"Well, yeah. We got plenty of women faculty and residents."

"Any ill treatment? Anybody there seem to be, I dunno, rude, mean, biased?"

"Who?"

"Well, I don't know. I'm asking you."

"No. I think the attitude from the top down is, pretty much, 'If you can give a good anesthetic and not let the surgeons bully you around, I don't care what color you are, what you eat for dinner, or if your sex is one of the usual two or something altogether new.' I know our chair has a thing right now about one of the female residents. She's close to getting kicked out. If that's what you're asking about, let me say I'd have thrown her out months ago. She's ham-handed and can't antici-pate the next problem. Her anesthetics are always playing catch-up. She scares me."

"Why hasn't he thrown her out?"

"Don't know for sure. Probably an ego thing. Dr. Miekle probably thinks he's good enough to make an anesthesiologist out of anybody."

"What about Charlie Ryan?"

"Charlie? I don't know that he feels one way or the other about her."

"How is he toward you?"

"He's great. He's always been fun to work with, a good teacher, es-pecially when his mood is good."

"He's got nothing going about women in medicine?"

"Charlie? I was told he was pushing my name for Chief Resident. I didn't get it, they gave it to that idiot Scoponich because he kisses their butts, but it was nice to be nominated."

"Is Dr. Ryan married?"

"Yeah, I think his wife's a doc, too. In fact, I think I heard she's a radiologist over at St. Elizabeth's. Probably pays all their bills. But why are you asking about him?"

"I heard a rumor that he's this old-fashioned knuckle-dragger who thinks women belong at home."

"Jesus. If that's Charlie he's a damn good actor. I work with the guy and he'd be about the last one I'd lay that on. Besides, he pretty much says what's on his mind. Who's laying out garbage like that?"

"Well, I'm on neurosurgery this month. My Attending is Miriam Lyle. She had—"

"And she thinks Charlie Ryan is out to get her?"

"No. Let me finish. There's a stink going on over a guy who died after an aneurysm operation. Apparently the stink started when your chairman, Ted Miekle, sent a letter to the Chair of Neurosurgery, Joe Kellogg. Dr. Ryan was the anesthesiologist on the case. There wasn't any resident. It's been suggested that Dr. Ryan doesn't like women in high places. I'm just trying to ask around."

"Well, you're noble for defending Dr. Mimi, but she's another one who scares me."

"How so?"

"All the stuff I've heard."

"I've heard a lot, too. But that's what bothers me. She's got a reputation."

"She sure does."

"But that's what I'm wondering about. It's like an 'Everybody Knows.' 'Everybody Knows' she's a problem. So when a case goes bad, which is apparently pretty common in brain surgery, people say, 'There it is again.' But when a case goes bad for a, you know, 'good' surgeon, people say, 'Oh, it must have been a really tough one. They happen.' "

She said, "I'm sure there's some of that, but mostly I think people deserve their reputations."

"I suppose so, for the most part. But still, how can you hang somebody over a single case?"

"I guess you can't."

"Yeah. Thanks for the info. I will say, though, if she gets any more paranoid about the Anesthesia Department, she's going to have me doing her anesthetics."

"Now that would be scary."

"Yeah, especially for me."

"Always remember, Ishmail, like I showed you, 'half the big syringe, all the little.' "

"I thought it was the other way around."

"Whatever," she said.

"I guess you have to draw up just what you want given," I said.

"You're getting it."

Over the next several days, I continued to ask, as discreetly as I could, some of the OR people I most trusted about Mimi's reputation and who her enemies might be. Nurses, techs, and other doctors alike—all were ready to recite the same stories I'd heard at the outset—wrong side, wrong level, hours and hours deep in a hole—but little new. There was a consistent thread that if she booked an aneurysm the OR staff would all call in sick or find themselves indispensable somewhere else. But real data were hard to find. The beast of Reputation was clearly riding around on my mistress's back.

Time with Mimi began to feel surreal. Most minutes of my days were entirely focused on very real patients with potential neurosurgical problems, so my clinic hours didn't have clocks melting off dead trees, but our personal time began to have the taste of a siege. Over dinner or curling into bed, we the oppressed verbally abused, in their absence, her supposed tormentors. Charlie Ryan and Ted Miekle were the obvious villains, but Joe Kellogg and Marshall Bullock were certainly on the edge of suspicion.

One night, as she dangled her hair in my face, again loaded on wine, riding me with a savoring slowness that invited free association, my deeper imagination saw us as jungle-bound comrades in army fatigues and berets, struggling to overthrow the Oppressor, spouting immortality-bound slogans, only taking a well-earned break to fuck for the Cause.

6

From here in Nebraska, way beyond being too late, it's easy to see signs that might have steered me away. Walter Bryant—one of the more miserable and bitter bastards I ever met—tried to warn me.

Walt was Chief Resident on the surgery team at the San Diego VA when I came on service as a third-year medical student. On Day Four of the rotation, when he found out I wanted to grow up to be a general surgeon, he told me, employing a few expletives for color, what foolishness that would be. This from a man not three months from the end of a six-year general surgery residency.

"You're supposed to be excited," I said. I still was.

"More like relieved, after this, but the next few years don't look any better, anyways," he said.

"Where are you headed?"

"An ER job."

"What?"

"There are no surgery jobs in San Diego County."

"What about opening an office—what do they call it? Hanging out a shingle?"

"Starving to death for two to five years, borrowing yet more money to pay office staff? In a town already over-doctored by about a hundred percent? Not me."

"So why not move? Bay Area? LA? Hell—Iowa?"

"LA is worse than San Diego. And any farther than that and I'd never see my kids. They are two and four and they live with their mom. In fact, that's the single shittiest thing about what this six years of residency cost me—my marriage. She's a wonderful woman, and we have two great kids, but she hated being alone all the goddamn time. And she did something about it."

"Sorry to hear that. I'm not married yet," I said.

"Don't. If you're thinking about surgery."

"I heard there's a program back East that won't even accept married residents."

"True. But it's in North Carolina. And there's the one in Houston where a guy in his fourth year—he'd made the years of cuts and everything—was doing his month in the Surge-ICU—and at this place you are forbidden, for the entire month, to leave the building. But one Sunday things are quiet so he meets his wife in the hospital parking lot for about twenty minutes. The Chief finds out about it and shit-cans him right there. Over. Kaput."

Still believing I was a born surgeon—my professors said so—I knew my track would be different. But I did make a mental note to avoid Houston when looking for a residency.

THE BOOK OF MIMI, CHAPTER FOUR

As my fortunes rose with Miriam Lyle, so they fell with the other woman in my life, Mary Ellen Montgomery.

Mary Ellen—better known in our medical school circle as Monty—and I had been best friends since I stood behind her in the lunch line at med school orientation two days before classes started. Through four brutal years we relied on each other for academic help and advice, occasional meals, sleepovers, odd loans, rides, and more advice on the opposite sex than one would ask of an in-house Ann Landers. We were never romantically involved.

Not that I was not attracted to her—quite the opposite. Though shorter and a little rounder than the magazine ideal, her face was classically pretty and her hair was striking—long and flaxen with a natural curl that was difficult for her to control and for us men within her aura to avoid touching. Best, though, was her smile. When she had it on, the world felt right as a Norman Rockwell painting. Pure magic.

Only once did I try to transform our relationship into something "more." That effort left a scar with a sore spot underneath.

Romances left over from college rarely last long. Three thousand miles of separation and a disgustingly handsome campus fireman back at the Old School were quickly lethal to mine. I went on a regimen common among medical students—flings both quick and cheap, interspersed with long weeks of longing. Mary Ellen was kind enough to give no sign of knowing what I was up to, but her amused smile when she caught me begging a phone number from a grocery clerk in Del Mar reminded me how unattractive are the desperate.

So I probably should have known she would shoot me down. At the end of second year we found ourselves on a blanket by a fire on the Del Mar beach, late at night, left alone by tired friends, each of us months past any romance and each pretty beered up. We were sitting close. I turned her head to me. I looked into her eyes. I thought I saw some hint of "yes." I moved to kiss her.

She said, "Hey, Don Juan. Trying to fuck up a really great relationship?"

"I won't do it again," I said. "Scout's honor."

Ever after I tried to avoid repeat embarrassments. I've held religiously to the first rule of that kind of "really great relationship"—no kissing. The second rule became: Any respectable dalliance for either of us was to be a source of mutual happiness, not jealousy. That was the theory.

At the end of medical school comes a sad time when once-fast friends must move on for internship and residency, scattering like dandelion fluff. Mary Ellen and I decided to try to hang together, aligning our applications geographically. Fate smiled. The computer match that shuffles the puppies put us both in Phoenix. I suggested to Mary Ellen that we rent a place we could afford. It seemed efficient, I said. And friendlier. She nodded. We found a town house. It was natural and all organic.

As it worked out, of course, we saw little of each other. Internship means never having to say you're home. Nonetheless our paths crossed at work and often enough in the town house, or at least the parking lot, that we could keep up with each other's major doings, including any significant romantic possibilities.

My affair with Madame Lyle, though, was, of course, off-limits even in the general, making-conversation sense. When it became apparent that Mimi and I were going to be sleeping together as often as not, Mimi insisted we develop a detailed cover story with Mary Ellen in mind. I told her Mary Ellen and I barely saw each other and only talked about our love lives when seeking advice. I told Mimi I could not imagine needing advice from Mary Ellen about her.

I warned Mimi I had always been bad at carrying off a lie. She said that was all the more reason to plan ahead: She fabricated a "cover" girl. Mimi called my house at odd times and left messages from "Lisa." Usually something girlish, like, "Hi, it's Leese. Just thinkin' of you. See you tonight." Mimi even grilled me on "Lisa": "How old is she? Where does she live? What does she do? Where did you meet her? Is she from here?" She told me, "Have your facts so they'll be there when you need them."

I told Mimi that Mary Ellen never would have asked all of those questions, and with our hours usually in complete asynchrony, our few communications were by notes on the refrigerator. I erased the telephone messages as soon as I could get to them.

Still, when I thought about it I knew I was again embarrassing myself, whether Mary Ellen saw it or not. The rule of *omerta* required to play the Game with Mimi necessitated more than one lie to Mary Ellen, a violation of our friendship that left me more ashamed than anything else I did with *la Profesora*.

One evening there came a baby to rub my face in my own mess.

A newborn was brought to the ER; the mother said he quit breathing for no apparent reason. Physical examination of the baby showed the problem: There was massive bruising on the top of the head and easily felt fractures around the rim of the skull where a hat would touch. Someone had hit the baby straight down on top of his head and broken the skull like an eggshell.

The ER doctor got the infant on a ventilator, put in an IV big enough for a major resuscitation, and called the Pedes team—Monty at the helm. Protocol for head injuries said she would need a consultation from the neurosurgeons. In a hopeless case it should have been a formality.

The mother was a girl of seventeen sporting the attire and tattoos of one of the more vicious gangs. She spent her time in and out of drug houses. In a wheelchair. She had broken her spine at the mid-chest in a car wreck seven months earlier. Her ER X-rays then showed a tiny assemblage of bones growing in her uterus—she had been unaware she was pregnant. During her stay in the rehab hospital she and her sister were arrested for assaulting the staff.

When she delivered the boy at thirty weeks gestation he weighed two pounds, nine ounces. After yeoman work by doctors, nurses, and techs and hundreds of thousands of tax dollars, he had been discharged. All of a week later he came to us via the ER.

By the time I got to Maricopa that night, the little boy was "tucked in" in the PICU. I found the CT films of his head on the viewbox. It was ghastly. The fractures were eerily symmetric. The brain underneath had lost all signs of structure. It had been rendered gelatin. Indeed it looked as if the top of the head had been flattened with a frying pan, though the child abuse text we consulted showed a drawing of a human fist doing the deed, hammerlike.

The PICU social worker told me Mary Ellen had already called the police. When I came into the family waiting room to find her and see where we stood, the baby's aunt was shouting at the mother, "I told you you shoo't'na brought your baby to no motherfuckin' hospital. They're gonnna take him away from you! No fuckin' shit!"

Mary Ellen was standing like a statue, unwilling to be cowed despite the woman's superior size and indubitable experience in matters violent. Nonetheless she seemed relieved to see me.

"Who the fuck are you?" the aunt yelled at me.

"I'm Dr. Ishmail. I'm a resident working with the neurosurgeons—the brain surgeons. We've been asked—"

She turned back to her sister and said, "Did you call a brain surgeon?"

"No, I didn't call a brain surgeon," she shouted from her wheelchair. Then, to Mary Ellen, "What I've been trying to tell you is the baby fell, from my lap, when I was changing his diaper. From here to here. And he hit his head. He hit his head here on the leg rest of my motherfuckin' wheelchair. Do you hear me?"

"Was the floor carpeted?" Mary Ellen asked. "Where your son's head hit?"

She looked at her sister. "Yes, it's carpeted, but he had hit his head here, on the leg rest."

The aunt moved around behind the wheelchair and started to leave. "I'm not going to stand here and listen to more of this bullshit. It's goddamn bullshit. You all think she hurt her *own* son!" And they were gone.

Monty and I looked at each other. "Bullshitter," I said.

"Yeah, right. You know me."

"What did you say to them?"

"I told them we were concerned that someone had hurt the baby, intentionally, and the police would be asking them some questions. You heard the rest."

When we went back to the Unit, Mimi was leaning on a counter by the scans, reading the chart. She looked up at us. She got a look of recognition; I was not sure if she knew Mary Ellen or felt somehow that she had caught me in infidelity.

She looked down her nose to read Monty's name badge. "I see— Dr. Montgomery is it?—that you have met my resident." The way she said it made me feel like chattel.

"Yes, I know Dr. Ishmail."

"Good. I'll be having him write the orders, then, on this baby. This unfortunate little . . . *abortion*. How, do you suppose, they could have let this unfit . . . *child* . . . in a wheelchair . . . take home a tiny infant?" Her tone was accusatory.

"I'm sure I don't know, Dr. Lyle. But we were not interested in transferring the infant to your service. Pedes will still be writing the orders. We called you because we needed your opinion on the chart, confirming what we thought—I mean I'm not trying to put words in your mouths—but it seemed pretty obvious that this was a fatal head trauma. We've already called the organ donor team. But we need to have on the chart—"

"If you know the answer why call me in?" Mimi said.

I spoke, hoping to prevent further inflammation: "Dr. Lyle, I can write—not write—whatever they want. Unless you think we should operate on the baby. If we operate I think they would understand if we wanted to assume primary responsibility, like always. . . ."

She shot fire all around. "We will not be operating, Malcolm. There's nothing surgical here. The baby's brain has been crushed."

To gain closure I needed to venture another question. "Is it our opinion then that this is a fatal injury?"

She said, "Yes," and turned on her heel and left the Unit.

I blinked and glanced at the ceiling. Mary Ellen said, "Oh my God. Do you have to put up with her every day?"

"Mostly she's not like that. She gets stressed around pediatric stuff."

"Well, this case is as shitty as they come. None of us is real happy around a dead baby."

"No. But you'll see her better side tomorrow. She can be charming."

"Charming?"

I blinked. "Yeah."

She stared at me. "Malcolm . . . you're defending a witch."

I looked at the CT pictures.

"Malcolm . . ."

"She's not so bad. You're seeing her at her worst."

"If she's the reason you haven't been home at night, I'll never speak to you again."

I said, "Oh, yeah, right."

Mary Ellen said, "Just try to keep her out of my ICU."

Omerta, self-protective for Mimi, would be self-protective for me, too.

The next morning the infant was declared brain-dead. His heart went in an ice chest to LA, there to be implanted into a different kind of trouble. There were no takers that day for a liver or kidneys so small. The remainder was autopsied on the infant's due date. The mother was later arrested on suspicion of murder and the aunt was arrested on an outstanding warrant for assault and battery.

As I stood in the PICU wondering what to do for a dying infant, feeling the mutual repulsion between the leading women in my life drive them simultaneously out of my sight, I had a glimpse of a certain line of logic: Anyone despicable to Mary Ellen must be despicable to me.

Another part of me argued it down, though: As I'd said to Mary

Ellen, Mimi had shown only the raw nerves. Surely Mary Ellen was caught up in the Reputation game. Being closer to the core, I could better see the truth: It was a persecution.

The next day, five days after my meeting with Dr. Kellogg to discuss Mimi's handling of the Coles case, came tangible proof of the other side of Dr. Miriam Lyle: the second Case of Extraordinary Teaching. I saw Mimi—I think—save a child's life. I believe, from what I had seen of other such cases, another neurosurgeon might have failed.

We were bogged down in afternoon clinic, about an hour behind the schedule, when the ER paged me about a kid with a head conk. All calls went first to me, the resident on neurosurgery, even if they knew good and well they were going to need the Attending in short order. That's what residency is: You get to play doctor with a real patient in front of you and real doctor behind you.

The ER resident was playing it cool, telling me without saying so that he wasn't really too wound up about this kid, but her mental status was a little funky and he thought he'd get a CT and call us just to cover all the bases. And then, also without saying so, the potentially life-and-death decision of whether to admit her for observation by expensive professionals or send her home for observation by Mom would fall neatly to us.

Mimi asked me what the call was. I told her the little I knew: a nine-year-old girl, on her bike, struck by a delivery van going a reported twenty-five miles per hour. Banged her head. There apparently was no loss of consciousness, and her vital signs were okay, but she was now perseverating, asking over and over again where her grandpa was.

"Normal CT?" she asked.

"In process."

"Are you concerned?" she asked.

I hesitated. "Well, the ER resident wasn't too concerned. He's the one who's seen her."

"Right. You need to see her. Go."

"I was in the middle of the post-op for your Mrs. Bourke, cervical fusion six weeks—"

"I know her. Go. I'll handle it. Call me as soon as you've seen the CT." I turned to go. I accelerated my pace when she called after me, "And don't let them fuck around. This kid is now *their* first priority."

The ER was on the other side of the campus from the clinic building, effectively a block and a half away. I walked at about half "intern speed," about as fast as most people would go if the bank were about to lock them from their money for the weekend.

I found the girl on a gurney, lying at a cocked angle, half tangled in a sheet. I got to her at the same time the X-ray tech did, ready to wheel her off to CT.

"Hold just a sec," I told him. He scowled.

Her mother was there, holding the girl's hand, her face flushed and her eyes red-rimmed but dry. "What's her name?" I asked softly.

"Darla," she said without looking up at me.

"Darla," I said loudly. Nothing changed for a few seconds, then the girl kicked her legs and shifted to her other side. "Has she been responding to you?" I asked the mother.

"Yeah, pretty much, but she's been confused like. She's been asking for her Pa-Pa. He been dead two years."

"Darla," I said, louder. Nothing. I picked up her hand and felt the pulse in her wrist. Slightly on the slow side. I pressed hard on a fingernail bed. She flinched and pulled her hand away, but said only something like "ahmm, ahmm, ahmm."

The tech said, "Look, Doc, if this is going to take too long, I got a list of patients waiting. . . ."

The girl was on the edge of a coma. I gave him a look intended to say "Shut up and stay put," but I said, "I'm almost through. And I think Darla probably needs your services about as badly as anybody right now." I was suppressing several good curses. I got an otoscope from the wall and shone the light into her eyes. Both pupils reacted and they were still the same size, but she barely flinched from the light. "Better get her to CT kind of *stat*," I said to the tech. He knew the usual translation of "stat" and got her stretcher going out the door.

When they were on their way I introduced myself quickly to Mom, a rotund woman in bold-patterned clothes, and told her about

Dr. Lyle, the attending professor. When I got to the part about we were doing everything possible, she cut me short.

"I know all about this shit. Her older brother like to be the death of me. He had bad concussions twice. He done all right though. I mean, he's back to his normal self and all, not that that's *all right*."

Then I made a mistake: an invitation to full disclosure. I said, "Well, this seems to be worse. We certainly hope that a concussion is all this is, nothing really serious." I should have nodded and smiled and gotten back to Darla and the CT.

"What you say?" she said. "You mean she's maybe worse? She had some kind of stroke or blood clot or something?" She was beginning to steam. "She gonna be okay?"

Sometimes, when asked to predict the future, I am tempted toward overwhelming frankness; something like, "I have no idea: We haven't done the CT yet, brain injuries are less predictable than sunspots, and I'm only a general surgery resident whose concept of the brain is that it's Jell-O that bleeds." Urges like that tell me I'm way too tired.

The party line is, thankfully, available to suppress trouble: "I'm sure she's going to be back to her normal self soon. She's going to get every possible thing done for her to make her her normal self again." I was backing away down the hall. "I'll come talk to you just as soon as the X-rays are done."

As I got to the CT control booth the first cut was just being constructed on the screen. That many years ago, it took the computer half a minute to construct each cut.

The pictures start at the bottom of the brain and work up. The first slices show the brain stem, and then only poorly because of all the surrounding bone at the base of the skull. Everything looked normal as far as the tech, the ER nurse, and I could tell. Each successive image was equally boring, or reassuring, and I was beginning to think about dinner when the tech muttered, "Uh-oh."

"What?" I said. "Uh-oh what-oh?" He drew his pencil tip around the inner edge of the skull and I saw the Uh-oh, a lens-shaped rim of matter pushing on the brain—blood.

"Subdural?" I asked.

He paused. The techs are not supposed to read the scans, but this was probably fairly basic. "Probably epidural," he allowed. "Got a little shift, too." The next cut had just popped up, and the midline structures of the brain were clearly being pushed to the side. The tech reached for his phone. I knew he was calling the radiologist even before the scan was completed. I ran out to the ER to find another phone and called Mimi.

That's when things got unusual.

Mimi told me to "consent" the kid for a crani; she would head right over to the OR and we would be pushing the gurney ourselves if we needed to to get this case started within thirteen minutes. I started to ask if there was some data that supported thirteen minutes versus fifteen or twenty but she had hung up.

"Consenting," the verb, means getting the standard written consent form signed. I found a form, stamped the top with Darla's plastic ID card, and found Mom. "Mrs. Winthrop, Darla's going to need emergency surgery to release—"

Her face screwed up in all three dimensions and she wailed, "Nooo."

"I'm sorry to have to tell you so bluntly, ma'am, but there's an expanding blood clot on the outside of the brain and it's pushing her brain pretty hard right now. That's why she's not herself. What we— Dr. Lyle, primarily—will do is take off a piece of the skull"—I was making a circle with my finger around the top right side of my own skull—"remove the clot, ligate any bleeding sources, and then put it all back together." I was well aware that some of that deserved more explanation, but I could not take the time. An autocratic approach was completely appropriate in the circumstances.

She wailed again.

"I'm really sorry, ma'am, I'm sure she's going to be just fine, but the sooner we get this started, the better her chances are." One of the transparent lies of medicine: She's going to be fine, but I'm worried about her "chances." "I need you to sign this consent for surgery, ma'am. It says that Dr. Miriam Lyle and her associates are authorized by you to perform a craniotomy, the operation I described, on your daughter, Darla."

"Ain't signing."

I almost fell over. "What?"

"Ain't signing it. Least not till I met this Dr. Lyle of yours and hear it from her."

"But Mrs. Winthrop, this is really an emergency. One of the rare cases where minutes count."

"I know you ain't the real doctor. I wanna see the surgeon. You go run and find her and get her butt down here."

I went back to the central desk and started the phone calls. Mimi was at the OR control desk, booking the case. "Mom won't sign till she meets you. She's up here in ER Eight."

"Fine. Wheel the kid down. Now."

"You coming up?"

"I will when I finish lighting a fire under some butts down here, but you should have that kid on the table, asleep, and shaving her head within six minutes. You better get her moving."

"But the mom is right over her. And surgery without consent is assault and battery."

"We have two licensed doctors agreeing it is an emergency. We'll write the chart entry after the clot is out. Hell, we could get half the medical staff to sign for an epidural." That was true enough. "And if Mom wants to sue my ass, I'd rather have her daughter standing behind her whining for a new toy than lying beside her drooling."

Braced for battle, I went back to the bedside. Darla's mom was stone-faced. She was not happy to see me again.

"Ma'am, I need to ask you again to please sign the consent. I've spoken with Dr. Lyle. She's right now at the control desk of the OR getting everything arranged to do emergency surgery on Darla. It is imperative that this operation begin as soon as possible, and I mean in a matter of minutes." She just twitched her mouth up around her nose but didn't look at me. "Ma'am . . ."

"Five minutes gonna make a big damn difference?"

I hesitated. "Yes."

"Let me see the goddamn paper."

I handed it to the woman and immediately kicked up the foot release on the girl's gurney, freeing it to roll. As Mom was reading the consent I began to maneuver it toward the door. She got the message. "Gimme a pen."

As I pushed the stretcher through the double doors to the OR suite, I could hear Mimi Lyle's distinctly elevated voice at the control desk: ". . . *now!* We'll do it without anesthesia! She's in a fucking coma, for God's sake!" She saw me with the patient. To me: "Wheel her on into Six." I paused. I wasn't in scrubs, had no hair cover, no mask. "Get her into the room, then go change." I moved out. Mimi to the nurse: "Just send in one of the float nurses and a basic neuro set. But it has to be now. This is a Level One center, is it not? We do deal with life and death emergencies!" She stormed toward the women's locker room. I was glad to be able to do as I was told and not have to fabricate out of the ether an employable body or a sterile instrument set that didn't exist.

Nakedness would feel more normal in an OR than street clothes. I reasoned backwards from Mimi's instructions, though, that sometimes minutes are more important than sterile technique. I backed into OR 6 with the unconscious girl, wheeled her stretcher around 180 degrees, and immediately had the most palpable sensation I had ever had of being alone. Only half the room lights were on. In the middle of the room was the narrow operating table with an intensely white sheet freshly tucked in at the corners. Someone had left one of the surgical spotlights on full power. It was pointed at the head of the table. No one else was anywhere in sight. It was churchlike. I shuddered.

All I could do was push the stretcher sideways up against the table in anticipation of moving the unconscious child over to it if ever help arrived.

My moment of silence was thankfully short-lived. The door from the OR core banged open loudly, and two men issued forth with oaths and a tray of instruments the size of a suitcase, wrapped like a cynical Christmas gift in dimpled aquamarine sheets of some paperlike material not found in nature and held together with tape the color of baby poop. I realized why I had brought the patient into the room wearing my street clothes, even though there was nothing to do on arrival: OR staff will do just about anything for a patient-in-need in one of their own rooms.

These angels in my time of need were normally the heathens of bone surgery: One nurse and one scrub tech, both ex-military, who spent most days helping in the major orthopedic cases because these employed the biggest and coolest power tools. I was quietly thrilled to see them.

"Fucking gotta-go-now," muttered Ansel, the tech.

Robert, the nurse, looked up at me standing there like a guppy, my mouth opening and closing, apparently in search of oxygen. "We don't have anesthesia," he said. "Anesthesia" in this case referred to the person, not the state of insensitivity. "They're all tied up. Ellerby is first to finish but Ganiats is taking fucking forever to finish that knee. It'll be a half hour easy."

Ansel said, "Hey, maybe she'll have you do the anesthesia."

"Me?" I said.

"Well, I meant Robert, but you'd be okay too. Hell, you've probably at least intubated before."

I had, at the time, intubated precisely three tracheas. Though the procedure didn't scare me to death, airway management was always of paramount importance and a child in a coma was not the person on whom I wanted to be expanding my role. I shuddered again. "Let's get her moved over," I said.

I knew at least how to get the basic monitors attached. Her EKG looked normal but slow, and her blood pressure was high.

I looked at the OR crew. They looked at me. I shook my head. The door burst open again: Mimi in scrubs, hands and arms dripping water. Right behind her was Dr. Ellerby, one of the anesthesiologists, huffing and puffing. "Go get changed," she ordered me with a nod.

I heard Robert say, "Hey, good to see you, Doc." I knew he was talking to the anesthesiologist.

By the time I got back from changing clothes and a ten-minute hand scrub compressed to two, the child was intubated and on a ventilator. Dr. Ellerby was putting in an arterial line, and Mimi was drilling in the skull, having just peeled back the skin and clipped off the bleeders. By the time I gowned and gloved, Mimi had sawed out the bone flap. She handed it to me: a concave saucer of skull with irregular edges. I gingerly passed it to Ansel. After it was safely in a tray on the back table, I asked him, "What happens if one of us drops it on the floor?"

"You mean after Dr. Lyle gets through kicking your dead and lifeless body off of a very tall building?" he said.

"Assuming it was my fault," I said.

"Oh, it would be your fault," he said, laughing.

The resident is always wrong. "Okay, after my dead and lifeless body hits the concrete."

"Funny you should ask," Robert said. "What did we do, Dr. Lyle, when that bone flap hit the floor a few years ago?"

I felt a bit sick.

She hesitated. "We called the Tissue Bank."

Another pause. Mimi was washing clot off the dura, the lining of the brain, and buzzing little bleeding points with the cautery.

"And . . . ," Ansel said. He was clearly enjoying this.

"They advised resterilizing the bone in the steam autoclave."

"Wouldn't that kill it?" I blurted out.

"Already dead," Robert answered. He had heard all this before. "Loses its blood supply when it's cut out of the head."

Mimi said, "You're right, Robert." She didn't look up. "So, Dr. Ishmail, why do we return dead bone to the skull at the end of these procedures?"

If the answer to one of these questions is obvious, it's either wrong or prologue to the next, harder question. You're obligated to answer anyway. "To protect the brain," I said in the pious tone I had learned in fourth-grade Catechism.

"Ultimately, yes, but what becomes of the flap? I mean, why go to the trouble of resterilizing a bone flap that's been on the floor when we could protect the brain with a helmet?"

I was thinking. She answered for me. "Growth matrix. The dead bone provides the matrix for the osteocytes to move in and reestablish themselves and re-create living bone."

"Same as it does in ortho when we use chips from Bone Bank," Robert said.

By now Mimi was standing with her arms folded and staring at the wound to see if any of the tiny vessels was still daring enough, under her gaze, to bleed. Satisfied that all was dry, she guided me through putting it all back together.

As I was sewing skin, Mimi broke scrub to dictate the Op Report. Darla's pulse picked up as Dr. Ellerby lightened the anesthetic.

Within two minutes of getting her to the Recovery Room she was crying for her mom, moving everything appropriately and nodding to questions.

I found Mrs. Winthrop in the waiting area. I smiled. "She's doing very, very well," I said. She was biting her index finger. I knew she didn't know what to believe. "She's still waking up from the anesthesia," I said, "but already she's moving her arms and legs, she answers simple questions, and she's been asking for you."

"Can I see her?"

"Not for a while. When she comes out of recovery."

"But she gonna be okay?"

"It certainly looks that way. Dr. Lyle did a wonderful—"

"That surgeon lady? I still ain't seen her. If she thinks I ain't worth talking to then Lord have mercy."

"That is absolutely not the case," I said. "It's been a very busy day. She has a lot of patients. I know you'll get to meet Dr. Lyle on rounds this evening." I paused, wondering if it was wise to veer again toward full disclosure, but decided with good news it couldn't hurt. "I think you should know that Dr. Lyle didn't meet with you ahead of time because she was in the OR suite whipping them up into a frenzy to get Darla's operation started before anything else could happen in there. She made us all break a few rules. She upset some people. They don't like having their plans changed suddenly. None of us does. But it may have made a big difference for Darla."

I think she thought I was feeding her a line.

I found Mimi in her office. I asked her how often she threw fits at the OR control desk.

"About once a year or so," she said. "Whenever I get an otherwise salvageable person with an isolated epidural or even a subdural. And this was a little kid. With babies and kids I get especially pissy."

"Because they're harder to manage?"

"No. For basic trauma stuff like this kids are no harder. Easier in some ways. They bounce out of the hospital in three days. The ones who do well."

"Do you think thirteen minutes to get to the OR is a magic number?"

"Only to the OR staff. If you say fifteen, people think you're saying 'about a quarter hour,' which could just as well be a half hour, which could be three quarters of an hour, which could be an hour. If you say thirteen minutes, people believe you mean thirteen minutes."

"But I've never seen that kind of push from a surgeon before."

"I'm perfectly happy to play nice for meningiomas. I'll even wait my turn at night for VP shunt revisions. But I had a man arrest and subsequently die from an epidural while waiting for the next available OR team. It happens with epidurals. I realized then that that man needed me to be drilling on his skull more than anything else, more than anesthesia, more than sterile technique. Did five or ten minutes make the difference for that little girl, what was her name?"

"Darla."

"Darla. Did shaving a few minutes make any difference? I don't know. If they don't die maybe you could have gone slower. You never know. Unless you run like the wind and they die anyway. Then you know you weren't any good. You know you didn't make any difference."

As I walked out she said to my back, "And I will not be irrelevant." I turned but she had turned her face back into her work.

7

Walter Bryant's warning about his bleak future as a surgeon was easily dispatched with a dose of naive optimism. The one who really should have given me pause, though, was Joe Baltz, a man who never said a word to me.

We met on the shiny new Monday starting my medical school Surgery rotation at the San Diego VA. At the start of rounds the interns were dividing up the patients on the service among us hopeless students. We were to "follow" patients as if they were our own, doing as much of the work for them as we could before seeking the sage counsel of our superiors—practicing for internship. We started at the pinnacle of acuity—the ICU. When they sneeringly asked for a volunteer, I stepped up first, green and transparent as a tropical sea. I wanted the full experience. I was going to be a surgeon. I won Mr. Baltz.

He was most of my workload and my emotional albatross for the next five weeks. He had come in with some blood in his stool and was found to have a plum-sized cancer in his transverse colon. The resection was a complete success and probably cured him of his cancer. Unfortunately, for years he had been intoxicating his liver by "tipping the jar" with greater vigor than anyone knew. Going into the operation his liver was still functional, but, unbeknown to his doctors, had zero reserve capacity. In the stress of recovering, it made the unilateral hepatic decision to check out.

While I had read about the consequences of liver failure, I was, as I had come to expect as the norm for a medical student seeing organ failure for the first time, unprepared for the reality. Chemical wastes run rampant. Everything turns a greenish yellow.

For reasons unknown to anyone, without a functional liver the kidneys shut down, too. Mr. Baltz required daily dialysis to stay alive.

Without a liver one of the worst accumulated toxins is ammonia. As the level rises the patient is pushed into a coma. Comas are graded on a scale of 15 down to 3, 15 being "normal"— awake and knowing who, when, and *where you are—and 3 being neurologically indistinguishable from a chair. Mr. Baltz was a 3.*

Not surprisingly, the immune system practically runs and hides. The patient is a setup for major infections. Napalm-like antibiotics are given every few hours to prevent this. These kill off all the usual suspects, the staph, strep, and E. coli. But, with the normal competition gone, the unusually hard-to-kill stuff get to have their own chance to shine. Mr. Baltz was widely septic with one such bug, Pseudomonas aeruginosa, *the day I took him on—sixteen days after his operation—and stayed that way until he died.*

Pseudomonas, *not surprisingly, smells bad. It also turns pus a sort of lime green. Mr. Baltz had green ooze at every unnatural body orifice we had made for him—his surgical incision, his tracheostomy, his chest tube, abdominal drain sites, and dialysis catheters.*

The antibiotics we use on pseudomonas only fight the bugs to a standoff. They definitely, however, kill kidneys. While kidneys will recover from hepatic failure alone, we were pretty sure Mr. Baltz—should he survive—was ensured lifelong dialysis from all the "mycins" we poured in.

From Day One of my tenure I thought he should be allowed to die. I grumbled on rounds. I grumbled to Mary Ellen. On about Day Eight I spoke up: "Why are we doing this?"

Walter Bryant blinked at me, then gave only a paternal smile. "You're new here, aren't you?"

The interns laughed. I scowled.

"We're doing this," he said, "because it's what we do."

I scowled harder.

He made a sweeping motion around the ICU. "Intensive care. We fight sepsis. We fill in for the organs that have failed. We replace all the missing elements."

I said, "But this man is dead."

He said, "He's not dead till we say he's dead."

I said, "I vote he's dead."

"Medical students don't get votes, Doctor," said a pimple-faced intern.

"Then don't call me Doctor."

He did a melodramatic version of looking shocked. "It's considered a sign of respect."

"Well, it also carries a certain responsibility," I said. "And if I don't even get a vote, I don't want anyone to think I have any responsibility."

"Lighten up, man. You take this shit way too seriously."

I blinked at him, then looked over at Mr. Baltz.

Dr. Bryant said, "Each of this man's problems is recoverable. We're giving him a chance."

"What about his kidneys?" I asked.

"You don't know they won't recover. And he could live forever on dialysis."

"Total liver failure is recoverable?"

"In theory, it can be."

"In what proportion of cases?"

"Oh, it won't happen. It's less than one percent."

I said nothing. We moved on to the next patient.

When I complained to Mary Ellen, she was, of course, sympathetic toward the patient and me. She said, though, "Remember why you're there."

"To help the man?"

"No, they're the ones doing that. Or trying to. You're there to learn how to be an intern. Help if you can, but don't make it too hard on yourself. The patient has the disease."

I looked for something—anything—to do. When I saw his wife I gently brought up the idea of withdrawing care. She was more than receptive, she was grateful. "He's hating every bit of this," she said.

"You know that?" I was expecting her to recount an earlier conversation.

"He tells me," she said.

I looked at her.

"When I'm praying I feel him there."

Next morning on rounds I reported her reaction. "You know his family is suffering," I said.

"They don't realize he could still live," Dr Bryant said.

We repeated our earlier argument. Dr. Bryant again ended by disavowing any hope for success: "Do I believe he's going to live? Not for a second."

"Then why are we flogging him? They're in real pain."

"Because we don't know he's going to die."

"Seems to me we do," I said with self-assurance, though I felt like a schoolboy expecting a beating for being right at the wrong time.

"But we can't prove it," he said, again moving on toward the next unfortunate.

My only recourse was to spend more time talking to Mr. Baltz's wife and daughters. I explained medical details and let them voice their frustrations. They seemed to appreciate the time and it made me feel like I was doing something.

Each day at rounds, when we got to Mr. Baltz, my contribution was an update for the team on the emotional state of the man's family. The intern told me to knock it off. I ignored him.

It took another month for Joe Baltz's heart to quit, too, so we could pronounce him dead. Not once did his coma score budge off of 3.

THE BOOK OF MIMI, CHAPTER FIVE

Even as Mimi and I imagined we did everything for The Cause, suffering, even in bed, the imagined slings and arrows of Drs. Miekle, Ryan, Kellogg, and Bullock with the grace of martyrs, patient care went on. And on. Our siege-state mentality was often superseded by the numbing repetition of all-consuming crises and the bone-bending hours of clinical neurosurgery.

We had a night in that stretch when three head traumas each needed surgery. The first was a routine clot on the brain from a head conk. We were near the end of it when a call came for Numbers Two and Three, arriving simultaneously from the same wrecked pickup. This was slightly unusual because it wasn't yet 2:00 A.M., so the bars were still open and people shouldn't have been on the road. Mimi said to me, "Put this guy's head back together," told the scrub nurse, "Watch him," meaning me, and broke scrub for the ER. By the time we finished the identical operation on Number Two and put a pressure bolt in Number Three, it was time for morning rounds, which we began with the usual walking breakfast of donuts and bad coffee.

The investigation of the Coles case and Mimi's abilities took an interesting twist before completion. Mimi was told, completely off the record, that Marshall Bullock, the Chair of Neurosurgery, had been forced to form an ad hoc Committee of Three to review the facts and make the final call.

Academic tradition says that any question of fitness for a faculty member belongs solely to the chair, but because of the nature of the department structure—split across two campuses less than two hours apart by high-speed freeway—he had largely turned it over to Joe Kellogg, the local vice-chair.

Dr. Kellogg related his findings to Dr. Bullock, Mimi was told, then phoned Ted Miekle in the Anesthesiology Department and told him he had found nothing to be concerned about. Dr. Miekle then apparently made enough of a row about the whole thing being a whitewash that Drs. Bullock and Kellogg had to agree to bring in an "objective" third person to go through it with the two of them and prepare a written report. They invited a neurosurgeon who was said to be "well-respected" to fly in from Seattle.

When word of this reached the residents, speculation ran wild among them. One evening at The Longhorn, our version of a student commons, I witnessed a memorable deliberation.

That night there were members of the usual bunch: representatives of future surgeons, radiologists, internists, anesthesiologists, et cetera. No one had heard of the neurosurgeon from Seattle, so there was a rumor-based, fact-free argument about just how impartial this third party might or might not be. The most important unknowns to the debaters were his marital status and the likelihood he had bedded Mimi, or vice versa, at some convention of brain surgeons. I kept my mouth shut.

One wag pointed out that such a coupling, had it occurred, would not by itself guarantee either a favorable or unfavorable review. He pointed out that her degree of bedtime willingness and expertise might have colored their ultimate parting in any number of unpredictable ways. It occurred to me that *his* talents were more likely to be a limiting factor than hers, but I kept my mouth shut tighter still. "The only thing I think we can guarantee," he said, "is that the facial expressions around the committee table would be really interesting to watch." To this I agreed wholeheartedly but silently, maintaining my mask of disinterest by keeping my face in my beer.

Mimi referred to the whole thing, naturally, as The Inquisition, though she expected complete exoneration of her judgment and skills.

Via Cynthia Blachly, I had been able to keep track, at least loosely, of whom the committee had interviewed and what records they had pulled. I shared my intelligence with *mi capitana* during our dinner dates.

The list of faculty and staff numbered around fourteen, but all were thoroughly predictable names and at least moderately predictable in what they might have to say.

The list of patient records, though, was more enigmatic. There were about thirty names, less than a fourth of which Mimi recognized. It looked as if all had been to the OR sometime in the preceding five years, all in the care of a neurosurgeon. Some for spine surgery, some for head bleeds, some for tumors, some for aneurysms. I assumed they were looking for some equivalent cases to compare to Dr. Lyle's. To Mimi, who lived within that context, it looked scattershot. "They're fishing," she told me. "They have nothing. Nothing." The siege state was lifting. We drank wine.

She acquired, in slowly emerging victorious, a quasi-magnetic field, the aura of strength of a warrior queen vanquishing the dreaded Hun. She became impervious to all the usual small aggravations of the clinic and the OR that would have tripped her agitation switch in more normal times. One minute she smiled beatifically at her office assistant's bungling a message and the next sat sipping coffee in the nurses' lounge, chatting amicably with two young and virginal scrub techs while awaiting the decision of an obstructionist anesthesiologist on a potential case cancellation. This was, to me, a new woman.

Fortunately, her ionic charge extended to the bedroom, and on one occasion her office. Among other things, she rediscovered her infantile oral fixation, regularly suggesting some manner of a reciprocal devouring.

Eventually she was told the final letter would be in everyone's hands on that coming Friday. She got a wink with the message. In anticipation of the Parting of the Clouds, she said we were going to take a weekend away. She told me we were going to a mountain cabin because, she said, juniper-scented mountain air and pine burning in a fireplace made her feel romantic. She told me to sell my soul if I needed to, but I had to get someone to cover my call. I got it arranged without summoning Lucifer, though it took a three-way deal that would have made a professional baseball manager proud.

I thought Mimi and I had done everything there was to do, but I was young, naive, and decidedly wrong.

Friday came, and with it, the promised letter. The summation of findings read more like a citation than a review of an investigation. She was, naturally, ecstatic. We closed up shop that afternoon as quickly as we could and made plans, within earshot of the clinic staff, to meet Monday morning for rounds.

By three-thirty Dr. Lyle had signed out her two inpatients to the neurosurgeon on call for the weekend; early even for her. We left separately, as we always did. I went home to pack a few things, and then to her condo. She was nearly through a beer when I got there. She insisted I catch up and then, as if throwing sand in the face of Death, our everyday rival, we popped two for the road.

She threw me the keys to her Mercedes and said, "Go east, young man."

"Where to?"

"It's a secret hideaway. I should be blindfolding you and packing you in the trunk but you seem trustworthy. Can I trust you?"

"Completely. Besides, I don't get out of the hospital much, much less out of town. I won't know where the hell we are."

She pointed us east on the Superstition Freeway through the suburbs, then we continued on Highway 60, climbing scrubby hills onto scrubby plateaus. I asked if we were headed to Sedona. She said no, Sedona was the other direction and just over-photographed cliffs and overpriced restaurants. She said nothing more. The highway signs, though, gave decreasing distances to towns named Superior and Globe.

We talked mostly shop-related stuff: my academic record, which general and vascular surgeons I respected, weird experiences in the ICUs, *The House of God*—a thoroughly cynical account of one man's internship, it was every resident's bible for bad attitude—and who, among the hospital folk, was thought to be fucking whom. She started pumping me about which nurses or classmates I had slept with, but I was mum. I recognized that she cared much less about my amorous past than testing my will to keep my mouth shut. Besides, I wasn't about to open up. This was for fun, not for keeps.

In the middle of nowhere, it seemed to me, she started watching the side of the road. "What are you looking for?"

"It's coming up. Now. Slow down, slow down," she said. Then, "There. Just past that Tonto National Forest sign. About a hundred yards. There. Turn there."

I turned the Mercedes down a gravel road, made a right, took a left fork or two, up a hill, around a bend, off gravel onto dust, and kept going, climbing into some desiccated badlands. We crossed a cattle grate. The terrain had become noticeably dryer; prickly pear instead of oaks, and some sage. Just as we lost sight of the sun over the ridgeline, we eased onto a barely-there trail, through a thicket of mountain junipers. We bounced another quarter mile down into a canyon, around a hairpin, to an honest-to-God adobe house tucked into the middle of a long grove of cottonwoods.

Mimi explained, as we were unpacking the car, that the house was probably eighty years old, at least the walls—the roof had burned eight years prior in a range fire. It was part of a privately owned inholding on what was otherwise National Forest property. She had operated on its owner, a commercial banker from Tempe. He had been able to buy it about ten years earlier from an aging recluse who had wanted to move to the California gold country because he'd read that, with gold over four hundred dollars an ounce, people were starting to destroy the rivers again to make money. The banker patient, grateful to Dr. Lyle for removing the pain from his neck and apparently prone to fits of bad judgment, told Mimi about his secret getaway and half offered her occasional use of it. She had gratefully accepted, I'm sure to his surprise.

"Can you start a fire?" she asked.

"Eagle Boy Scout! Goddamn right." The beers had soaked in.

"You and Ed Adams. Fucking Boy Scouts."

"Learned to swear at my first summer camp. Eleven fucking years old. And start fires. Lashings, too."

"What are lashings?"

"Wrap thrice, frap twice. Long twine, two small logs or poles. Lashings are the wraps and knots you use to tie them together. Make things."

"That could prove useful," she said with a come-fuck-me look. She poured us each a double shot of gin and disappeared into the bedroom while I lit a fire and unpacked the deli picnic she'd brought. Mimi reemerged in a long yellow silk robe, lace-topped stockings, and slippers with modest heels. Her hair was down. I consciously swallowed.

She tossed a small package to me. Professionally gift wrapped in a manly pattern of deep brown and silver. "I thought you needed this," was all she said. Inside was a beautiful sterling silver belt buckle, cast into a bear's face in an oval shape. I was gushy: "Wow. This is really beautiful. I've never seen anything quite like it."

"I thought you would like it. It's made by a Hopi man I've known for years. He does a lot of unusual stuff. Part shaman, part silversmith. He told me the face is that of a bear spirit that came to his aid when he was on his first vision quest. The bear became his 'guide,' helped him find his right path. He's so full of that voodoo stuff. I put the receipt under the cotton in the box if you want to go look for something else."

"No. No. I like this."

We ate and drank. The alcohol and Mimi's self-presentation put my hormonal state on spin cycle. We kissed a lot more than usual. She looked at me carefully between kisses, as if she thought she recognized me but couldn't find my name. She suddenly got up and began rummaging in her duffel. She produced a leather sack with a drawstring and carefully laid its contents on the low table beside the couch: a long glass smoking pipe, smudged from prior use but wrapped in tissue, a long thin chemist's pipette, a shallow glass dish like a huge watch lens, some small glass vials and jars, matches, and a bottle of Pharmacists' Ether.

"Ever freebase?" she asked without looking at me.

I hesitated. "I don't think so."

"You'd know if you had." She went to the kitchen cupboard for a box of baking soda and filled a jar half full of water. She mixed the water, baking soda, some of the ether, and the contents of one of the vials and shook. She lectured: "You remember ether extractions in organic chemistry?" I must have looked blank. "You dissolve an organic salt in water, add acid or base, depending on the organic compound you're after, then add a lipophilic, hydrophobic, immiscible liquid, preferably a highly volatile one . . ."

"Like ether," I interjected.

"Like ether. Shake and bake." She smiled, bit her lip, and shook her concoction with self-conscious glee. "Draw off the lipid layer, evaporate the carrier, the ether, and you're left with the free organic acid or base, which, in this case, is cocaine base."

"I knew that year of organic chemistry had to be good for something," I said.

"Oh, it is. It is." She was demonstrating the drawing-off part by now. She laid the ether on the glass dish in successive dribbles with the pipette, then gently blew across the top of the liquid. The layer of ether visibly shrank away and a small semisolid white mass accumulated on the glass. She blew until it appeared to be dry. "You want all of the ether gone," she said. "We'll be playing with matches in a minute. And it is not good to burn your face off."

She scraped up enough to half fill the bottom of the pipe bowl, then put the pipe in my mouth. She said, "When this melts, inhale slowly and don't stop until it's gone. Hold it as long as you can, then we'll kiss and you can exhale into my lungs. We waste none of this stuff." She struck a match and held it under the bowl.

I did just what she prescribed. Even as I held my breath I felt a rush of pleasure ride into my head like nothing I'd ever felt before. As I leaned to kiss her and exhale into her lungs, I was trying to remember exactly what orgasms felt like so I could compare the two. After a minute she blew out the exhausted vapors. She smiled at me and waited for a reaction. I grinned broadly and lay back into one of the big chairs.

She scraped another pipeful, lit it for herself, held her breath for an unbelievably long time, then motioned me to kiss her. She blew softly into my lungs. I held the stuff until I thought I must surely pass out, at which point I let out an explosive breath. Mimi laughed.

"So this is pure cocaine," I said.

"No, dear, it's been stepped on. Cut with lidocaine and mannitol and all kinds of crap. Some of it comes out with the base. If it's really pure you get better crystals when it dries out. With all the shit in it you get goo."

"Can't you get hospital stuff?"

"Are you crazy?"

"I heard people talk about it. Pure and cheap."

"Yes, it's pure and cheap. You sign it out of the narc cabinet, all full of reassurances to anyone willing to listen about it still being the best at what it does for the schmo with the broken nose, but someone gets the idea that *maybe* you're keeping the leftovers and rumors go around. Whether they can prove them or not, rumors, if they're true, are deadly. No, you're better off never even ordering the stuff up. Even for legitimate use. Then, no rumors."

With the lecture, she gave me another bowl and I was spinningly euphoric. She repeated her own dose, then sat on the couch with a dreamy-eyed look of self-satisfaction. She was watching me. I kept closing my eyes, smiling, opening my eyes to look at her, and smiling again.

"Okay," I said. "I'll bite. What are you thinking?"

She smiled and closed her eyes. "I like fantasies," she said.

"Sounds good to me. Am I in any of them?"

"Oh yes," she said. "In fact, I was just now trying to decide if I want you on the top or on the bottom."

I half laughed. "Of what? Or whom, maybe I should say."

"I won't tell you his name."

"His?"

"Oh yes, his. As long as I've been sexual I've wanted to watch two of my lovers have a go at each other."

"Me and another of your boyfriends."

"An ex. And the one I have in mind was also a doctor. An orthopedist I met at a spine convention. More than a few years ago but not at all forgotten. Tall and blonde with liquid eyes and the greatest ass God ever put on a man."

"Good, then I'll be on top," I said with sarcasm.

"Mmmm. For a while, I suppose. You're not homophobic, are you?"

"Not particularly. But I'm not too homophilic either."

"Well, this is my fantasy."

"Am I drunk in this fantasy? I really hope I'm drunk."

"You can be even higher than you are right now."

I smiled. "Whatever became of this tall, light, and well-rounded stud of yours?" I asked.

She sighed. "Time. Distance. You know."

"You ever see him?"

"Actually he was in town last year. He called. I was all excited to get together until I found out he had gotten married. I guess he wanted to cheat. I told him to fuck off."

"And now you think he and I should fuck each other."

"As long as I get to watch. And direct. All's fair in fantasy, Malcolm."

I just shook my head. "I don't think I've ever been that drunk," I said, "and I've been pretty drunk." She smiled and closed her eyes. Then, making sure I was watching, she slowly slid her hand all the way down her lower abdomen and just kept going. I sat and watched and drank it up and smiled.

Mimi's manual display was certainly enticing but before long I was mentally wandering, trying to remember the nerve pathways involved in the microvascular control of blood flow to the genitalia. But I was still smiling. The coca euphoria I'd read about was real, though after the first rush, not as intense as I'd expected. I realized my mind was running around, playful, happy, unconcerned. More than anything else I felt a carefree invincibility.

She told me, "Take off all your clothes," which I quickly and gladly did. The fire had warmed the cabin well, and nakedness, once achieved, seemed like such an obvious choice I was mildly embarrassed I hadn't thought of it myself. She motioned for me to do as she was doing and got a delighted smile when I gained full posture.

Among its many attributes, though, cocaine is an anesthetic. Officially, a topical and local anesthetic—the chemical precursor of novocaine—it certainly seemed a sexual anesthetic, too. I could find no tension, nothing compelling me to move forward, only satisfaction in that exact moment.

Which left her to direct. She motioned me onto her and pulled me inside. "Feeling passive tonight, Malcolm?" she whispered directly into my ear. I could only smile and quicken my pace.

She put her hands on my hips and forcibly slowed me. "On this high," she said, "we go slowly. Mmmm. Slowly." She rolled us over, raised herself to sitting, and stayed tautly still but for a slow rhythm of pelvic squeezes. I closed my eyes, smiled like the fool I was, and whispered, "I love your pussy."

"Mmmmm. You're a bad boy."

This was possibly the longest fuck on record. Eventually we moved to the rugs in front of the fire. In my altered state the whole focus became fucking: the feeling, groping, probing, kissing, licking, tasting, smelling, working, sweating pleasures of the acts of fucking. As opposed to coming. I could not have cared less about that, and by all available signs, she felt the same way.

After what seemed to be hours, however, I realized that such an encounter deserved a climax. There were clear signs of exhaustion in both of us. I felt the inevitable falling drug level with its counter-euphoria and figured that it would have to be soon or not at all. I began to work in that direction, and work it was. With much concentration and finally a bit of grunting, I achieved a short and ragged orgasm, then fell to my side, gasping. It was clear Mimi was not so inclined. She murmured something unintelligible and began to fondle my rapidly departing organ. I reflexively jerked away. She made a pouty face and went into the bathroom.

Evidently the neurohormonal mechanism in the male brain that insists on sleep postclimax is stronger than cocaine. I remember a minute or two of drifting exhaustion, the fire needing wood, Mimi going to pee, then returning to our "bed" with a big sheet and two blankets, and the next thing I knew I was startled—painfully—awake. It was pitch black and my head hurt. I was waking up to the sounds of a woman alternately shrieking and sobbing, but no bed under me bouncing, only the stiffness of the floor. I bolted to sitting. It took me at least three long gasps and blinks to remember where I was and who was beside me.

When the "Mimi" part of my memory woke up and engaged itself in the fray, I came very acutely face-to-face with my place in our relationship. I, the subordinate and the invited guest, facing a superior in mid-breakdown. How familiar, how presumptive should I be? I hardly had the emotional stature there to take the role of mate, despite our frequent matings. Very clearly though, she needed something, someone, and I was the only possibility. I put my arms around her. I needn't have worried: She immediately turned into my chest, now just sobbing and gasping.

"Mimi," I said. "What's wrong?" Just sobs. "Nightmare?"

"Um-mmm."

"It's okay, we're here. I'm here. Malcolm. I've got you."

A stuttered "Malcolm."

"You're okay." We rocked gently and the crying ebbed away to an occasional staccato sigh. I gently broke away to tend the fire. I stirred the ashes in the fireplace and threw in some newspaper and kindling. A single tail of smoke began to wind upwards. I got a cold washcloth from the bathroom. She rubbed her eyes.

"I keep having this awful dream," she said in broken cadence. "Way, way the worst tonight." She wiped her eyes with the bedsheet. "I'm sorry, Malcolm."

"Oh Jesus, Mimi. Don't be sorry. I'm just glad I'm here to hold you. What was it?"

"You don't need to hear it," she said.

"No. You should tell me. Get it out." I was trying to be polite.

"It starts out the same. I'm in the OR. Lost."

"I had dreams like that during the first half of internship," I said. "Whatever service I was on, I'd have dreams about some patient there crashing, and me having to do some emergency something that I didn't know how to do yet."

"But . . . No, it's different. I remember those dreams, too, but this is different."

"How so?" I said, yawning.

"It's awful," she sobbed again. "I'm lost in a maze of ORs. I go out one door and it's another OR. And they're doing heart surgery in one and spine surgery in one but brain surgery in most of the others. Everyone stares at me. The nurses, the other surgeons, the residents. Everyone. In one of the rooms there's blood on the floors and the walls and even the ceilings. I woke up this time when I saw the blood dripping from the ceiling. And the nurses and all the surgeons are staring at me!" She burst into tears again.

She gathered herself together and sat up. "Tonight, in tonight's dream, I'm naked from the waist down. Running around the OR half-naked. And one of the nurses is laughing, pointing at my leg, saying that must be 'come' running down my thigh." She was sobbing again. "And I say, 'Oh, it's okay, it's Dr. Dreamboat's,' " she practically wailed. "But she doesn't hear me. None of them can hear me. They're just laughing and pointing."

I had wrapped her up again and began gently rocking again. "It's okay, it's okay," I droned.

"I get so lost," she sobbed.

"You're not lost," I said.

"I do. I get so lost. In the OR."

"What do you mean?"

"I can't . . . I can't . . . I can't find exactly where I should be," she sobbed.

"Is this like that dream of being chased? Somebody's after you and you're stuck to the floor?"

She leaned away from me to the end table and a box of Kleenex. "Something like that."

"But you can't find your way to the OR?"

"No, worse . . ." She blew her nose.

"What? Feet stuck in the quicksand? Monsters chasing you?"

"Inside the head." The newspaper and kindling I'd laid on the grate burst into flame with an audible *poof.*

"What?"

"I get so lost inside the head. I can't see things in three dimensions. I've never been able to. I stare at the head. I try to line it all up, just like McWhorten taught me, but nothing comes." She was crying again.

I was staring at her in the fire glow. She looked terrified.

"I start each operation bright-eyed. Full of optimism. 'This is going to be the one. This time it will all work the way they say.' I make an incision, turn a flap, dive in . . ."

"No. You know the anatomy better than anyone. . . ."

"Sure, I can recite it. But I can't see it. In my head, like I should. I memorize the fucking CTs, cut by cut, but I can never stack them up again, you know, in my mind to re-create the whole. I can't roll things around in three dimensions and see what's on the other side. I never could. I just don't think in three dimensions. Ever. It tortures me, knowing it, having to hide it. I wall up." She stared through me. "I'm *so-o* tough," she sobbed.

I put my arms around her again. I stared into the flames, my faith in my chosen profession burning around me. I thought of Keith Coles and his wife and children. Casualties. I needed something to hold on to. Even straws would be good.

"Mimi, I've always hated analyzing dreams. They're nothing but anxiety playgrounds and I have more than enough anxieties when I'm awake," I said, trying to laugh a little. I realized my face was in a knot. I closed my eyes and made my forehead and cheeks relax. When I opened my eyes she was staring at me with fear. I could only stare back.

She pulled away. "It's my daytime nightmare," she said, trying to laugh, too.

I cringed but forced a short chortle. "Yeah, we all have them." My throat was closing down. I mustered a pathetic smile. I escaped terror by redirecting the conversation. "But who is this 'other man'? The guy you call Dr. Dreamboat?"

She half laughed through a sob. " 'Dreamboat' is my code name for a neurosurgeon I know—kind of. He's out in Scottsdale."

I gave her a quizzical look. "What's my code name?" I asked.

She laughed again. "You don't have one."

"Yet," I said.

"Yet," she agreed. "But it will be a good one. Promise."

"I'll look forward to it. So who is Dr. Dreamboat?"

"Oh God. A great man. Busy practice in the ritziest hospital in Scottsdale. Must make a fortune. He was on backup call, covering for Ed Adams one weekend when Ed was in New Mexico getting some Grand Old Man award from the fucking Boy Scouts. I got into an aneurysm case, up to my earlobes, again. It was a Friday night. At first I thought I had the thing, but my view kept slipping away. I had to call for help, again. He was the one who answered. I had not met him but I knew of him, knew who he was. He came to help. He scrubbed in, sat beside me. Smelled nice. Had incredible eyes. Mmm. That's all you see over a surgical mask, but in his case it's enough." She was just staring.

"And what happened?"

"He moved a couple of retractors and slid the clip under and around that little . . . pulsating . . . cherry . . . like he was born to it. I just kind of sat there in awe. I think he was a bit surprised that it turned out to be really fairly easy, at least for him. Maybe there is such a thing as a routine aneurysm for a man like him."

I said nothing.

"Anyway, he's an absolutely gorgeous man. I got kind of a crush. Actually, I got a raging crush. Why not? He was a white knight. My white knight." Her voice tailed off. She turned to stare into the fire. The dancing red light bounced from the wetness in her eyes. She said quietly, "I told you I like fantasies." I had only to think back to her lying on the sofa not too many hours earlier to have what I thought was a clear idea of what she meant. She smiled at me.

"A few nights later, when I was home alone and feeling sorry for myself, especially after some wine, I wrote him a thank-you note. Not just a simple 'Thanks, you're swell.' No, I practically spread my legs for him. I had drunk too much. I suggested a date of some kind. I don't even remember exactly what I wrote, but I was so far gone into the fantasy of it all that I walked to the mailbox at midnight and sent away my little missive, sealed with a kiss."

"Did he ever say anything?"

"No. He never replied and I didn't run into him for probably three years. It was at a Western Society meeting. I tried to be, I guess, entirely professional, and he did, too. He didn't bring up any of it. Didn't ask for a date, either."

"Probably all for the better," I said.

"Well, it just left the thing hanging out there. I almost wish he had laughed at me or something, so I could have defended myself, or at least known what he thought about it. Or if he even remembered it at all."

She lay back down and curled up on her side. I laid in some firewood and went to the bathroom. Once back in bed I lay flat on my back, makeshift pillow stuffed under my neck to give it some stretch. It felt like my brain was trying to pound its way out of my skull and my gut was toying with the idea of something cathartic. Sleep was slow to come.

8

There are rules, maxims, and Lessons for Life to be had, working in Adrienne's Quiet Little ERs Where Nothing Ever Happens. A gem I've noticed about fathers who run over their sons' heads with trucks: They always get them twice. I've seen three in my career. All three were dads and sons. Sons ranged from six months to fourteen months. The first, from my intern days, happened at the continuous summertime party along the Salt River outside Phoenix. Along a ten-mile vestige of river left only as a conduit between the last of the dams and the city's intake diversion, ten or twelve thousand revelers float in inner tubes, cavorting on their future drinking water, pretreating it with beer, sunscreen, and pee.

The baby brought to us had been set, in his car seat, under the back of the Jeep for a nap in the shade. Later, probably getting low on beer, Dad hopped in and backed up. Big thunk. "What was that?" Go the other way. Big thunk again. Massive head trauma doesn't always kill you right away; it can take twenty-four hours or longer. I imagine, though, that the recrimination, the divorce, the suicide fill up years.

The one brought in from the prairie hinterlands last month was a fourteen-month-old. We guessed he was crawling under the truck to fetch a ball, or maybe hiding from his older brothers. Dad went to reposition the truck so he could get the barn door closed. Big thunk. "What was that?" Go the other way. Big thunk again. The surgeon I called said it's a natural choice in driving—if you might be up against something, better go the other way. He said we all do it.

I have a different theory: I think it's our need to make certain that we're really, truly in a world of shit before we'll get off our butts to try to change something.

The Morning After.

After beer and wine and cocaine, after exhaustive sex, after Mimi's nightmare and after teasing sleep on a stone floor, I came to consciousness with considerable fear and loathing. Our quaint and timeless adobe hideaway had mutated into a chilled and fireless old mud hut lost deep in a desert canyon.

Mimi was up and making coffee, wearing an extra-large sweatshirt and bags under her eyes. There was a palpable presence of something unwelcome.

I went naked and shivering into the bathroom, avoiding contact until I could at least crank up my defenses. I took my time peeing so I could run through what each of us had done and said and convince myself before I had to speak that it had not been my own special nightmare.

I managed to reemerge with an upright, seemingly self-confident stride despite my covering of gooseflesh and my shriveled and hiding manhood. As I pulled on my jeans and boots she handed me a mug of the coffee and a toasted bagel. We tried some friendly small talk revolving around the lighthearted notion of "Boy, didn't we have a great one last night."

We were made prisoners in our private canyon by the real possibility of seeing someone we knew should we venture up into Globe. We spent the day on a pair of short hikes. We wandered among the cottonwoods up the little stream, took a nap in the sun on the patio, then did a second stroll down the stream. The springtime sunset came late enough that it was still daylight when we realized we needed to venture at least as far as a supermarket to avoid going hungry. Reasoning that her car might be as recognizable as either of us, our only choice was for the hostess to go to town for the steak, leaving me to stay back to build and tend a fire in the outdoor *chimenea*.

Time alone, recovering from an epic debauch, poking burning logs with a bent stick of cottonwood, is an experience in self-hypnosis. Lying on a wooden bench by the outdoor fireplace, I drifted along the edge of sleep. The embers radiated their searing heat and every spectral color from white to gold to blood red. I caught myself wondering how Sister Edith dealt with her mustache. More awake, I reasoned that I had been pondering hell, because it was the graphic description of hell in second grade by Sister Edith that always made me most apprehensive, and if I had been staring at combustion and thinking of Sister Edith, I had certainly been considering hell.

Fortunately Mimi brought back enough wine that we were able to contentedly avoid any substantive conversational topic, sticking instead to sex, drugs, religion, and politics. Bedtime was an asexual collapse.

In the car ride back the next day, I laid claim to a moderate hangover. Really I just wanted some silence. Mimi, too, was still blearyeyed. She copied my excuse, fatigued even to the point of letting me drive.

On the route down from our borrowed mountain, the junipers thinned out, giving way to sage. As we approached Phoenix the sage gave way first to some misbegotten cotton fields, then to a few ragged, bullet-ridden saguaros left there to herald one's return to the Land of Subdivisions, the Valley of the Sun and its suspect claim to civilization. I wanted nothing more than to be able to turn her Mercedes around and go only north. Someplace relatively sane: Flagstaff. Las Vegas. Death Valley.

We got to her condo by early afternoon. Our goodbye was brief. From there I drove straight to my home, which was, thankfully, empty. My sorry secrets would remain safe from my better half for at least one more day.

I did my laundry, sat down and read four pages of a chapter in a surgery text, managing to rally myself before falling completely asleep. I went running and cleaned out my car. Evening came. I was finding solitary time pleasant: I had no urge to go back to Madame Lyle. Our lust was spent—tired and flaccid. I went to the supermarket for a fish steak and a bottle of white. There a brunette was smiling at me. She was slightly overdressed, apparently on the make, but I wanted a new entanglement, even a short one, like I wanted syphilis.

Denial is a wonderful thing. I guess I was hoping we could muddle through, at least until the end of my rotation. Maybe not have to go trekking deep inside anyone's head while I was still the witness. Nonetheless, when the new workweek began with a pair of routine operations, I found myself double-checking everything I could: which wrist needed the nerve released, which side and exactly what level the lumbar disc was offending, and what palpable landmarks a gloved hand might feel to be sure to find the proper vertebra on the first try.

At first it seemed to work. Things went smoothly. I began to believe the warning in the canyon would, after all, dry up and blow away in the desert winds. I told myself that giving it any significance was just my own version of a self-flagellating nightmare. The guilt of a recovering Catholic after a weekend of sin.

In clinic the second day I kept looking for another Darla Winthrop; someone we could rescue from the jaws of Death, someone who would go forth, reanimated, singing our names. Instead I saw a man in for his routine post-op visit. Madame Lyle had worked on his lumbar spine a week before I joined her team. The pain and weakness in his legs had, unfortunately, grown worse since the surgery. This is a known possibility, clearly explained to every patient before they lie down for us, but my faith in Mimi Lyle as a technical surgeon was, like my lust, withered.

Mid-afternoon I met Susan McKenzie, the woman who would unwittingly make painfully apparent the exact depth of the mire I was in.

Our doctor-patient relationship began like any other. I pulled a nascent chart from a slot and read the intake nurse's notes: A thirty-two-year-old mother of three, referred by Gyn Clinic for a suspected pituitary adenoma. Three years after weaning her last child she had spontaneously resumed lactating. They got a brain CAT scan, which showed quite clearly a tumor at the front of the base of the brain, obliterating a pocket of bone that would normally cradle the pituitary glands. It was almost certainly a benign growth that kicks out a hormone, in this case the one that tells breasts to make milk.

She was stoutly built, blonde, and fair-skinned almost to albinism. In our conversation, besides the relevant history of her symptoms, I learned she once participated in rodeos but now chased her children and made quilts in front of the TV when they were asleep. She had come in alone because her husband had just found a job at a construction site sixty miles away. Her readily visible anxiety gave our conversation an extra urgency.

Benign tumors often grow in very malignant places. The pituitary sits just beneath the point where the optic nerves cross and comingle on their way to the back of the brain. When Ms. McKenzie was seen in Gyn Clinic three weeks earlier, the gynecologists tested her vision and found it completely normal. On my exam, however, she had clearly lost parts of her peripheral vision, more on the right than the left. The adenoma was apparently growing very quickly, pressing on the optic nerve fibers.

I presented the case to Dr. Lyle. In the classic format for a medical description, probably first prescribed by Hippocrates, I told her the few pertinent identifying data, why Ms. McKenzie had come to see us, and a complete description of her symptoms, all in maybe two run-on sentences. Then the pertinent past medical history, social history, review of systems, and a detailed description of her physical exam—completely normal except for the visual field cuts and freely expressible breastmilk. I would have described the findings on the CT scan, but Mimi had already put them on the viewbox and had pored over them all the time I was talking.

"Pretty clear-cut," was all she said, and opened the door to Ms. McKenzie's exam room.

When the conversational niceties were again uncomfortably cut short, Susan began looking at me as if I could save her. It occurred to me maybe Mimi did not like women. She cut directly to the You-need-an-operation part, and described how we would work up through her nose, cut away the bone at the base of the brain, and pluck out the tumor. The "vision nerves" were right there and blindness was a possibility, but Susan "shouldn't worry about it." I almost dropped the chart. I'm sure my mouth fell open.

Fortunately this was not entirely new to the patient. Her earlier doctors had given her the overview, and she was bright and aggressive enough to have found some information on her own. She had even arranged for a month off from her receptionist job, beginning a week hence, knowing this was coming. "Better make it two months," Mimi said bluntly.

Back in the hallway, where most clinic decisions are made, Mimi was curt: "Book it. Trans-sphenoidal resection of pituitary adenoma. Five hours." Turning away from me, I'm certain she said, "God, here we go again."

I went back to Ms. McKenzie to go over the pre-op details—the consent, the tests, the diet proscriptions. She looked confident, expectant, innocent.

When I called the OR scheduler, asking where we could fit a major case in—soon—she said their computer database showed Dr. Lyle averaged well over eight hours for this type of operation, and she would be required to block out a full day. I wondered if their database had not mixed in aneurysm operations. One or two fourteen-hour cases could seriously skew one's profile. Having already lost every OR scheduling argument I ever started, though, I said only, "Whatever works." Fortune smiled: The scheduler moved a vascular case to another room and came up with an available slot the next Tuesday, a week away. I gave the date and time to Mimi's assistant.

When lunch break came Mimi was on the phone, being syrupy with someone, discussing a grant proposal. Open on her desk was a thick file marked "NIH." She waved me away.

On my way into the cafeteria I met one of my internship classmates, Gene Woods. We had become good friends while sharing a rotation in the ICUs. Gene was born with the cynicism one needs to succeed in surgery. He called neurosurgery "spudification." He was headed for a professorship somewhere. "How goes brain surgery?" he asked. "Turned anybody into a potato yet?"

"You mean today?"

"Well, this week."

"No, but it's only Tuesday." Then I got a shiver—Susan McKenzie. "Talk to me next Wednesday, though," I said.

He wondered what I was getting into, but I had already said too much. I changed the subject but could not shake the foreboding.

Before diving back into the afternoon patients, I went to talk to Mimi. She was standing just inside her private office. "Excuse me, Dr.

Lyle," I began. "That woman this morning. What did you mean about 'Here we go again'?"

She gave me a vague though stern-faced look. "Nothing. I didn't mean for you to hear that, Malcolm."

"But . . . Is there something here . . . something more . . . problematic?"

"No. These are difficult cases. Always. I've seen them turn into nightmares, is all, but that's part of the job. It's unavoidable." She gently closed her office door in my face.

Standing alone in the corridor I replayed our explanations to Susan McKenzie. Of all the absurd doctorly inanities I had heard, Mimi's mention and simultaneous dismissal of blindness was memorable. When I remembered the look on Susan's face, I was not certain I could play my part again with the necessary professional wall. I felt dishonest.

As soon as I finished with the next patient—another walking (poorly) proof that the evolution of the human lumbar spine is far from complete—I called the operator and asked her to page Dawn Stelfox, my friendly anesthesiology resident. Five minutes later, when Dawn's voice announced from my hip an in-house extension, I found a secluded phone to make the call.

"So what do you know about Dr. Mimi doing pituitary cases?"

"Never had the pleasure," she said.

"Any way to ask around? Quietly? Say, for a hypothetical patient needing a hypothetical pituitary adenoma taken out."

"A purely hypothetical patient?"

"A purely hypothetical young mother of three. Trans-sphenoidal approach—straight up through the nose. You know, leaving no externally visible evidence you've been there."

"I'm sure I can get an informed opinion, in a hypothetical sense. I'll call you back."

Two hours later I had the answer I most feared. Dawn was working that afternoon with an ENT resident who had heard a tale from two of his seniors. Once upon a time there was an extended flog wherein the ENT folks had done the trans-nasal exposure without a glitch, then waited five hours for Dr. Miriam Lyle, using the finesse, in his words, of "a bull elk fucking a cow," to remove the little bugger and, miraculously, leave only one side blind in her wake. She had not, in this instance, solicited help from any other neurosurgeon.

That night, at 3:15 A.M. I was suddenly wide awake. I had been dreaming about going blind from watching Mimi masturbate on cocaine. I lay there for a half hour before I could again drift off, only to be slapped awake by the clock radio. Until then, I had not, since starting my internship, been awake while lying down for any period longer than a minute.

In the shower that morning, I realized I wanted help even if Mimi Lyle did not. In times of trouble I had a close and highly reliable resource: Mary Ellen Montgomery.

Mary Ellen and I were used to crossing the Styx together. I'd once been her sounding board through a confrontation with an Attending, albeit in less explosive circumstances.

It's still a touchstone case. Nancy Madsen, an eleven-year-old girl, had had a brain tumor removed when she was nine, but had not been "right" ever since. She was admitted to the Pedes ICU during a bout of nonstop seizures. An unusual complication of severe brain dysfunction is pulmonary edema—water in the lungs—which Nancy developed in spades.

While her doctors scratched their heads about the diagnoses and prognoses, she was teetering on the brink of dying from her lung disease. After three full days of innovative heroics with Nancy's ventilator, Monty convinced one of the cowboy-souled anesthesiologists to help her shoulder portable, full-scale life support and get the girl to the MRI scanner—a block away—and back. That by itself was a nail-biting feat, but the pictures they got proved to be critical in their decision making.

Most of the girl's brain stem had somehow lost its blood supply and infarcted—died—a particularly awful kind of stroke. Except for vision, smell, and hearing, all sensation was permanently lost. All movement and outward expression were equally obliterated. This meant, if she were to "wake up"—not likely in itself—she would be permanently locked into a personal hell: awake but absolutely paralyzed, ventilator dependent for eternity, and completely unable to communicate with anyone—not by voice, not by hand, not by encoded eye blinks.

Mary Ellen had been quite persistent in wanting to let Nancy die of her lung failure. The consulting neurologist was noncommittal. He said, "Let's see where we are after the lungs clear up." Mary Ellen said, "It'll be too late." Translation: The stroke would kill neither her higher brain nor her body, just the connection between the two. The lung disease was the way to let her go. Mary Ellen asked the professor if they could get the hospital ethics committee involved. He gave her a flat "No."

No one had asked the family what they wanted. Mary Ellen explained everything to them in detail and broached the idea of letting go. She was, no doubt, graceful in leading them to the idea, but Mom went nuts when she realized what Mary Ellen was getting at. That's always a risk you take when you bring it up, but if you don't bring it up you may be assuming the wrong thing.

The mom vented to the PICU social worker. He passed it up the ladder. Mary Ellen's professor then went nuts, even writing a letter of reprimand for her file. All for caring enough to be involved.

As feared, at two weeks the girl's lungs had recovered. She would have been completely off the ventilator, but none of her muscles could be made to move. I saw her from time to time in the hospital: The girl lay in her bed and stared, or seemed to stare, at the ceiling. Mom learned to get her into an electric wheelchair and strap the portable ventilator underneath the seat. They went for tours of the lobby and the wards. When it was cool out they went to the parking lot. Nancy had the face of abject apathy. If there was more cooking behind the mask, no one could have known. Eventually they took her remains home, everyone the poorer for it.

As it was playing out, Mary Ellen vented to me. Unfortunately my sympathy was matched only by my impotence to help, but she said it was helpful to talk. After our talks she would get eerily quiet, put on a veneer of fuck-you determination, and go back for more. She could be scary.

Mary Ellen still sees the girl for routine care in her own follow-up clinic. She won't let her go. She said to me, "She needs me."

"How does the mom treat you?" I asked.

"Oh, pretty fair. She acts like we never had a problem. We chitchat about men. She got divorced after the girl went bad."

"Don't they all?"

"Well, most."

Unfortunately, Mary Ellen's view of me had been tainted by the little ménage à trois in the Pediatric ICU involving Mimi, Mary Ellen, and me. Still, I needed her. I paged her as soon as I got to the hospital.

"Suppose," I said, "you were teeing up a nice young woman for an operation you did not think your Attending could do well."

"Which Attending? Or should I say, 'the Witch Attending?' "

"Never mind that."

Long pause. "Can the Attending do it at all?"

"Well, the grapevine says that said Attending makes a complete hash of it."

"Sounds bad. How's your relationship with said Attending?"

Long pause. "Mixed."

Another pause. "And I assume there's serious risk to the patient or you wouldn't be calling."

"All the usuals: brain damage, death, extreme disability."

"Like what?"

"Like . . . extreme disability. Like being buried after a nice funeral."

"Malcolm, why are you being so coy? You're usually full of details."

"I can't really go into detail, Mary Ellen. That's part of the problem."

"Malcolm. Hello. It's me."

"Oh hell, Mary Ellen. I can't. Can we leave it at that?"

"Yeah. If that's what you want. We can leave it at that. But I don't think I can be much help if I don't know what you're up against."

"It's a shitty ethical thing."

"You know how much I love ethical dilemmas."

"Sorry. But it's where I'm living right now."

"It's certain you're not living at home. Got a new HO?" "HO" was Mary Ellen's term for "Hot One," a romantic prospect.

"Mary Ellen, I'm sworn to secrecy. But it could be the radiology resident with the long black hair."

"The Chinese woman? You thought she was untouchable."

"I've been wrong before. I'll be wrong again."

"Well, who is Lisa? She's left a really cute message. Sounds like a high schooler. You're getting worse, you know."

I'm a terrible liar; I had forgotten about Mimi's prefab cover story. "She was a mistake. Never should have shown any interest."

"Well, tell her. She seems to think you're in love."

"Yeah, I will."

"And call me again when you want to talk to me."

"Yeah, I will."

I hung up, lonelier than I had thought possible.

I prayed that in Mimi's clinic I would see only patients with "simple" problems. Of course, if you're seeing a neurosurgeon, your problems are not simple, but some are easier than others. Entrapments of peripheral nerves. Even low back pain. It's the bane of life for any orthopedist, neurosurgeon, or even a family practitioner, but, figuring it never killed or blinded anyone, I was hoping for only back-pain patients.

First on my schedule that morning was an easily forgotten lecture on state-of-the-art treatments for metastatic prostate cancer. The professor could have made it very short: They all die, slowly and painfully. As he droned I conjured what might have been another option for Ms. McKenzie: I could phone her with a not-quite-anonymous warning:

Me: "I'm not sure you remember me. Dr. Ishmail, the resident you saw with Dr. Lyle."

Her: "Yeah."

I imagined an uncomfortable pause. "This call is entirely unofficial. No one knows I'm making it, and it would be a really good thing if you could forget my name and face."

She might chortle. "Sounds kinda serious, Doctor."

"I guess it is. I'm calling with, um, a suggestion. Some serious advice."

"What?"

"The operation I booked you for . . ."

"You don't think I should have it?"

"Oh, no, you really need the operation. But you need to find someone else to do it."

A silence, then, "I don't have a choice. We don't have insurance. We go to the County Hospital. And they said I would get a professor from the university there."

"Well, you did," I would say. "And she's smart. Really smart. But in certain types of deeper operations she has a lot of trouble. More trouble than just about any other neurosurgeon would have. It's an unusual kind of problem she has, but your brain, your sight, is not something somebody should be messing around with."

"But they already scheduled me. What would I do? You can't do this!"

"Please try to be calm, ma'am. I'm just trying to help you. I have a lot of respect for Dr. Lyle, but you really want somebody else to be doing your specific operation."

"How? How could I do that?"

"Get a second opinion. Find another brain surgeon. Use the yellow pages if you have to, but get someone else to see you. Say you just want a second opinion. Then stick with that surgeon. Listen, that happens all the time with second opinions. Patients tend to go with whom they saw last. No one will think anything of it."

"But we can't pay for that! That's why we go to the damn County."

"I don't know what to say about that, ma'am, but you have to try."

"I'll talk to my husband."

"Yes, of course. And, if you could, forget we had this conversation."

She would not have said "Thank you."

In fact, she probably would have decided that I, the learner on the team, was just a miserable lout out to cause trouble. With no financial resources, she would have ended up back at Maricopa, back with Mimi Lyle, but now doubly frightened. She probably would have reported me to anyone and everyone who would listen. Then she would have sailed through the operation unmarred, and, in repayment for her extra anxiety, would have hunted me down and set me on fire.

The days progressed. Slowly and painfully.

I told myself I would find the right time to go see Joe Kellogg. A moment's lapse in the schedule, an operation canceled. Something.

But nothing intervened. In afternoon clinic the day before the scheduled operation, I realized why I was avoiding the meeting. Joe Kellogg would no more hear bad things about his star recruiting success than he would about his own mother. I would inevitably be the one wearing shit.

At Mimi's that night I spent my last dollar: "You remember what you told me in clinic the other afternoon," I began. Her face became wooden. "About pituitary cases turning into nightmares?" No response. "I was wondering . . . well, it occurred to me, if they can go so bad, maybe you could get another neurosurgeon to help us with the case, to, just in—"

"Do not ever, ever, bring that up again," she said, very quietly. I sat silently. "I am fully capable of getting a pea out of its pod."

I nodded.

She went on, slowly, distinctly: "I'm not sure what you think you heard me say. But I have no problem whatsoever with this kind of case. I have never said otherwise."

Again, I nodded.

The subject was changed and we miraculously carried on as if it had never been brought up. At bedtime I was feeling anything but sexual, but I think she wanted to reassert the underlying premise of our relationship. Once she fellated me to attention I obliged her with a thrashing performance she apparently mistook for passion. I then left for my own town house, fabricating enough detail in my cover story to show my professor I was learning.

Once home I showered.

On the appointed Tuesday morning Mimi and I met for morning rounds just as we always did, large coffees in left hands, pens in right hands. We left notes and orders on our patients, then found Ms. McKenzie alone in the Pre-Surgery Holding Room, looking scared, lying still under a sheet and two thick cotton blankets.

"All set?" I asked her.

She said only, "Mm-mm."

"Will any family be here, waiting for you?"

"My husband is just getting the kids over to their grandmother's, then he'll be here. I was hoping he'd be here before they take me." She looked past me toward the door. "The kids wanted to be here but I knew I couldn't take that."

Dr. Denny, the assigned anesthesiologist, came over to the gurney. "I'm holding off on giving her anything until her husband gets here," he said, letting me know we would be waiting for him.

I said, "I'll tell Dr. Lyle about the minor delay." I went to the back room and paged Mimi. I told her to go to her office and work; I would call her when she was needed. I did not want her getting inflamed. I hoped she could again be optimistic for at least the beginning of the operation.

Ultimately Ms. McKenzie was thoroughly sedated, wheeled into the neuro OR, anesthetized, and cannulated in all the right places. For a major case this can take an hour. Then a team of three from the ENT Division—an Attending, a resident, and a medical student—did the first shift, spelunking their way, headlights and all, up the nose to the thin plate of bone that separates the mucus from the brain. "All yours," they said. "Page us when you've got it out." And they were gone. I called Mimi in her office.

She smiled at me as we scrubbed, then settled in behind the operating scope humming very softly, just as I had heard before. At that point I buoyantly believed that my earlier worries had been ill founded.

Our view in the scope, once it was irrigated and suctioned, was bone. We stared at it. She seemed hesitant to break through it. Even to me it was obviously the next step. After fussing about the way the scrub nurse had certain instruments arrayed on her stand, she finally, with an audible sigh, began sticking long-handled bone crunchers up Ms. McKenzie's nose and chipping away.

The hole in the base of the skull grew one small chip at a time. My view of the proceedings, through the 90-degree teaching arm of the operating microscope, looked like an indeterminate stew of soft pink lumps dotted with frequently changing sharp edges of white bone, all bathed by lipstick-red blood alternating with a clear wash.

When Mimi was through the bony layer, she put in long thin brain retractors. It wasn't long until the humming stopped and, having been through it before, I sensed the early return of the familiar, palpable sense of frustration. Dr. Denny's face was impassive, stony. Terrie, the scrub nurse, was staring at the wall.

Time passed but the view in the scope stood still.

Mid-morning Joe Kellogg ambled into the room, tying up his mask as he came to the table. Mimi's eyes—all of her face I could see—told me his arrival had locked her ponderous steps into ice.

"How's it going?" he asked.

"Oh, I think it's going just fine," she said without looking at him. "We're getting there in bits and pieces, you know. Muddling through, despite ourselves." It was the overstated modesty of the highly skilled, misapplied.

Dr. Kellogg came to my side and nodded to me—my signal to get up. He sat and looked through the scope for a couple of minutes, then stood. He went to the wall and studied the CT pictures on the view-box, then looked around the room like he was lost.

He said, "Well, Mimi, I'm around all morning if . . . if it gets interesting. I've just got a straightforward laminectomy down the hall." A pause. "We don't see a lot of these." Another silence. "You know Ed Adams is in England—that visiting professorship. . . . Call me if it gets interesting." He left. I stared after him.

By noon Mimi had already gone to the viewbox twice to study the scans. What I could see through the microscope had not changed in at least an hour.

We were in the middle of another cross-country trek without a compass. She was muttering to herself again. Making tiny adjustments in the retractors and angles of view, then undoing them. It was, for me at least, a horrifying déjà vu. Though I initially assumed Mimi must have been just as upset, it occurred to me she might be resigned to it or even used to it.

By Hour Six I considered leaving: silently rising, pulling off gown and gloves, and disappearing. It would not have been wrong in the ethical sense. If one is powerless to stop a robbery, one does not have to stand and hold the door.

But it would be a showy form of breaking ranks. Everyone in the room would know of my distaste for the proceedings at hand, if they did not know already, and the Powers in Surgery, should Mimi or the OR crew choose to pass along even a casual report, would see my behavior as serious insubordination and equate it to abandoning a patient.

I recognized, too, that dramatization of my feelings would embarrass Dr. Lyle but would not improve her anatomic visualizations. It would certainly have negative repercussions on my tenure as a surgical resident and just at certainly would not help Susan McKenzie.

Instead I rose and stretched. Mimi glared at me. I raised my eyebrows and moved my head slightly in the direction of Joe Kellogg. With only her cold, contemptuous eyes she directed me with irresistible force back to my stool.

Around three-thirty, just after the nurses changed shift, my own version of brain stew had me almost catatonic. The only thread I had left to grasp was the hope that Susan McKenzie still would be lucky. That she would fall within that group of patients—probably the majority portion—who actually did well despite a poor draw on the assignment of her brain surgeon.

Suddenly things began to pick up. There was a flurry of activity in the hole and Mimi mumbled, "Now we're getting somewhere." BB-sized chunks of tofu-like tumor began parading out. Within forty-five minutes she was satisfied that she had it all. I had no way of knowing.

She looked at me, stupidly victorious, and, attempting humor, uttered one of the trite phrases of medicine: "Even a blind pig finds an acorn now and again."

I lied my smiling approval.

Just when she said "Let's pack up and go home," something unexpected broke open. Bright red blood began to pour from the nose. Mimi muttered, "Oh, for fuck's sake," then shouted, "Clip. No, cautery. No suction. No. Not 'no, suction.' No, there is no—no fucking suction!" The suction had stopped. We were unable to evacuate the work area.

Through the scope I got a highly magnified view of the headwaters of the red stream running down the plastic drapes. It was a kaleidoscopic gush that looked like a clear mountain brook running over a spring of molten cherry candy. The clear stuff was cerebrospinal fluid, signifying we'd torn through one extra layer. This meant Susan would be at risk for a chronic leak of brain fluid out her nose.

I was of course useless, frozen in my role of ignorant supplicant. Mimi was apoplectic until the scrub nurse got a new tip on the sucker and we could see tissue again. She laid into the electrocautery, changing my view to highly magnified, swirling brain smoke. I held the sucker. She ultimately put a tiny titanium clip on the bleeding source, a point I guessed to be an artery, hopefully of the tiny, insignificant type, which she referred to as "that little prick."

She gently laid in a strip of a white, bioactive gauze that was supposed to stop bleeding from outside of the source, something our physiology professors in La Jolla had said was impossible. When it appeared to have worked, she packed a wad of Styrofoam-like stuff in the gap where the tumor had been.

While sitting and waiting, making sure the bleeding didn't start up again, she told Dr. Denny, the anesthesiologist, he would need to put in a lumbar drain before we left the room. This would help the hole in the lining of the brain heal by keeping the cerebrospinal fluid from flowing through it out the patient's nose. Mimi's tone was peremptory. Dr. Denny didn't look up. He barely nodded.

Away from the table, Mimi allowed herself a quick, self-congratulatory grin as she pulled off her paper gown and latex gloves and stuffed them in the trash with a small flourish.

The ENT team trundled in and put Susan McKenzie's nose back together. One of the OR nurses, the anesthesiology resident, and I, the wordless zombie witnesses, wheeled Ms. McKenzie to her ICU cubicle. When the physical part of the delivery was complete and the life support functions were being methodically assumed by the ICU nurses, I went to the desk and hid my face in the chart. I carefully lettered the "Brief Op Note" that memorializes the collected labors until the transcriptionist can type out the verbose spoken version. I followed that with a comprehensive set of orders—everything I could think of, from ventilator settings to a laxative if needed. Unfortunately I was too good at it. Having done it hundreds of times it took no more than ten minutes. I'd wanted it to take longer.

Under proper resident protocol I would have paged Dr. Lyle and asked where and when she wanted to start rounds on her other patients. I couldn't. I just went and saw them, wrote progress notes, and updated orders. For one Pilgrim in Pain, I acquiesced to his wish to be discharged. He was angered that being in the hospital for back pain meant he'd be getting fewer narcotics than at home.

Just as I was finishing, Mimi walked onto the ward, looking just as she always did, as if the day had been routine. I avoided eye contact.

"Go home, Dr. Lyle," I said. "I'll take care of rounds." It was what an overreaching resident would have said to show off broad shoulders, but I honestly did not want her around. When she answered by taking a chair next to mine, I gave her a succinct status report on each of our half-dozen patients.

She smiled. I was afraid she was thinking of celebrating her "victory" by having me for dinner again. Unfortunately all I could come up with were exactly the same things I would have said had I been creating cover for a later rendezvous and clandestine fucking, something that would have been beyond even the most testosterone-soaked imagination at that point.

"Go home," I said again. "I'll page you if anything comes up."

"I am tired," she finally allowed. Then the way she looked as she said "I'll see you for morning rounds" told me she wanted to see me for morning rounds and no sooner.

When she was gone I finished the charting on the last of our patients. Then I went home and threw a few things in a duffel. I got in my car and drove east out of the Valley of the Sun.

9

On my first Friday night, years ago, in the Quiet Little ER Where Nothing Ever Happens of St. Petersburg, Nebraska, I got two maxims from one case. The first: Be careful where you put your head.

We received a guy who'd been pouring some kind of rocket fuel into the open carburetor of his old pickup, trying to get it to turn over and buck. The ensuing fireball took all the hair off his face, eyebrows included, and left his cheeks and lips raw and blistering and on the verge of shedding very many layers of skin, some of them only partially formed at the moment of their death. His left hand was just as bad.

My surgical training had been truncated before I got to the Burn Unit rotation, so I lacked experience. I'd done my homework, though, reading the textbooks and studying the pictures. I knew to slather the raw parts with a standard concoction of antibiotics and silver salts that would stop the Chinese army, were they in bacterial form, then wrap thickly with soft cotton and ship the whole package to a Burn Unit where the resident experts could graft and grow him some new skin.

The hard part, though, was his airway. Anyone who has ever done a CPR course knows airway comes first. Anyone who has put his face into that kind of heat may have inhaled enough hot gases to have scorched his throat and trachea to the temperature of the exhaust pipe on a hot rod. Significant swelling there can close down his breathing passage, which would be particularly bad in the back of an ambulance halfway between Hooker and Lincoln. He would die. Standard treatment, according to the books, would be to put him down with drugs and pass a breathing tube to keep open his airway.

Easy to read—or write—considerably harder to do. This gentleman weighed about 280 and lacked any visible neck. His mouth looked relatively small. While I was sure I could figure out what drugs and how much to use to get him to be still, at the time I was not at all sure I could get a view of his lar-

ynx and get a tube in. That is a mechanical skill we practice on plastic man-nequins, none of which has the anatomy I expected in him, that of a bull elk in rut. If I failed there he would die unless I did an emergency tracheotomy—something I had never done before—and if I failed there he also would die.

They say good judgment is based on experience; experience is based on bad judgment. To date I had made no judgments, good or bad, regarding poten-tially burned airways.

I sweated and procrastinated for a good ten minutes before the sign lit up over my head with Maxim Number Two: You can call for help.

The senior doc in the Burn Unit in Lincoln, when I answered in the neg-ative each of his questions about labored breathing, coughing, hoarseness, and throat pain, was quite reassuring. He said the man would "probably" make it just fine to Lincoln. We packed him into the ambulance and said, "See ya."

I called the next morning to see if "probably" had been good enough in his case. Better to pester Lincoln immediately than be surprised by the subpoena in six months. Fortune had smiled on all of us: Mr. Fireball would live to get that dang truck going yet.

THE BOOK OF MIMI, CHAPTER SEVEN

Flight from Phoenix and Mimi, of course, solved little and made many things worse. I knew when I started the car and left town that simply failing to show up for morning rounds could be tantamount to quitting the residency. Short of vomiting up whole organs, one's physical pres-ence is always expected. Still I felt I had no choice. Theoretical conse-quences were as nothing in the face of the reality of Susan McKenzie.

In my Datsun in the evening sun I sprinted east. On the edge of the suburbs my pager chirped. A woman's voice asked me to call the Maricopa operator. I turned the pager off, something I'd never done before. I crossed the Salt River dust plain twice to get to the highway up into the mountains.

My strength was exhausted. Maybe it was the McKenzie case or the Coles case, maybe the long hours of emotionally demanding med-icine mixed with long hours of an emotionally demanding relationship at the edge of disrepute. In more normal times I would have conferred with Mary Ellen, but I'd made her counsel off limits to myself.

I passed the Tonto National Forest. I passed Globe. I ascended the Mogollon Rim in the gloaming. I found Interstate 40 at Holbrook and lowered my head for the distance. There is little traffic across the high desert. Excessive speeds are the norm. I focused on my drive, refusing to examine all internal signals to slow down and think about what I was doing. Trepidation was for the timid.

I slept a few hours at a rest stop between Gallup and Albuquerque. Just past Las Vegas, New Mexico, the sun climbed above the flat, stiff bed of the Great Plains, screaming all the way. I hurried through a drive-in for a late-morning meal in Colorado Springs. Once my head is down, food, gas, and peeing are like speed bumps.

It was night again when I got to Hooker. I went by Dad's office. It was dark but for the small light over the sign—his "shingle"— "Nicholas Ishmail, MD, Physician and Surgeon." I walked from my car and stood and peered in the window at his desk. Neat stacks of journals and charts and correspondence awaited his attention there.

I drove to our house. Even nothing-towns like Hooker have beautiful old houses. Ours was built in 1910 by a successful merchant and had survived with minimal tinkering by its few owners.

When I walked into the kitchen, Mom dropped her dish towel and almost ran to hug me. "Malcolm! What are you doing home? Why didn't you call?"

"Uh, Mom, kind of a spur-of-the-moment thing."

"Are you in trouble?"

"No. Not really. I mean yes, a little. But I think I can handle it. I came home to think about it. Maybe talk it over with Dad."

"Medical trouble?"

"Yeah. Residency trouble."

"Have you eaten? Did you sleep this time?"

"Yeah, some of each."

"Not enough of either, I'm sure. I'll get you some dinner. Your father's in the living room. But you'll have to tell me, too."

Dad was staring at a crossword, pen in hand. He raised his head to show he knew someone had entered, but did not look up at first. When he did he blinked and slowly let a smile build.

"Malcolm. Home from the war already?"

"Seems so."

"I didn't know it was over."

"It might be. For me."

He sat up in his chair. "Sit down." He waited.

"Tell me again how you handle it when you get into an operation over your head."

He frowned. "I know you didn't come all this way for a bedtime story."

"I'm AWOL."

"They aren't kind to deserters, Malcolm. I'm surprised you got as far as Gallup without some horseback posse getting you roped and hung."

"I've got a real dilemma, Dad."

"And you think an old country doctor can help?"

"I think you can."

He bit his lip but smiled slightly. "You want a drink?"

"Yeah. Yes, please. I'm pretty wound up. I get that way when I do these drives. I'll get it. You want one, too?"

"Yes, please."

"Scotch?"

"Sure." I poured two drinks. He said, "Every surgeon gets himself into jams. You know that."

"I know I do, but tell me again what *you* do." I said.

"I get help. It's not that hard."

"But where is the point when you say to yourself . . . what does it take to say 'I can't do this'?"

He rubbed an eye. "Okay. Here's one you haven't heard before. Last year I was going in for a simple abdominal hysterectomy. Fibroids. Bleeding and painful. Simple. I did what you're supposed to, though, I looked and felt all around and lo and behold the poor woman had a lump in her descending colon. You know I've done hundreds of bowel operations, probably dozens of partial colectomies. But she'd not been worked up for cancer. I don't do surgical oncology anymore. It all gets sent to Lincoln or Denver. But I was facing a woman, in the flesh, anesthetized, with her belly open."

"Who is there to come help you in Hooker?"

"You know, Malc, we got phones here a couple of years back. I got her covered up, broke scrub, and got on the phone. The guy in Lincoln I send cancer patients to was off fishing or something, but I had a nice chat with the man covering for him. He told me what biopsies she would need for staging and to go ahead and do a wide resection with a primary anastomosis. Of course I could sew two ends of a colon together. It's basic surgery. I suspect even you have mastered that by now."

"Yes, Dad."

"But when I was doing this kind of work I would never have done a primary anastomosis for a cancer patient. Everybody got a colostomy. But times change.

"I went out and told her husband what I thought we should do. He agreed, of course. And she got what she needed—two fairly simple operations at one go-round. She didn't need a second admission, a second anesthetic, a second incision, any of that."

"And she did okay?"

"Cured of both problems. Not every surprise cancer is such a happy case, though. I've also had to close up and send patients on down the road by ambulance. That's more humbling. Not sure I told you about each of those." He drank.

"So those guys in Lincoln aren't thinking you should be quitting surgery altogether."

"They think I do okay. When you call another doctor for help—if you've been careful up to that point—not been stupid in thinking you can do an operation you have no business doing, or burned an anatomic bridge inside the patient before you realized what you were up against—a good surgeon, a good doctor, will help. There's no judgment—it's about the patient. Sure, you'll be explaining step-by-step how you got to where you are, but if your logic is sound you get the patient taken care of and you can still live with yourself."

I said, "Of course."

"Your pride isn't worth a gnat on your ass compared to the patient's well-being."

"I know that."

"And your pride will be ultimately better off with healthy patients, anyway."

"I know that, too."

"I know you know that. But you asked me."

"Yes. But what . . . ," I said, "what if you can't do an operation you are supposedly trained to do?"

"Well, now, that's a totally different ball game. I'm sure you're not talking about yourself, because you're not finished training, yet."

"No, it's my Attending."

"Your current Attending? What service are you on?"

"Neuro."

"A neurosurgeon."

"Yes."

There was a silence. "What can't he do?" he asked.

"She. She can't find her way around deep inside the brain."

"Malcolm, think about what you're saying."

"Dad, I have thought about it. I have thought about nothing else for the past week and a half. She gets lost. That's what she told me. Her words. She told me it's always been this way. She does her homework. Studies the scans. Sits and thinks and tries and tries and I guess just nothing comes. She can't, in her mind, put one slice on top of the other and make it look like brain, see it from different angles."

"That's not . . . She's a trained neurosurgeon, for God's sake."

"Dad. I've seen it. I didn't know what it was at first, but I've seen it."

Another pause. "Give me a case."

"She's been known to open the wrong side of the head or start a laminectomy at the wrong level, though I haven't seen that myself."

"Carelessness. Unacceptable, but just simple human carelessness. Not some deep flaw."

"Yes, I know. But the deep flaw is there. It first came up in an aneurysm case. Supposedly fairly routine for an aneurysm. Anterior communicating artery. I scrubbed and held hooks till she got them all bolted to the table. Then I sat for hours blinking into the microscope. Dad, she was lost. I didn't realize it at the time, but it went on for hours. She had the dura open for over ten hours. And they say that's not her record. There was even an inquiry over this case." I told him about Mr. Coles's death and Drs. Miekle, Ryan, Kellogg, and Bullock. "In the end they just said, 'Bad disease, bad outcome. What do you expect?' Then, after her exoneration, in a moment of, I guess, uninhibited self-awareness, she told me she gets lost and it's always been that way."

He rubbed his face. "She told you this?"

"Yes, Dad." I looked away. "She was feeling vulnerable. Weak for a moment."

He stared at me. "She trusts you."

"Yes, Dad."

I was afraid he would want to know why, but he stuck to the clinical issue. "She needs to get a second surgeon. Someone to help her."

"That's what eventually got us out of there. After that endless wait they finally called in another surgeon and, bang, it was done. So when we were setting up another patient for a deep-sea expedition—this time a tumor but practically in the same place—I suggested she get another surgeon to scrub at the outset, and she about threw me out of the clinic. The operation . . ." I was talking too loud. "Dad, it was so painful. It was like being stuck in the sand. Wheels turning and nothing happening. I knew she was lost again. I asked her if we should call Dr. Kellogg—the Chief. He had even stopped in the OR earlier to say he was available. She almost killed me."

"And what happened?"

I described the culmination of the operation. "And after rounds I left for here. No excuses made. I'll tell them I was dying with the flu and couldn't get to the phone. It'll be a black mark against me but I don't care." I paused, then said, "I imagine the patient will be okay. They say most are."

He nodded and sipped his drink.

"Dad, she was put at real risk. Aren't we supposed to try to minimize risk? Where we can?"

"Of course, Malcolm. That's our job."

"And one of the next ones won't be lucky."

We were quiet a moment. I said, "How did she get this far?"

"Well, I imagine she can take blood clots off the surface of the brain. From what you're saying that wouldn't provoke her deficit."

"No, not as long as you pick the correct side of the head. I could probably do those by myself by now. You cut off part of the skull and it's right there in your face."

"Don't be flip."

"Okay, but you know what I mean."

"Yes, I do."

I went on, "And she can drill straight down on a spine and usually find the chunk of disc rubbing on the nerve. She can probably find most aneurysms. You look under the right—the correct—lobe and there it is. It's when it's a little around a corner she has trouble. She gets lost."

"So most of her patients do fine."

"Exactly, Dad. Except aneurysm patients. Most of them do lousy, anyway. Everybody knows that."

He said, "Look at it this way. All we have as scientists are probabilities. You took statistics in medical school."

"Sure."

"So you learned about coin flips as the basis for everything in medicine."

I laughed a little. "Well, that's not how they put it."

"But, have you ever told a patient or his family you knew for sure how something was going to come out?"

"No."

"Of course not. Because you know all we have in medicine are probabilities—coin flips. Or rolls of the dice. But each individual patient gets only one. You know it's a single patient lying in front of you. One case at a time. Some patients buck the odds, some succumb. That's what we doctors do. We don't have yeses and noes. So we try to make the odds as favorable as we can for our patients."

"And the odds she gives aren't good enough. That's what I'm up against."

"Right," he said, "but when a case goes bad she can say it was just the odds. A run of bad luck. If she's getting lost in there on the tough ones, who would know?"

"Me."

He nodded. "Do you know of any other cases? Like the aneurysm? I mean is this a pattern?"

"No. I mean I know other cases like that one have happened. She's kind of a legend around the OR. But I don't have specific names and dates of birth."

"Do you think she's hurting patients?"

I hesitated. "I'm not a brain surgeon."

"You're a doctor. You have your patients to think of."

"Yes. Dad, I *think* she's hurting patients. I know, if that's true, as I understand the problem, that it is preventable. But I can't prove it's true."

"Do you believe it's true?"

"Yes. I believe it is. It all fits."

"It fits the data."

"Yes, it's the only explanation for what I have in front of me."

He said, "Is there a need to act?"

Again, I hesitated. "Most wouldn't," I said.

"You're not most."

He had spent his entire life winnowing integrity from natural tendencies. That was why I'd come. "Yes, I believe there is."

"Have you thought about your options?"

"It seems the only thing left is to go to the heads of her department."

"It seems. But think it through, Malcolm."

"I will, Dad."

"And don't ever forget how proud we are of you."

"Thanks. I won't."

The next morning I called the Maricopa Surgical ICU. The charge nurse told me Ms. McKenzie was waking up, though slowly. She was still on the ventilator but there were no gross neurologic deficits. Her family had been in to see her.

I clicked off and sat with the receiver in my lap until the piercing tone came on to remind me the phone was off the hook. I would have done anything to help Susan McKenzie, but her die had been cast. I said to the ether, "For the next one, then."

I needed an appointment for a meeting.

I little relished the idea of a second session of incestuous politics with a Professor of Brain Surgery. Having tried Joe Kellogg with little to show for it, I would have to go to Dr. Marshall Bullock, the über-boss, and from everything I'd heard, a real fingers-in-the-light-socket kind of guy.

His reputation among the U of A medical students was unique. He was said to be an exemplary gentleman teacher to medical under-grads—tolerant of relative ignorance, patient with uncertainty, and never failing of manners. Apparently, though, the initials "MD" be-hind a name made a man or woman fair game for any and all sorts of embarrassment and invective. It was said that newly minted interns were regularly reduced to blubbering under his withering assault of obtuse questions, mid-level residents clambered over one another to avoid him, and chief residents survived by memorizing his personal repertoire of physiologic fine points like kindergartners learning the Pledge of Allegiance.

I called Cynthia Blachly, our residency coordinator, my Mom-away-from-Mom. Besides being the one who could arrange my sit-down with Dr. Bullock, she would have been the first to know about my having gone AWOL from Mimi. Expecting a shocked response I said, "Hi, Cynthia. Malcolm Ishmail."

She said, "Hi, Malcolm. What's up? You sound far away."

"It's a cheap phone."

She said, "What can I do for you?" in a normal tone. Apparently I was still alive as far as the Residency Office knew.

I inhaled deeply and asked if I could meet with Dr. Bullock early the next week.

"Rethinking your story?" she said.

"I just thought of something I need to add."

"Disclaimers?"

"You're such a help."

"Dr. Bullock is in Tucson, honey."

"I know."

"He's not coming to Maricopa any time soon."

"I was thinking I should go to Tucson."

"Well, I can try to set it up, but I don't have direct access to his schedule and your schedule is not exactly wide open. Besides, Dr. Kellogg was supposed to be handling anything that comes up here. He was a little testy, I understand, about not being in on every interview and every message that came out of his backyard. You sure you don't want to meet with him?"

"I already did."

She sighed. "Wanna pick up a phone? You don't want to drive to Tucson. It's an ugly drive."

"I'll risk it."

When I called her back Cynthia had set up an appointment for me the next Monday afternoon. She still gave no sign that Dr. Lyle had ever mentioned my absence. Maybe Mimi was happy to be rid of me.

For two days I lived in Hooker. I went to Dad's office. The locals—all shapes and sizes—came and went, some jaunty, some on crutches, some hunched over walkers, all smiling.

I hiked along the river. I ran on the high school's oval track. I did push-ups and sit-ups. I ate home cooking. I caught up on my sleep. I made no excuse to Cynthia nor Mimi nor anyone else for missing most of the last week of my time as a brain surgeon.

That Friday I left on the return trek. I intended to perform my usual head-down sprint, but somewhere on the eastern slope of the Rockies, driving in the dark, I began to cry. It didn't interfere with my momentum, steering on the interstate being practically foolproof, and no one could have seen, so I just let it flow, examining, as they came up, the notions and images that made it throb.

Certainly I feared for my career. Medical academics, like everyone else, do not like having their major mistakes exposed. Even messengers can get killed and in my case I might be mistaken for more of a problem than a messenger.

More aching, though, was the loneliness. It was not as acute and searing as being dumped by a lover, but more pervasive. Even more formidable. Intellectually, after a breakup, one knows the pain is finite—there will be another lover. This, on the other hand, might never go away. Always—high school, college, med school, internship, and residency until now—I had been able to rely on my *compañeros* in times of trouble. There had always been those among whom there were no secrets, no lies.

I stopped for a sit-down meal and a cheap motel. I wanted to call Mary Ellen.

When I got to Phoenix Sunday afternoon, I went to Maricopa to check on Susan McKenzie. I found her chart and read Dr. Lyle's notes. Mimi's tone was completely self-satisfied.

The patient was not in her room, but her nurse said her husband had taken her for a walk. Maybe a good sign. I found them just outside the cafeteria. Her husband, looking aged since I had met him in the presurgery room, was pushing her IV pole. I spoke briefly to both of them. It was obvious she did not remember me. It was unclear whether she knew her husband.

Her acute mental vacancy, while not necessarily permanent, was frightening. Much of the good stuff of brain function—memory, personality, sexuality, impulse control, sense of humor—lives where we'd been pressing. It sometimes takes weeks or months to reappear. Sometimes parts of it are gone forever, the gaps invisible to the doctors who do not know the subtleties of the person.

The calendar having ended our academic relationship, my tour with Madame Lyle was over. There was neither party nor speech. There never is—residents come, residents go, easily forgotten. I had ended our personal relationship with my insubordinate absence from the last few days of clinics and rounds. I'm sure we both knew that any further words between us must necessarily begin with an apology from me, something I was not planning. If she wanted to lodge a complaint or add a nasty letter to my file, I would deal with it as I could.

Monday at 0700 sharp I stopped being a faux–neurosurgeon, transforming instantaneously into a faux-vascular surgeon. After morning rounds I made my scraping apology for having to leave for most of the day on an administrative matter. My Attending snorted. "Hell of a way to start a new service, Ishmail."

"I know, sir. But I have to meet with the Chairman of Neuro-surgery. It's pretty serious."

He gave me a hard look but waved his hand dismissively.

The interstate out of Phoenix, south to Tucson, cleaves vast expanses of dust speckled with the occasional chancre of industrial farms and a seemingly random smattering of abandoned farmhouses and road-houses, anachronisms in the age of the sixteen-row tractor and the interstate highway. It invites a heavy accelerator.

The only remarkable thing about Dr. Bullock's office was his Executive Assistant. A woman best described as "huge," sporting a tower of lacquered hair, but with eyes sparkling from beneath the folds of flesh. She was kind and grandmotherly and called me "Dear." She insisted on getting me coffee, then brought cookies along for good measure. I waited in the relative warmth and safety of her maternal domain. When I was almost asleep in the armchair she gently called my name and nodded me in the correct direction.

I faced the office door. I paused and steeled myself before knocking. The portal to purgatory, I discovered, looks just like something you see every day.

Marshall Bullock was sitting sideways to his desk, bent over an old typewriter. I remembered having seen him at Maricopa once, being led around by a stiff-looking team of doctors and their hangers-on, each gussied up in something more formal than usual, each in a brightly clean white lab coat. He looked to be of above-average height with broad shoulders and a thick, athletic neck. His face was tanned and lined, his reddish hair sun-streaked.

Before I could sit down he asked, "What brings you to Tucson?"

He did not look up. I hesitated. "I don't want to be rude," he continued, "but our report on Dr. Lyle is all written. And the Chief Resident has made a mess of this paper we were to have in press next month. If I don't get it in the mail by four-thirty this afternoon, the editor is going to come out here from Yale just to have a go at me with a switch."

I smiled. One could sell tickets to such a meeting. "Sorry, sir. It's not really a straightforward thing." I sat. "Since I talked to Dr. Kellogg two weeks ago, I've been thinking about the implications of what he was asking me."

"About Dr. Lyle." His voice had an unnerving booming quality.

"Yes. I thought about the nature of the questions and all." Silence but for the typewriter. It occurred to me that if I quietly left he might not be certain I'd ever been there. I ventured on: "It seemed the issue was probably bigger than just the Coles case."

He typed on, but finally said, "It may have been. In some people's minds."

"Actually, Dr. Bullock, something came up. She said something to me that got me worried about another patient. . . ."

He glanced up briefly. "A particular patient."

"Yes, sir. I mean, as an example of the problem . . ."

"Someone . . . in the hospital? The ICU?" He turned toward me.

"No, sir, not exactly. She's in the hospital, was in the ICU. A woman I saw in clinic and scheduled for surgery. We did the case last Tuesday."

"A completed case?"

"Yes, sir. But something she said . . ."

"What kind of case?"

"A pituitary adenoma. Trans-sphenoidal approach. Thirty-two-year-old mother of three."

He rocked back in his armchair but stared at me intently. I got the impression I might have touched a sore spot.

I said, "Something Dr. Lyle said, too. I mean we both felt bad for the Coleses, and she was kind of getting down on herself. . . ."

"That's a natural reaction for a good surgeon," he said.

"Oh. Of course," I said. "I've been wondering ever since his operation if I could have done anything differently, you know . . ."

He waved his hand. "Of course."

"But she said a couple of things that got me wondering. And it's been like a rock in my shoe ever since." He waited. It was time to shoulder the load, but I stumbled. I said, "In clinic she said, 'Here we go again.' "

He frowned. I scrambled: "Since I met with Dr. Kellogg and he pointed out how long Keith Coles's operation had taken—I mean, fourteen hours—how she had ultimately needed help, and all that, I got to wondering if this might turn out the same way. If that was what she meant." His frown tightened. "I checked around with some OR people and they told me about one of these adenomas she did a few years ago that turned into a disaster and left the man half blind."

"You were concerned about this woman being made blind."

"Well, yes, sir."

"Dr. . . . Ishmail, is it?"

"Yes, sir."

"We all know Dr. Lyle does some operations slowly. All of us like to be meticulous."

"Yes, sir."

"And the OR people do not like slowness," he boomed, "unless it's their own."

"Yes, sir."

"And blindness is a known complication of that operation. It's in the texts. It's part of the explanations we give these patients ahead of time. It's not like that man was the first."

"No, sir." A pause. Sink or swim. I blurted Mimi's secret: "But what else she said was, 'I get so lost inside the brain.' "

He looked up slowly. Our eyes met. I went on, in a slow careful tone: "She said to me, 'I memorize the CTs, cut by cut, but I can never stack them up again to re-create the whole. I can't roll things around in my mind in three dimensions and see what's on the other side. I never could. I just don't think in three dimensions. Ever.' " He stared at me. "She said it's a 'daytime nightmare.' Apparently recurring."

There was a long silence. I sat still. Dr. Bullock was leaning heavily on his elbows on the desk, but said nothing. He had both hands cupped over his chin.

"I tried not to think much about it at the time. But then Ms. McKenzie came into clinic. I was the one who worked her up for Dr. Lyle. It really began to bother me. I realized that, well, if there's one place you really need three-dimensional thinking, it's got to be brain surgery. Maybe surgery inside the heart, too, fixing a valve, but . . ."

"Yes. Quite." He cut off my nervous prattling. There was silence as he stared. "She told you she cannot reconstruct anatomy in three dimensions. Mentally."

"Yes, sir."

"She said she 'gets lost in the brain.' Her words."

"Yes, sir, essentially."

" 'Essentially' or exactly?"

"Well, I guess exactly. 'I get lost inside the brain.' What I just said. It's kind of seared in my head." He stared through me. "And I think it's accurate," I said. "It explains the kinds of problems that have . . . that have been reported. It seems to fit what happened to Mr. Coles. And maybe others, I guess, from what I've heard. And I think she thinks she's being fair to the patient. She said she tried for 'a couple of hours' before calling for help. I think she believes that. But at least in the Coles case it was what—over ten hours with the dura open?"

He sat in thought. Again, I waited. His eyes were focused on things I could not see. He massaged his upper lip. I was sure that he was well aware of Mimi's reputation around the OR. I imagined he was thinking through the implications. Clinical. Political.

"What is this woman's name again?"

"Susan McKenzie."

He scratched it on a notepad. "And how did the case go?"

"Well, it was sort of mixed, I guess. It began okay, but then it turned into that same sucking and buzzing and sucking and buzzing and nothing happening. Just like in the Coles case. It was déjà vu."

"Did she get help?"

"No. I sort of suggested it, but she . . . didn't appreciate the suggestion. Eventually, kind of suddenly, she got into the tumor area and started shelling out what she said was the adenoma. Then she closed up. There was a lot of bleeding, though, really suddenly. Bright red. And we were into the CSF."

"How did she handle that?"

"There was some yelling. The suction quit at the worst time but she handled it. Started buzzing a lot and finally put in a clip. The bleeding stopped."

"And the patient?"

"So far, no overt stroke. Slow to wake up, though. Pretty vacant."

"She will clear," he said.

I sat. That is a brain surgeon's favorite prediction. After a second I said, "I mean she's walking but she's not there. They're optimistic, but she's certainly not as awake as some patients are at this stage, and from what I understand a lot of the frontal lobe stuff is subtle. Personality things."

"Sometimes subtleties have to be sacrificed to save the greater portion."

"Yes, but not if they don't have to be."

He glared. I said, "This woman is the mother of little kids."

"Each of our patients is important to someone."

"Yes." I said. I almost added "Precisely so" but thought better of it.

I felt I was about to be dismissed. I wasn't going home with any unfired shots. "It even occurred to me I should have sent the woman away. Told her to get another 'opinion' from somebody and not to come back to Maricopa."

"You would have told her that?" Thunderheads swirling between his eyes.

"No. I did not. It occurred to me, but I knew that wouldn't be right. But I'm feeling like I would have to if I saw another complex case walk into her clinic. That's why I'm here. I feel like I have to try to do something."

"You're thinking you know more about brain surgery than your professor!"

"No, sir. Not at all. But I mean I am a doctor. This woman was my patient, too. And I had knowledge about potential harm. Harm that might, for all we know, have been done. And might have been avoided. At least made less likely. What should I do? I know I can't send away one of Mimi's patients. Or at least I shouldn't. Or maybe I should. I did ask Mimi if, considering what she had said about 'Here we go again' and the Coles trouble and all, if she might not ask someone to help her, or even send this woman on to another surgeon."

"What did she say to that?"

"She made it pretty clear that that was not an option and that I should never bring it up again." I was sitting up very straight. "So I had no choice but to come to you."

He glared.

I said, "Dr. Lyle even has insight into her own problem. But she's not going to stop, not on her own. Maybe Ms. McKenzie will be perfect in six months, but some patients aren't going to be lucky. How could I do anything else?"

"You're suggesting, Dr. Ishmail, that a respected professor of neurological surgery has some kind of innate flaw, some absence of ability—of even normal everyday ability—to think and see things in three dimensions."

"Well, sir, it's what she herself described to me. And it fits the other . . . the events . . . in the OR."

"Does your diagnosis have a name?" he sneered.

I was well inured to belittlement. I said, "There are all kinds of apraxias. Some inabilities to do a specific task would be obvious, some would be subtle."

"She's a brain surgeon, for God's sake."

"Yes, sir."

"She does not have an apraxia. It's impossible."

I said nothing.

"And the operation is finished. The patient is recovering."

"But what about the next one?"

"Oh for crissakes." He was silent, then said, "Does she know you're here?"

"No, sir. I'm off of her service as of this morning." Again, a silence. "I saw a man in her clinic two weeks ago. He had a redo lumbar spine fusion before I came on service. And now he's worse than before the operation. I know, like everyone else, that bad outcomes happen. Especially in neurosurgery. It's all a matter of percentages. X percent of our patients will get worse. And when someone dies or lives in pain we all tell ourselves it could not have been helped. I'm feeling like it could have been helped."

His look was hateful. "Like you could help."

"No, sir. But maybe you could improve the odds for these patients."

A long pause. "Why, Dr. Ishmail, do you think . . . what possessed Dr. Lyle to tell you—a mere resident, if you'll pardon me—of this *inability* of hers?"

My ice was thinning out. Still, I knew I needed to keep the personal separate from the professional, keep our superiors focused on the real issue. "Like I said, she was in a weakened state. She's been stressed a lot lately. Mr. Coles died, then this inquiry got going. Dr. Lyle hid it all, but she's been really affected."

He stared at me. "And you know this."

"Yes, sir."

"You've been calling her 'Mimi.' Are you on familiar terms?"

"Well, sir. We spent a lot of time together. It was just me. I was the only resident on the service."

"You saw her every day."

"Well, nearly so. It's a busy service. We always had several patients."

"What is your relationship?"

I hesitated. "Sir. With all due respect, that is probably not relevant to the question."

"Your relationship—how you might have come to know certain things—is not irrelevant."

"Well, sir, it's—"

"Because your credibility is not going to be impeccable, no matter what."

"Her word versus mine."

"Yes, and she's a professor."

I rubbed my eyes. I thought. "She told me. She told me exactly what I've told you. She was upset about the Coles case. That's all there is to say."

He stared at me, hard. He took a huge breath.

"And when I go to Dr. Lyle—Mimi—and ask her about this—I will, of course, have to get her version—if I ask her about getting lost in the head, what do you imagine she'll say?"

I thought. "Within the logical bounds of possibilities, sir, she could, as an honest physician, ask for appropriate help. For the good of her patients. But more likely, I suppose, she'll just flat-out deny it, then ask who said so."

"And surely you're not hoping that could be kept secret."

"I know that would be asking too much."

"And it would be unfair to her. One gets to know the source of one's accusations. Also it would be fully impossible."

"Yes, sir."

"So when she finds out it's you . . . ?"

"I don't know. I'm sure it will be unpleasant."

He waited a second, then said, "Are you going to be able to stand up to the process? Have you any idea what's going to happen?"

"I'll do what I have to."

He turned his chair to look out his window. There was a long silence. Without turning back to me he said, "Dr. Ishmail, you know, do you not, that Dr. Lyle is as an Associate Professor of the University of Arizona?"

"Yes, sir."

"That she is on track for promotion to full Professor within a year?"

"No sir, I didn't know that, but if—"

"That she is well respected by her colleagues around the country? The world's best academic neurosurgeons?"

"Yes, sir, or, I mean, if you say so. But with all due respect, sir—"

"She is. And, you also know that our little ad hoc group has answered Dr. Miekle's *damnable* letter. Her outcome in the Coles case, however regrettable, was to have been expected given the patient's disease state. The man had suffered a massive stroke going in and no surgeon in the world was going to make that better."

I was silent. He turned back to me. He said, "Keep in mind, Dr. Ishmail, it will not help Mr. Coles, nor Ms. McKenzie—nor you—to be going around spreading stories about a faculty member."

I nodded slightly.

"I don't know where this . . . *maelstrom* got started—this goddamn anesthesiologist's letter and all this. A tempest in a goddamn teapot." He said "goddamn" as I imagined an angry Creator might. "It gets to be impossible to control. People want to gossip like old ninnies."

I said nothing.

"It will not help anyone for you to contribute to this . . . this defamation. This character assassination." Apparently Mimi's reputation was to be our concern. "So . . ." He closed his eyes and took a deep breath. "I thank you for your concern. For your coming here."

Dismissal.

"Yes, sir. Er, you're welcome."

He stood up. "I'll give this some thought. Believe me, I will."

I nodded.

"I know where I can find you if I need to."

We shook hands. I drove home in the dusk knowing I had started a wildfire behind me, with little reason to hope that what I had done would help Miriam Lyle's patients, and knowing just as surely that I had done only the bare minimum.

10

Hundreds of weekends ago Adrienne sent me to one of her favorite stops on the Western Acute Tour of the High Plains: Hoacham, Nebraska. Hoacham is the "Scenic Hub of Agriculture for the Republican Valley," population 5,952, considerably more when there's a cattle auction.

On my first stint in that Quiet Little ER Where Nothing Ever Happens, I came upon a telling example of innate medical talent, or maybe lack thereof.

The nurse rousted me out just after midnight. An itinerant Salvadoran farm worker was found in a roadside ditch with four small stab wounds at the base of his neck. If you picture a slender knife entering flesh, then leaving, you realize the visible slit in the skin is only a point on a line. The tip of the blade might have angled just about anywhere, and it could have reached many inches deep. And the base of the neck, anatomically, is tiger country.

The one farthest to the right apparently went down into his chest. When I parted the skin edges, I had the distinct impression I saw lung moving. Whether that was correct or just overwrought fantasy, his right lung was down, so I put in a chest tube to suck it back to attention while the nurses squeezed in enough fluids to get his blood pressure up into human ranges. This allowed him to begin to wake up, which allowed us to see that he was drunk beyond recognition. It also provided enough driving force to reopen from the inside one of the stab wounds in the left neck that had partly clotted shut; it started pumping out bright red blood.

Every time I tried to part the edges to find the pumper, the hole filled before I could see a thing. It seemed to be coming from well below the skin and sub-Q; it was definitely coming fast. I needed help. I pushed a finger into the hole and asked the nurses, "Who's on call for surgery?" They looked at each other.

I clarified the question: "Whom do you call when you need a surgeon?"

"Whoever you want."

It occurred to me to mention my mother—or my father—but I restrained myself. "Who's on call?"

"Well, we don't really have a call schedule or anything like that." I'm sure I just blinked back at them stupidly. "You just call who you want," one said.

I blinked. "Okay. What are my choices?"

"Well, there are two surgeons in town. Dr. Yates has done a surgery residency and Dr. Latta has not, but—" she looked over her shoulder as if the wrong person might hear "—Dr. Latta is the better surgeon."

It took a few seconds to digest that. If the ER nurses were willing to impugn the one despite his far superior credentials, that was an exceptional bit of intelligence. "One has done five or six years of residency, but the other one is better?" She nodded emphatically. "No contest," I said. "Get the better surgeon, please." I smiled, picturing Dad traipsing out of our house in the middle of the night.

I stood there pressing on the poor guy's neck, trying to figure if I was pressing too hard and cutting off flow to one side of his brain or not hard enough and letting his entire blood volume squirt down into his left chest cavity where I wouldn't know about it until it was way too late.

Fortunately, Dr. Latta did not live far away and was apparently sober. An old-style GP just like Dad who had evidently been doing surgery since before there were residencies, he had glowing silver hair and the smiling unflappability of a doc who has survived probably four decades of bleeding drunks.

He eschewed gloves and essentially dove into the wound with two long sterile Q-tips to see what he could see. Which was nothing. Every time he parted the skin edges the hole immediately welled up with more lipstick-red blood. After three such tries he looked up at me and said, "Vertebral artery."

The vertebral artery is one of four that feeds the brain.

"That's not good," I said.

"But, don't you think so?"

"Hmm-mmm?" I replied. I was wondering why the devil he was asking me.

"Don't you think that's probably what it is?" he went on. "Comes up off the subclavian right under there."

"Yeah, I guess so. So what do we do?" I was praying we would not be opening the man's chest in my ER.

"Punt. It's fourth and thirty-four." Fortunately I had grown up with football as metaphor for life. *"Fly him to Lincoln. They'll fix him."*

And that was that. I kept a finger in the dike for another half hour waiting for the helicopter. We gave him two units of blood, switched out my finger for one of the flight nurse's, and said adios.

When our nurse called for follow-up, the trauma surgeon in Lincoln, a Dr. Karlgaard, confirmed as correct Dr. Latta's diagnosis-by-presumption. He had opened the area, found the severed ends of the vertebral artery, and, to keep any tension off the repair, sewn in a short segment of the guy's leg vein. He said, *"Count it. It's a win."*

THE BOOK OF MIMI, CHAPTER EIGHT

The Book of Mimi, in an ideal world, would have been finished.

Immediately after returning from Tucson and Dr. Bullock's light socket, I resumed being a faux–vascular surgeon, again doing well the job of the supplicant. By Day Three of that rotation, however, the arrogance and bombast of my new boss had me missing Mimi at every level, even the professional. After his third casual reminder that he had, you know, trained at Harvard, I almost said, "Isn't that in Ohio?"

The hours wore on. I heard nothing from Drs. Bullock, Kellogg, or Lyle about my report to Dr. Bullock on Mimi's "3-D Problem."

On Day Four, though, the end began. In afternoon clinic, still talking over my shoulder to a kindly local "dirt farmer" unfortunate enough to have a tobacco-induced stricture of the artery that fed his left leg, I opened the door from the exam room and was face-to-face with Doug Goodbout.

"Hello, Dr. Goodbout," I said, closing the door.

"Good afternoon, Dr. Ishmail. I act today in my role as Vice-Chairman of Surgery." His breathiness was in full force. "Our Chief, Dr. Hebert, is not yet returned from the nation's capital, where he has gone to testify to a congressional subcommittee on the role of the County Hospital System in Arizona. As you know, we are the only state not participating in the federal Medicaid program."

"Yes, sir."

"My task here is rather unpleasant, I fear. Could we find an empty exam room?"

"Of course," I said. A patient was just leaving the room two doors down, so we went in there. He closed the door.

He clasped his hands in front of himself and sighed. "I must ask you for a specimen of your own urine," he said.

"What?" I asked. "Is this some kind of sick joke?" though I knew Doug Goodbout would never participate in any kind of joke, sick, healthy, or indeterminate.

"I'm afraid not. Dr. Ishmail, there has been an assertion from a highly credible source that you have been—and possibly are—using illicit drugs."

I was spinning. "Maybe I should see a lawyer first. I mean, this is a pretty serious accusation. I have nothing to hide, but—"

"I hate to be the one to remind you of this," he interrupted, "but your employment contract with the universitly does specifically allow for spot checks when the supervising authority has any legitimate reason to suspect such activities. Actually, the same is true of all public employees, including myself."

"And who's the supervising authority here?" I was pretty sure he was right. I was trying like hell to remember how fast cocaine and its metabolites were cleared.

"There are potentially several here, actually. The Department Chairman, the Residency Director, the Committee on Graduate Medical Education—any could make the request. In this case, the matter was brought before the GME Committee Chairman. She called the Residency Director and me—acting for the Chair of Surgery. We all agreed a spot check needed to be done expeditiously. The matter will of course come before the full GME Committee."

"Who—or what—is the credible source?" I asked, though I knew very well. It had been over two weeks since we had done the coke in the canyon, and I should have been clean. Still, the stakes of the game had gone beyond my means.

"The committee is not obligated to identify sources," he said.

"Do I have a choice?"

"Of course you do. I cannot make you micturate into a specimen container, can I?"

"But . . . surely there's a catch there," I said.

"A refusal is a direct and willful violation of your terms of employment and, given the nature of the issue and the extent of the accusations, I believe your employment would be terminated very soon indeed."

"I'd be presumed guilty."

"Not precisely, but the net result would likely be identical."

"I'm clean, Dr. Goodbout."

"I surely hope so."

"But I object to this process."

"Unfortunately, there is no better. Your vindication, of course, would be quickest with full cooperation."

I held out my hand. He got a urine cup from the exam room cupboard and stiffly handed it to me. I reached for the door latch.

"No, no, Dr. Ishmail. Here."

"Here?"

"Unless you would prefer that we walk together into the lavatory at the end of the hall, which I imagine would be significantly embarrassing for you, in front of the clinic nurses, and all, and may well begin a flood tide of rumors."

"Better not to do that," I said.

Dick in hand, self-consciously working not to overfill the cup or spill, I had a flashback to the occasion of a similar posture in the same building, Mimi kneeling in front of me, sucking me into total submission. At that moment in the surgery clinic, picturing the scorched earth that would come from whatever version we chose of the final battles, even that memory was rendered painful.

Once I had peed into the cup under Doug Goodbout's gaze, the rest of the clinic seemed entirely banal. As soon as I signed off the last patient I bolted home and grubbed through my boxes of files and papers that had been forgotten in the corner of my bedroom. Miraculously I was able to dig up my employment contract and the papers I'd been given on Day One covering Rules and Policies. Finding it was a painful victory.

At least it was entertaining: Under the heading "Unprofessional Conduct shall include," it said, ". . . (d) Habitual intemperance or excessive use of cocaine, morphine, codeine, opium, heroin, alpha- or beta-eucaine, marijuana, novocaine or any of the salts, derivatives, or compounds of the foregoing substances, or of alcohol or alcoholic beverages, or of any other habit-forming drug or substance. " I had to look up eucaine. I could imagine no recreational use for novocaine. I wondered what use of cocaine they would consider to be not excessive, but thought it best not to ask.

I left a message at the office of a Dr. Anita Montoya, a gastroenterologist who chaired the GME Committee, asking her for a meeting as soon as she could spare me ten minutes, and would it be possible to get copies of whatever she had about me in writing?

I thought about trying to get a lawyer but I had no money and probably no case. From my reading of the contract, Section VI, "Employment at Will," pretty much gave them the right to fire me any minute of any day for any reason they chose or for no reason at all: ". . . may dismiss at any time without notice and without specific cause . . ." I found that painfully convincing.

Dr. Montoya's secretary paged me at precisely 9:00 the next morning. Dr. Montoya was hoping I could get away from whatever I was doing at noon so we could chat. When I asked my Attending on the Vascular Services if I might be excused for a time for "an administrative matter" it was clear from his facial expression and tone of voice he was at least as aware of the details as I.

Dr. Montoya could not have been nicer, but the message was still brutal. We first danced around who my accuser was; I wanted to look surprised that Mimi Lyle would have anything bad to say about me.

Of course I was hoping for confirmation that my urine test had been negative, but here the acting was even more important—I had to pretend I knew it would be. She did not mention it.

Next we reviewed the way my ass was hanging by a thread: "From my reading of my rights," I said, "you could fire me this instant for, say, wearing brown shoes."

"Technically, yes," she said, "I guess you could put it that way. It's part of everybody's employment contract here."

"You have the same clause?"

"I think everyone employed by any government body in Arizona has it. That does not mean, though, that you do not get heard. We are ethical."

"So, ethically, I get due process," I said.

"Believe it or not, we want to treat you fairly. Primarily, though, you and I are meeting to discuss process. How the allegations will be handled."

"Okay."

"And first on that list"—she checked some notes—"I am to go over the allegations." She handed me a copy of a letter. "Dr. Miriam Lyle, your Attending recently on Neurosurgery, has made this formal complaint."

It contained nothing surprising:

Dear Dr. Montoya and Members of the Committee:

I wish to bring to the attention of the Committee on Graduate Medical Education a most disturbing and inappropriate set of actions by Dr. Malcom Ishmail, a PGY-2 resident in general surgery.

For a period of six weeks, Dr. Ishmail was the resident on my service. This, of course, entailed working closely. I was polite and pleasant. I would be guessing were I to attempt to say how Dr. Ishmail could have mistaken this for even simple flirtatiousness, but apparently he did.

On or about the third week, Dr. Ishmail began to ask me for dates. Because of our faculty-resident relationship, this was, of course, extremely inappropriate and I politely but firmly declined all invitations and told him directly that his requests were inappropriate and unwelcome.

By the fifth week, however, Dr. Ishmail's "tactics" had changed. When otherwise alone in my office or in clinic, he several times put his hand around my waist or on my hip and made verbal suggestions

*of ever-increasing explicitness. This happened several times despite
my telling him on each occasion that his behavior was inappropriate
and unappreciated.*

*The last straw came during the final week in clinic when we
were momentarily alone. He came up behind me, put his hands on
my shoulders, and said very quietly, "I've got two grams of pharmaceutical freebase and a very lonely hot tub at my condo. Want to
fuck?"*

*I should have slapped him, and now wish I had. I have since
learned that "freebase" refers to crack cocaine.*

*Between that incident and this writing I have been able to avoid
being with Dr. Ishmail in any more private situations. It is my sin-
cere hope that Dr. Ishmail's behaviors be dealt with promptly and
forcefully; I do not believe immediate termination from the residency
would be too harsh a measure.*

Respectfully yours,

Miriam Lyle, MD

When I looked up Dr. Montoya was watching me intently. I tried
to look puzzled, knowing I'm not enough of an actor to have suc-
ceeded at looking shocked.

"All right," I said with a deep sigh. "Process. Do I answer this
now? To you?"

"No. Well, I mean, you can, but you'll probably want to give it a
little thought." She explained my options under the University Discipline Policies. I told her I wanted the shortest course to exoneration.
She smiled and nodded.

"The full GME Committee is set to meet next week. We could
give you a hearing then."

That night at home I got a surprise call from Dr. Dick Hebert, Chief
of the Trauma Service and Chair of Surgery—my boss. He and I had
hit it off well when I'd come to Maricopa as a fourth-year medical stu-

dent to interview for the residency. He was the main reason I had chosen Maricopa over the better-known hospitals in California.

Dr. Hebert was, in his version of events, a "Cajun castoff," someone his swamp brethren would not take back into the family once he got a couple of degrees "out West" in Texas. He told us his only choice was, like a vagabond of the last century, to keep heading west. He eventually found Phoenix, where Texas credentials were at least preferable to those from either coast.

He would speak among his personal favorites with a thick twang, then turn it off in favor of thoroughly proper academician's diction and pronunciation when he had to face—again in his terms—the "unwashed." We residents rapidly learned that the twang meant you were on his team and in favor. If it stopped, you were about to get a new bodily orifice or the equivalent of a pink slip.

He was still in Washington and—most important—still twanging:

"Ishmail, boah, what the hell kinda trouble you causin'?"

"I—"

"Neva mind. I know what kinda trouble you causin'. I heard all about it. I'm not sure you know the size o' the gator you done grabbed onto. That woman, shit, son, she had a gun I'm thinking she might try to keel you."

"Yes, sir. I obviously . . . felt pretty strongly that she was . . . has a problem. . . . And ethically—"

"Son, I would hate to lose you. Especially over her. She ain't worth it to you or me or anybody else. Now I dictated a letter to the damn committee. Told them you were a goddamn shining star of surgery, never had a problem, excellent reports from all your rotations, promising future, all that."

"Thank you, Dr. Hebert."

"Well, it's the by-God truth. But it ain't gonna be worth a fuck if they think anything she is sayin' about you is true."

I swallowed. I said, "Well, she seems to be pretty good at lying."

"Mostly, way I hear it, she been lyin' about why her patients ain't doin' well."

"That's what I've been trying to get—"

"You got any ammunition?"

"Ammunition?"

"She's tryin' to fuck you, son. You gonna sit in front of the GME Committee pissants and say, 'No, no, no, I never done it?' 'Cuz if that's all you bring to the party they'll shit-can you right on the spot. You better be firin' both barrels. You better be explaining *why* she's tryin' to fuck you."

"Yes, sir."

"And Malcolm . . ."

"Yes, sir?"

"I will not be able to snatch your ass back from the fire if the GME Committee says AMF."

"AMF?"

"*Adios*, Mutha Fucka."

"Yes, sir—er, no, sir."

Fortunately, or unfortunately, I spent the next day, a Saturday, helping Brett Elliott, a part-time faculty member, do a portacaval shunt, a particularly long and dreary operation done to reroute blood away from a cirrhotic liver, usually on alcoholics. Such shriveled livers allow little blood flow through them and the back-pressure in the gut becomes its own problem, leading eventually to massive bleeding into the GI tract. Given the dismal prospects of people with liver failure regardless of our interventions, surgeons have vehement and entertaining arguments over the value of such operations.

I was well removed from that specific fray; my entire role was to pull—hard—on the pickled liver so the real surgeon could see under it. Most of what I saw for six hours was the large brown mole on the back of Dr. Elliott's neck. It was mindless, stupefying. My own problems resumed their rightful place in my vision.

Dr. Hebert said I would need both barrels. I didn't have a single barrel.

It was not difficult to figure out the new Game. A direct denial from Mimi could only go so far; she needed to discredit the report. Her twisted version of our relationship—me a suitor, offering drugs, spurned and hurt, now wreaking his revenge—recolored my accounting of her. And just mentioning drugs guaranteed an overblown response. While she probably figured we were too far out from our trysts for my urine to light up, it cost her nothing to roll my dice.

All of which nicely turned the tables. Just like her, I would be left, after denying every red-blooded act back to and including masturbation in puberty, having to satisfy my judges that her version of me was all smoke screen and deflection.

What to do? I couldn't have backed off if I had wanted to. My only hope lay in substantiating my claims about her.

Brett Elliott's mole bobbed and waved in front of me.

Stupor can be productive. Notions at the lost edges of consciousness can leap forth: What do you need to make a case? Witnesses.

Other than OR staff, who, as nonphysicians, would carry no weight, there *were* two possibilities: Ed Adams and Dr. Dreamboat.

At home that night, despite the late hour, I typed out my formal denial, though I knew it to be lame from the start. In any dance, after all, each partner must keep step:

Dear Dr. Montoya and Members of the Committee:

It is with shock and dismay that I read the heinous accusations you have before you. The members of the Committee may or may not be aware of the recent investigation of Dr. Lyle's clinical abilities. It seems she has fabricated these charges as retribution for my participation in that process.

All I can offer at this point is my most fervent denial of any such unwanted sexual advances, of any "groping," of any such lewd suggestiveness, and of anything to do with any illicit drugs!

I beseech the Committee to conduct its investigation thoroughly but also promptly. I want my name cleared as expeditiously as possible, but also want the falsehood of these accusations brought to light and these lies dealt with appropriately.

Respectfully,

Malcolm D. Ishmail, MD

The next day, Sunday, I found a Faculty Directory on the ward during rounds. I phoned Dr. Adams's home.

His wife answered, fairly shouting: "No, dear, I'm afraid he is still in Europe. He will be for the next two weeks. Off on a lecturing tour. Some 'visiting professor' thing they like to do, don't you know. He wanted me to go along, too, but I've just gotten so I don't enjoy traveling anymore. Not the way I used to. Not the way you would need to to get around over there, you know. Is there something I can help you with?"

"Gee, that's too bad. I mean that you couldn't go along."

"Yes, well, it really is okay. I have plenty to keep me busy here. Our garden, don't you know."

Maybe she could help. "Actually, since Dr. Adams is not available, you know it's possible one of his associates could help me. I heard a reference to someone . . ."

"What?"

"I said I heard something about a certain one of your husband's associates. Unfortunately, I don't know his name."

"Well, if you'd like to talk it over, I may be able to help, I don't know. I don't do well on the phone, though. It's too hard to hear. Why don't you drive over here and we'll figure it out together," she said.

Their house was an older ranch style in one of the unpretentious parts of town. I knocked. A statuesque woman answered. Her brilliant silver hair was pulled straight back and lacquered, forming a helmet. Mrs. Adams fairly lit up when I gave her an opportunity to talk about her husband.

"Did he get an award from the Boy Scouts?"

"Well, dear, he has been given several. You know he has stayed very active with the Scouts, even after our boys moved on to college and all."

"Did he get one in New Mexico?"

She pondered. "Well, yes, at Cimmarron Ranch. He got his Gold Oak Leaf. Quite a major honor, you know. Thirty years of service. Cimmarron, don't you know, is that wonderful ranch they have in the mountains. Thousands of acres."

"Yes. I was there myself, not too many years ago. I was a Scout, too. Do you know when he received it?"

"Well, I could find out. Let me see." She went into the den and I heard a file cabinet slide open. She came back with a tattered manila folder. "Here it is. The little certificate that came with the pin." She handed it to me. I memorized the date.

We chatted about the wonders of Scouting over coffee and a muffin, I thanked her profusely, then made an escape.

I screeched my Datsun to Maricopa and ran down to Medical Records—the chart keepers. I knew too well the night and weekend crew; it was only on their shifts I seemed to get my butt down there to sign off orders and dictate my incomplete notes, usually under threat of suspension for tardiness.

Barbara, an especially friendly taskmaster, was at the desk.

"Oh, Barbara," I said, cocking an eyebrow.

She looked at me sideways.

"How good are you with mysteries?"

She eyed me back. "Will this be . . . something unusual?"

"Strictly unofficial. Neither of us is even *here*."

"My favorite kind of job."

"You're a star, you know that?" I jotted down the date. "Find me a cerebral aneurysm taken to surgery within two days of this date."

She leaned back in her chair and scowled at me. "Hoo boy. Any other clues?"

"Miriam Lyle, MD, would have been primary surgeon. And it was done on a Friday."

"You know charts this old are off site, on microfilm, or usually just plain lost. Even if I knew who I was looking for."

"Don't you have a surgical database?"

"Not on computer. Not that far back." A pause. "But!" I could see the light go on. "We do have a database. The old-fashioned kind. On paper."

Barbara paged me not an hour later to say one of her minions had located the OR logbook for that period. A courier would have it there from the off-site records storage at 8:00 A.M. the next morning.

I flogged my intern through morning prerounds, managed to keep our Attending on track during his rounds, then made an excuse to be a few minutes late for clinic. In Barbara's basement dungeon the chart maven of the day shift pointed me to a large clothbound ledger book, smudged with black marker declaiming "Surgery" in big handwritten block letters on the cover.

I quickly thumbed through to the memorized date, then backtracked to the Friday, read down about thirty lines in the "Case" column and found one listing "ACA aneurysm clipping." In the column for "Surgeon" it showed simply "Lyle/White."

The yellow pages, under "Physician: Surgeon, Neurological" listed only one Dr. White: Steven White, MD. I phoned the number listed—his answering service—and asked that he call me on my pager. I gave my name only as "Dr. Ishmail." Employing the title usually ensures a return call. Fifteen minutes later, as I was rechecking some X-rays on one of our patients, my pager chirped. A slow and resonant male voice with frequent overtones of gravel said, "Returning your call, Doctor," and gave me a phone number.

I dialed it from a dictation booth. Dr. White listened graciously as I quickly gave the high points of the trail of conversations that had led me to him. I then said, "Really, I'm calling about Mimi Lyle. Are you the Dr. White who helped her clip an aneurysm one Friday night, years ago, when Ed Adams was out of town?"

A pause, then, "Yes, that was me."

"Then I expect you remember her."

"Mm-mm. Yes, I do. Fabulous woman. Fabulous looking, especially for a brain surgeon. Not one to forget."

"No, not easily forgotten," I said. "But there's been, um, kind of a flap around here. There's some question about her surgical skills." A silence. "I was wondering if I might be able to come talk to you."

More silence, then he said, "Can you drive out here?"

"Yes, absolutely. Where's 'here'?"

"Paradise Valley. How soon can they get along there without you?"

"Late afternoon. It's just a clinic day."

"You come on out here. We'll talk."

Dr. White's house had an air of roomy dignity and affluence. The owner was easily six foot two, even with a marked stoop. I had expected his silver hair and patrician dress but his clothes hung loose on his wiry frame and his breathing seemed labored. Somehow I'd pictured bulk and ease.

He offered me a drink. "Scotch? Milk of the Motherland!" he rasped.

I hesitated. "No, sir. I'm on call."

"Well, I'm not, by God." He fairly boomed the last two words. "I'm going to, if you don't mind."

"No, of course not."

As he poured he said, "How did you get involved with Mimi Lyle?"

"I was a resident on her service."

"Yes, you told me that. But a resident's job doesn't usually include making inquiries about his professor's past." His voice filled the home without being intimidating.

"No. I suppose not." I recounted the halfhearted investigation of Mimi's operating skills. He nodded as if he were hearing an old joke.

I said she had confided in me when things were difficult. "She woke up," I said, "from a nightmare—she told me about it—apparently she has this recurring dream—where she feels like she's in a maze of ORs, lost. And everybody is laughing at her while they're doing surgery. That was when she mentioned you. Then she told me. She said she gets lost inside the head."

Again, he nodded. Knowingly. "Yes, I think she does," he said, watching my face.

"Then, not even two weeks ago, we hit the same quicksand." I told him about Susan McKenzie's adenoma removal. I said, "I felt compelled to pass that on." He still watched me. "To the powers-that-be in neurosurgery—Dr. Bullock and Dr. Kellogg. When I told Dr. Bullock about her he said, 'She will clear.'"

"That's what all brain surgeons always say. It's our motto."

"So she's grossly okay; it was still horrifying. I realized I just couldn't do it again. To somebody else. And still be a doctor."

He nodded. "What did they say? When you shared this? What did Marshall Bullock have to say about it?"

"He talked about it in terms of an apraxia. He wanted some sort of a diagnosis. But then he said it would be impossible."

"Oh shit, Malcolm. Do you think it's impossible?"

"No. I mean, from what we learned about brain function: Some people can't read. Some people can't understand time. Or get certain kinds of verbs, talk in certain settings . . ."

"Of course. It's very possible. The brain is capable of remarkable *inabilities* as well as abilities. It's the opposite of talent."

I nodded. His ability to articulate my thoughts reminded me of Dad.

He said, "So what happened? With Marshall?"

"Well, nothing."

"Precisely."

"Pardon me?" I said.

"Exactly the only thing they can do. Nothing. They have no response. They don't have the slightest idea what to do with intelligence such as that."

I could only nod, slowly, hoping for more.

"Oh, they probably mean well. But the system has no structure for it. It cannot deal with the underlying problem." He whispered loudly, "She's in the wrong specialty."

"How's that?"

"She's smart. She means well, but she should be in pediatrics. Or radiology. Or even vascular surgery. Something two-dimensional or maybe even just plain linear."

"Something strictly left-brain," I said.

He half laughed. "Yes, yes."

"Well, Dr. White, one thing they did with my 'intelligence'—I mean they had to—they went and asked her about it. She told them, in a letter, that I had made a series of clumsy come-ons to her in clinic and offered her drugs. And groped her. I got rousted in clinic a few days ago for a urine sample and I have a meeting with the Committee on Graduate Medical Education and all their ass-kickers in a week." I blinked a few times. "I've seen the letter. Which is why I came to you."

He looked into his drink. I went on: "She said once you had a case—maybe more than one—that you helped her with." There was a silence. "Some years ago, when Dr. Adams was in New Mexico."

He twitched his mouth in a circle. "You screwing her?"

I thought to try to look shocked, but knew right away, under Dr. White's grin, what foolishness that would be. I mustered a rueful half-smile. I said, "Was. Not anymore."

"Ha. It fits the story," he said, taking a pull on his drink. "And the clues. Good man. Well done."

"I don't know. It seemed harmless enough when it started but now it's looking like one of the dumber things I've ever gotten into."

He snorted, "Take it from an old man, Malcolm. Some of my biggest mistakes are among my fondest memories."

I laughed slightly. "Yes, sir."

"Don't 'Yes, sir' me. I'm too old. Never liked formalities."

"Okay.

"So your 'come-ons' must not have been too clumsy."

"My part, Dr. White, was rather passive. Acquiescence."

"Ha! Perfect. Now you get the blame."

"Yes, sir. So it seems. Which, again, is why I called you."

"All through the whole thing—this mock investigation—was she completely confident she would be cleared?"

"Yes."

"Totally exonerated? Never in doubt?"

"Yes."

"Blamed some . . ." he waved his hand, "some, conspiracy against her?"

"Yes."

"Always the same," he said. I waited. "A gaping hole in a surgeon's abilities—hell, anybody's abilities—is like the blind spot in your vision—" again he bellowed a whisper, "—you have no clue it exists."

"Yes, sir."

He had a spell of racking cough, then went to his bar to pour another drink.

"Sir—Dr. White—when Mimi told me that night . . ." I hesitated. "You know, I didn't really want to cop to my affair with Mimi when I met with Dr. Bullock. I think he suspected something was up. He all but asked me directly. I wanted to keep it to myself, though. It was as if I still wanted to protect that part."

He looked directly at me. "It's not that romantic."

"What do you mean?"

"It's not about protecting your private affair. It's the issue. Your affair with Mimi is not the issue. Patients are the issue and you know that."

I smiled and sighed. "Yes, sir."

"Because you're a doctor."

"Yes, sir."

"And your affair with Mimi was not—I am going to guess—the great love of your life."

"No, sir."

"You said, 'She woke up from a nightmare.' That was the clue."

I nodded.

"So you went to talk with Marshall Bullock. Marshall never once let any aura of warmth build around himself."

"No, I suppose not." A pause. "Anyway, Mimi woke up one night, all in a panic. That's when she told me about getting lost in the brain. We'd been partying pretty hard that night. That's one of the things that makes it hard to come out with this. I have to kind of dance around exactly how this came out between us."

He nodded his understanding.

"But she also told me about you. Well, indirectly, anyway. She never used your name. Called you 'Dr. Dreamboat.' Apparently she—"

He walked toward me, motioning me to stop. "I was going to get to this." He leaned to open a large book on the coffee table and produced from it a note card, still in its envelope, still bearing a faint remainder of Mimi's musky perfume. "This was my other clue about your affair with our Dr. Lyle. There's tragic loneliness there. I've known about it for years."

He handed me Mimi's thank-you note, then sprawled back on his couch. He added, "She also has insight into her own problems. At least some of the time."

The note was dated two weeks after their shared aneurysm operation, written with a fountain-pen script in Mimi's flowing hand, though somewhat scrawled and crooked on the card. It read:

Darling Steve,

Just a quick note to thank you for coming in last Friday night to help me with—what was her name?—Mrs. Schaer's aneurysm. I know you had thought to have a quiet weekend on Ed's call, but your good graces allowed me—us—to save an otherwise awfully bad situation.

I imagine I did wait too long to ask for help. Someone from the OR suggested later that I had been several hours trying to find the aneurysm but I'm certain it was not so terribly long. They can be so mean. Next time I will call you sooner.

I do get lost—sometimes have trouble constructing things in my mind in three dimensions. I study the scans and the angios, then go look into the brain, and I cannot for the life of me picture where the thing lies or a way to it. I was just born that way. It's not really anybody's fault. It's kind of a secret shame.

Fortunately, with the help of dear friends such as Ed Adams and you, we can get these difficult situations handled and help save these patients.

It's a shame your practice doesn't bring you to Maricopa more often. I would like to see more of you. Call me sometime soon. I could make you dinner.

Fondly,

Mimi

I slowly raised my eyes to Dr. White's, fighting the urge to smile. I said, "She mentioned this."

He nodded. "I was not married then. Not even attached. It occurred to me more than once to follow up on that, well, 'invitation,' but I never did. Probably all for the better, but right now I do kind of regret some of my scruples."

I said, "A remarkable thank-you note."

"Extremely so. Imagine a neurosurgeon who cannot navigate inside the brain. Ah, the ramifications! Brain surgery is about precision." He sat forward again. "Precision, Malcolm. Those gray and white lobes in your way when you're looking for something are all damned important to your patient. This is not *belly* surgery where you can bag up all the chitlins and swing them off to the side so you can get a clamp around the aorta. Or put your entire hand around some tumor before you lop it out."

I nodded.

"To be a good neurosurgeon—hell, even an adequate neurosurgeon—you don't have to be lightning fast. But you do have to be *precise*. Expedient. This is not goddamned fishing. You have to know exactly where you're going, how you're going to get there, what you're going to do, and how you're going to get back out. And if you don't know those things before you start, you sure as hell aren't going to get some miraculous *vision* halfway there."

I nodded. I looked again at the letter. "Extraordinary. It's almost like a Freudian slip."

"Hell, Malcolm, it looks and reads to me like she was legs-in-the-air drunk when she wrote it. It's more than Freudian. It's confessional. She let out her deepest secret. She *unburdened* herself."

I nodded. He sipped his drink. "Would it be all right for me to get a copy of the letter?" I asked.

"Hell, take it. I want it gone." Then, "I know what you're thinking, too. 'How come the old fuck squirreled this away for so long?' Unfortunately it's a simple question with a very complex answer.

"The short version is, I had nothing to gain and everything to lose. If the world sees me as attacking the reputation of a peer, my reputation suffers, not hers. On top of that, it would be said, by her lawyer, that I did it for monetary gain. Technically we were competitors, according to the law. She could get some prick trial attorney and try to take everything I've ever earned. Malpractice insurance doesn't cover restraint of trade, Malcolm. And at the time, my daughters were at Cornell and Bowdoin. And they're vastly more important to me than Mimi Lyle. No other neurosurgeon could be seen as completely impartial, but no one but a neurosurgeon could know the difference, or could tell her to stop or change her practice. Quite a bind."

"A catch-twenty-two."

"Yes. Worse. With deadly implications."

"But now you don't mind if I . . ."

"Malcolm, I'm through with practice. I'm going to be dead in six months. Mesothelioma. *Abdominal* mesothelioma. Even heard of it?"

"No, sir."

"Neither had I. They're giving me all their cis-platinum goddamn poisons and buck-up platitudes, but I'm dying."

"I'm so sorry, sir."

"Yes, we all are." He looked at me. "You ever study the stages of dying? All that happy horseshit?"

I nodded.

He nodded back. "I'm having a hell of a lot of trouble with it, Malcolm. I hurt like hell and I puke a lot. Losing weight daily. All those years of medicine. Watching people die. I always said if someone told me I had cancer they couldn't cut out with a scalpel, I'd say 'Fuck you all' and hit the road. 'Screw your chemofuckingtherapy. It's been nice, see ya round.' But goddamn if I ain't in there on their schedules getting shot full of that crap. All to try to buy just a little more time. See, Malcolm, my younger daughter's been trying to get pregnant. And she thinks she might be—finally. So if I can hold on for eight more months, I just might get to see my first grandchild." He coughed a long racking spell. "Ha, with luck the kid'll be premature! Ha! Shit . . ."

I was silent. He had a few tears in his eyes from the coughing jag. "So what they say about your time scale for what's important changing on you is sure as hell true. It surely is, Malcolm. Things that matter to me now are very near term and *very* long-term. Cancer is like that. Besides, it will be hard for them to sue a dead man."

"Yes, sir."

"So have a drink with me. They told me to lay off but I told them to fuck off." He laughed.

"No, thank you. I'd love to but I think I need a pretty clear head."

"Yes, I suppose you do."

"Maybe a rain check?"

"Anytime, Malcolm. You're welcome back anytime."

"I'd enjoy it. I really would."

11

Timing—usually bad timing—is, logically, the lifeblood of emergency medicine. Accidents, by their nature, are all about bad timing, often on more than one level. Like Henry's asthma choosing the wrong day to act up.

Last week in the Quiet Little ER of Ogallala, Nebraska, another of my regular stops, we had a little girl with "Failure to Fly." While there probably is no good time to have your two-year-old daughter wriggle out of her car seat and open the car door, one of the worst has to be when you're taking a curve too fast, with her on the outer arc. She may think she's flying, but it won't last.

By the time Dad, who was driving, got stopped and ran back to the would-be Amelia Earhart, she had regained consciousness and was bawling appropriately.

The local medics brought her to me for a good going-over. The nurse and I peeled her off her dad long enough to determine, despite Dad's inability to do much more than stammer, that she had apparently been launched with enough velocity to have cleared the gravelly part of the roadway and made it straight to the grass. Our evidence, besides the grass stains, was her complete lack of any injury worse than a good goose egg on the side of her head. Still, one is compelled to get a CAT scan.

While my little Sally Ride was in the scanner her mom arrived in my ER. Not fully hysterical, but significantly louder than Dad had been. That's when things got interesting.

Seems they don't like each other. Stood along opposite walls and worked entirely on blame issues. Lawyers' names came up. Neither was wearing a wedding ring.

The little girl checked out completely and I sent her on her way. Mom had a pretty good grip on her. I learned by observation a Useful Maxim of Marriage: The worst time to launch your two-year-old daughter out the backseat of a moving vehicle is when you're in the middle of a custody fight. There's bad timing.

THE BOOK OF MIMI, CHAPTER NINE

Now, mercifully, I can end *The Book of Mimi*.

After meeting Steven White, I went straight back to Maricopa for a unique kind of rounds: In the ER office I photocopied Mimi's thank-you note. In the library I scrawled out three pages of recitations and explanations addressed to Marshall Bullock. At the ICU nurse's station I made photocopies of the whole package—a set for Joe Kellogg and one for me. In the OR Business Office I sealed theirs into interdepartmental mail envelopes and dropped them in the "Campus Mail."

I checked with my intern. All was quiet. I went home.

I spent the evening staring out the window of my town house. I pictured the faces of nameless professors at my upcoming meeting with the GME Committee. A Give-'em-hell call from Dr. Hebert would have been nice, but unlikely. Recalling his advice to come out firing, I sat down to plan strategy.

In outline form I wrote lists of everything "Mimi" I could remember: her phone numbers, the personal artifacts one would find in her condo living room, her kitchen, her bathroom, her bedroom, certain nonobvious aspects of her anatomy. From my Surgeon's Case Log and personal datebook I found a few clues to prod my shoddy memory. I was able to construct a passable list of our ventures to restaurants, each of which I knew to have been paid for with a Platinum Visa in the name "M M Lyle, MD, PC." I found the receipt for my silver belt buckle still tucked under the cotton in the gift box. I added it to my file.

I went out and made ten more copies of Dr. White's note. I made up a list of the committee's probable questions, tried to think of all the angles they might take, then think through the implications of every possible answer and select tactics that would build my case. I tried to prepare my arguments, to anticipate Mimi's unspoken counterarguments, to plan for anything they might throw at me. Both barrels.

When the day came I thought I was prepared. I was not, of course, calm. If there exists a medical resident—in actuality still a schoolboy despite years of full biologic adulthood—who could be calm in such a setting, he—not I—should be drug-tested.

Dr. Montoya was politely professional, almost friendly, pointing me to my chair and introducing each inquisitor individually, smiling.

"You know why we're all here," she said.

One of the Unknowns, Dr. Aaron Kerlin, a graying man with half-glasses perched at nose tip, interjected, "We have charges of cocaine—"

Dr. Montoya cut him off. "Aaron, please. Dr. Ishmail, you've read Dr. Lyle's letter. We would like to hear your version of these events."

"Thank you, Dr. Montoya." I looked about the group and took a deep breath. From my folder I took my yellow pad and flipped several pages to my final outline. It said at the top, "Slow down!"

I recounted my weeks as a faux-neurosurgeon. When I got to the faculty inquiry over the Keith Coles case, I said, "Initially I sided with her—we were, well, on the same side. We talked a lot about the case. Tragic as it was, though, it seemed to us to be just another bad outcome in brain surgery. It seems to happen all the time. You all know, I presume, the investigation cleared Dr. Lyle in the case. That might have been the end of it but for something Dr. Lyle said to me after the inquiry was finished." I looked around at the faces. "She told me the reason those types of operations go so badly for her is she gets lost inside the head."

Some committee members were staring at me. "Her words: 'Lost inside the head.' At first . . . well, at first it scared me. I mean, lost in someone's brain. But I more or less shrugged it off. Everyone has self-doubts. Especially after a patient dies."

I then described Susan McKenzie's case, working my way to, "I heard Dr. Lyle say to herself 'Here we go again.' I got scared again. I remembered what she had told me. I asked around among the OR people. They told me about a similar operation she had botched a few years ago. I tried to get her to seek some help with the adenoma—asked her directly—but she wouldn't hear of it."

"Yes," one muttered.

"I tried to rationalize away my fears. I couldn't come up with much else I could do. The operation went ahead but it didn't go particularly well. We spent a lot of time spinning wheels. I realized in that OR that she was again lost." I looked around again. "I sat and watched and realized that was exactly what was going on. 'Having trouble constructing things in her mind in three dimensions'—again, her terms. It also explained the Coles case.

"I gave this a lot of thought. Believe me. But I had to do something. I felt I had to bring forth Dr. Lyle's troubles with three-dimensional thinking. It occurred to me that someone with this kind of relative deficiency probably shouldn't be cutting into people's brains, at least not too deep. I set up an appointment with Marshall Bullock, the Chair of all U of A Neurosurgery, in Tucson. I told him all of this, exactly what she'd said and what I'd seen. I felt she needed some kind of surgical help, or backup, or a restriction of privileges, or something."

"What did he say?" a stout woman asked.

"He told me he would, you know, take it under advisement. I did think it made something of an impression, though nothing seems to have changed. He seemed interested in maintaining her reputation."

Two of them nodded. I went on, "I didn't really feel I had done enough, but it was all I could do."

"And since then? Have you heard anything more?"

"The next thing I heard was Dr. Goodbout knocking on my door in clinic for a urine specimen." Two of them began leafing through the folders they each had in front of them. I saw one pull out a hospital lab printout, no doubt the report on my drug test. I kept my poker face.

Dr. Kerlin was finally allowed to speak: "There are written allegations from a respected faculty member that you proposed a date with her, saying you had some 'pharmaceutical grade cocaine' to share with her."

I nodded.

"And this comes on the heels, within three weeks, anyway, of a reported discrepancy in the drug count in the OR lockbox. Two 10-cc vials of 10 percent cocaine have been reported missing."

That was staggering. I mouthed to myself, "Oh fuck." I had not heard about that little heist, the perfect coincidence of bad timing. Without mentally calculating it out I knew each vial would have been worth thousands of dollars on the street.

"What say you, Dr. Ishmail?" he said, feigning a smile.

"Complete falsehood." I said, trying to find a tone of voice neither too vehement nor quavering.

"Is that it?" he asked.

"Dr. Kerlin, I didn't steal the OR's cocaine and I never offered drugs to Dr. Lyle. If there's some other evidence, something more than an accusation . . ." I held up my hands.

Dr. Kerlin frowned at Dr. Montoya. She sighed a bit.

"By the way," I said, "Dr. Hebert said he was going to send a letter to the committee."

"Yes, we each have a copy," Dr. Montoya said.

"Good. I appreciate Dr. Hebert's support. Anyway, it's easy for me to imagine being on Dr. Lyle's hit list. I reported my concerns to Dr. Bullock. I presume she knows about that."

Another of the ensemble spoke, a nerdy-looking man with a sparse mustache and a squinting face. "But you and Dr. Lyle have not spoken about this, had any confrontation, say, about your having . . . 'turned her in,' for lack of a better term?"

"No. It certainly became clear to me, though, when Dr. Goodbout came around for a specimen."

"Yes, yes, I suppose so," he said.

"But, if I may add something," I said, looking at Dr. Montoya. She nodded. "I realized that other neurosurgeons have seen what I've been talking about. When Dr. Lyle is struggling to find her way, she usually calls Ed Adams to assist her. He helped on the Coles case. I wanted to get his thoughts on this, but he's been out of the country.

"Dr. Lyle did share with me, though, that one time, some years ago, when Dr. Adams was also unavailable, she had called in Dr. Steven White. Dr. White is—has been—practicing primarily in Scottsdale. He came in late one Friday to help with another aneurysm and, according to Dr. Lyle, had little difficulty getting it clipped.

"I met with Dr. White, a few days ago, at his home. He shared his opinion that Mimi is in the wrong specialty. He gave me this note." I pulled the card, still in its envelope, from my folder. "He referred to it as 'confessional.' In it she describes her own inabilities." I passed my stack of copies to Dr. Montoya, then waited.

Several nodded as they read. The nerdy man said, "Have you shown this to anyone else?"

"I got it a week ago. I sent copies to Dr. Bullock and Dr. Kellogg."

The stout woman said, "You, a resident, seem to want to sit in judgment of your professor."

"No."

"You want her to be, what? *Error-free?*"

"No. That's not it. I thought the thing about mistakes in medicine was, whether they're bad judgment or lack of information or lack of experience or whatever, that you're supposed to learn from them. Not hurt somebody the same way twice."

They were staring at me.

A wiry-haired woman said, "And how did the patient do? The young woman with the adenoma?"

"Okay. She woke up a little slow, I guess, but she was grossly intact when I saw her."

"So, do you think you were wrong to have worried?"

"Not at all. I'd be just as worried about the next one."

"Did you speak with Dr. Lyle about your concerns?"

"Like I said, I asked her about getting help. When the case was booked. She made it very clear she didn't want to hear suggestions from me. I just went off service a few days after that, started my vascular rotation, and next thing I know, this."

"And you contend that her letter is . . . what? A complete fabrication? Pure lies? For some sort of retribution?"

"Apparently so. Yes. I think she is—obviously—trying to disgrace me. Make it seem that what I told Dr. Bullock was a stupid attempt at revenge for having been spurned."

Dr. Kerlin spoke: "Okay, perhaps so. But let us go through her allegations." He looked at Dr. Montoya. "I think we need to do that." She nodded. To me: "Did you do the things in her letter?"

I looked blankly at my notepad. This was expected. "I may have made mistakes, sir. Certainly. In my residency. In my life." I looked up. "Fortunately I can say with a clear conscience—and I was once an altar boy—that not one of them is in that letter." Two of them smiled.

"Okay. You never asked Dr. Lyle for a date?"

I hesitated. "No. Certainly not as she describes it."

Dr. Kelin sat forward. "What do you mean by that?"

"Just that. I did not ask Dr. Lyle for a date."

Dr. Kerlin looked at Dr. Montoya. He said to me with obvious frustration, "Did you seek dates? Seek sex? Other than asking for a date?"

My ground was shaking. I looked at my notes. They held no solace. "I'm not trying to be cute with the wording. Dr. Lyle and I had a relationship." I felt my face burn. "It never involved any of the kinds of things she says in her letter."

A pause. Dr. Kerlin: "You—you and Dr. Lyle—you had 'a relationship.' But you did not ask her for a date."

"Yes, sir. That's a fair statement."

"Will you care to elaborate for us? Help us understand . . . ?"

"Sir, with all due respect, the particulars of our relationship are not really germane."

"Are we to understand that you two are, or were, lovers? And this letter is, according to you, part of a lovers' spat?"

"No, sir. I mean, we are not lovers. Whether we were or not is irrelevant. And the letter is her retaliation for participating in the process of trying to ensure good patient care."

"But you were lovers."

I hesitated. I took an involuntary sigh. "Yes, sir. Were."

He looked about as if he were resting his case, victorious.

"For how long?" asked Dr. Wiry Hair.

"Well, of my six-week rotation there, take out the first week or so and most of the last two weeks," I said.

"But you never asked her for a date?"

"No, ma'am. I acquiesced. I said yes."

"She initiated it?"

"Yes, ma'am."

"When did this happen?"

"Middle of the second week of my rotation. We hit it off. But really, how it began, how it ended, none of that is important. What is important is that she told me why she has so much trouble. I acted on my obligation to patient care. She is apparently seeking revenge."

"And no one knew of this? You did not tell Dr. Bullock?"

"It's really irrelevant. It obscures the real issue." A pause. I said, "I think—I guess I'm sure—she feels betrayed."

Dr. Kerlin: "She initiated this affair."

"Yes, she did."

Two were shuffling their folders. One said, "How did you manage to keep this a secret for—what—a month?"

"She had it pretty well thought through. How to put down cover and hide tracks."

They were all staring. "Had she done this before?"

"You mean with a resident? I have no idea. You'll have to ask Dr. Lyle." They continued to stare. Dr. Montoya nodded.

"And just to be completely explicit: Yours was a . . . sexual relationship?" The questioner was a nearly child-sized man with a thick beard and a bow tie.

"Entirely so."

"Did you, at any time, make any objections?" The haughty expressions I'm sure were meant to convey professorial disgust, but it was not difficult to imagine a tinge of fascination behind the Victorian veneer.

I hesitated. I had trouble believing any of them really expected a young man to put very obscure academic scruples in front of a very tangible erection. Besides, the professor's ethical obligation in such a case was much the greater. "No," I said, "why would I?" Several of them smiled.

"You would have, Doctor, because it was the right thing to do," said Dr. Kerlin.

"By some standards that may be true, sir," I said. "But the ethical problem arises from the power one holds over the other. And I believed from the start she would never abuse that power. She never did. I was no victim here. That was something between consenting adults."

"You're not here to lecture us on ethics."

"No, sir. But my relationship really is not the issue."

"You're here to answer allegations of drug abuse," he went on. "And harassment."

"Yes, sir."

"You deny offering drugs to Dr. Lyle, but say she was your lover?"

"Yes, sir."

"Were there drugs involved in your alleged relationship?"

"That's not Dr. Lyle's allegation."

"No, she alleges that you repeatedly offered her cocaine."

"I did not offer her cocaine."

"But were there drugs involved in your relationship?"

I sat silently. I knew dodging to be a virtual admission, but better than an outright declaration.

"Other drugs? What . . . marijuana? Opiates? Pills?"

I sat quietly, trying to convince myself the obvious logic of the greater issues would prevail.

"Cocaine?"

Still, I sat quietly.

"You will not answer whether or not there was cocaine involved in your relationship."

Every movement I made, every blink, swallow, glance, weight shift, or roll of a finger hurt. I felt like crying. I said only, "No."

"Then, were there or were there not drugs used between you two?"

A long pause. "I think," I said as calmly as I could, "I am entitled to withhold certain answers."

The nerd said, "Well, I think we have an answer."

Another pause. "Your urine test was entirely clean," Dr. Montoya said. She was apparently the ever-compassionate doctor, giving me a bit more rope that I might not hang myself.

I only nodded, pointlessly clinging to the strategic notion of seeming to know all along that it would be. Another pause.

"How could you satisfy us," said Dr. Kerlin, "that you have never used drugs?"

"Well, Doctor"—I took a deep breath—"no disrespect intended, but I could no more prove that than you could prove you've never molested small boys."

He snorted, "That is outrageous."

"I mean, sir, in a purely logical way of looking at it, it's awfully hard to prove you've never done something."

"Have you ever used drugs?" asked Dr. Nerdly.

"If I smoked a joint in college, would that bother you?"

"Did you?"

"Does it matter?"

"Yes. I want to know if you smoke marijuana. I want to know if you ever did."

"I do not. I don't like marijuana. On the question of my past, I suppose I should again decline to answer. It's a self-incriminating question. And irrelevant to the issue."

Another pause. Dr. Montoya: "You paint a somewhat suggestive picture in the way you answer some questions and not others."

"I'm being as honest as I can."

"Do you know anything about the cocaine missing from the OR?" the nerdish one asked.

"What I know, sir, is that drugs come up missing around here with some regularity. In the Medical ICU, about six months ago, they found that someone had slit with a razor blade, or maybe a scalpel, the cellophane at the back of two boxes of Demerol injectable vials, put a needle through all the little rubber stoppers in the backs of the amps, and sucked out ten 100-milligram doses of Demerol. He—or she—then put the boxes back at the bottom of the stack with the intact sides facing outward. Those boxes were counted as 'full and correct' at every change of shift for days or maybe weeks. But to answer the question directly, no, I know nothing about the missing cocaine. This was the first I heard about it."

"How do you know so much about the Demerol?"

"I work here. Stories like that usually go around faster than cold viruses. I guess the missing cocaine was too mundane."

Another pause for breath.

Dr. Nerdy: "So. You were . . . intimate." He was struggling.

I pictured us in her bed. "Yes."

"And your . . . relationship . . . was ongoing, consensual, mutual."

"Absolutely."

"And how are we to believe you? You said yourself some things are impossible to prove."

I felt myself shrinking. I looked through my folder at my pages of notes about our time together. I read down the myriad intimate details. Clinging to the top was the credit card receipt from a jeweler's store bearing Mimi's signature. At this, the obvious point to pull it out, to bolster my case, I hesitated. I drew a breath. Her gift to me had been the single moment of honest romance between us. In my mind I focused on the bear's face, my shamanistic guide. For the second time it occurred to me I might not want to be a surgeon.

In that pause Dr. Kerlin spoke. "It hardly matters. We have a, a, a confession of grossly inappropriate behavior. And probably, use of illicit drugs." The others looked unconvinced but I was still silent, shaking slightly, skewered by my incurable clinging to one last hopeless intimacy.

I heard little else. Voices went on, back and forth at each other, like gunfire across a killing field. It seemed nothing further was required of me. Soon enough they thanked me, then sat in silence, awaiting my departure so they could decide my fate. I trudged back to vascular surgery.

To their slight credit, they did not dismiss me on the spot, nor, technically, ever. Of course, they didn't have to. They just did not renew me for the next year. Years ago all surgery residencies used a pyramid structure. They would take in six or eight or ten interns, then choose, each year, selectively fewer from among them to advance to the next level, until they had only two or three to graduate each year.

In theory, this left only the cream to be full-fledged surgeons, but in the reality of ass-kissing academic politics, it left only those who stayed the farthest from trouble. Precisely because many promising young doctors were abandoned after one to four years of dedicated service, most training programs had dropped their pyramid structures. At the time, though, Maricopa, to prove they were a serious residency, still did some pruning after the first and second years. A perfect way to be rid of a young doctor of questionable character, never mind his talents for surgery.

To the question of my having used cocaine, they politely wrote that there was insufficient evidence to act. I heard secondhand, though, that one of my crusty old inquisitors had commented, "No low-life resident—an admitted druggie—is going to bring down the reputation of a highly respected academic surgeon." Given the chance, I would have pointed out, again, that they were mixing unrelated issues. They would have, again, ignored me.

The coincidence of their annual process and my morass was, for them, perfect timing. I got the notification of nonrenewal and the effective end of my career as a surgeon by registered mail exactly forty days from the last time Mimi Lyle and I—and I use the term advisedly—fucked each other.

THE CASE OF
HENRY ROJELIO

12

HENRY ROJELIO, DAY TWO

Henry Rojelio, my asthmatic unfortunate from Glory, on the morning after his "event"—"event" being a common medical understatement for "cataclysm"—lay in the Pediatric ICU at my old "home," Maricopa, in a coma, on a ventilator, theoretically alive.

I'd found Glory simply for employment. After the banishment of being "nonrenewed" in my surgical residency, I entered a written appeal to Maricopa and made applications to half a dozen other training centers, but no one was crying for a tainted, one-third-trained young doctor. The process was going to take a long time.

Though unemployment meant more sleep and exercise and less grease in my diet, I needed to eat and pay my rent. The work most readily available to licensed doctors with no firm specialty was then what it is today: hourly coverage in ERs, especially those in the smaller towns where there is often little to do. The hospitals must pay an hourly rate to keep a doctor there, and can't be overly choosy if they are going to keep their costs in line. A gold-plated residency and board certification are not required.

When my "nonrenewal" came, I called two of my former Maricopa coresidents who were known to moonlight, Gene Woods and Darryl Reichley. Sometimes guys are tight-lipped about their sources of cash, but these two recognized my dire need. They not only gave me names and numbers but put in phone calls on my behalf.

Through these two I was given a somewhat reluctant interview with the lead doctor in the Glory Emergency Department. Mustering all the eloquence I could to explain my current professional hiatus, I landed a "trial" position. This seemed to me the perfect place to gain experience and keep a low profile, while staying close enough to Phoenix that I could avoid another uprooting and keep on top of my appeals and applications to other residencies.

And it worked, until Henry Rojelio.

Day Two in the Debacle of Henry began for me, appropriately, with minor malfeasance. Henry's "event" kept me awake most of what was left of that night. Since internship I'd been able to collapse into sleep given any opportunity, even on the tail of running codes. Most codes, though, are merely the flailing endpoints of predictable diseases, not inexplicable "events" materializing out of the ether.

At 0740, when I was finally getting some REM in the call room, the Glory hospital housekeeper banged on the door wondering if it would be a good time to change the sheets. She was apologetic—noisily so—and offered to let me sleep. Once freed of my shift, however, I wanted utterly to be someplace—anyplace—else. I dressed and shuffled off to the parking lot half asleep, but remembered I'd left something in the ER. I trundled back in to retrieve from the med refrigerator my packaged adrenaline syringe from Henry's code. I slipped it into my duffel, barely remembering, given my lack of sleep, exactly why I'd wanted it. "It's the Rosetta Fucking Stone," I mumbled to myself.

Back in Phoenix my half of our town house was its familiar wreck. Mary Ellen was long gone to the 'Copa. I stumbled around the stacks of mail, the piles of laundry, and the equipment residue from a photographing trek up in the Mogollon Rim completed three weeks prior. I stashed the syringe in the refrigerator and opted to sleep the rest of the morning.

When I got up, there was a knot in the impossible-to-reach muscles running from under my left shoulder blade up into my neck. I tried unsuccessfully to stretch it out, loaded up on ibuprofen, and went for a painful and halfhearted workout. Post-shower I went over to check on Henry.

I knew I'd be free to visit Henry at the 'Copa, if not exactly welcome. No hospital in the world is going to keep a licensed doctor from visiting a patient he has referred there. Still, it was a relief to see my parking pass was still functional, and, with my ID badge and white coat for camouflage, I felt almost at home skating through the main lobby—forever known to the residents as the Lobby of the Seething Masses. As far as Maricopa security would know without looking in some obscure file, I still worked there. I went into the Admitting area to find a phone.

I paged my housemate. On Henry, Day Two, Mary Ellen was my only true confidant, though our friendship was still suffering from the chill of my need to hide my affair with Madame Lyle. When I paged her she might have been anywhere on the hospital campus. As a third-year resident, about to "graduate," her responsibilities when rotating on the in-house service ran her from the ward to the PICU to the ER and sometimes to the clinics if a kid needed to be admitted from there. While the interns were supposed to be responsible for the sick kids, doing the dirty work, making the decisions, talking to families, practicing for a practice, she was the one directly responsible for *them*. Often not a pretty spot.

The phone rang back almost immediately.

"Dr. Montgomery?" I said.

"Oh, Malcolm. I was expecting Horrible Harry."

Harry Upchurch was a prominent pediatrician, successful if somewhat officious. "He's coming to Admitting?" I said.

"Well, I'm expecting him in the ER. He insisted he lay eyes on this dehydrated little prune before I admit him."

"VD?" I asked.

She humored me. "Yes. You're cute. Vomiting and diarrhea, Doctor. A pediatrician's lifeblood. Also has a fever to 104 so I sicced my intern, sweet little Michelle, on a spinal tap."

"You gotta love a screaming baby."

"Actually, this kid is pretty quiet. Sick, you know."

"Sounds bad. When they'll lie still for a needle in the spine, they're not feeling too awfully well, I suppose."

"About it," she said. "Like I'm thinking ICU for this kid."

"I was about to head up there. I came over to check on my work from last night. Any changes?"

"Not that I would know. I haven't had time to check on him. I asked his nurse when I ran through there this morning and she said 'Stable.' "

"Stable" is a medical descriptor with no real meaning and had long been a joke between us. Dead people are "stable."

"Sorry," she continued, "I knew you'd want to know, but it's been the usual frantic Monday."

"Mary Ellen, it's not Monday," I said.

"Really? Who knew? Sure feels like a Monday."

"Well, I doubt they'll throw me out of the Pick-U. I'll go up and view the damage."

"I'll be up there if this ditzy twerp with the big eyelashes can ever get us some spinal fluid."

"Want me to come over? I still have the strong arm of a surgeon, you know."

"No, thank you very much. I think we little old pediatricians can muster the strength to overcome a two-year-old."

"At least a lethargic one."

"Yes, at least—uh-oh. The kid is seizing." The line clicked off.

The world has nicer pediatric intensive care units. The one at Maricopa was created from an old ward the hospital didn't need when cost containment became a battle cry and they stopped keeping patients around until they actually felt well. The county couldn't afford a down-to-the-studs makeover, but they put in enough money to at least get partitions and doors so each patient would have privacy. That was a big improvement, I was told, from the original unit, where kids were packed in next to each other like an old-fashioned charity ward, replete with ventilators alarming all at once, and IV lines seeming to braid from patient to patient.

With my old UAMMB name badge clipped to my pocket, I knew no one would challenge my visiting Henry. The chart rack was, as always, empty, contents scattered to the winds. I found the name Rojelio on the grease board—Bed 2. I walked into his cubicle. The room smelled of antiseptic and cheap cologne. I scanned the traces on the monitor and smiled at the nurse there, whom I did not recognize. She barely acknowledged me.

I plopped open Henry's chart on the bedside table. There was little in that day's entries to suggest he was seriously ill.

I read, too, all the narrative notes of the others who'd been called to help. After a disaster you always wonder if they're saying bad things about you, soon to be replayed in court. Some grand old professor writing "thirteen-year-old asthmatic nearly killed by bungling incompetent in referring ER" would be painful, as well as false, but the worst you ever see are vague generic references to prior caregivers. It's tempting but pointless to try to read between the lines.

Henry's nurse was eyeing me. Critical care RNs, working with only one or two patients for eight or twelve hours straight, can get highly proprietary.

"Are you consulting, Dr. Ishmail?" She was looking at my ID badge.

"Not really. Not currently," I said. "I saw him in the ER when he came in. Just following up." She lost interest.

"He doing okay?"

"Stable," she said. I smiled.

"Stable good or stable bad?"

"Well, BP and pulse and the like have been just fine. Neurologically he's kind of stable bad. He had a couple of seizures as soon as he got here, but none since they got him loaded with meds. Not exactly waking up, though."

"It's still really early, though," I said. Such optimism may be cliché but it is too often all we have: *He'll get better. The swelling will go down.*

"Yeah. Well, plus he's young, too." A second cliché: *The young aren't brittle. He'll get better. Who knows? Maybe he'll grow a new brain.*

She said, "I think they expect he'll do okay." She put a dollop of eye protectant gel in each eye, opened and closed each lid twice, then left.

Intensive care, properly done, reduces human existence to bare physiology; the parts of it you cannot describe in numbers are of little use and soon forgotten. The sickest, longest-term patients get physically inundated with tubes and wires, tubes and wires, and more tubes and wires.

Henry was not yet that bad. The monitor screen hanging on the wall verified, via numbers and waveforms, Henry's "stable" normal cardiovascular status. His heart, lungs, liver, and kidneys were working, according to the numbers on the chart. He had his share of tubes and wires: the big tube in his mouth, two IVs—one of which was capped off—a blood pressure cuff, EKG wires, a pulse oximeter wrapped around a finger, a gastric tube down his nose, and a urinary drain in his penis—straightening it. Still, he appeared to be sleeping, and he had a little color in his cheeks. This was a far cry from the hair's-breadth code of eighteen hours earlier. His heart, at least, was recovering.

I went back to the central station, planning to wait for Mary Ellen. Henry's nurse had his chart there doing her paperwork.

"Any family around?" I asked her. I still needed to sit with them for my explanation of Henry's plight. I knew if I didn't soon put a face to my name, their suspicion that I was the devil incarnate would gradually solidify.

"Mom and Dad were in not long ago. They seemed kind of in shock. Pretty angry, too. Didn't stay too long, but said they'd be back before lunchtime."

The door to the Unit whirred open to let in a sorry parade: At the center of a full-sized ER gurney lay a flaccid infant. Surrounding her was a committee of hospital folks. At the foot were a nurse and a respiratory therapist. At the head Dr. Montgomery was disgustedly fussing over a bright-faced young blonde woman with too much eyeliner and fake eyelashes, the short white coat of an intern, pockets a-bulge with crib notes, squeezing the breathing bag like she feared it would squeeze back. Bringing up the rear was Harry Upchurch, looking as distinguished as a man can in a seersucker suit and bow tie.

Monty saw me and just shook her head slightly as her platoon passed the desk. I followed them in and stood against the back wall as they got the baby moved to the hospital's chrome-plated crib on shopping-cart wheels, changed over from the transport monitor to the wall-mounted version, and connected him to his ventilator. Keeping an eye on the hubbub, Monty backed up to stand beside me.

"Sodium one-twenty-two," she said.

"Rice water?" I asked.

"Yep. Just like always. Long time vomiting and diarrhea, then just replace precious bodily salt water with a little carbo-water and you, too, can seize."

"Well, you ought to have the admit note memorized by now," I said. She made a face.

"How's your boy doing?" she asked.

"Practically off all drips. Not waking up. Stable," I said, making a face myself.

"I still don't understand what happened to that kid," she said.

"Well, I'm open for ideas."

"Yeah. But I don't have any. Do you think he aspirated?" she asked.

"Well, it would be a reportable event in the pediatrics journals if he didn't. There was plenty of stomach content there where it didn't belong. I sucked out the pharynx as much as I could."

"What did you see below the vocal cords?"

"Frankly, my dear, I was just damn glad just to see the cords. This was not the slickest tracheal intubation you've ever seen," I said.

"No, I'm sure it wasn't fun. It doesn't matter much. If it's in the lungs it'll blossom and rear its ugly head by tonight."

I nodded.

Henry's nurse poked her head into the cubicle to tell me the Rojelios had returned and she had asked them to wait for me in the private family room.

I mumbled to Monty, "Speaking of no fun."

She took the cue to turn back to her own troubles, but not before giving me a sympathetic shake of her head. "You'll *love* them," she whispered. On my way to the nurse's desk I pilfered some of their overcooked coffee in one of the ubiquitous Styrofoam cups.

I tried to prime myself for what a cynical med school classmate had dubbed a "compassionate moment." You're supposed to have simultaneous professional detachment and deep personal empathy. An oxymoron carrying, in this case, very high stakes. I was coming up blank about what I could actually say. The Rojelios knew me only as the party responsible when their son nearly died.

Empathy. A laugh. How could I empathize with a parent whose child had just suffered a near-lethal event? I, who was years from having children or even a romance I would be willing to tell my mother about?

Styrofoam coffee in hand, I ventured to the family waiting room where the Rojelios waited. Such rooms ought to be soundproofed and have rubber walls. They are the places of wailing and gnashing of teeth. This one was like most: poorly furnished, with plaid-clothed and multi-stained chairs and sofas, proffering the faint but unmistakable aromas of body odor, old cigarettes, and what was probably aged vomitus.

I found an apparent mother and father, a school-aged boy, and three children under five. The adult male had to be Daniel, Henry's father. He was leaning on the far wall, arms crossed, scowling, and tapping one foot with a machine-gun pace. The only light in the room was a fluorescent bank in the middle of the ceiling.

Henry's mother had barely made eye contact with me before looking to Daniel for action, but it was long enough to convey her fear. He sneered at her ever so briefly before turning to me. "Yes?" he said.

"I'm Dr. Ishmail. I was the physician at the Glory Emergency Department who treated Henry last night. We didn't get to meet then. I guess you had left."

"Yes. I do that. He goes to your ER all the time. You never make him better. Anymore I just drop him off."

I sat down and looked back and forth between the two of them, not struggling for words, but wondering how much to tell them, and where to begin. They took the chairs opposite mine, shooing away two small children. Apparently Daniel was the source of the cheap cologne in Henry's cubicle.

I leaned forward in my chair, wanting soothing words to flow right out, but they didn't. They never do. It's always forced. There was an awkward pause, then finally I used the standard opening: "He's going to be fine." It's better to stretch the truth than kill the hope, we're told.

"They said he quit breathing," Daniel said.

"Yes, that's true. He did quit breathing, though we don't know exactly why."

Henry's mother blew her nose.

"But then you . . ."—Daniel waved his arms—"you revived him, shocked him back, whatever. You got him back again."

I explained Henry's code in short form. Henry's mother spoke to Daniel in Spanish. He turned to me and said, "She wonders when he wakes up."

"Your son . . ."

"Stepson," he corrected me. "My name is Mendoza. He is Rojelio."

"Your stepson," I said, "is, well, his brain is sick. Injured. He's in a coma." Henry's mother obviously understood the term. Her lip began trembling. "It is very early, though. Many times such patients wake up fine." Daniel's eyes narrowed.

I went on, "Frankly I'm not entirely sure what happened to Henry. As you probably know, asthma is a severe constriction of the tiny muscles around the small air passages inside the lungs. It's an overreaction to something. Something inflammatory, like a virus or a pollen or something."

I was making my hands into tubes and squeezing them progressively tighter. "Patients don't move enough air. They get into trouble from lack of oxygen. Some get into serious trouble. Some die. It's called bronchospasm. Spasm of the bronchioles, the tiny airways."

"Yes, we have heard all this."

I took a deep breath. "In any case, your son had stopped breathing, and I'm afraid his heart had stopped also." It made me feel better to unburden even this much.

Daniel's eyes were ice. "They did not tell us this. That his heart stopped."

"We got it back. We did CPR—chest compressions." I put my hands together and mimicked pushing on my own sternum. "It was a little rough, but we got his heart going again."

He said something to his wife in Spanish. She replied, casting glances at me. "Did he have a heart attack?" he asked.

"No. That is entirely different. That is when one of the arteries to the heart gets blocked off. There is no sign Henry's heart muscle has suffered any lasting injury. For a while we had him on a drip—a continuous infusion through the IV—to stimulate the heart, but they've been able to turn that way down and off now."

He began to translate to Henry's mother but she nodded, staring only at me. "Then why he is not waking up?"

"Well, that's not entirely clear right now. For some period of time—a short period, but we can't say exactly how long—there was no blood flow to the brain, then during the CPR, the rescue work, there is some flow, but it's less than normal. The brain needs constant oxygen. It may have been injured. Possibly permanently. How much, we won't know for a while."

"A stroke?"

"Well, something like that."

"We have a lawyer, you know," he spat at me.

"Well, no, I did not know, but okay, now I know." Lawyers are not generally helpful in ICUs, but there was nothing I could say.

"Ted Priestly. Perhaps you have heard of him." Apparently Daniel wanted me to feel fear.

"Will he be involved in any decisions?"

"What do you mean, decisions?"

"Well, decisions about how to proceed. How far to go. Your boy is critically ill. He could need surgery. He could need care for many weeks. Even years. Ultimately he may not live. You may have to—at some point—decide . . . decide how far to go, when to let go," I said, realizing only too late that much less would have been more than enough.

Henry's mother jumped from her chair, swallowed a loud sob, and began pacing the little floor space available. Daniel's face was impassive, though. He stared at me and narrowed his eyes. Mrs. Mendoza crossed herself and prayed to the ceiling as she paced. Daniel spoke to her and she froze. She turned to bore into me with her eyes and said, "*No máquinas.*" No machines. I nodded very slightly.

Daniel said, "Sit down, *corazón.*" His tone was cold. She continued looking at me. I nodded again. He made an emphatic gesture to the chair. She sat.

Daniel turned to me. "You will not let him die."

"Of course not." I said. "First of all, I'm no longer his doctor. The Maricopa doctors are in charge now. You will be talking with them. But I can assure you they are doing everything possible, everything imaginable to help your boy. The main doctor in the ICU will be Dr. Montgomery. She's a friend of mine. You can trust her completely." I was aware my reassurance was empty since they had little reason to trust me.

"Can we see him?" his mother asked in halting English.

"Yes, you'll be able to see him almost any time," I said. My beeper went off. It was a number I didn't recognize.

The door opened and a man in a clerical collar came in. Henry's mother jumped up and ran to him. They clasped their four hands together between them. He murmured something to her, then said to me, "I'm Father O'Donnell, the parish pastor of the Mendozas."

I introduced myself. "I was just explaining to the Mendozas what we think might have happened." Daniel barely looked up at the priest.

"They can fill me in. I'm here mainly to pray with them, anyway."

"Yes, I'm sure that will be helpful for them. I was just finishing— gotta go answer a page. Mrs. Mendoza asked about visiting in the Pedes ICU. They can go in almost any time but the nurses always want you to ask if it's an okay time. There's a phone by the door. Sometimes they need a few minutes to get him taken care of, sort of 'tucked in.' "

There was a silence. I rose to leave. I said, "I'll try to be around to help keep you up on any developments as things change, but, like I said, the Maricopa doctors are now making the decisions."

Daniel glared at me, then looked away.

My belated rapport-building was a four-star failure. We'd gone from mild suspicion to poorly suppressed acrimony.

To get out the door I had only a second lame cliché: "Let me know if there's anything I can do for you."

They stared.

Reentering the PICU, I kicked at the slow-moving automatic door but missed.

Mary Ellen was writing in a chart at the nurses' station. I said to her, "Thought you'd want to know: Seems I started a fire in the waiting room." She looked up. "Let's just say Henry's family seems a bit hostile right now. And Dad—Stepdad—made it a point to tell me they have a lawyer already."

She shook her head, looked back at the chart in front of her, and said, "A lawyer, huh? Maybe he's cute."

"Hey, no cruising for HOs on my disaster."

"Sweetheart, hot ones are few and far between. A girl's got to get 'em where she can."

"Yeah, perfect. On the tails of my disaster he'll get rich on a contingency fee from a settlement for a life sentence *and* lucky with you. Maybe I can give him a blow job, too."

"Malcolm, I've never even laid eyes on the guy. Don't be so paranoid."

"Paranoid? Any reason you can think of I might be paranoid right now?"

"Sorry, Malcolm. You have been having a bad run lately."

"Yeah. Maybe the *Book of World Records* has a category for Medical Black Clouds."

She smiled her sympathy.

I picked up the phone beside her and answered my page. When I hung up I sighed. Mary Ellen asked me what it was.

"The Glory Hospital administration," I said, "kindly requesting I find a time in the next few days to sit down with one of their higher-ups and 'make some notes' about what happened to Henry Rojelio."

She gave another sympathetic look.

"So be sure to let me know if you figure it out," I said. "I could use an answer or two."

I didn't want to leave just yet. Being at Maricopa, bent to a tough case with Mary Ellen, was still more "home" than our town house. "What else you got in here?" I said.

She looked up at me. "Celia Weatherill is back." She nodded over her shoulder to the middle cubicle.

I peeked around the partition. There lay an infant, wide-eyed, puffy-cheeked, and hooked to a ventilator via a tracheostomy.

"She's the ex-preemie you've been talking about?"

"Uh-huh. Brain hemorrhages. Went home, despite her bad lungs, for all of eight days. Got respiratory syneytial virus, went on to bronchiolitis obliterans."

"Wherein . . . your terminal bronchioles . . . ?" I waved my hand in a circle.

"Get obliterated . . . Right. And she suffocates internally."

"Might as well smoke," I said.

"Yeah, but this is like four packs a day for fifty years."

"You know, I think you're kind of a magnet for these kinds of cases."

She eyed me. "We all have our talents."

I nodded.

"She hasn't been free of some flavor of pneumonia—nor home, mind you—for the seven months since then. We had her over to the St. Elizabeth's home for about five days, on a portable vent, but she bounced."

"Seven months?" I said.

"She was only supposed to have been born four months ago. But here's the good part: Single mom. Dad was none too sure about this fatherhood thing to begin with. Took a powder when the going got tough. She has a new man and . . ."—she leaned toward me—"I think he's trying to whore her out."

"Lovely. And why are we doing this?" I said, motioning toward the baby.

"You know, that's exactly what Dr. Frank asked me not more than two hours ago."

"Who's he?"

"He's the pedes infectious disease guy. We haven't even consulted them formally, but he knows what bugs every kid in the hospital is growing out 'cuz he goes and checks on all the cultures."

"Yeah, I remember him," I said, picturing him in my mind, a tall, gangly professor with a short beard, thick kinky hair, and eyes that sparkled when he was discussing an interesting germ.

"Well, on his way through here, while we were writing up notes and orders after rounds, he kind of grabbed me by the elbow, jerked his head toward Celia, and said, 'Why are we doing this?' I just kind of shrugged. He said, 'She ever going to get out of here?' I said, 'No. Not in my lifetime.' He said, 'Just a tragedy. Seems she ought to die, doesn't it?' I nodded. He turned to go, but then he turned back. He said, 'Almost forgot. The sputum culture you got on her two days ago is growing resistant stuff. Why don't you put her on gent and ticarcillin? Better get peak and trough levels, too,' and he left." She stared at me.

I nodded and smiled. "The great medical oxymoron."

"Exactly," she said. "We're doing the wrong thing keeping her alive, but here's the right antibiotic to kill off her pneumonia. It's classic. The drugs are accomplishing the wrong ends, but it's all we know how to do. We've lost our ability to not treat things."

"Nah. I don't think we ever had it. It's a primitive reflex we can't suppress," I said.

"Pure brain-stem? Maybe. But I thought there was a rumor going around that we had evolved."

"Only our feet," I said.

She laughed. "You know it used to be said that pneumonia was 'the old person's friend.' "

"Sure, but I imagine our ancestors would have happily killed a lot of pneumonia if they'd had ticarcillin," I said.

"I suppose. Now if we just grow little Celia some new lungs, then she can grow up."

"Oh, I know what you mean. We're dragging out her death. Celia is an ongoing tragedy."

"No, *her* tragedy is over." She squinted slightly. "For the mom it goes on and on."

I smiled. Mary Ellen was every bit the doctor I remembered. What might have built up to an internal warm glow got squelched when I remembered the new booby traps I'd put inside our friendship. I had to keep fresh exactly what details Mary Ellen was likely to know about my ouster from the residency and what was still unclear. I hated the secrecy.

Thus cooled, I took one more peek at Henry, "sleeping," and said my goodbyes.

The elevator ride down from the PICU was a painful reminder of what I had lost. Stopping at every floor, the car took on, person by person, a gathering of pale patients and their sweating, hopeful family members, of lost-in-thought doctors and giggling junior volunteers.

They packed into the elevator as if I weren't there. The struggle was going on without me. It seemed the combined weight of Henry's debacle and the coma of my career would crush me.

The bell dinged, signaling Floor 1, where my claustrophobia would be relieved. The crowd decompressed into the Lobby of the Seething Masses. I was last out, about to be able to breathe deeply again, when I came face-to-face, with my mouth open for special effect, with Robin Benoit, the Glory ER nurse, a seeming alien on turf I still thought of as mine. She was dressed for something athletic, but looking like the desert had blown sand in her eyes.

13

Here in Hooker, besides watching thunderstorms while I'm on call in the hospital, I am witness and sometime participant in the decline of my father.

Not long after the Trouble with Henry and my skulking retreat home, Dad had his first stroke. In my darkest hours I fear the former caused the latter, but that's just superstition. In reality his vascular disease is directly linked to his addiction to cigarette smoke—he quit a hundred times—and the fact that he completely ignored his own blood pressure.

That first "event" did little harm, though, and would have been a godsend had he taken it seriously enough to change his ways. But the old fuck, like most doctors, thought he knew everything, even—without measuring it—what his blood pressure was at any given moment.

Last Christmas he had a big stroke. Now he is profoundly damaged. Unable to practice. Unable to speak or, for that matter, do anything that would imply intent on his part. The irony of that is too much to bear.

Mom—after the stroke, after the tears, after we sat and wailed and gnashed our teeth—sold his practice. There was no choice. I lacked the credentials to do what he had been doing.

The only possible buyer was a local favorite son, a three-sport letterman from Hooker High, well thought of in the banter of the town barbershops, Brant Kudamelka. We were afraid it would kill Dad. He thought little of Brant.

Brant, after resetting the records for accuracy in passing a football at a state college of little academic renown, and earning a third-string All-American rating in his division, failed twice to win a spot in an American medical school. Undaunted, he flew to a spot in the Third World where American dollars supplant test scores as admissions criteria. He completed the course, then came Stateside to an obscure surgery residency teetering at the edge of extinction. He has not passed his Boards.

*I remember Dad, when confronted with Brant's parents' bubbling joy at
their son's "success," always smiling broadly and congratulating them loudly.
Alone later he would mumble to me general worries about the future of medicine. Though I knew he was not thinking of me at such moments, I was inevitably chilled with chagrin.*

HENRY ROJELIO, DAY TWO (CONTINUED)

Once I thought about it, stepping off the Maricopa elevator to see
Robin Benoit emerge from the Seething Masses should not have been
shocking. I knew of no connection she had there, but the medical
world is small enough, even in Phoenix. There are dozens of legitimate
reasons any particular nurse might show up at the County Hospital.

Once I mentally slapped myself for being paranoid, I was glad to
see her: She was my own latest Hot One.

When she started working at Glory, a month before our Henry
Event, we were both unattached. She was a stylish and pretty brunette,
shapely, friendly, not annoyingly talkative, and intelligent. My low-key
if unsubtle flirtatiousness seemed to be well received, though she politely declined a suggestion one afternoon that we share a drink after
her evening shift. I called her the next day to suggest dinner and a
movie. Apparently upping the ante worked; she accepted.

Unfortunately our date got postponed when she had to work because one of her colleagues phoned in "sick." Nonetheless, in the idle
hours in our quiet ER, we had gotten to know the basics about each
other. I knew she came most recently from an ER job in the San Francisco Bay area to Phoenix to be with an unnamed male. Something like:

"What brought you to the Valley of the Sun?"

"Hmmf. I thought I was in love."

"And . . . ?"

"He thought he 'needed a little space.' I was apparently cramping
his style."

I nodded sympathetically—to both of them—and sipped my
Squirt.

Our embryonic romance gave our chance collision in the Maricopa lobby an extra dimension. Trying not to blink and fumble like a seventh grader, I came up with, "Seeing an old boyfriend?"

"No. If they're old they're not my boyfriend anymore."

"Okay. Seeing a young boyfriend?"

"Could be." She mustered an enigmatic grin. "How about you? Seeing anyone special? Avoiding anyone special?"

"Well, I just saw our mutual friend Henry Rojelio. That was special." Her grin died.

"Yeah, I was going to go up there, too," she said.

"Well, brace yourself. It goes from bad to worse. The family is all there. That was more special. There's, um, more than a little hostility there. Dad told me they've got a lawyer already."

"Oh God."

"My words exactly."

She frowned. "How is the boy?"

I filled her in on the progress. I said, "Not waking up, though."

She bit her lip and turned away for a second. When she tuned back she blinked back tears. "He should . . . It's still early, isn't it?"

I found her apparent lack of the usual emergency worker's cynicism endearing. "Sure, Robin. He should still be okay."

She sniffed. "I got a call from the Glory Hospital. Administration. Sally Marquam, the Vice-President of Clinical Ops, wants to meet with me tomorrow, before my shift, about two in the afternoon. They told me I'm not supposed to talk to anybody about this, but I really want to talk to you first. I don't know what to say, what happened."

"Yeah, they beeped me, too. Told me the same thing."

"I'm so, I don't know, jumpy about it. I hate *meetings* with bosses."

"It shouldn't be that big a deal. Sick kid crumps; happens all the time."

She curled her mouth. "Yeah, but I'm still real nervous about what they might be thinking. Maybe I shouldn't be, but I am."

"So, we'll talk it over if you want. That's not against the law. They probably say they don't want any of us to talk to each other thinking we're going to cook up some cover story, but we don't have anything to cover."

"Of course you're right."

"What are you thinking—about us getting together? We could go get coffee or something." I gestured toward the door.

"Sorry. Time crunched right now. And it should probably be in private." Her expression changed. "You know, I'd love to make you dinner tonight."

"Can't. I got a twelve-hour night shift out at St. Greenbacks' in Scottsdale. Covering for a doc with a herniated disc."

She thought. "Maybe breakfast then. I do great waffles."

"Geez, Robin, sounds great, but after a night in that ER, I'm pretty sure I'll be asleep, no matter where I'm sitting."

"How about tomorrow night?" she said. "I'll just blow off the meeting till the next day. They can wait."

"What about that evening shift?"

"I meant after that."

"Elven-thirty? Yeah. Late dinner. Sure. I'll sleep all day and be wide awake about then, anyway."

"Meet me at work," she said. "We'll go from there."

My night in Scottsdale was depressing. At 2:00 A.M. they brought in the dangling harbinger of Henry, Day Three, an apparent suicide someone found hanging from a scraggly cottonwood tree behind a strip mall. The medics cut him down and ran him in, bells and whistles on full display, "Code Three."

I was unable, despite much pulling, pushing, fighting for leverage at ridiculous angles, and grunting, to get his mouth open to intubate him. As I struggled—hunched over an engorged head, marveling at the purple snake of a bruise encircling his upper neck, my own adrenal glands on "turbocharge"—the muscles under my left shoulder blade began to cramp. On my fourth try to pass the tube the knot imploded with a racking and painful finality.

The spasm in my shoulder opened my internal memory file on the physiology of muscle tetany. From there it was no leap at all to figure out why the patient was so damn stiff—he was in rigor mortis. Needless to say, the code was unsuccessful.

Once home, I slept, though poorly. I blamed the knot in my back, though Henry might have had more to do with it.

At ten-thirty that evening I drove to Glory. Crossing Phoenix is another source of a bad mood. The urban mass goes from horizon to horizon with no meaningful structure, points of interest are miles apart, yet much of the area is vacant. Desert, in small broken plots, stripped of all interesting cacti and variously littered with urban residues, looks a lot like dirt, sand, and trash. Were there a Poster City for Contemptuous Land Use, Phoenix would be it. One of my residency mates coined a facetious motto for the city: "Phoenix: Where Land Is a Disposable Commodity."

Normally, the most depressing part is the river dividing Phoenix from Tempe and Mesa: You see only its desiccated bed. They suck what was the Salt River absolutely dry to grow bluegrass in Scottsdale. The Salt, that night, though, was running full. The winter rains in the mountains east of town had been exceptionally generous.

I got to the Glory ER as the nurses were changing shift. Patty Kucera was at the control desk. I limped in, head and neck cocked rigidly to my left. "Ooh, you look stiff, Doc," she said. Robin came out of the med room.

I said, "I got this knot in my shoulder from a corpse. Did you know rigor mortis can be contagious?" While I recounted my 2:00 A.M. code Robin stepped around behind me to feel the offending muscle.

"Ooh, that's a bad one," she said.

I quietly let out something like "Unnnh."

"We better get you into something comfortable." She leaned over the desk toward Patty and added in a stage whisper, "We have a date!"

Robin, in her Chevy Camaro, led the way to her house, a stucco bungalow in an older tract development in Mesa, most of the way back to town from Glory. As she unlocked the door to let me in she said, "Will you have a drink with me?"

"Absolutely. What are you pouring?"

"Well, I have a couple of choices: There's some Bailey's in the fridge, a couple of beers, and some white wine. It should be champagne, since we can finally get together, but I'm not feeling that much like celebrating." Robin had on worn jeans and a snug knit top. She looked great.

I said, "Enh, who needs bubbles? Got any Scotch?"

"Sorry."

"The wine'll be fine." I sat at the breakfast counter.

Opening the refrigerator, she said into the top shelf, "Yeah, I have a thing about bubbles anyway." She poured us each a glass. "You're such a dear. I've been so wrung out. I mean, to come and put up with me after a night on call," she said.

"Oh, I got some sleep today."

"I barely made it up to the Pedes ICU yesterday, after we ran into each other, and then they wouldn't tell me much. You said you thought Henry was going to be okay though . . . ?" She gave me an inquiring look.

"I guess that depends on your definition." I tried again to stretch my neck.

"Oh God," she said, "I thought he was doing pretty good by the time he left the ER." She got out salad makings, a wok, Baggies of chopped vegetables, and a plastic container of marinating fish.

"His heart was doing okay."

She laid into some radishes with staccato knife strokes. "What do you think could have happened to him?"

"Freak things, I guess. Arrhythmia from the epi. Laryngospasm. Exacerbated bronchospasm. Maybe his asthma was just way worse than we knew and he coded from garden variety hypoxia, good old lack of oxygen. Since it doesn't make any sense, it could have been anything."

She said, "I mean, I gave him the shot you ordered, and he—he codes. They're going to think it was me—that I did something wrong." She studied my face. "And then, what should have been a routine code apparently goes all wrong and he barely makes it back. I mean, he was young and all, he should have bounced right back, whatever it was."

"That's what they say. But the only routine I've ever noticed about codes is that most of them don't work."

"But he should have been . . . recoverable." Her voice quavered slightly.

"Yeah, but things don't always work out the way they're supposed to, eh?"

She said, "But it's all got me so . . . I mean, they can't wait to have a private little chat with me, the one who gave him the shot." Again the look.

"You shouldn't be worried. Really. You were just doing your job. They're going to do theirs—get it all on the record. They can hear the lawyers coming."

She turned away. "But you know how people talk, and I know the nursing administration has been asking questions in the ER. I can't help be worried."

"Are you feeling like you did something wrong?"

She looked at the ceiling and stammered, "I—I don't think so, Malcolm. You know how you wonder, though, after something goes bad? I mean, a sub-Q shot of epi is something I could do in my sleep. I probably have done it in my sleep. I've given so many of them they all run together in my mind, you know?" She served the salads.

I said, "Logically—I mean in a purely analytic sense—there are really only two things you could have done wrong. You could have drawn up the wrong drug—say, grabbed the wrong amp from the drawer and cracked it open—but that's pretty unlikely, since they're mostly different colors and different sizes and shapes. Or, you could have given the epi IV instead of sub-Q. Hit a vein. That's really unlikely, too, but if you did, it's a whopping big dose for IV. He could have gotten his pulse so fast he arrested from a tachy-dysrhythmia. Or got acute heart failure from the blood pressure. Hell, with that much epi IV it's possible he shot his blood pressure through the roof and had a stroke. I'm just thinking out loud, but he could have bled into his brain from the sudden surge in blood pressure. Nah, that's getting way off into fantasyland. And they're getting a CT of his head, so they'll know if that happened, but I really doubt it's going to show much besides the usual—'diffuse edema, consistent with global ischemic insult.' " I took a bite. "But all the other possibilities are *his*—I mean, something his body did that most wouldn't. So all in all it's pretty unlikely that anyone could seriously blame you."

She forced a smile. "What do you think? That's what I want to know."

"Like I said, I can only guess. Pick one. Take laryngospasm. It's as good as any."

"Vocal cords close . . . spasm and . . ."

"And he can't move air in or out. Shut off. And in his stressed state, his heart . . ."—I waved a hand—"checks out."

She drained her wineglass, then refilled it. "Hope you don't mind," she said.

"No. Of course not."

"What does your friend think? What's her name? Dr. Monty?"

"Dr. Montgomery, Mary Ellen Montgomery. Everybody calls her Monty. I think she's about as unclear about it as any of us. We only talked about it for a few seconds. She was up to her ass in alligators when I was up in the Pick-U."

"So what's the lowdown between you and this Dr. Monty?" She sipped her wine and gave me a coy look. "You didn't mention you lived with her."

"It's true," I said. "I don't hide it. I guess it just didn't come up. Mary Ellen and I have been friends since we started med school together. We were lab partners in gross anatomy and paired up for the class on physical examination. I got to listen to her heart and peer deep into her eyes. And ears. With the right scope, of course.

"Then we both got residencies here in Phoenix and decided to share a town house. That means we've been roommates going on three years and friends for seven." I reached over for a chunk of the tomato she was quartering and popped it in my mouth. "We've never been lovers." I took another swallow of wine.

She said, "You haven't heard anyone say anything about me, have you? I mean, people can be so mean sometimes. I'm just really worried."

"God, you're being skittish. I haven't heard a peep, Robin."

She went to the stove and turned on the flame under the wok. "I just hope all this fuss doesn't hurt you."

I chortled. "My reputation ruined? A wrongful death suit? Permanent vegetative state?"

"We can talk about something else, if all this is . . ."

"It's all right. I suppose I could get sued over this. You don't need to do anything wrong to get sued. A third of all doctors get sued eventually. Maybe I can get mine over with early. I've heard it's a real eye-opener about what a joke the legal system is. The courtroom as a one-ring circus. Illusion as your goal. But I have insurance. Not as much as the hospital's twenty million dollars, but if they run through my policy limits all they'll have left to go after will be an old Datsun and a pile of debt."

"There wasn't any other Attending on the case, was there?"

"Just me. That family doesn't really go to regular doctors. No insurance coverage and an intractable psychiatric condition," I said. "Very bad combination."

She poured the vegetables into the hot oil. "So how would they pay their lawyer?"

"You kidding?" I thought any nurse would know how that worked. She looked at me blankly.

I said, "The *abogados* line up for cases like this."

"Oh, right, contingency fees. They get half?"

"Half, or maybe only a third. What's a couple o' mil?" I said. "But that's a depressing topic. So I hear you're meeting with Sally Marquam tomorrow."

She shot me a look. "Speaking of depressing."

"Yeah. Precisely. It seems to be where we're living today."

"What should I tell her? Can she get my license taken away?"

I thought any nurse would have known how that worked, too. When answers are obvious, though, I try to be polite. I said, "The State of Arizona issues your license. She could report something to the Nursing Board, but they're your boss. You're part of 'them.' They don't want you looking bad."

She said, "Get yourself some more wine, if you want." She added the fish to the stir-fry. I went to the refrigerator and refilled my glass, then stood beside her as she toyed with the sizzling food.

"Will I get sued, too? I mean, am I going to have to go to court?" Robin asked.

"You wouldn't be named in the suit. Since you work for the hospital, the hospital is responsible for you. If they think you did him in, they go for the hospital. I think it's called *respondeat superior* in legal jive. It's Latin for 'deep pockets, baby.' But you would have to testify. That is, if it went to trial. I guess most of these get settled out of court, though."

"You think this would?"

"I don't know," I said. "On the one hand we know we didn't do anything negligent. It certainly looks like there was a bad outcome, but that's not the same as malpractice. The question is, can you convince a jury that you—we—didn't do anything wrong. If Henry doesn't die and he's just left with permanent brain damage and they let some plaintiff's attorney wheel a comatose teenager into court, most juries will go nuts, no matter what the facts are."

"This *is* depressing," she said. She looked over at me. She put out a hand, taking mine. I stepped behind her and put my arms around her waist. She nuzzled her head back onto my chest. I leaned down and kissed her neck. She turned to me and our mouths met, softly at first, then wet with full intention.

"Time to eat," she said, pulling away.

The coy looks melted into inviting smiles. Halfway through the plate of stir-fry I was cocking my head right, eyes closed, and digging my fingers into the golf ball in my left trapezius again. She suddenly stood up and said, "You need a back rub." She held a hand toward me. When I took it she pulled me up and kissed me. I hadn't planned on a sudden shift to the physical but it didn't seem like a bad idea. She disappeared into the back of the house and returned with a sheet, a towel, and a bottle of oil. She put the oil in the microwave, then pointed me to her bedroom. "Promise not to look at the room. It's a mess."

"It'll remind me of home."

She called after me, "You're going to have to take your clothes off."

"Oh damn," I said.

Her bedroom furnishings were minimal: a bed, a nightstand, a dresser, and a bookcase. There was nothing on the walls.

I pulled off my shirt and sneakers and lay facedown with my feet at the head of her bed. She came in and lit two candles. Her massage oil was slightly hot, her hands very strong. She kneaded both my trapezii and all the strap muscles of my neck until they felt like they could never again raise my head. I could still tell where the knot was, but its angry barbs were gone.

"You're amazing," I said through the pillow.

"I took an extra-credit course in nursing school," she said.

She worked down each arm individually, then back to each shoulder. She worked down my back to the lumbar curve, then wiped her hands, reached under my stomach, and undid my pants. These she slid down and off, then pulled off my socks, leaving me naked. I turned my head and began to rise up slightly but she said, "Lie down and relax."

It occurred to me: Why did I even start to get up? To what, exactly, was I going to object?

She straddled me and laid her hands back in the exact spot she had just left. From the small of my back she began deep circular strokes around my buttocks. "That feels amazingly good," I said.

"These are your biggest muscles. And fine ones, at that."

I was smiling like a fool. She worked down my thighs, calves, feet and toes. I was feeling whole and perfect, as if my flaws had disappeared.

"Flip over," she said. I hesitated only an instant. She worked from the tops of my feet up my shins and the front of my thighs. She spread my legs slightly to get to my inner thighs and worked up to my abdominals, barely brushing my half-erect penis. She went on up my chest, working over my chest muscles, did the front of my neck, then my face, with small circles around the temples.

"Now you rest," she said, and was gone. At that hour I should have fallen asleep in seconds, especially after the two glasses of wine, but my biologic clock was inverted and the procreational parts of my brain were on alert. I just drifted along, smiling drowsily. I did not, however, move.

Piano music came from the living room. I became aware of her moving beside me just before she touched my lips with her index finger, then straddled me again. Her legs were bare. She rubbed my chest again, then bent down and brushed her lips against mine. I smiled, eyes closed. Her cue. She kissed me, well. She had an urgency.

I kept my hands at my sides, my reciprocation strictly in my lips. She slid down my abdomen to kiss, lick, and soon enough suck my near-painful engorgement. She took me well into her mouth with a vigorous rhythm, but stopped just short of culmination.

I opened my eyes to see Robin's breasts suspended over my face, but for a second I only smiled. She returned the smile and kissed me hard on the mouth. She rubbed her nipples around mine, then slowly rose over my face again for me to suck and kiss her breasts. They were wonderful, despite the obvious presence of silicone implants.

I got her to lie back so I could take a turn with my own mouth. I said, "It seems you have some redheaded genes on the back of a chromosome somewhere."

She pulled me up to her again, saying, "It's just the candlelight." Then she rose, saying, "I need you in me." She went to an old bookcase built into the far wall, retrieving what looked like a large pair of matching books, glued together. "Toy box," she said. She took a tiny key from the drawer in the nightstand and put it into a nearly invisible slit in the edge of the upper book, turned it, and the cover popped up slightly.

"I got this at a place in North Beach in San Francisco called the Kitsch Kitchen. Isn't it great?" she said.

Inside the box were some papers, a small stack of money neatly bound with a white paper strip, some silk scarves, condoms, spermicidal foam, and a dildo-shaped vibrator. The bill on top of the stack was clearly a hundred. I said, "Jesus, you must deal drugs or something."

"Oh shit," she said, "you're not supposed to be looking." She gave me an exasperated look. "My parents have a lot of money and my dad insists on sending me some every month. He doesn't want Mom to know, so he sends cash. I never deposit it so the IRS doesn't think I'm 'dealing drugs or something.'"

"What are the scarves for?" I asked.

"If you're bad I tie you to the bed," she said with a smile as she tossed me a condom and took the foam into the bathroom.

I called, "What if I'm good?"

"Then I tie you to the bed to keep you here," she called back.

Completion of our lovemaking was exquisite, if conventional. I topped it off with a quick lapse into total unconsciousness. When I came around I opened my eyes to see Robin up on an elbow, staring at my face. The candles were still burning; little had changed. I offered an expectant smile.

She blinked, but said nothing, still looking at me intently. She kissed me briefly, then went to the bathroom.

Her prodding me gently in the arm woke me up a second time. "It's time for you to go home, sleepyhead."

I frowned. "What time is it?"

She was wearing a plaid flannel nightgown now. "About one-thirty. I need my beauty rest. And you just need some rest, period."

I looked at her. "I kinda like sleeping here."

"But we hardly know each other."

"I thought we were getting along pretty good."

She smiled. "We are. So let's not rush things."

I scowled. I said, "Me-e! What about you?" She kissed me again, then pushed me out of bed.

At her door I hesitated to leave, pulling her toward me to kiss her. Her response was cool.

I rubbed my eyes, stumbled to my car, and drove back home, across the flooding Salt River.

14

Hoacham, Nebraska, Scenic Hub of Agriculture for the Republican Valley, has a unique bar. It's at one end of the main street. When you approach it from the town side, the sign reads "Last Chance Bar and Grill." From the other side, logically enough, it reads "First Chance Bar and Grill." The locals are onto the ruse. They call it simply The Chance. Now that's down-home.

A few weeks ago I was back in the Hoacham ER, seemingly condemned to relive a key clinical part of my story. That weekend Hoacham was the Scenic Hub of Asthma and its nasty little cousins. In the span of twenty-four hours I admitted to the hospital three little ones with unrepentant wheezing.

The worst off was a baby of eight months, never before sick but that night unable to adequately exhale. Probably set off by a common virus, but in his body, life-threatening. We gave heavy doses of nebulized inhaled drugs and crossed our collective fingers. In an hour he was worse.

Never having actually given an epinephrine shot myself, I asked the nurse to let me watch her do it. She was amused. I did not bring up my experience in Glory.

When he continued to deteriorate I knew he needed to be on a ventilator and flown to Lincoln. I knew he needed chemical paralysis. I looked up my med choices in a text, chose one that would last long enough for a lengthy flight, got him drugged and intubated, and the helicopter came and rescued us all. As he sailed into the night I kept thinking how simple a sub-Q shot of adrenaline really is. I bet in the old days Dad gave them all the time.

HENRY ROJELIO, DAY FOUR

Arriving home from my early hours with Miss Robin, I stumbled directly into bed and did not wake up until almost eleven. Despite rising to unresolved career trouble and finding the mailbox holding only the usual solicitations and bills—the Daily Disappointment—I felt the midnight beginning of Henry, Day Four, might turn out to be a gold-star harbinger of things to come. I hadn't the faintest niggling that the whole encounter was more or less than it seemed.

I went to a downtown park for a pickup basketball game, then home for a shower and something canned for lunch. In the middle of the meal, as I was trying to relive certain moments from our "date," I realized I'd left my jacket at Robin's house with my notes about Henry's code and billing records from the Scottsdale ER tucked into the inner pocket. The perfect pretense to call too soon. I caught her by phone just as she was leaving for her meeting with Sally Marquam.

"Hi, you sweet thing," I said.

"Oh. Look, I'm running out the door. You know: The Meeting."

I explained about the jacket.

"Yeah," she said, all business, "it's on the couch."

"If you could bring it with you to the hospital, I can get it then. I've got a four o'clock meeting with those same folks. Actually, though, I'd prefer to take you out to a late dinner after your shift."

"Mmm. I'd love to but I can't. Best thing would be for you to come by and get it sometime. There's a key on top of the outside light on the wall over the front terrace. You walk by the terrace coming to the front door. Just step over the rail."

"When will you be home?"

"Oh, any time. Just come by."

"If I'm letting myself in, what will the neighbors think?"

"They would call the police, so you better be quick."

"Should I have waited a day or two before asking for a date? You know, be a little harder to get?"

She laughed. "I'd have been heartbroken."

"But you might have said yes."

There was a pause. "Call me soon." She hung up.

From that inauspicious start, Day Four really went south.

At three-thirty I drove back out to Glory, moderately deflated over Robin's deflection of my date request, trying to reinflate myself by imagining her acceptance of the next invitation and where that might lead.

Glory was an odd town. It sprang from nothingness in the 1880s as the hub for the three copper mines in the nearby mountains. When the ore ran thin, though, the only things the mine companies left behind were tailings—mountainous piles of ugly, sterile dirt and rock, as if whale-sized moles had run amok. The town shriveled.

Glory was resuscitated a decade before my arrival. Ultra-cheap land just over the hills from Phoenician sprawl and a developer's whispered-to-be-corrupt permission to tap into a cross-desert water conduit had turned the key. Laws were ignored. Fortunes were made.

With putting greens green, tennis courts hosed off, and swimming pools sufficiently chilled, the "culture" of leisure moved in on top of the old tailings. My patient population there was a mix of the over-sunned, over-jeweled wives of the over-leisured, concerned about the pain and swelling under the new face-lift, and farm workers who brought to the ER their sore throats and sore backs because they had no other doctor to see.

Ten minutes late for my appointment with Sally Marquam, I pilfered a cookie and coffee from the doctors' lounge. I thought I was going there for a friendly review of a bad case. Even when outcomes are horrible, all the participants usually line up on the same side. As I searched out the administrative wing I asked myself how Dad would handle this. He would stand erect, speak carefully and accurately, disparage no one, and invariably be right. Being old school, he would also be better dressed than I was.

From the first open door I passed, a female voice called, "Come in, Dr. Ishmail. Please have a seat. I'll let her know you're here." Evidently the woman was Ms. Marquam's assistant. I did not know her, though she seemed to know me. She said, "I'm Valerie."

I sat in her anteroom. "Hi. I'm Malcolm." I smiled weakly in her direction. She was young, busty, and blonde with impossibly long fingernails painted meat red to match her earrings and necklace. She smiled back. I rubbed my eyes, then spread an arm in each direction along the back of the couch and rested my head backward against a concrete planter. With my vision contained on either side by a small palm plant, I closed my eyes, trying to conjure a vision of Robin's breasts, ignoring the silicone.

"Are you asleep?" There was a pause, then again, "Are you asleep, Dr. Ishmail?"

I saw ceiling and palms, just as before, blinked a few times, then lifted my dead-weight head. Through the blur I could see standing sideways in front of me a female, half bent over at the waist, one hand still pointing to where she had touched my knee to waken me.

"I guess I must have dozed off," I said as I pulled my arms into my lap and stretched my neck to either side. "Too many long nights lately."

"So I understand. Please step this way, into my office. I'm sorry to have kept you waiting," she said over her shoulder.

The office door said "S. J. Marquam, Vice-President."

"I don't want to be curt, but they've had me booked rather tight all day. I've still got a lot of people to see—please go on in and sit down—mostly about this incident of the other night." She called to her assistant.

I sat in an armchair by the only window. With my eyeballs clear I got a better look: Ms. Marquam was probably in her early thirties, just under six feet, trim, wearing lightweight flannel and gold-rimmed eyeglasses and good-looking in a handsome way. Valerie, as her backup, sat cross-legged, notepad in hand.

Ms. Marquam laid out the objective—get it down in detail while memories were freshest. She said, "Sometimes something like this will generate a lawsuit years after the fact, and it's best to have as much detail written down as possible."

"Yes, and whatever I say can and will be used against me," I said.

"Actually, not so. This is done as part of the hospital's quality assurance process and is protected under state statute from discovery in court. The law protects formal quality improvement work from being used in lawsuits. They made it that way to encourage people like us to speak freely when problems arise." She looked at me. "You will speak freely?"

"Of course. There isn't anything to hide. Nobody did anything wrong. There wasn't any malpractice."

"I'm sure that's true, but that does not prevent lawsuits. We may need to prove it, in other words. Why don't you just tell us what happened, in narrative, then we can go back over specific issues."

I sat back in the big chair and closed my eyes. I was tired. "Henry Rojelio. Thirteen-year-old kid. Apparently crazy, but probably pretty normal physiologically—except for his asthma. Came in with a wheeze. Doesn't seem to want to use his inhalers. Apparently prefers the ER. Some people like ERs. Dad brought him in, dropped him off, disappeared."

Sally began to interrupt me but stopped herself. She took a sheet of paper from Valerie's pad and scribbled something, then nodded to me.

I went on to detail my encounter with Henry and his crooked penis and our one go-round with a neb. "He told Robin he wanted sub-Q epi. He seemed to think that was what he had come in for, and he seemed to know all the rest was a waste of time. She suggested we jump to that. I mean, we could have tried more nebs or continuous nebs or changed to a different drug in the inhaler, but they all do pretty much the same thing. I checked his chart. He'd gotten good results with epi each of the two visits I checked on, so it seemed like a good idea to sort of jump to the end, especially if we knew it worked and he had tolerated it well before."

Sally wrote again. Then she said, "Go on."

"I told her to go ahead."

"Who?"

"The nurse. Robin."

"Did you write it out? The order?"

"No, I don't think I did. Verbal order." She wrote again. "I think I was on the phone." I waited. She looked up. I went on. "Next thing I know, Robin says he's turning blue, and all hell broke loose."

Another pause. "That's it?"

"Pretty much."

"Could you explain about the code?"

"Well, not much to explain. He was in full arrest—we ran a code. Took a while but we got him back."

"You thought things went pretty well?"

I hesitated. "I guess you can't say things ever go well at a code. That would be like saying you had a really nice funeral. But the procedural stuff went okay. They got a line right away. The drugs went in. I got him intubated." I waited, but they were just looking at me. "He eventually responded. In fact, we were about to quit. It had gone on too long. We tried one last round of drugs and that time they worked." She reached over toward Valerie, who handed her several photocopies in a stack. She flipped two pages.

"Doctor, these are copies of the ER record and the code sheet. The originals, of course, are in the locked file." I nodded. "The nurse's notes on the code sheet are fairly unremarkable. Who was the recording nurse again?" she asked Valerie.

"Dianne Tonneson."

"Right. Miss Tonneson wrote in times and drugs and over here in the Comments column in several places she wrote 'EKG—asystole,' then 'EKG—fib,' then 'shock times two,' then 'sinus tach.' That sort of thing." She handed me the copies. "Look that over and see if that's how you remember it."

I read the drugs, times, comments. I shrugged. "It seems right. I mean, that's why we have someone at codes who does nothing but take notes. You can't remember all the details afterward."

"I'm sure." She leaned forward and pointed to the bottom of the page with her pen. "Read the next page."

I flipped it over. Stapled to the code sheet was a copy of a note originally entered on a blank page as an "Addendum to Code Sheet." The date was identical, but the time would have been an hour or so after Henry's ambulance had left Glory. It was in a different hand from the notes of the recording nurse. Heavier. Swirly and loopy. "Informed Dr. Ishmail of arrest at 2055. Slow to respond. In face of cyanotic patient appeared uncertain how to proceed. I suggested Code 99. Dr. Ishmail had trouble intubating patient. Refused DC countershock. Note also, he ignored my question during asthma treatment about advisability of epinephrine in boy already on Ritalin. R.B."

I felt my face burning. I felt what was left of my career being skewered. I felt like the flesh was falling off my bones. I closed my eyes. I tilted my head toward the ceiling.

When I opened my eyes Sally was watching me. She said, "The initials R.B. refer to Robin Benoit, the nurse who was caring for Henry. That was her chart entry, her writing, her initials." I stared. "I think you can see why I need your version of the events in greater detail," she said.

I leaned forward, breathing heavily, struggling to restrain myself. I closed and opened my hands and bit my lip, replaying our night, looking for clues. I loosened my jaw barely enough to speak. "No one writes that in a patient chart. No one. I mean, it's an engraved invitation to a lawyer to take your firstborn son." They stared at me. "Christ, I've known of doctors practically killing people and no one will even talk about it, much less put it in writing. Forget about putting it in a legal document."

"I am sorry to have to go through this with you, Dr. Ishmail, but it is for your protection as well as the hospital's. Who is your malpractice carrier?"

"Um, Twentieth Century Casualty, I think. It's through the ER group." She was calming me by getting me back to answerable questions.

"You'll probably want to contact them soon and get them involved, too. I imagine they'll want you to create a report just like this one, but they probably have a specific form you would need to put it in, like a letter to an attorney."

"Yes, I'd better be calling them."

"But let us try to get your accounting of the code."

"Absolutely."

"She writes first that you were slow to respond."

"Oh Jesus," I said. I took a deep breath. "That could mean anything. If I saw that in a chart I would probably figure the doc was on the golf course or getting laid in the call room and ambled in an hour after the call."

"That might be one version."

"I was sitting right there. At the charting desk in the ER." My voice was rising, so I took another breath. "I think I was on the phone," I said, "and I may have been skeptical about her report, but I essentially got right up and went to the patient."

"Essentially?"

"I was on the phone. I probably said, 'Gotta go.' I looked for my stethoscope. I *essentially* ran right in."

"Why, if you had to guess, would she have written that you were slow to respond?"

I was silent. All I could think of was a conceit I had been taught about the diagnostic skills of nurses. When I was a junior medical student just beginning my clinical rotations, Cheryl Hemminger had passed down, in didactic format no less, a bit of wisdom I thought at the time to be rather chauvinistic. As Chief Resident of the medical service, hers was a mountainlike enlightenment that seemed lifetimes beyond us. She chided me once for relying on a nurse's interpretation of the breath sounds of an old man with emphysema. She said I should rely on my own. "Nurses are many good things," she said, "but they are not trained diagnosticians. You are." I knew I wasn't, yet, but I also knew I wanted to be like Cheryl. I definitely acquired the attitude. It was part of the course.

I said, "I have no idea why she would have written that." I also thought to myself, *And I'm thinking seriously of giving up women.*

"What do you mean you were 'skeptical about her report'?"

"She said the kid was turning blue. It seemed so ludicrous I'm sure I thought she was wrong. I maybe made a face."

She paused. "How long would you say it was between the instant she came to get you and you got to the patient?"

I thought. "Ten seconds. Fifteen max."

"You had been on the phone. Do you remember who you were talking to?"

"Does it matter?"

She shrugged. "Whoever it was might be able to corroborate how quickly you got off the phone. That's the kind of thing that may not seem important now but could be later."

"It was a friend. An an ex-girlfriend, actually. Shelley Batista, a nurse at Maricopa."

"Could we contact her?"

"I imagine."

"Do you remember what you were talking about?"

"Her ex-husband. She was telling me what a 'dickhead' he was, still wanting to see her."

"If it's too personal . . ."

"And her periods." I was emotionally flailing. "Problems with heavy flow, and days of cramps . . ."

She cut me off. "Dr. Ishmail, I understand your being upset about all this. Any of us would be. The only reason to ask to reconstruct the conversation here is to be able to refresh her memory later. If she doesn't remember the specific instance of talking to you that evening, I could say, 'You were talking about your ex-husband the dickhead and some problems with your periods and at some point in that conversation the ER nurse apparently interrupted to say that a boy was turning blue. Do you remember that? And then about how long was it until Dr. Ishmail hung up?' Do you see?"

I laughed a little. "Yeah, I suppose that might tweak her memory."

"Apparently this Miss Batista and I could have quite a conversation. I believe 'dickhead' is the universal term for ex-husbands."

I smiled. "Wouldn't know."

"Trust me."

"All right, this delay, alleged delay, was fifteen seconds max. Half of which was spent getting from point A to point B. What else am I accused of?"

"She wrote, 'I suggested Code 99.' "

"Well, I guess maybe she did. So what? It's not like I was looking around wondering what to do. That's the implication here, isn't it? That I had no idea what to do? I was assessing the patient, trying to decide the proper course of action. She could have suggested high-dose vitamin C and a coffee enema. She could have suggested we skip out for a drink. I'd like to think I would have decided that a code was the better choice."

"Again, it will seem from what she wrote that there was an inordinate delay."

"There wasn't."

"Again, how long would you estimate? How long did you take to assess the patient and decide the proper course of action?"

I took a deep breath. "It always seems longer than it really is. I guess it would have appeared that I was standing and looking for ten or fifteen seconds again. But I was feeling for breathing, feeling for a pulse. To anyone else it might look like you're just standing there."

"Were you doing anything? I mean, physically. Moving in any way? Anything that another person could have seen? Something besides thinking."

"Well, little things with my hands. To feel for a breath you put the back of your hand under the nose, but then you stand really still. The unwashed of the world may not see what you're doing. Really, I was maybe praying or cursing to myself."

"Then what? I mean, what did you do?"

I shrugged a little. "She asked if he was breathing. He wasn't."

"And what did you do then?"

"What did I do then? I did mouth-to-mouth breathing. I put my mouth on the boy and blew, just like they teach in CPR."

"Wasn't there some kind of apparatus there in the ER?"

"It wasn't there. We got to that when the RT got there and found us one. But he needed a couple of breaths. I was there. I breathed for him."

"It was not there? You looked?"

"There was a piece of tape hanging on the wall where it normally lives. No breathing bag. I looked rather hard. I expected to find mouth-to-mouth unpleasant, and I was right."

She frowned at Valerie, who nodded that she had indeed gotten that down. Someone in the ER would be hearing about reloading supplies.

She turned back to me. "When did you call the Code Blue, or Code 99, or whatever?"

"Code Blue. At least, west of the Rockies. I think Code 99 is an East Coast thing."

"Okay. Code Blue."

"Calling a code is like calling an army. You get four times as many people as you need. You might need a big response, in theory. But you don't want to call for one if you're not sure. Besides your looking like a jackass, you've taken a lot of people in the hospital away from other work, some of which might actually be important to other patients. And you've called wolf. Next time they walk slower. Time after that a few don't show up at all."

"So you delayed?"

"No I did not delay. I was assessing. He needed basic CPR first. Calling a code is not the first step. Basic resuscitation is."

"Okay," she said, "but, again, time frame, if you can. How long did you do basic resuscitation before calling the code?"

"Less than sixty seconds. He didn't have a pulse, he did not get a pulse right back, so we called the army."

"And the rest . . ."

"The rest, I guess, is what's on the Code Sheet. Continuous CPR. An IV. Drugs. Blood to the lab. Intubation. EKG strips. Drugs. All the usual shit. We were about to quit, like I said, but that 'one more time' seems to have worked. At least for his heart."

Sally drew a deep breath, then asked her assistant for "the report." She plopped on the desk a stapled stack of several sheets, the top one a hospital form of some type.

"I'm afraid it gets worse. This is Robin Benoit's full report," she said. "Formally, it is an incident report—that's the form on top—but she attached a two-page narrative. She gave it to me at our earlier meeting. It is, I'm afraid, very damning of you, your management of the emergency and all."

I began to read, but she continued, "I made notes of the main points. Some of it brings up the earlier . . . allegations, but in more detail. If I may . . ."

"Go ahead," I waved my hand.

"Robin begins by saying she hardly knows you, being here only a month and a half, but she had several concerns about Henry Rojelio's care and, especially considering the bad outcome so far, she felt compelled to make a report."

I closed my eyes and nodded, wondering how I had managed to end up in bed with another pathological liar.

"The first item of concern is this 'apparent reluctance' on your part to respond. . . . We already addressed that, but if you have anything to add . . ."

I shook my head.

"She repeats that you were—quoting—'very slow to comprehend the situation and, even scarier, slow to think of what to do.' She goes on, 'At one point I actually had to point out to Dr. Ishmail that the patient was not breathing.' " She looked at me.

I looked back. "We've covered that, too. I was assessing. I made conclusions. I began treatment. What else?"

She gave me a long look, then returned to her notes. "She described you as hesitant and unsure of protocols in running the code."

I shook my head but made no other response.

"Could you respond to that, please?" she said.

I bit my lip. "Protocols are written to take thinking and decision making out of the loop in a crisis. They are not an end in themselves. I know enough from the protocols to help me make decisions. The nurses wanted to give certain things, I guess because they've been told 'we always give them.' Narcotic reversal to treat overdoses. Glucose to treat hypoglycemia. I hesitated. I said, 'Okay, if you want to,' knowing they were just a waste of time. It was clear that kid was not OD'd on heroin or insulin. Then one of them suggested a high-dose epinephrine regimen she had just read about. It's new. She knew about it, I didn't. We adapted the dose to his size and gave it a shot. That seems more like good teamwork to me."

She nodded, then looked at Valerie, who nodded to signify she had recorded my explanation. Sally said, "She says you failed in your first two attempts at tracheal intubation, at one point dropping the laryngoscope on the floor. Then picking it up and reusing it without washing it or calling for a new—"

That was it. I blew: "That's just fucking beautiful," I said loudly to the ceiling. They were silent. "It's a perfect example—one sees the glass half full—the other . . . goes and pisses in it. In a high-stress, literally life-and-death situation . . . Can you imagine if the parents saw that?"

"They shouldn't be able to," Sally said.

"Well, I should certainly hope not. You know, two people watching that entire code—one could walk out to the parents and say, 'Dr. Ishmail is such a putz. He nearly blew the intubation and your son would have died.' And the second could walk out and say, 'Dr. Ishmail saved your son's life.' And you know what? They'd both be right."

Sally took a deep breath. I realized I was bouncing in my chair, so I consciously stilled myself, then looked up. "What else?"

"She claims you made several derogatory comments about the boy, referring to him as a 'loser' and a 'future slimeball of America.' She says the nursing team ultimately instituted a protocol of high-dose epinephrine, which you had apparently never heard of, and it was this that brought back his heart. You addressed that . . ." She flipped her note page.

"In the final paragraph she says she still wonders if the whole event might not have been avoided if you had not insisted on giving the epinephrine. She says she asked you if that might be not a good idea in a patient on such a high does of Ritalin, but you told her not to worry." A long pause.

"Is that it?" I asked, eyes closed.

"Yes."

I scooted back in the chair and leaned forward onto my knees. "And what becomes of this report?" I asked. "I mean, it's obviously damning. It's totally false. I feel like throwing up, like I've been kicked in the kidneys. I have to know, though, to whom or I guess in what form I have to respond."

"For now, to me," she said. "It is my job to investigate all serious or potentially serious incidents and allegations."

"But then what?" I said. "I mean, I suppose my job here is on the line, but you don't—no disrespect intended—you don't have that final authority."

"No, that's true. But I am required to report immediately to the Executive Committee any situations I believe should be dealt with immediately."

"Who is on the Executive Committee?"

"Jerry Schteichen, the CEO, Stu Bernhard, the President of the Board, and Morris Cunningham, the President of the Medical Staff."

"When does the full board next meet?" I asked.

"This needs to be dealt with immediately, Doctor. I know you're scheduled to work most of next week. As you know, you were taken on here on a conditional basis. Your credentials are not sterling and it will not take much for the medical staff officers and the board to terminate the arrangement."

"So, I give you my response right now? She takes notes? This is it? Judge, jury?"

"We're just trying to find out what happened. Any actions will only be taken based on what happened."

"Lovely," I mumbled. I straightened up. "Okay, I'll respond. But I want the notes to say, too, that I don't think this process is fair. At all. I was invited here to discuss the events and make mutual notes. Now I am to answer charges. I should have time to give a more complete, better-prepared response. I mean, I want the right to add, to change, later."

"So noted." Sally nodded to Valerie, who just went on scribbling as fast as she could.

"Jesus, where to begin . . . One," I ticked my finger, "Ritalin. She never said a word to me about Ritalin. I don't think I ever knew he was on it. You should check my chart notes . . ."

"They're there," Ms. Marquam said, pointing to the stapled stack.

"Well, you check them. Believe me, I write thorough notes. If Ritalin came up I would have mentioned it."

"Shouldn't you have known all his meds?"

"I'm sure I did. That is, I'm sure I checked. He's a pretty disturbed adolescent and he may not have told me everything. His parents weren't there. Ms. Benoit *never* said a word about it to me. More important, though, it would not have made a twig of difference. Not one iota. If a kid's asthma is bad enough to need sub-Q epi, he gets it with or without Ritalin. For that matter Ritalin and epinephrine are chemically related. In one sense Ritalin might do some of the same things. In any case, I've never heard of that as a contraindication, but if I had more time I could research that for you. But I do know for sure breathing comes first, and asthma, when severe, is a state of not . . . fucking . . . breathing."

I paused to catch my breath. "Two. The shot. I never insisted on giving him anything. He apparently has needed epi before, got good results, and now both he and the staff think that's what he needs. He has no patience for inhalers. Probably why he's always in the ER, won't use them at home, either. So, in truth, Robin came to me asking for an order for sub-Q epi. She told me that's what it had taken before, that in fact he *wanted* a shot, and being as weird as he was, we're all better off if he's home from the ER."

"Why do you say he's weird?"

"Her words. Not mine."

"Was he weird to you?"

"Well, exhibitionism at thirteen, pseudo-seizure syndrome, and he apparently likes getting needles."

"Do you think this supposed weirdness got in the way of his getting good care?"

"Oh Jesus! He got excellent care."

She was staring at me.

I took a deep breath. "The facts now: Subcutaneous epinephrine is still the best, most immediate, most effective treatment for an acute exacerbation of asthma. Sure, we'd rather get it under control with lesser treatments, but when you don't have time, because the kid's too sick, or reason to think the lesser treatments are not likely to work, as in Henry's prior ER visits, it is perfectly acceptable to 'jump,' if you will, straight to the gold-standard treatment. So, no, I'd say Henry got excellent care, despite his 'weirdness.' "

"Tell me about pseudo-seizure syndrome."

I recounted what I had read about the intractable course and progressive nature of the disease. When I ended with the predictability of early death, Sally Marquam sat staring blankly. Finally Valerie leaned over and pointed to something in Ms. Marquam's notes. She looked up. "What about the names?"

"The what?"

"Slimeball, loser . . ."

"I did not ever use those words about Henry. Actually I kind of felt bad for him even while I was trying to treat his asthma. He seemed neglected. God knows names like those are pretty common in ERs, especially with patients who seem to live there. Maybe she figured I must have used them. One of your nurses used the term 'loser.' ERs are the last refuge for people with inadequate personalities, and we all get pretty jaded. But like I said, I don't think I used those terms about Henry."

She was again still. Again Valerie pointed to something in Sally's notes, but she shook her head. After a few seconds Marquam asked, "Why do you think it happened?"

"I really don't know. There's a long list of physiologic events that can give kids sudden dying spells: laryngospasm, bronchospasm. Epiglottitis for crissakes. Unfortunately it's all guessing. We have no evidence, no data. Not a single physiologic fact we can rely on."

"What about an allergic reaction?"

"No one is allergic to epinephrine. It's the body's internal signal for 'red alert.' It jacks up all the control dials to Max. It's a naturally occurring hormone," I said. "Everybody has it. It's probably the same chemical compound from earthworms on up. Hell, we use it to *treat* allergic reactions. Real ones."

"What about the other, the nebulizer?"

"Albuterol is chemically related to epinephrine. Maybe it's possible but I've never heard of an allergic reaction to it. Besides, he's used it a thousand times without problems and got into trouble well after the neb."

She nodded, staring beyond me. There was an odd pause. She suddenly looked at her watch, then said, "It's late. I need to return some calls. I think we've covered what I needed. I will present your explanations to the Executive Board tonight." She rose and gave me her hand to shake. "We'll be in touch. Let's be sure to continue to work together on this. Not make enemies of each other."

"Sure," I said with a hint of sarcasm. Then, despite myself, "As soon as your people quit lying."

Sally Marquam turned stony, then pivoted on her heel and disappeared.

Valerie and I stared at each other. She said quietly, "A reporter's been calling." She rolled her eyes toward her boss. "She promised him she'd call before five."

I mustered a tin smile. "A reporter? Like—news reporter?"

She nodded.

I wanted to die.

15

Four weeks ago I did an odd thing: a nine-to-five work shift. Who would have thought I could do it? Eight hours. We even had a regular lunch hour and a sort of coffee break. The horror, again.

This playing Pandora and peeking into the Box of my past has unsettled me enough that I'm thinking I might be able make some changes, shift the end results a bit. Figuring I was qualified to do "urgent care" kinds of things, I called the woman who runs the family clinic in little Othello, twenty-seven miles due west of Hooker, wondering if they needed any part-time help.

Turns out they were looking to expand their hours. Their doctor, Annie Parrott, knew I had the reputation in the area as the local boy with all the potential. She kindly left out the local intonations about my having blown it along the way. She had heard good things about my ER work. Maybe we could try a couple of midweek days. She sounded pleased. In my shoes it was flattering.

When I met with Annie and the clinic director, Cathy Schendt, I made no bones about my lack of training in primary care. They said half of what they did in the clinic was identical to my ER work. Which was to say that most ER work in a small town is primary care. The rest would be preventive counseling—which most patients would ignore—and long-term management of usually stable conditions like hypertension and diabetes. We all acknowledged I didn't know enough—yet—to be independently functional, but Dr. Parrott would mentor me along. She would work with me side by side for the first few weeks, then be available by phone for an undefined stretch of weekdays if we all wanted to keep up the program.

In the outback of the prairies, full printed credentials apparently aren't necessary if you seem to know basic medicine and have someone to back you up.

Even the first day I had a Case Worth Talking About. Mrs. Jenny Gabrekiewicz, though eighty-three, did not present much of a physiologic *challenge. She came into town from her ranch for—her words—"a little poke and a prod." She said, "I left them boys out there with all them cows, so God awmighty knows what's going on." Then, in anticipation of her pelvic and Pap smear: "Doctor—hell, you ain't old enough to be no doctor—you better get me up on the rack and check the dipstick. And no funny stuff."*

I explained we would do that last; I needed to go in order, top down. As I was looking in her ears she said, "I'm down to one tit, you know. They lopped off the left one some twenty years ago. Hell, you was probably in diapers."

"Naw, I was, let's see, well, it's a good guess I was in school. Now I'm gonna listen to your chest, so don't talk. And take deep breaths, please."

"Aw hell . . ." She waited until I took the stethoscope from my ears.

"You can talk now," I said.

"Good. I hate it when I can't talk."

I smiled at her. "I might have guessed that."

She grinned.

Her exam was entirely unremarkable except for the mastectomy scar. The older operations took most of the underlying muscle, and the deformity and weakness are impressive.

I wrote the prescriptions to refill her medicines. "Guess you're all okay for now. Come back and get your blood pressure checked in a few months."

"You married?"

"Not yet."

"Well, my granddaughter is getting a divorce. Coming up from Colorado Springs next week. Her and the baby. You oughta get on her dance card pretty quick, young man, 'cuz she is a real looker."

I smiled.

HENRY ROJELIO, DAY FOUR (CONTINUED)

From Sally Marquam's meeting-turned-trial, I stormed out of the Glory administrative wing, mouthing silent epithets to myself as I went. As painful as the allegations in Robin's report had been, there were just enough grains of truth underneath to make them extraordinarily dangerous, however false the implications.

Slow to respond? As I said, I may have paused a second or two. Professional machismo à la Cheryl Hemminger. Still, nothing I would want to try to explain to the Glory Powers That Be, nor a jury.

Bungled the intubation? Threw the blade on the floor? Or salvaged a bad situation to save a life? Some invasive procedures go so well they look deceptively easy. The tip of the big needle finding the center of the jugular vein in one light poke while the surgeon is telling a ribald joke. Michael Jordan draining game-winners in the playoffs or Jack Nicklaus knocking a 2-iron pin high. Easy. Some procedures never get accomplished despite great blood, sweat, and tears from all parties. Most are in-between. Maybe the doctor on the Glory Executive Committee would relay that to the others.

Even though there was some risk of my attempting to throttle Robin if I saw her, I thought I could contain myself enough to go ask her what the fuck she was up to. She was to be on duty in the ER. Her shift was less than two hours old and probably not even good and warmed up yet. I found a bathroom and splashed some cold water on my face, then shambled into the back of the ER.

There was no one in sight. I checked the patient log. A seventeen-year-old girl had just come in with a headache. Robin was probably checking her in. I sat at the doctor's desk, folded my arms, closed my eyes, and waited.

"Hey, Malcolm." Adam McEwan, another part-time ER doctor, was walking in.

"Hi, Adam. Keeping things quiet?"

"You know. The usual."

Robin came out of an exam room. She stopped moving and clenched her face down tight as soon as she saw me. We stared at each other. Adam looked from face to face. I said, "Hello, Robin."

She said, "Hello, Dr. Ishmail."

"Is that the way it's going to be?"

She shot me a glare. "Is *what* the way it's going to be?"

I gave Adam a wan smile. To her: "Hot one night? Cold the next?"

"Look, I don't think this is very professional. Coming to bother me when I'm trying to work."

"I didn't come to bother you."

"What did you come for?"

"I'm trying to find out what the hell you think you're doing." My voice was rising. "Why you wrote out those goddamn lies about me. Especially after last night!"

"Last night! You—you practically raped me! You—"

"I what? You practically raped me!"

I looked at Adam, palms upward, offering my incredulity. He looked like he'd really rather be in Philadelphia.

Robin said, "I think you should leave."

I said, "I think you should tell me what you're trying to do to me."

She said, "You leave or I'm calling Security. Right now."

I looked about. I realized that nothing was going to be salvaged from that meeting. "Fine. I'm going. But I'm not through with you. I *will* get an answer." To Adam: "Sorry. Sorry, but watch yourself around her. You can't be sure what she's going to say about you."

I drove back to town, quietly raging in my head. I replayed our night together. The quaint seeds of paranoia Robin had shown before dinner apparently had taken root and grown to full flower: She was going to make the whole debacle my fault before anyone could even accuse her of a mistake.

A light was on in our town house; Mary Ellen was home. Thinking I couldn't show her my sullied self, I got back in my car. Interestingly, in Phoenix all roads lead to the 'Copa, or at least they do on my internal autopilot.

Once in the parking lot, I thought to go up to see Henry. I was still his referring doctor—legitimate enough reason to see how he was faring. In my current mood, though, it seemed the risk of tripping into more trouble, say, offending a priest or a lawyer, should one happen to be there, was far greater than the chance of doing anything that helped anyone's cause, especially Henry's.

Rather than burn gas wearing ruts in the streets or sit in the parking lot staring at my steering wheel, I walked the perimeter of the hospital campus. I watched the night sky for a while. Clouds were blowing through, reflecting the glare of the city back down as they passed.

Lightning flashed in the west and the wind started gusting in circles, whipping sand and dust and trash into my face. I wished it would rain.

I ducked into our old bad habit, The Longhorn, thinking I could avoid potentially painful encounters with old friends by sitting at the bar and keeping my head down. Maybe some food and a beer would help my outlook.

Barely into a *cerveza*, though, I was visited by a ghost of long hours past. Two stools over was a nameless fellow pilgrim, nursing a beer and a shot, sporting a gauze head bandage just beginning to show a medallion of blood over the left ear. Sticking out of his back pocket was a triplicate form I recognized as a Maricopa Emergency X-ray requisition. Apparently he knew from experience the best place to wait out the queue.

Putting my head up long enough to admire the man's situational awareness, though, made me visible. Gene Woods, my former surgery mate, spotted me as he came by from the john. He slapped me on the back and said, "Holy living shit, look who's back. Just couldn't stay away?"

"Oh, you know . . . where else can you fuel up for a week at a time?"

"C'mon to the table, man."

"Oh, I don't think I—"

"Aw bullshit. Anybody survived internship is a life member. C'mon."

I trailed Gene to the back and joined a half dozen of the regulars. They were eating the usual combination plates oozing enough oil to heat a small home for a night. I picked at some chips and salsa.

Being back among the brethren felt surreal, despite the baseline bonhomie apparently carrying over from year to year. Ed Bonderant, a senior resident in Family Practice, was imitating his physiology professor from med school in Seattle. Ed was a local hero: Stories abounded about his ability to maintain an amused equanimity in the face of the worst hospital firestorms: rampaging residents passing shit down the totem pole, cirrhotics hemorrhaging simultaneously from both ends of the alimentary canal, and physically combative psychiatric patients being carried to rubber rooms by mass assemblages of doctors, nurses, and students. Ed credited both his meditation practice and having grown up in a large and dysfunctional family. His vision of medicine was holistic, especially primary care: Western pills liberally spiced with bits of Oriental philosophy selected strictly on the basis of what he liked. That evening it occurred to me I should study his ways.

Ed had his head tilted back so he was looking down his nose. He wagged his index finger in random arcs, saying with tunnel-mouthed diction, "Ah, um, would you explain, um, to us, for us, for all of us, here assembled, the 'Bonderant-Altoona reflex,' um?"

Alex Bass, an Internal Medicine resident, said, "That's William F. Buckley, Jr."

Emily, Ed's wife and apparent soul mate from several previous lives, if that's karmically allowed, said, "No, that's Dr. Porter. We had him *forever* during first year. Ed has him *down*." Ed and Emily had been classmates in medical school. The story went that they had fallen into bed together during their orientation and taken up a new version of tantric love: They *never* separated, except for work. They married just before third year.

Emily was in her third and final year of Pediatrics, and had decided to sign on for two years of Pediatric Oncology. Anyone who can do Kids-with-Cancer—about as depressing as medicine can get—has the unspoken awe of the rest of us. She was also an adventurous and studious cook who enjoyed doing up big meals for weekend gatherings. She had a broad bosom and long dark hair. Part gypsy, part Madonna. Having the thing closest to a home and hearth that any of us could see, Ed and Emily became sometime parent surrogates for any of the tribe prone to shifting living situations and occasional heartbreaks.

"Okay, I'll bite," Gene said. "What's the Bonderant-Altoona reflex?"

Emily said, "First, you have to know that Altoona is my maiden name."

"Oh, this will be good," Gene said. "Something sexual, for sure."

Ed, changing his adopted speech style to East Indian, said, "Ho, Nho, nuh-ting like daht. Nho. Nho sex. Never."

"Okay, what then?"

He said, "Schtooping," rolling a Yiddish lexicon into his Indian accent. "Yahh."

Emily said, "Ed says his blood pressure and pulse are lower after sleeping with me than after sleeping alone . . ."

This brought hoots.

"No, wait, not after sex . . ."

"Schtooping, yahh," Ed said.

"No! Not that. Just sleeping together. Even if we sleep in the call room at the 'Copa."

"You have sex in the call room?" someone said.

"No," Emily said.

"Nho," Ed said. "Nho sex. Schtooping." His grin was pure Cheshire Cat.

Emily said, "Not in the call room!" A pause. "Well, not often. Anyway, Ed says it's unhealthy to sleep alone. He says when he's with his 'proper mate' he feels some kind of brain waves that—"

"Hippocampal-septal slow waves," he put in, in his Dr. Porter–William F. Buckley, Jr., persona.

"Right," she said. "Like maybe sex is not the basis of the pair bond. It's the brain waves."

"No. It's schtooping," Gene said. They all laughed.

Gene said, "So you guys will live to a hundred and eight with pair-bonded slow waves. The rest of us will be dead at forty."

I thought of my personal litany. It was going from bad to hideous: Aborted residency. Career hinging on improbable appeals to unsympathetic academics. Robin, what I had for a love interest, now the acute salt in a chronic sore. A neo-nemesis. A walking, talking, kissing, cock-sucking, internal contradiction. Any warm glow I might have kindled from our night together had been put out cold.

The conversation around me had suddenly stopped. I realized they were all looking at me. I raised my eyebrows. Ed said, "How 'bout it, Malc? Surely you got a significant woman hidden away somewhere?"

I laughed. "Yeah. A couple of 'em, in fact."

Emily said, "What do you think, Ed? Medically Arrested Development?"

"Yhess! Egzellent!"

"What?" came a chorus.

Emily said, "Ed's into creative diagnoses. He calls this one 'MAD.' It's a common condition."

Ed, as Dr. Porter, said, "The cost of becoming a doctor, it is often said, is your twenties. Some, um, would say the prime decade. So. Simple math. Lose ten years. Thirty-year-old doctors acting like, um, twenty-year-olds. Arrested development."

"We're collecting lots of data," Emily said. "Most of our friends. Ed's going to write up an article and send it to *The New England Journal of Medicine*."

"Great," I said to Ed. "We'll all be over to your clinic in the morning to get registered. Get our IDs and our pictures taken."

Gene said, "Great. Yeah, I want to be a case study. My fifteen minutes of fame and I'll have to be photographed in front of one of those measuring grids, naked, with a black rectangle covering my eyes."

Alex said, "You know, I think my mom suspects I've got a character flaw. Maybe having a diagnosis will help. You know, I can say, 'Oh, it's just my MAD acting up again.' "

Emily said to me, "Malc, I don't think you're a textbook case, though. I think you're in love with your roommate but won't admit it to yourself."

I said, "Nah. My roommate isn't all that interested in philandering ex-doctors with no prospects."

She said, "You're not an *ex*-doctor. And maybe you have to give up the philandering first."

"She knows me like she knows how to manage kids with diarrhea. And I'm not going to walk the straight and narrow for its own sake. You need a reason."

"Like that slogan from the sixties," Ed said. "'Chastity is its own punishment.' " He held up his hands. "Personally, though, I wouldn't know." He grinned.

The salt was stinging in my open sore. Robin was all dichotomy. While my personal radar told me she was on my side, the printed materials called me a fool. She—at least one side of her—still owed me a huge explanation. Despite the halfhearted mutual defense alliance between Sally Marquam and me, I was clearly the one standing on the trapdoor. And with my earlier performance in confronting Robin inside the Glory Hospital, I was likely as good as gone.

Still, even more than I needed that job, I needed at least a passable reputation. If I wanted to overturn Robin's portrayal of me, I needed some idea why she'd made it. I had little to lose by trying again, presuming I could stay out of another *mano a mano* inside the walls of the Glory ER. Maybe I could still get something sensible from her. Or at least something I could use.

I made an excuse to the Oval Table and drove back out to Glory.

The nursing shifts were due to change, so I waited in my parked car. I saw the night nurse go inside. Twenty minutes later Patty Kucera came out and headed for her car.

I rolled down my window and called a hello.

She walked over but eyed me suspiciously. She said, "Hey, Doc."

"Is Robin around? I thought she was supposed to be on."

"She was, but she had to go home after a couple'a hours. She was feeling sick. Cramps and nausea. They called me in."

"That's too bad."

"Yeah, she looked pretty bad. Claimed it was her period, but I think she's pretty stressed, what with that kid coding on her the other night and now all the questions. I heard your date might not'a gone so well, either."

"Actually, we had a nice time."

"Uh-huh. Anyways, I told her to get some rest."

"Did she go home?"

"Well, I hope she did. She better have. I gave up a night off."

"You don't have her address, do you? I really need to talk to her, and I could see if she needs anything."

"No. I don't."

"Well, I can probably find her house again. She drove me there last night."

"Yeah. If you find her, tell her I hope she's okay."

"Yeah, I will."

She turned to go, but turned back. "You know," she said, locking together the fingers of both hands and stretching her wrists, "my arms got really sore from all the CPR the other night."

I smiled, but she wasn't joking. I said, "Well, maybe if you get more practice . . ."

She smiled back.

With only a few wrong turns and several lucky guesses, I found Robin's house. The neighborhood was shut down, though a late-night dog-walker passed as I got out of my car. Her house was totally dark. I knocked at her door, waited, called her name and knocked again. No answer.

I backtracked from her door. Her key was just where she had promised. I went in quickly and quietly, shut the door behind me, then called her name again.

I had a sudden creepy feeling to watch behind myself for clubs, knives, and guns, but that was silly. So far I'd been attacked only with a pen. I was also nervous about neighbors and maybe the police, but I reminded myself I had a legitimate reason to be there and, for that matter, an invitation.

Still, I didn't want company. I waited a minute for my eyes to accommodate, then edged my way from the entry to the kitchen. I called her name again. I turned and bumped something, creating a crash behind me as the metal salad bowl and a wineglass hit the floor, the glass shattering. I said, "Oh fuck," and groped for the light switches.

With the place lit I made rounds. Her bed was not only empty, it was neatly made. She was not in the bathroom, not asleep on the couch, not in the house, period. In fact I found no jacket on her couch, as she had promised. Nor was it in the kitchen, nor the bedroom.

I bent to the mess, picking up the larger shards, being careful not to cut a finger as I did so. I found a broom and dustpan and cleaned up the broken glass, but even after sweeping up I made no move to leave. My quest for explanations had created only more mystery.

The kitchen was only partly cleaned from our supper: dirty dishes in the sink, the wok still on the stove, the empty wine bottle next to it. I checked the refrigerator: half a carton of milk, bread, cheese, a brown banana, most of another bottle of white wine. There was little on the counters: sections of the *Arizona Republic,* half a glass of water, a blank scratch pad by the phone. The cupboards held a predictable array of dishes, glasses, pots, and pans. It all looked as if the owner was due back any minute.

Her bedroom gave the same impression: a bath towel in a heap on the floor, beside it a pair of slacks. In the dresser were socks and panties in one drawer, sweaters and jeans in others. I found a few blouses and dresses hanging in the closet. The bookcase was still full of books, neatly arranged by size. There was a gap, though, where her "toy box" had been.

I sat at the kitchen bar where we had eaten. It flashed in my mind to call Mary Ellen, see if she had any ideas. That was a laugh. What would I tell her? My latest choice of lover had, after our first sexual encounter, declined my request for a second date, dumped on me at work, then left home, sex toys and contraceptives in tow? I could just imagine the chuckling "Hey, Don Juan" that would bring.

I stared at the phone. It seemed contaminated. Maybe there was some kind of evidence there. Fingerprints. A secret phone number. Memory of clandestine conversations.

I told myself I was being superstitious. Beyond the fingerprints none of that was possible. I got a napkin and picked up the receiver. For the full duration of the dial tone I stared at the keypad. A recording came on: "If you'd like to make a call, please hang up . . ." I looked at the "Program" and "Redial" buttons. I interrupted the whining voice by pressing the receiving cradle, got a fresh dial tone, and pressed "Redial." The phone spat out its quasi-musical notes, then the tone of a phone ringing. A woman's voice: "Providence of Glory Hospital. How may I help you?"

"Who is this?" I asked.

"This is the hospital operator. How may I help you?"

"I'm afraid I have the wrong number." I hung up.

I played with the "Program" button, too, but all I got regardless of sequence or digits was a dial tone.

My eye fell on the notepad there. Though the top sheet was blank, it was imprinted with the image of widely looping handwriting I recognized as Robin's. I found a pencil. Laying it nearly flat, I swept a light layer of graphite over the scratches. A phone number emerged.

I mentally rehearsed another "Sorry, wrong number," and punched in the number.

The same woman's voice: "Providence of Glory Hospital. How may I help you?"

"Oop. Sorry. Me again."

"Better check that number."

"Right. I will. Sorry."

I wanted a shot of Scotch but settled for a glass of wine from the refrigerator. I handled the bottle through my napkin and figured I'd take the glass with me. Whatever Robin was up to, professionally and socially, did not include me, at least not on her side.

Papers, I thought. I checked every wastebasket I could find. They were all empty. I returned to the drawer nearest the phone. Piece by piece I went through perhaps twenty scraps and notes and found nothing.

I went back to the bedroom. There was no wastebasket, but in the drawer in Robin's nightstand I found a page of hospital chart paper. The top was stamped with a patient imprint whose name I did not recognize. I examined it at an angle to the light, looking for impressions, but there were none.

I poured a dash more wine and sat. I wondered where help might be had.

I came up blank.

I closed all the drawers and doors, killed the lights, and tripped on out. I put the key back in its wide-open hiding place.

Driving home to the heart of Phoenix, I realized I still had no explanation for Robin's blind-side assault on my handling of Henry Rojelio. Henry's dying in the ICU was an ever-ready reminder that maybe after all I truly had fucked up the case. I have learned very well that each of us is blindest to his own defects. Still, every time I ran through the decision-making tree for Henry's care, it came out the same way.

I took to bed two distractions: a Hemingway book I was limping through and another glass of wine.

16

Three weeks ago in Othello I met Fred Sommers. Fred came to the clinic under protest. A neighbor virtually dragged him in. The neighbor recognized shortness of breath, involuntary weight loss, and coughing up blood as fearful things.

Fred looked bad, but his chest X-ray pretty much told the story: A lemon-sized mass of something bad was growing just to the right of his heart. It had choked off most airflow to the bottom half of the right lung. When lung lobules don't get air certain bad bacteria run rampant. These isolated parts of the lung were socked in with pneumonia. The combined inflammatory effects of infection and cancer had stimulated his chest to fill with fluid.

When I gave Fred the news he merely nodded. He was willing to acknowledge that it hurt, but mostly he wanted to get back to his farm. His kids were at the neighbor's and he didn't like the imposition. His wife had left him five years earlier. His kids needed him.

I convinced him, with help and promises from his neighbor, to stay with us for a little while. He did allow that the oxygen I had running to his nose seemed to make his breathing easier.

Once we had all the culture specimens in the lab, I got an IV going, ordered the right antibiotics, and called Annie Parrott to get her input. I figured Fred needed some high-end oncology help in Lincoln or Denver. She concurred and said she knew just the person to call. While she made arrangements I put on gloves, washed and anesthetized the back side of Fred's chest, stuck him with some big needles, and drained off a liter and a half of blood-flecked fluid that looked like moldy maple syrup. He took a deeper breath and thanked me.

Fred went that night by ambulance to Lincoln. I heard no more until Annie called me last night. She said the pathologist called the biopsy so "anaplastic"—a descriptor for malignant cells that connotes a raw, primitive origin, usually fast-growing and highly refractive to treatment—that he was unable to classify the cancer. Treatment would have to be by "best guess."

Thoughts of a cure were zero. The oncology team hoped only to shrink the tumor enough to clear out the pneumonia and get Fred home to see his kids. They hit it with industrial-strength radiation. And nothing happened. The tumor kept growing.

Fred got sicker by the day and died nine days after I had seen him. He was fifty-one.

The Hooker bank has a little fund going for the kids. I wrote a check for about what I made the day I had seen Fred, acutely aware of my insignificance.

HENRY ROJELIO, DAY FIVE

Henry, Day Five, had a painful beginning. Anxiety and anger had churned my dream loop into a froth I hadn't seen since early internship, so at seven o'clock I thought to try prolonging the night's half-sleep by lying in bed with the sheets over my head. It seemed a well-reasoned choice, but I knew I could never pull it off. I'm wired to get up.

I found my bathrobe and banged around the town house, putting away belongings and scrubbing the bathroom with a fury, trying to tell myself as a mantra that the truth would prevail, never mind its no-show at the end of my residency and truancy now.

At 8:02, as I was brushing my teeth, minty white foam dripping from my mouth, the phone rang. I spit and rinsed and ran to grab the handset as the answering machine was kicking in. It was Sally Marquam.

Even at a dink hospital like Providence of Glory, I guess you have to have certain *huevos* to make VP. I'm sure she hated doing it—I would have—but apparently between supper and breakfast she had reported to her Executive Committee, counted the votes—all three—and hardened her stones to call me to tell me the bad news, doing it as if she did it every day. My working privileges at Glory were suspended indefinitely. There would be a full investigation of the ER incident involving Henry Rojelio. Fourteen days hence they would all have a meeting. I was invited, for the second half only.

Sally Marquam was all desiccated professionalism. I suppose any warmth would have been shocking and no doubt wasted on a doctor quickly spinning out of her orbital plane.

As I was about to hang up, she added, "And don't talk to any reporters."

I said, "You must be joking."

"I wish I was. We've gotten calls from a reporter from the Phoenix paper. He seems to know some of the details already. Press coverage will not be good." She told me the CEO, already having conniptions over yesterday's announcement of Medicare's latest nonpayment foolishness, had reacted to the prospect of adverse press like the world was ending. The President of the Medical Staff had been more philosophical, saying something about their patients' generally ignoring newspapers. I figured they were both wrong.

She added, "I must also tell you we will not tolerate you harassing any of our staff."

"I was looking for some explanation for your staff's lying about me."

"Whatever you may think, please keep away from Miss Benoit. It will be better for both of you."

I thought, *Yeah. Where were you when that advice might have helped?*

My personal inventory was in free fall: I knew I wasn't just losing a job. A formal termination of privileges at the Glory Hospital would have to be reported to the Arizona Medical Board, which, in my case, could readily metastasize to a loss of my license. If that happened my appeals to residency directors, regardless what state they were in, would be instantly vaporized.

Through an interesting quirk of karmic timing, the day's mail contained a notice that my student loan repayments were to begin in two months. The grace period they allow after one's termination of student status was expiring, and would I please call them at my earliest convenience to discuss repayment plans?

I tried a five-mile run. I churned along the canals that parse out the Salt ex-River into its bluegrass support role, but my legs were pegs and my shoulder seared from stray reminders of its earlier ball of fire. It was more an exercise in frustration than exercise. I think the gods don't grant an endorphin high to one who would shake the firmament of his superiors.

I gulped water back at my town house. I popped a can of Squirt and took it to the shower. I stood bent under the hot spray and breathed the steam and was still. I became aware of my heart slowly hammering under my ribcage.

I thought I should adopt a scientist's approach—analyze and verify whatever evidence I had. My only link with Henry's mysterious event lay in my refrigerator, the epi syringe. It seemed I could begin by getting the contents of the syringe verified. Though I knew it to be grasping at straws, I was indeed drowning and drowning men will do that.

Once dried off, though still not dressed, I noticed that the cut on my hand from my display of disgust during Henry's code had started oozing again. I improvised a fresh bandage as I called Maricopa and asked the operator to connect me to the chemistry lab. I asked the lab woman, "Who would know about ordering a complex chemical analysis of the contents of a syringe?"

She transferred me to a supervisor. He confirmed my fears: Complex analytics get run once a week. It would have to be sent out. To a State of Arizona lab. Three-hundred fifty bucks minimum, considerably more if they have to analyze "unknowns." For billing she would need either the patient's Maricopa Hospital account number or a research account number. And the State Health Division keeps copies of anything and everything medical. I didn't ask if they would accept a postdated check and my jar of pocket change; the thought of having my name on yet another eyebrow-raising piece of paper on another clipboard anywhere within the Health Division was ample deterrence.

Gravity drew me to the 'Copa. I had no particular purpose. I didn't look at a clock. The hour of the day, the day of the week, *schedule*, to me, was nonexistent.

But Mary Ellen Montgomery, my only local confidant, was somewhere there, locked in hand-to-hand combat with all the usual foes—

death, disease, bumbling interns, indifferent professors, and the odd passive-aggressive nurse. She did not and could not, if she were going to respect me, know every detail of my demise, but she still gave off warmth and good ideas.

I started at the PICU. Henry himself might have something for me. His chart might be full of clues. He might even wake up. I was not optimistic, but should he be one of the lucky few, my own luck would be considerably improved.

Henry was alone in his cubicle. A boom box was softly playing some syrupy piano music. The ventilator made its rhythmic whish-clicks; the IV pumps silently blinked their little green lights. Henry had acquired a long, triple-channel catheter in the garden-hose vein living under his left collarbone; his milky "food"—"hyperalimentation"—was being pumped through it.

He lay still, except for his chest rising and falling with each whish-click. The nurse had just washed his face and combed his hair. He was pink. Peaceful looking.

I checked his medication sheet; the list of drugs required to support the patient is a backdoor indicator of the patient's problems, but the quickest. He had morphine and Valium ordered "as needed," but he had needed none. His unconsciousness was all his own. He was getting only peptic ulcer prophylaxis and a suppository laxative; hardly teetering on the physiologic brink.

His daily chart notes were equally unenlightening:

Hospital Day 4.

Subjective: Naught.

Objective:

Vital signs stable. Off all drips.

Normal cardiac function.

Pulmonary: On minimal ventilator support, breathing room air. Checking blood gases only twice a day. All values within normal limits.

GI: On ulcer prevention protocol.

Renal: Good urine output. Chemical waste levels within normal.

Metabolic: Electrolytes normal. Ramping up IV feeding to achieve full nutrition soon.

Neuro: Remains comatose. CAT scan shows no hemorrhages, no masses. Brain edema consistent with diffuse hypoxic injury.

We—I use the grand collective medical "we" since I was not then actively involved in Henry's care—were in the wheel-spinning phase, waiting out the brain, "waiting for the swelling to go down," waiting for it to declare itself good, bad, or a total indeterminate mess.

As I stood staring, one zombie to another, the Rojelio/Mendoza family traipsed in to see their son and brother. When Daniel saw me his frown tightened and his neck straightened.

It was the bleakest of assemblies. From Daniel on down, each looked more haggard than the one before. Even the baby, barely walking, seemed to have bags under his eyes. I nodded a professional hello, then left them, wordlessly, to their private hour of pain.

I paged Mary Ellen, but instead of calling back, she came into the Unit, towing along her bubbly intern, Michelle Rosenbaum.

"Malcolm. You're alive," she said.

"That depends on your definition. I guess I'm at least as alive as our boy in Bed Two."

"Any change?" she said.

"No, pretty comatose."

"Sorry I'm not more on top of him, Malcolm. We've been buried. He's one of those we're taking care of by assumption. You know, 'We haven't heard any cries for help so he must be okay.' "

"Yeah, of course. You can't do much for a brain injury, anyway."

"We're expecting a patient transfer any minute. He might interest a surgeon such as yourself."

"Thanks, but I've given it up."

"Oh, Malcolm. Don't be a wuss."

"Okay, I'm not a wuss. What are you getting?"

"Gunshot. Four-year-old supposedly shot himself."

"Where?"

"Casa Grande."

"No, where in the body?"

"Oh, belly. Flank, actually. Through and through. May be a classic flesh wound. No surgery indicated. At least that's what the transferring doc thought. We'll see."

"Yeah, we'll see."

"And we'll see how he got a gun."

"I can tell you that," I said. "Dad set it down and turned his back—only for a second."

Henry's mother hurried back out of the Unit, streaming tears, dragging along behind her the oldest of Henry's half-brothers. The boy, who looked to be eight or nine, was hitting her back and shoulder as hard as he could with his trailing fist, but her grip on his forearm was nonnegotiable.

"Oh Jesus," I mumbled.

Mary Ellen said, "Lovely. Fucking lovely."

Dr. Rosenbaum said, "Geez," giving it two syllables.

After deep breaths all around I said, "How's the rest of your service? That baby with the obliterated bronchioles?"

"Little Celia," Monty said. "Same. Spikes a fever at least once a day. We send cultures. Nothing grows."

"Her creatinine is going up," Michelle added.

Mary Ellen gave me a look. "Dying kidneys, you know."

"Dialysis?" I said.

"Not if I can help it," Mary Ellen said.

The doors whirred open again and a tall, middle-aged man wearing a tan suit came in. I took him for a drug company rep. He stopped at the control desk, casting about to see who might be able to direct him. His glance settled on Michelle, who was closest to him and the most formally dressed. Michelle silently looked to Mary Ellen for help. The man's eyes naturally followed hers.

"I'm Ted Priestley," he said. "I'm a close family friend of the Mendozas. They asked to come up and look in on their son Henry."

Monty introduced herself, then said, "I'm the senior resident here. I'm more or less in charge of Henry's care on an hour-to-hour basis."

"I understand. I met with the Mendozas last night and discussed the situation at some length. I promised them I would come by and see the boy." He nodded to her, then me. "I'm sorry to interrupt your rounds, or whatever."

Mary Ellen pointed him to Henry's cubicle. When he was safely gone I said, "That would be their lawyer."

"Just who we need," Monty said.

"Well, he's not a fanged ogre," I said. "What do you think? Cute guy?"

"Him? Gawd no. But the priest. Did you see him? He was in this morning. Oh my Lord. What a waste. Did you see the eyes?"

I looked blank, so she turned to her intern. "Am I right?"

"Oh yes. Yes," she bubbled.

I rolled my eyes and sighed.

Mary Ellen said, "Malcolm, you have no taste in men."

I looked at her. "No, I don't. And don't ever tell anybody otherwise."

Monty's pager went off. While she took the call, I thought again about Robin's sneak attack. Perhaps she was just the killer type. I idly asked Michelle, "So, how would you know if a syringe of epinephrine had epinephrine in it?" I expected vacancy.

Michelle said, "The epinephrine signature."

I looked at her. "The what?"

"You know. Like in dog lab. In med school? Didn't you guys do dog lab? In physiology?"

"Yeah. We did," I said.

"And did you inject epinephrine? And neostigmine and isoproterenol and all the other drugs that affect the controls? And graph out the changes? The sympathetic and parasympathetic, the agonists, antagonists, alpha, beta, dopaminergic . . ."

I said, "Uh-huh. We did that. Most of what I remember from that, though, was one of our classmates bawling and practically screaming when we made the hearts fibrillate and the dogs died."

Michelle said, "We had two crying at my medical school. But don't you remember the epinephrine signature?"

"Refresh me."

Michelle said, "Beta first? You know, just as the first few drug molecules hit it's still in a low concentration. At low concentration the beta effects dominate. Beta opens up the vessels—vasodilation. You get a real quick little drop in pulse and blood pressure. But then the alpha effects, when the full dose hits, do the opposite. Rising pulse and blood pressure. You don't remember that?"

"It's coming back to me," I said. Mary Ellen rejoined us. I said to her, "Michelle has been refreshing me on epinephrine." To Michelle I said, "Only epinephrine does that biphasic thing."

"Right." She smiled at me and batted her fake eyelashes. "Only epinephrine has alpha and beta effects like that."

I said to Mary Ellen, "From the mouths of babes." I thought to myself, *Now all I need is a dog lab.*

17

After a few years of ER work here on the plains, I thought I had seen enough
to pronounce the Quiet Little ERs Where Nothing Ever Happens different
from their citified brothers only in the pace of events. I knew that broken fe-
murs showered just as much marrow into the pulmonary arteries in St. Petersburg and Ogallala as they did in San Diego, that headaches were just as
aggravating for all concerned in Hoacham as in Phoenix, and that bleeding
was messy everywhere.

It took me years of experience to notice that one type of case was different—the patient "found down." These are people found by someone else, unconscious, unable to give a history. I have learned that local knowledge makes
those "found down" not only more interesting—knowing who they are and
why they got into their current messes—but they get more accurate and efficient diagnosis and treatment.

A few months ago in Ogallala the medics brought in, at midnight, an
unconscious middle-aged woman, smelling heavily of regurgitated alcohol,
some of her partly digested dinner clinging to her hair. Where I went to medical school and did my aborted residency, the history from the paramedics usually would have been very short. Something like, "Middle-aged female, found
down, no blood visible, no signs of violence, no incontinence." The unsaid part
was, "No one has any clue who she is."

But in my Quiet Little ER the medic told me her name and age, what
antiseizure medications she was supposed to be taking, and why she doesn't
take the pink ones—she hates pink. The RN told me the woman always said
she was allergic to "tranquilizers" but in fact thought highly of Valium.

We sent a toxicology screen, got her stomach cleaned out, got her rehy-
drated, got her head scanned, and got her cleaned up. Diagnosis: Acute (and
chronic) intoxication with alcohol and Valium. Not (acutely) life threatening.

The nurse phoned the woman's son, saying "Mom's here again." He said *he'd be there, leaving the time unspecified, implying Mom would be sleeping it off in one of our bays. That seemed to be the routine. I realized any objection would be counterproductive—the woman's "rest" would be the highest and best use of the space that night.*

I learned another maxim: If you're going to be "found down," you're better off doing it where folks know your name.

HENRY ROJELIO, DAY FIVE (CONTINUED)

When I said to myself I needed a dog lab, I was being facetious. Then, suddenly, it seemed like a good idea. Maybe, in fact, just what I needed.

Any medical center doing research has animal labs. They're used for everything from studies of subcellular metabolism to developing new surgical techniques. My problem was not going to be finding an animal lab, but finding one on very short notice with an appropriate animal prep and a supervisor who might be willing to let me play.

I didn't have time to work up from the bottom. Rather I needed to cash in my few remaining chips at the top. From my talk with Monty and Michelle, I went up to Dr. Hebert's office.

His secretary said he had just "gone down to a trauma." That meant he was leading the cast assembled in the ER to receive an acutely injured patient directly from the EMS crew.

I shuffled into the back of the ER and blended into the hind end of the crowd. The paramedic in charge was just rattling off the patient's story: a fifty-six-year-old man who crashed his delivery van into a power pole at fifty-plus miles per hour. He was properly belted, so he was alive, but his bald pate and fleshy face were peppered with small, angular lacerations from the sharp edges of busted glass. He was screaming.

Dr. Hebert was sitting quietly in the corner of the room, reading something handwritten. The Chief Resident was conducting the team through the paces of handling the patient.

I waited quietly beside Dr. Hebert. He looked up at me as he flipped a page. "Ishmail! Goddamn. They ain't kilt you yet?"

"No, sir. But it seems they're trying."

I explained, in vague terms, that I needed his help. "I think I can clear up a goodly chunk of this mess in a good old-fashioned dog lab. Run a sample, check the vitals. I knew the Surgery Department would likely have studies going on in different—"

"Shit, son, we got studies! We oughta be so smart we hurt." He looked at the wall clock. He shouted at the resident, "Avery, the clock is *tickin'*. I ain't heard just yet what you plannin' on doin' with this old boy."

Avery said, "Yes, sir. I was thinking about sending him to the CT scanner."

Dr. Hebert said, "Not very original, but I guess that's what I'd likely do, too." To me he said, "What'a you up to?"

"It's kind of a long story."

The patient shrieked. Dr. Hebert said to me, "You think this old boy is hurt?"

"Not bad." He was starting to grin at me. I went on, "Hebert's Law Number Two: You gotta be healthy to be loud."

"Goddamn, you was payin' attention."

"And Hebert's Law Number One: Never fuck with the pancreas."

"That's right, but now I can't take credit for thinkin' that one up, but it's a good one to frikkin' remember. You get yo'self back on the team here and I'll let you in on a couple other dandies."

"Yes, sir, I'd like that."

"So you say this man is 'not bad hurt.' Right, Doctor?"

"Yes."

"Good, I'll put you' name on the chart, too. 'Consulting—Dr. Malcolm I-S-H-M-A-I-L.' "

"That would really upset somebody."

"That's *exactly* why I'm goin' to do it."

He scribbled a chart entry, scrawled his signature at the bottom, and told Avery to "hurry the fuck up, son." He called up to his secretary and asked her to phone the animal lab in Tucson to find a time I could run a quick test. To me: "How much time you going to need?"

"Ten minutes."

He frowned at me. Into the phone: "Marie, get Alphonse to find a half hour for a unique piece of research. Dr. Ishmail needs to run some potion through a dog. He'll be up to get Alphonse's number from you." To me: "Alphonse Emmerick is so smart he ought to frikkin' glow in the dark. And he ain't bad with his hands, even with the tremor. Unfortunately he has trouble makin' up his frikkin' mind. Stand and hem and fuckin' haw long enough to have finished both the operations he was tryin' to decide between."

I nodded.

"Knows his science, though. If you got too much time on your hands, get him to tell you about what pulmonary immune mediators do in endotoxin shock. *Chingalamadre*, that will make your eyeballs *spin*." Dr. Hebert pronounced the Mexican curse with no hint of Hispanic inflections.

"I can imagine."

Dr. Hebert's secretary gave me Dr. Emmerick's phone number and directions to his lab in Tucson. She said he had been adamant that I be there by seven-fifteen in the morning; he was not going to disrupt the day's schedule for any "dilettante science."

I headed home. Unlocking the door to my town house, I sensed the walkway darkening behind me. I had company. Strongly backlit in the portico was a man with a police badge in his hand. I squinted at the shiny metal, then at his face. He identified himself as Will Borden, a detective from the Mesa Police Department.

"Are you Dr. Malcolm Ishmail?"

I frowned and squinted again. "Yes. Yes, I am."

"May I come in?" He looked to be in his early thirties. Easy smile, perfect teeth, very little belly, and a crewneck Italian sweater over expensive slacks. Not, to my mind, a typical detective. I looked past him to a second man watching us from ten paces back.

"My partner," Detective Borden said. "We're like nuns. We always travel in pairs." The second man was looking at the sky, hands in his pockets. "Does he want to come in?" I said.

"No."

I nodded and let Borden in.

I looked again at the second man, but he seemed to be studying the way the low light angle set off the cheap construction of the town houses. I closed the door. "Sit down," I said, motioning to the couch under the front window. "I just need to go pee."

"This will only take a minute," he said.

I looked at him. "Still, I gotta pee."

"Okay, but leave the door open. If you don't mind."

I frowned but did as he asked. I called from the bathroom, "What is this about?"

"Just needed to talk with you. Thought maybe you could help us."

I went to the kitchen and put the coffeepot in the microwave. "What with? Did I do something?" I half-laughed.

"Well, Dr. Ishmail, we're doing some checking around. We're trying to find someone who may or may not be missing. Robin Benoit. A nurse. We were told you knew her."

"She worked in the ER where I worked."

"Uh-huh." A pause.

I said, "Is she missing?"

"The Glory Hospital people phoned us. Her boss is worried about her. Apparently she left work last night feeling sick."

"Coffee?"

"Yeah, sure. Thanks."

"Would your other half like some?"

"I doubt it. He's stretching his legs."

I envisioned him watching the back windows for any impolite egress. I got two mugs. I stared over at him.

"Is that a police matter? I mean, nurses go home sick all the time."

"Well, that's what we're wondering." He sipped his coffee and looked up. "When was the last time you saw her?"

I thought through the sequence. Minutes seemed like days. "Yesterday."

"Uh-huh." He smiled at me. I waited. He said, "When yesterday?"

"In the afternoon. Five-ish. Why are you asking me?"

"You two worked together. May have been friends. Someone at the hospital thought maybe you had been to her house. We just thought you might have some idea where she went."

"Did she go someplace?"

"She doesn't seem to be at home. And she didn't show up for her shift this afternoon."

"Really. Well, I don't know where she may have gone. Wish I did, though."

"Why do you say that?"

"I've got a few questions for her myself."

"How's that?"

I thought a second. Maybe I was stepping into a hole. "She kind of dumped on me yesterday."

"When you last saw her?"

"No, just before that. She filed a report with the hospital people about a case we worked on in the ER that went really sour. She pretty well fried my ass. And for no reason I can think of."

"Over a patient? A case?"

"Yeah. A teenaged boy with asthma. Kind of a messed-up kid. We were treating his asthma and he curled up his toes and tried to die." I waited.

"She 'dumped on you' . . . Did you two—you and this nurse—have any disagreement about the boy? About the way things went?"

"No, not at all. At least I didn't think so at the time. She was concerned about what people were going to say, wanted my opinions. She made me dinner, though. She certainly didn't seem pissed at me."

Another pause. He said, "The woman at the hospital was concerned there had been, maybe, some kind of disagreement between you two."

A silence. He smiled slightly and sipped his coffee. He waited.

I said, "No. Not directly. I mean, yesterday afternoon, the last time I spoke with her, was at the hospital. When I found out about her report I went to the ER to see . . . well, if you'll excuse me, see what the fuck she was trying to do to me."

"Uh-huh."

"I tried to be friendly but she wouldn't talk and I kind of blew up at her. I guess I shouldn't have done that. I went back out there later, to try to sort of apologize, but she was gone."

"And?"

"And? And what?"

"How are you feeling toward Miss Benoit now?"

Again I hesitated. My proclivity for hyperbolic responses to obvious questions—"I feel like throttling her"—would not be a good idea. "Well, let's just say I'm waiting for an explanation."

"Have you thought of any possible explanations?"

He was using the same open-question techniques we had learned in medical school "How to Take a History" lectures. Again I paused. I thought, *Maybe I screwed it up and she's calling it the way it is*, but again kept that to myself. I said, "Well, Officer, I had thought we were on good terms. Then we weren't. I'm wondering why I'm getting two completely different sides of the same woman."

He smiled. "Sometimes they're like that."

I nodded my complicity. "Do you know that she's missing? I mean, how do you know she's not visiting her mother or something?"

"Maybe that's all it is."

"But you drove up here first thing after you're called, to talk to me, just to be sure."

He shrugged. "Covering all possibilities, is all."

"But did you go to her house? Go check on her?"

"For a missing-persons check we send a uniformed officer to knock at the door."

"Did he find my jacket and notes there?"

He was silent.

"On the couch?" I said.

"Sorry?"

"She said I left them on her couch. Or at least that's where she said she would leave them for me. Though I couldn't find them. Maybe your officer found them?"

"You were at her house?"

"Yeah. When they told me she had gone home sick, I drove back to her house. I really wanted to find out what she thought she was doing."

"You wanted to confront her again?"

"Not exactly. I realized I'd handled it wrong the first time. I thought . . . I don't know what I thought, except that she was the only one who would know what she was doing to me."

"You'd been there before?"

"She invited me there for dinner. Night before last. She said she needed to talk to me about the case that had 'gone bad.' That was when she seemed, like I said, so worried about what people would think or say."

"Uh-huh."

"And I guess I left my jacket there when I left. Brown leather. Aviator type. Torn lining. It had some billing stuff from Scottsdale and my copy of the chart notes from the asthmatic case in the pocket. Inner left pocket. And I called her the next morning to see about it. Asked her to bring it to the hospital where I could get it from her, but she seemed in a hurry. Said she would leave it on her couch for me and told me where to find a key to let myself into her house. It all seemed odd."

"Did you go get it?"

"No. That's what I said. I went there, last night. I had a meeting late yesterday with the hospital VP, then I went to the ER to talk to Robin. Like they told you, it turned into a little row. I got to thinking about wanting to find out if she really thought that disaster was my fault. So I went back out there; you know, try, try again. They told me she'd left work sick. Cramps and nausea. They had to call in another nurse to cover her shift. I had nothing else to do, so I drove out to her house, but she wasn't there, even as late as it was. No jacket either. Maybe your guy had taken it."

"No, he didn't notice it in her house."

"Maybe she stuck it in her car, meaning to give it to me at the hospital."

"Maybe."

There was a knock at the door. Will's partner entered with barely a nod, a thick and awkward man. Will said, "This is Ken May." We shook hands and he took a chair.

Will replayed the highlights of our conversation for his partner. I looked at the two of them. The big silent one had an intense stare and the faint hand tremor of early Parkinson's. When he looked up at me I smiled thinly. He turned and looked out the window. His breathing seemed heavy. Probably a smoker.

Will said, "And when, again, did you last speak with her?"

"I called her early in the afternoon, asked about the jacket. I asked her for a date, if you must know, but she said she couldn't. Didn't really give a reason. Told me to pick up the jacket, told me where the key was, and said to call her again soon. Then there was our 'conversation' in the ER, if you can call it a conversation."

Ken was staring at me again. Will said, "Had you been on dates with Robin?"

"Well, we were sort of starting up."

"Were you lovers?"

"Does it make a difference?"

"Not to me personally, but romantic connections can be pretty important to get straight when people can't be found."

I said, "We were, two nights ago, for the first and maybe last time."

"Why do you say that?"

"Say what?"

" 'Maybe the last time.' "

"You just told me she's missing. She was acting squirrelly toward me when I asked her for a date, even before I met with her boss and found out about her lies. I'd say I've been jilted."

He nodded. "Did she ever say anything to you about needing or wanting to go anyplace? Get away?"

"No. I don't remember anything."

"Visit friends? Family?

"No."

"Do you know of any friends or family? Did she ever speak of anyone she was close to?"

"She mentioned her folks were rich, though I never heard where they live. She used to work in northern California. ER nursing. That was about it. The other night most of the conversation was about the kid in the ER. I guess we never really talked about her family or friends."

"Do you know of any way to reach her? Besides her home?"

"Through the hospital, I suppose. But I guess you would have tried that. Or the Nursing Board."

"Yes." Again, he waited. "Can you think of any reason she might have taken off? Disappeared on her own?"

"Nope."

"No one was after her . . . ? Not in financial trouble . . . ? Not pregnant . . . ?"

"Not that I would know about."

Ken May got up and wandered around the room, breathing audibly, looking at things like a bored man whose wife had dragged him out shopping. Watching him, I said, "Look, I think I've already told you more than . . . well, more than I should have."

"But you said you wanted to talk to her, too."

"That's true. That's true. I really do hope you find her."

"But you don't expect her back?"

"You told me she has, what? Disappeared? Like I said, I didn't really know her. Not that well. I wouldn't know if she'll show up or not."

A pause. "When were you next scheduled to work?"

"Well, I had been scheduled for a couple of days later this week," I said, "but it sounds like you know that that's been canceled."

"What do you mean?"

"You said 'were.' 'When *were* you next scheduled to work?' "

"Yes," he said, "in the call we got from Ms. Marquam at the Glory Hospital, she told us your privileges, or whatever, there at the hospital are being reviewed. That was one of the things that prompted her concern."

"Ah, it's becoming clearer all the time. I guess I don't know when I'll be working."

"You apparently had some problems over at Maricopa, too, when you were a resident there."

"Yes, I was fucked over there, too. But that's a long story."

"We've got time."

"Maybe I'm a shit magnet. But really I'd rather not discuss it. It's not relevant anyway." Ken May was wandering out of the room, going shopping for God knows what. I said, "Do you need something?" He came back to his chair and flashed me a half-second grin.

"What's in the back?" he said.

"My stuff."

He grinned again, then resumed looking about the room, paying particular attention to the ceiling.

"Is he always this much fun?" I said to Will.

"He needs more exercise. Sitting still makes him nervous."

"Well, he's spreading it around. Should I have a lawyer present?"

"You could, if you want, but they charge an awful lot. And no one is accusing you of anything, and you're telling me you haven't done anything wrong."

"No. I have not."

He rubbed his face. "Do you know what kind of car Miss Benoit drives?"

I thought a second. "Chevy Camaro. An old one."

He sat waiting.

"I followed her home the other night."

"What color?"

"It was dark. I mean, it was night. The car's dark, too, though. Dark blue, I think."

"Ever been in her car?"

I thought. "No."

"Never gotten a ride someplace? Sat with her in a parking lot for a cigarette?"

"Don't smoke." Ken May was now staring at me again and breathing in big rumbly breaths. "Nope—never been in her car." I waited.

"To the best of your memory—I mean you did, apparently, see a fair amount of Miss Benoit's skin—did she have any identifying marks of any kind?"

"Not that I saw."

"No scars? Tattoos? Birthmarks?"

"Nothing I saw."

They watched me. I waited. Detective May said, "May I use the toilet?"

I hesitated, then said, "Yeah." As he walked past I almost added, "Leave the door open." I took a deep breath

"How'd you do that?" Borden asked, pointing at my hand.

"This?" I held up the makeshift bandage on the back of my hand. "I cut myself during the code in the ER. When that asthmatic kid arrested. Things weren't going well. I was flinging something and caught my hand on a wall bracket." I peeled the bandage back for Will to see the cut.

He looked at it intently.

"What did you say you cut it on?"

"A wall bracket in the Glory ER."

"How long did it bleed?"

"I don't know. Fifteen, twenty minutes. When we got the resuscitation done I put a bandage on it and it quit."

"Was it bleeding the other night? Last night?"

"No. I don't think so."

"Okay. But, it would be helpful if you'd be willing to come down to the station to give us a blood sample."

"I didn't think I was being accused of anything."

"You're not. But on the chance we find any evidence anywhere, it's always a good idea to know what came from whom. You know, a hair or something that, turns out, came from one of the good guys. That kind of thing."

I nodded, doubting he was as convinced of my innocence as he wanted to sound.

Then he added, "What are you planning in the next few days?"

"I don't know. Work is up in the air."

"Not going to be leaving town?"

"Wasn't planning on it."

He smiled thinly and reached into a pocket. "Here's my card. It would be good if you could keep in touch. Let us know what you're up to."

I nodded slowly. "Hard to imagine going anywhere right now, really. With the kid that went bad in the ER . . . He's in the Pediatric ICU at Maricopa."

"Yeah, that's what we've heard."

"I'm trying to stay on top of it. They may be making decisions . . ."

"When will that be?"

"In a few days."

Ken May came back to the couch. They looked at each other, then at me. Borden said, "Would you be willing to sit for a polygraph?"

"A lie detector?"

"Yes, sir."

"I thought those were . . . I don't know, useless. Discredited."

"Not at all. We use them all the time. The ACLU thinks it's better to have the bad guys out on the streets, so they've made sure we can't use them in court. But that doesn't mean we can't use them to fill in pieces to the puzzles."

"Well, not to be rude, but what's in it for me?" I was wondering if I was to be required somehow to have another personal visit with the officers.

"Well, you said you wanted to help us find your missing girlfriend. And, if you haven't done anything you would want to hide, this is the quickest, easiest way to help us clear you."

"Clear me," I said, "of suspicion?"

He shrugged.

"Is this something I have to do? Or something you think would be a good idea?"

"It would be a good idea."

Questions were coming faster than answers. I did want to find Robin, but I needed some time to think. "I'll call you," I said.

As they left, Will striding with athletic grace and Ken trundling with effort, I knew they expected me to cough up something incriminating, but I had nothing to give them. I envisioned them rehashing every inflection and word choice I'd made, wondering what I was hiding and how they would smoke it out of me.

18

Dad had a spill a couple of weeks ago. Since he is essentially nonverbal, it's impossible to know if he just lost his balance or passed out or something in between. Doesn't look like he had another stroke, but the old coot broke his nose, of all things. I was on the far side of the Sandhills taking pictures when it happened, so I was of no immediate use.

In the Hooker ER they wanted to call Dr. Kudamelka, the chump who bought Dad's practice, the only doctor in town who saw broken bones. Mom quietly refused. She called Dad's internist. He came and checked what needed to be checked—physical exam, blood work, X-rays. They told me in the ER he looked up nasal fractures in their text, then said to Dad, "This is gonna hurt," and muscled the hash of cartilage and bony bits back into something of a straight line. Dad's eyes teared profusely.

Mom called my motel only after they were back home. It seemed that all was medically okay, but they were both tired and she was scared. I drove all night.

The next night, after dinner, after we got Dad to bed, I brought up the idea of getting him to a nursing home. There was a long silence. I pointed out to Mom that she would not be physically able to care for Dad too much longer, and if she killed herself trying to keep him in one piece it would do neither of them any good.

Still just silence. "You always told me, Mom, if a situation is bad, you have to change it." She blinked. I went on, "You said, 'If you're not working for change, you apparently must like things the way they are.' "

She looked up at me. "I never meant you should change it to something worse."

"No, of course not . . ."

"And your father hated those places. It would kill him."

"If seeing Brant Kudamelka in his own office didn't kill him, he's beyond death from disappointment."

She stared at me. "He thinks you're going to make that better."

"Me? How?"

"He thinks you will."

"He doesn't think anything of the kind."

"You go ask him."

"Mom, he doesn't respond to anything I say. He sits and blinks."

"You're not saying the right things."

I went up to his room and sat him up. It took me a while, but I got around to "Dad, are you still hoping I'll be able to practice here?"

Of course there was silence. I looked at his eyes. He seemed clear. Clearer, anyway, in his facial expression than I thought he had been since the stroke. He looked like my father.

HENRY ROJELIO, DAY SIX

Watching the Mesa detectives drive away, I felt a hint of panic creeping around my throat. My pain litany now included a threat to my freedom to walk the streets based on the fate of a missing woman who apparently wore at least two faces. I had little doubt Henry's outcome would weigh in as well.

I was suddenly sure I had shared too much with those two. "Divulger's Remorse." Sometimes I seem to have the unjustified optimism of a daffodil in spring. Sleep that night was fitful.

Henry, Day Six, began at five o'clock, with a repeat drive to Tucson. I decided it's a better trip in the dark.

Finding coffee, finding parking, and getting my bearings in the medical center complex took, of course, longer than I had allowed. I got to Dr. Emmerick's office ten minutes late.

Alphonse was at least six foot five with board-straight posture. I guessed he'd had a large piece of stainless steel attached to his spine at a young age to arrest scoliosis. He was not happy, though, so there was no small talk. "Dr. Ishmail, we're planning on starting our runs at eight-fifteen. On schedule. I hope you can be quick with whatever this errand is." He was thin, dark skinned, had broad glasses and a frequent blinking tic.

"Yes, I'm pretty sure . . ."

"Let me show you in." He got up and led the way, practically trotting. Without turning back toward me, he said, "Dr. Hebert thinks this is all pretty cute, I guess."

We wound around the research wing to a stairway and down to the secured basement. Alphonse barely nodded to the bored security man at the steel doors. The animals in the lab sections need constant protection from the wackos. The man reached under his desk. The electric lock clicked. We ended up in a back laboratory, through a door marked "Anesthesiology."

"We stole their lab," Dr. Emmerick said, pointing at the sign. "They never did much of any consequence with it, anyway."

In the center of the room, strapped on her back on a large wooden bench, was a big brown dog with the hair and coloration of a Doberman and the size and shape of a retriever. There were two plastic lines running to blood vessels in the dog's groin and a plastic ventilator tube running straight down her throat into her trachea. She was asleep, presumably anesthetized, certainly not moving. A bank of dials and digital readouts stood beside her, along with a stack of monitor modules atop an eight-channel continuous printout polygraph. Three of the needles twitched with each heartbeat; one swooped lazily with each cycle of the ventilator. The paper was imperceptibly rolling forward and into a neat stack in a basket at the bottom of the machine.

Alphonse introduced me to the man at the table, Miguel, adding, "Dr. Hebert wants the young doctor here to run a quick sample of something to see what happens. You can help him, if you don't mind. Just don't let him take too long. We're still on for the planned runs." Dr. Emmerick left.

Miguel was young and smooth. He had a slight nodding motion most of the time, giving the impression he was hearing faint music inaudible to those of us who were less hip. He said, pointing to the dog, "She's about ready. I mean real stable vitals. You going to need anything special?"

I looked blank.

"Any blood draws? Metabolics? Hemodynamics?"

"Uh, no, guess not." I pointed to the slowly turning roll printer.

"Is that printing out blood pressure and pulse? That's about all I'll need."

"Yeah. That's on the polygraph."

"Is she asleep?"

"Oh yeah. She's breathing Ethrane. It's real cheap. Works fine. And she's on a continuous infusion of vecuronium."

"Is Ethrane the anesthesia gas?" I asked, dredging my mental records of ancient lectures.

"Yep. New and improved ether, though they got way better stuff for humans."

"And the vecuronium is for paralysis . . ."

"Yeah. Non-depolarizing muscle relaxant. The new curare. Muscle paralysis without the nasty side effects of the old drugs."

"Like respiratory depression?" I asked.

"Oh no. Lots of respiratory depression. Muscle relaxants relax all the muscles, Doc. If you left out the respiratory muscles you'd have the dog pushing on her diaphragm and belly. Wouldn't work."

"And 'non-depolarizing' means what again?" I asked. I had my face screwed up, trying to find lost records.

"Curare and all the ones like it disconnect the muscles from the nerves. They block the connection without setting it off. The muscles don't fire. Now, succinylcholine is a depolarizing drug. It sets off the muscles right when it hits them. Makes 'em twitch. It's too short acting, though, for something like this. We don't use it much," he said.

I nodded. "Okay to start?"

"She's all yours."

I looked over the setup. Hanging on the side of the polygraph was a beat-up clipboard holding the data on that dog. "Number fourteen" weighed 28.3 kilos. Ten micrograms of epi per kilo would be more than enough to send the vital signs flying. Three hundred mikes—three tenths of a cc.

I asked Miguel, "Can this print out faster?" He reached over to the polygraph and tore off the end and tucked it into the catch basket. He pushed a button and the paper picked up speed.

I tore open an alcohol swab and wiped off the rubber nipple on the IV line near the dog's groin. I bent close to the clear plastic line and pushed the hair-thin needle through the rubber, injecting the plunger slowly from the "0.70" mark to the "0.40" mark. A tiny air bubble came out of the beveled tip of the needle, then a small stream of fluid, visible only as waves of different refractive index, like the shimmers above distant blacktop in the summer.

I opened the plastic roller clamp on the same line, high up near the bag of fluid. The bubble accelerated down the tubing, around two bends, and disappeared into the dog. I readjusted the clamp, then watched the polygraph.

The ticks of the needles gradually came faster. The digital readout under "Heart Rate" rose from 82 to 110, that under "BP" rose from 115 to 177.

"There should have been a dip in pressure." I said, mostly to myself.

"Here," Miguel said, pointing to the paper. The graph showed a definite dip in both the top and bottom of the sweep of the blood pressure trace, but it was extremely short; there was an almost immediate rise in both. "It was quick, but it's there," he said.

I just stared. He said, "You would have missed it without the printout."

I watched the dog's vital signs drift toward their earlier values, then looked at Miguel.

"Epinephrine," he said in a tone implying it was obvious. I nodded, looking blank.

Miguel ran the printout through the rollers, tore it off, folded it over, and handed it to me.

"Prairie shit," I mumbled.

19

Annie Parrott dubbed last Wednesday in the Othello Clinic "Minor Trauma Day, Squared." "Minor trauma to minors." The day started with broken bones. A nine-year-old girl was hanging upside down from the family tree-house to make her toddler brother laugh. She fell, banging up her face up and breaking both bones in her right forearm just above the wrist, creating a disquieting swan's neck out of her arm. Annie turned her over to me. I checked the usual things and did a simple splint to keep the pain down while her folks took her on down the highway to an orthopedist. I imagined the brother, being both blessed and cursed with a Y chromosome, found the whole show to be quite a hoot.

Then, mid-afternoon, I got to show off my holistic version of laceration repair. There's nothing quite like a bleeding four-year-old, especially a little princess in her going-to-a-birthday-party pink dress, to get a pair of parents wound up like watch springs.

A drinking glass had broken on a counter above her and the big heavy piece found the inside of her forearm en route to the floor. Fortunately the gash was only through the skin. There were no tendons, arteries, or nerves involved, and I had clean, straight edges to work with. As a bonus it ran across, rather than parallel to, the underlying muscle. This means the tension of the muscles helps pull the edges together, not splay them open. Your repair will be free of underlying stretch and the scar will end up very faint.

I love these. The kid has sobbed herself into a dither. The mom and dad know in their minds it's only a flesh wound, but in their hearts their daughter is bleeding and wailing and they can't fix it alone.

The key to emotional success is to be sure to get all the painful stuff out of the way almost as soon as you see the kid. And lay in the local anesthesia for all you're worth. Some ER people try to soak in a cocktail of anesthetic stuff, but it takes forever and often just plain doesn't work. Besides, with the *microscopic needle I use for the local, she's hardly crying during the injection more than she was when I gently peeled back the bandages to view the damage.*

After the local, wait. Maybe ten minutes. See if they've got a Squirt. "The local takes a little time to work completely," I tell the folks, thinking to myself, And everybody's breathing can return to normal.

In some of the ERs they pull out a papoose board to lash the kid down like Gulliver in Lilliput. I tell them, "Naw, just have the kid and the mom lie on the gurney together." Mom holding Kid in a bear hug may not be as effective as a total-body mummy board, but it usually does the job, and besides, Mom feels like she's doing something to help, and Kid feels like this surely is the best place in the world. This instead of the instant terror the mummy board creates in child and parent alike.

Do the sterile wash with a gentle, rhythmic stroke, more like a massage than a scrub prep. Keep up a quiet prattle—anything. Ask about the birthday party. Was there a clown? Any balloons? 'Cuz I like balloons. What kind of cake? Start sewing in mid-answer. What songs did you sing? Will you sing it for me? If you got the local right, the sewing is all part of the massage.

On little girls I use really fine suture and a kind of double stitch that leaves the least scar. Boys get twine and baling wire. I figure they ultimately want a certain amount of decoration to show off when drunk—they're the ones who wake up from benders with big tattoos.

The double stitch is pretty slow and this princess, being fairly exhausted, fell asleep before I was done. They often do. I'm never so proud of being boring.

The dress looked like a total write-off. Still, the folks looked grateful.

I think the clinic nurse thought I'd put the princess under some kind of spell.

HENRY ROJELIO, DAY SIX (CONTINUED)

Henry, Day Six, was not shaping up as planned.

I had mixed feelings about the epinephrine syringe containing epinephrine. A big part of me still would have professed to the world that

Robin was incapable of trying to hurt Henry. Maybe that was the part of me that had wanted to date her. But clearly some other part of me doubted that. Perhaps the part of me that wanted exoneration and maybe a job. I did not want to give up scientific and professional detachment, though. Such weakness is only acceptable after it's proven correct.

I thanked Miguel for his help.

"Did you get what you needed, Doc?"

"Yeah, Miguel, I guess I did."

" 'Cuz you don't look too happy about it."

I gave him a thin smile. "There's adrenaline in that syringe, eh?"

"No doubt about that," he said.

Dr. Emmerick came in, waving a newspaper. "Ah, Dr. Ishmail. You're apparently famous." He handed me the "Regional" section of the morning's *Republic*. On the front page was a story about Henry Rojelio. There was a photograph of Henry's mother, a tear on each cheek, clutching the baby son and glancing ruefully over her shoulder toward Maricopa Hospital. The cutline said she had been praying for her eldest son, who was in critical condition in the Children's ICU.

The article was labeled as the first of a three-part series on emergency care in small towns. There was a nasty push going on in the medico-political circles to try to organize and consolidate emergencies and trauma care. The big specialty centers were arguing for improved survival, the smaller decentralized hospitals were touting local access to care. It is a common conundrum in health care: specialization versus immediacy. All of us had heard all the arguments a hundred times before.

The tale of Henry, at least what the reporter had been told about it, provided a convenient lead-in to the larger issues. He described an "unexpected" cardiac arrest in an adolescent with an asthma attack and a "complex seizure disorder." The hospital spokesperson said they were looking into the possibility of an allergic reaction.

The reporter noted that the attending physician on the case, "a Dr. Malcolm Ishmail," had not completed a residency, was neither a pediatrician nor an emergency physician, and could not be reached for comment.

The implication of the report, of course, was that the arrest might not have happened in the hands of a "real" doctor in a specialty center, or at least it was a good example of the type of case the arguing parties liked to chew on. To illustrate the counterargument, the reporter had added that the patient and his family were well known and "liked" by the local nursing staff. Poetic license has its place in investigative reporting.

If the reporter had tried to reach me at all, it had been halfhearted. I was never paged.

I asked Alphonse if I could use a phone to call Maricopa. He nodded to Miguel, who took me back to the lab, dialed the intercampus code, and handed me the phone. "It's ringing the operator," he said. I asked the operator to page Dr. Montgomery.

"Seen the paper?" I asked her.

"Not yet."

"Your patient and mine, Henry Rojelio, is the star subject of some creative reporting." I described the article to her. "Any messages at home from any reporters?"

"None that I've gotten."

"It's got his name here. Maybe I'll give him a call. I would like to comment on a couple of things," I said.

"Malcolm, be serious. Do you think they'd use it in the next installment to make you look better? Or maybe just leave it hanging out there like a lame defense from the hopeless?"

"I could explain some physiology."

"Yeah, that will get some big headlines."

We kicked around what he would have asked: What was my background? Why had I not finished a residency? What had happened to the poor boy? My smartest response to just about any question would have been "No comment." I realized there was a gulf between what I would have wanted to say and what would have been prudent to say.

"I suppose it was a good thing to have been 'unavailable,' " I said.

"Probably. Where are you?"

"Doing research." She probably took that to mean I'd been getting laid.

"You sound far away."

"I'm on a beach on a desert island."

"You're not the kind to run and hide."

"I'm thinking about getting drunk. I've been reading Hemingway. My new idol. I don't think he was sober all that often."

"You know, not everything he wrote was autobiographical."

"I suppose. But he does refer to lovemaking as 'We had a fine time.' I bet that was autobiographical."

"At least for him."

"Yeah. That's what I meant. Anyway I'm thinking of becoming dissolute."

"Never happen. You're not wired that way."

"Hey, I can change. I'm finished in Glory, anyway."

"What do you mean?"

"I mean they're going to hang me out to dry over Henry's debacle."

"Malcolm! Surely they don't think this was all your fault."

"They're going to give me a hearing. I'll get to tell them they're wrong."

"Then you've got a shot."

"Yeah. Pigs could fly. How's Henry?"

"Malcolm, you can still have a little faith in the system. You can't just quit."

"Mary Ellen, I had faith in the system. It's gotten pretty thin. But I'm not quitting. There are things going . . ." I sighed. "How's Henry?"

There was a pause. "You're not telling me what's going on."

"Mary Ellen, I will. I promise. I'll buy you a nice dinner. But for now, just tell me about Henry."

A pause. "You've seen it before. You could probably phone in my daily chart notes. Normal physiologic functions. No signs of significant life."

"What did the EEG show?"

"The usual. More slowing. Not flat, not human. But the day nurse today said he was twitching when she called his name. None of us could get him to do it, though."

"She a Right-to-Lifer?"

"Malcolm!" Mary Ellen and I did not always agree on the value of religion in health-care decisions.

"I know, I know. But they see things, sometimes," I said.

"Some pray for visions."

"Apparently effectively. He's starting to sound like that trauma kid we saw together when we were fourth years. What was his name?"

"Uhh, you got to give me a little more to work with."

"Head trauma. Vietnamese kid." Silence. "They were from Chula Vista. . . . You were on some elective—Infectious Diseases. I was on the Trauma elective. We consulted you guys when he spiked his hundred forty-seventh fever and we already had him on every gorilla-cillin in the place." Another silence. "Vu. Wasn't it Vu?"

"Nathaniel Vu. That's it."

"Twenty-year-old, horrid brain conk," I recited. "Crashed his little Chevy into an abutment at midnight. Probably a suicide. Only slightly unfinished. Neurosurgeon cut out half his upper skull to decompress the brain, cortex mushroomed out enough to strangle off its own blood supply against the edges of the bone, then it died back."

"But this isn't the same," she said. "He was a trauma."

"But it's going to be. It's the final common pathway: Twitching. He'd lie in a knot, eyes always open. Blinking a lot. No response to stimuli," I said.

"Well, now that I remember it, that was the debate."

"Yeah. His family thought he was in there. They thought he knew them. Every day, three, five, ten of them slogging in to sit and talk to him. Bringing cards and drawings and balloons and all that shit. It was terrible. They'd jabber away at him and he'd twitch and blink and they were convinced—convinced!—he knew they were there. Shit, they'd talk about all the relatives back in the old country, how things were where he used to work, who was dating his sister. His sister would cry and his mother would cry more. They'd finally leave and he'd blink and twitch still. And the therapists would come in twice a day and try to stretch him out straight, and they'd leave and he'd go *sproing* back into his knot. The family—shit, they were wasting their own lives on a man with no brain."

"Malcolm, people do that all the time. Besides, Henry is not as hopelessly chronic as Nathaniel Vu."

"Not yet. He hasn't cleared the edema yet. Started breathing on his own and blinking a lot."

"We'll have to see how he is when the time comes." Her tone was icy.

"So how is his family doing?"

"I don't know that they're any worse than average for this sort of thing, but they are louder than most. Lots of yelling in Spanish."

"Little kids still in tears?"

"I don't know, Malcolm."

"Bruises and broken bones?"

"Malcolm!" She took a deep breath. "The little brothers were acting out this morning. And Stepdad wants to challenge everything we say and do."

"Sounds lovely."

"Yeah, it's great. Their lawyer asked if he could read the chart. I said no. An hour later the stepdad had me paged wondering why not. He wants him to see it, it's his son's record, et cetera. So what could I do? We're going to have a big Care Conference at noon. Parents, priest, lawyer, nurses, social worker. Maybe a doctor or two. You should be there."

"Mmm. Sounds exciting. Maybe I should be there, you know, to keep you from salivating over the priest."

"Not possible." A pause. "What are you doing this afternoon?"

"I'm gonna go buy a cheap camera and work on my artistic vision. It's been in a coma, you know."

She said, "I know what you're going to do. You're going to go to the library. Do some real research."

"What library?"

"The Maricopa Biomed Library. I'm sure you still know where it is."

"And what would I be looking up? Assuming they let me in."

"Malcolm, pretend it's a school project. Look up all the pathophysiology you can think of. Do a differential diagnosis. Like in school, Malcolm. Make a list of the possible causes for what happened to Henry, look them all up, expand the list, look them up. You've done it all before."

I said, "Mm-mm. And it wasn't any fun any of the other times, either."

"Malcolm, do some homework for your hearing in Glory. Look up the drugs in the pharmacy texts. Sometimes they list all the weird stuff that's been reported. You know, the references. Pull the journals. Look for case reports."

She was right. Since my epinephrine syringe contained—as advertised—epinephrine, I was going to have to build my defense on dull science. "Well, the beach is all covered in sand, anyway. I suppose the library could fill a few hours."

Just outside Tucson, I hit a highway construction snag. The heavy posture of the woman leaning on the stop-sign-on-a-stick, a hardtack bottle-blonde sucking on a cigarette, was all I needed to know we would be sitting for a while. I shut off my motor and got out of the car to stretch. I walked up the embankment, found a spot that afforded a view of the activities up ahead, and sat on a rock, hoping I could enter a desert trance. Instead I got agitated. The sun hurt my eyes. I had trouble remembering what I was still fighting and why.

Back in football country we used to say "When in doubt, go long." I could make a U-turn over the median and head back to Tucson, then west out of town, maybe way out into the desert, see if the saguaros had been shot up out there, too. Maybe make LA or San Diego by nightfall; dull my brain with the So-Cal lotus leaves—days on the beach ogling a different species of bottle-blonde; then and only then start thinking about another job.

I pictured my Datsun skittering west across the desert; even with the cheery winter sun heating up the moving tin can, with the promise of Southern California, the home of instant gratification, even with the mindless babble of the radio at high volumes, it would be insufficient opium. I couldn't do it. I knew when the sun set, the gloaming would be painful: The primitive parts of the brain know night as the time of lions and tigers and bears.

I wanted a home. Running away wouldn't get me one.

I got back in my car, still parked on the freeway. The "Henry" section of the newspaper was on the passenger seat. I reread the article but found it no better reading the third time than the first two. But then, on one of the middle pages, right next to the story about Henry, a little one-column story caught my eye: "Police Seeking ID of Woman's Body." Someone had found the body of a young Caucasian brunette of medium height, floating in a culvert in the canal along Indian School Road. Her face was "distorted."

I sat and stared at nothing. The possibility of Robin's body lying on a slab in the morgue would explain Detectives Borden and May making early house calls. They no doubt would have heard all about my confronting her in the Glory ER. I couldn't remember exactly what I'd said, but I was sure it was enough.

Their lie detector suddenly seemed like a great idea. I pulled Will Borden's card from my pocket. When traffic got going again I found a pay phone and called the Mesa PD. A raspy, tobacco-infused female voice dragged out the greeting, "Homicide," making it sound like an offer.

"Hello. I'm looking for Detective Borden."

"The detective," she rasped, "is on another call. Would you care to wait?"

"I'd like to leave a message, if I may. I'm short on pocket change."

"Just a minute . . . okay."

"Please ask him—"

"Who is this?"

"Oh, sorry. This is Dr. Ishmail, calling from outside Tucson. Let him know I'm—"

"Dr. who?"

"Dr. Ishmail. Malcolm Ishmail. He came to see me at my town house in Phoenix a couple of days ago."

"Will he know what this is about?"

"Yes. Very much so. Please tell him I've decided—"

"Is there a number where he can reach you?"

"What? I mean, well, no. I'm calling from a pay phone. . . ."

"Honey, it's gonna be hard for him to call you back if I can't give him a number."

"He wanted me to take a lie detector. I've decided to do it. As soon as he wants to. Tomorrow. Today. I want to get it—"

"Uhh . . . He's off the phone. I'll put you through."

Will said, "You're in Tucson? I thought you weren't leaving town."

"Tucson hardly counts. I think it's a suburb. Besides, I'm coming right back." I repeated my offer to Detective Borden.

He said, "You're doing the right thing, coming in."

"Yeah. I seem to be stuck on that lately. It's a curse."

We set a time for two o'clock that afternoon.

I got to Maricopa just after eleven. I figured I had time to take care of Mary Ellen's homework project as ordered. With my old ID for cover, I ambled into the Maricopa Biomedical Library.

Despite being off in a corner of an upper floor, out of the way of any Seething Masses, and an oasis of calm, it was not a popular draw. Scattered around the stacks and computer terminals were only three other young doctors; two were asleep and the third was reading a newspaper and loudly slurping a large coffee. I worried that pulling texts and journals would give me up as an alien.

In the text section, I grubbed through the recognized bible of pediatrics, fishing for the True Physiology of Henry. I looked up *aarrhythmia*, *allergy*, *asthma*, *bronchospasm*, *epinephrine*, *laryngospasm*, *pseudo-seizures*, and *Ritalin*. The epinephrine subchapter contained nothing pertinent I didn't already know, but I photocopied several pages. I thought I could use them to support the idea of Henry's heart running away from him after the shot. While it was speculative, that scenario just might be accepted by a Glory administration hungry for ways to exonerate their staff. It was just plausible enough that I could present it in earnest. It was more plausible than an allergic reaction. What would be left unsaid was it was all I could come up with.

Standing at the copier, picturing the nefarious possibilities I would be asked about during the upcoming session strapped to Will Borden's polygraph, I hit a still untapped topic: poisons.

Figuring no medical gathering ever starts on time, I went back to work. In the reference texts I found lots of chapters on poisons and poisoning. Chapters and subchapters on general approaches to evaluation and treatment, a chapter on lye—drain cleaner resembles candy to toddlers and is hell on the esophagus—lead, arsenic, other heavy metals, organophosphates (insecticides), and toxic plants. I found a section on "evaluating for the presence of unknown toxins" but it was mostly about kids who had gotten into the wrong cabinet. In short, nothing pertinent.

I got to the Pediatrics conference room by twelve-fifteen, but Henry's Care Conference was already going. A middle-aged man in a jacket and tie stopped speaking in mid-sentence when I ungracefully barged in. It felt like most of the gathered family and staff were staring at me as if I were vermin creeping onto the picnic blanket. I was about to mutter an apology, but stopped when I saw the man's stare. With grating politeness he said, "I'm sorry. This is a family Care Conference," implying I should back away quietly.

"Yes," I said. "I'm sorry. I'm Dr. Ishmail. I was the boy's physician in the Emergency Department in Glory."

"Oh. I see."

Mary Ellen spoke up: "I invited him. Malcolm was a resident here. He knows most of the staff. I'd like him to sit in on the conference."

The speaker said, "Well then, if you're one of the boy's physicians . . ." he nodded to a seat.

I said, "I'm sorry I'm late. I was told it was going to be at around—"

Monty said, "Sorry, Malcolm. Everyone was here so we started. I wasn't sure you were going to be able to make it." Then to the group: "I've been in daily contact with Dr. Ishmail. He's been following the case closely, of course." To me: "I think you know who everyone is. . . ." She gestured about her. I realized from the grim and sweaty expressions that silent, respectful nods would be my best greetings.

I recognized most of the faces around the table: On one side were Henry's mother and stepfather, Mary Ellen, and one of the PICU nurses. On the other side were Ted Priestly, the lawyer, Mary Ellen's intern with the big eyelashes, smiling, again looking unaware, and another nurse.

At the head end of the table sat Monty's HO priest, Father What-a-Waste. Next to him, the speaker, who looked vaguely familiar. When

Monty introduced him as "Dr. Levi Strand, the consulting neurologist on this case," it came back to me: Dr. Strand had been the Attending who had argued with Monty over Nancy Madsen, insisting on keeping her lungs alive when her brainstem was gone. I sat down as quietly as I could and folded my hands.

Dr. Strand resumed speaking. "Well, then . . . Actually we're nearly finished, I believe. We have explained to the Rojelios, er, the Mendozas, about brain edema—the swelling we'd been talking about—and how their son may regain more function as the swelling resolves. As Dr. Montgomery probably told you, the EEG is not definitive for brain death. There remains some activity. The imaging studies, the CAT scans, show some loss of cortical mass." He gestured in a swirling motion over his head. "We had placed the boy on some heavy sedation when he arrived, to control the seizure activity. Some of those drugs have been, well, hanging around. The levels, though, have been coming down progressively and we are confident that we will be able to do the bedside determination—the examination of the most important reflexes for the life support functions—in the morning."

I nodded. Mary Ellen said to me, "Apnea challenge. Calorics." I nodded again.

The priest spoke, beaming his blue eyes around like searchlights. "I want to say again, we—the Mendozas, Mr. Priestley, I, our congregation—all trust you doctors and nurses completely. We know the Lord's hand will guide you to do the right thing." Dr. Strand nodded. Mary Ellen looked like granite.

The lawyer was staring at me. He looked around, then said, "I know all these considerations are very emotionally charged. As I said before, I'm here only as a friend of the family. I know Daniel wants nothing more than his son's survival. If I can be of any help at all here, it will be in that—helping my friend express his . . . his needs, his wants, and those of his family, of course."

Dr. Strand echoed, "Of course."

"The Mendozas want their son back . . ."

"Of course."

". . . any way the Lord will give him to them."

La Señora Mendoza bit her lip but didn't speak. She looked angry.

One of the nurses had been looking at each speaker and nodding her sympathy; the other was staring at the table. Dr. Strand looked about the group, silently asking if anyone else wanted to speak.

The conference room was linoleum-lined like a kindergarten. It served as the arts-and-crafts center for the children fit enough to do projects. The walls were covered with fresh paintings of roadrunners and Gila monsters in primary-colored tempera. I said quietly, "What about the other children? Henry's brothers and sister?"

Dr. Strand squinted at me. "What do you mean?"

"What do they need?"

Monty was shaking her head slightly. Ted Priestley looked at Father O'Donnell and then at Henry's parents, then at me. "They are children," he said.

"Precisely so," I said. "They're not here at this meeting because they are children, but their needs may be greater than anyone else's."

He looked askance. "They will be completely taken care of. I'm sure if you asked them they would say they only hope to have back their brother."

"I'm sure that's true," I said, intending to elaborate on the difference between the real and the expressed needs of children, but I paused when I noticed Mary Ellen glowering at me.

Dr. Strand cut me off: "I'm afraid we have to concern ourselves with the welfare of our patient here first. I believe we are all agreed upon the plan and we know tomorrow will be a difficult day no matter which path the Lord shows us." He nodded to Father O'Donnell. "So unless anyone else feels the need to speak . . ." He looked about. Everyone was silenced. He rose slowly and people scuffled out.

Mary Ellen and I made eye contact, signaling each other we needed to talk, then stood and waited by the door until everyone had gone. She insisted we sit back down.

I said, "Sorry I missed the main event, but I think I got the flavor. Seems the disaster may live on."

"You don't know the half of it." She looked more concerned for me than for her patient. "Old Smiley, the lawyer over there, just before you came in, was telling of us about a 'somewhat similar' case in Pennsylvania he had read about where the DA had pressed manslaughter charges."

"What? Are you serious?"

"Oh, he was all apologetic for even bringing it up, the slimeball, but said he wanted to be up front that he had 'received information' that could—*could*—turn this into a criminal case, especially if the boy dies. At one point he said something implying, in his roundabout Gee-I'm-sorry-to-have-to-mention-this way, that any decision to withdraw support could turn this into a murder."

I closed my eyes and took a deep breath. "What kind of 'information' did he have?"

"He didn't exactly say. Said he knew of a report on file at the hospital he was going to try to see, though."

"It's protected. If it's the one I know of, it's part of Quality Assurance and protected from discovery."

"Malcolm, what the hell have you gotten into?"

I took a deep sigh. "Mary Ellen. I wish I knew. I went out there, to Glory, two days ago, to go over the risk management stuff with the Glory administration and found out the nurse on the case had written up a report saying I'd fucked it up from top to bottom."

She looked incredulous. "You've got to be kidding. What a bitch!"

"Yeah. She made a laundry list of everything I supposedly missed in the workup, of things I didn't know during the code, of how I struggled with the intubation, then—poof—she's gone. Jesus, she made it sound like I was a butcher."

"You've never butchered anything in your life." I gave her a smile. "Why would she do that?"

"Well, that's the question."

"Covering her own fuckup?"

"Yeah, that's what I'm thinking." Since Mimi, I was accustomed to keeping things from Monty. There in the warmth of her fire, though, I could think of no good reason to keep all my current troubles secret, too. "There are detectives looking for the nurse, too," I said. "She's disappeared."

"Well, who could blame her for running and hiding? She must have done something fairly heinous."

"Yeah. Hit and run. Though I kind of get the sense these detectives are wondering if I know something about her disappearance."

She stared at me. "That's gotta be a joke. You're still half altar boy.

You wouldn't squash a cockroach. You have those detectives call me. I'll set their asses straight."

She was doing to me what she had done dozens of times, at key points in my life: notching me up a rung in my own understanding of who I was. We locked eyes. I smiled.

Then I sighed. I said, "So, back to reality. The nurse's report must be the information he's not supposed to know about, but does. But it's part of QA, so it should be protected."

"It's protected from discovery in a malpractice action, Malc. I'll bet you dinner it's usable in a criminal action."

"Oh shit. You're probably right. That would be just fucking beautiful." I looked at the ceiling.

She leaned toward me and took my hands. "You can see why I thought you should keep a low profile about letting the kid go. It might be best for everyone if he hangs around, regardless of how many neurons are firing."

I shook my head. "What did Mom and Dad say?"

"That was the interesting part. They really didn't say much. The lawyer and the priest did the talking for them, saying they want everything possible done. Though come to think of it, I didn't hear the priest use that language."

Now I was getting angry. "Let me get this right," I said, "if Henry 'lives,' for lack of a better term, the potential settlement goes up, what, tenfold? An annuity for eternal care? And he's in line for a fat percentage? Is there a conflict of interest here?"

"Might be. Hey, calm down. I didn't invite him. All I can do is play hostess for the Big Meeting while my Attending oils everybody up."

"You think the family really wants the full vegetable treatment? Lifelong ventilator? Tube feedings?" I said.

"Well, that's not exactly how they put it."

"But that's how you need to put it if they can't see the darkness at the end of the tunnel."

"Malcolm. Stop. It's too late. I tried. Herr Doktor Professor at the head of the table isn't about to take a stand. He's just going to play along. If Henry's brain-dead we'll be able to let him go. If he's not, it looks like we carry on, regardless."

I bit my lip and nodded. I turned to her for a second, then closed my eyes, then opened them and forced a smile. "Well," I said, "you can be proud of me. I went to the library and did my homework."

"What did you find?"

"I read every printed word I could find about epinephrine and asthma and damn if we didn't get a good education. There was nothing much in there I didn't already know." She nodded. I said, "I even looked up poisoning. Nothing there, though, either."

She was staring at me.

I said, "Can I buy you lunch?"

"I need to go check on some labs. I left a kid in Diarrhea Clinic. Where you going?"

"I guess the cafeteria. I kinda miss their secret sauce."

"You're sick." She rose to go.

I said, "Wait. So . . . The plan for Henry?"

"Brain-death determination in the morning. He's off all sedatives, relaxants, everything. If he's waking up, good. If he's not, we'll do what's right."

"I know you will. But he apparently ain't waking up."

"Yes, but we've no choice," she said.

"Well, don't dilly-dally."

"No, Malcolm."

"Those little Mendoza kids are suffering."

"So is Henry, Malcolm."

"No he's not. He's in a coma."

"Yes, Malcolm."

I went to the cafeteria. I'd missed the cracked vinyl seats, the buzzing fluorescent lights, the noise and the gooey arroz con pollo. All around the room interns and residents were inhaling their lunches. Talking with their mouths full. Talking too loudly about their patients' problems. Laughing at black medical humor. Struggling with burdens and succeeding. Just like old times.

20

From the time I could walk, I got to tag along with Dad on rounds. Some-times there was a reason—some family inconvenience that left me in his hands—but just as often it seemed he wanted the company. I came to under-stand I was more than welcome.

My grade-school pals said it must be yucky. I obliged them with exag-gerated tales of guts and things vomited up, leaving out any mention of my initial queasiness. By the time the chance to reshape the tale arose, I had mastered the queasiness. Often there were long stretches of boredom, watching him write in charts or talk on the phone. I learned to keep handy a coloring book or, as I grew, a comic book, a chapter book, homework, or a novel.

The good stuff generally happened when I was asked to leave the room. Dad would smile in a way that said he was sorry to have to ask, then later explain that it was only the other people who thought I shouldn't be there. He also explained what had gone on. I learned to look for a spot where I could eavesdrop and sit with my face buried in a book, staring at the same page for as long as fifteen minutes.

Once, when I was in about the fourth grade, Dad said there was some-one he had to go see. When we went into the hospital room he embraced a man his age—mid-forties. The man's eyes were tearing. In the bed was a child, asleep, but pale and ghostly with purple blotches on her face and shoulders that made me wince. Dad turned to me and nodded toward the door. I left it ajar.

I heard this: Dad: "She's comfortable, sleeping like an angel."

The man: "Yeah." He sobbed.

Dad: "Are you sure you and Gwen are ready?"

The man sobbed.

Dad: "I'm so sorry, Ed. They did everything they could in Lincoln. I think you made the right choice to bring her home now, though. We can help

her here. I'll speak with the nurse. Annie will get all the morphine she needs.
We won't let her have any pain."

The man: "I don't want it to . . . go on . . ."

Dad: "No. Of course not. It won't."

In the car I asked Dad if she was dying. He said yes. I asked if she was
hurting. He said no. I asked what the morphine was for. He said to make the
parents' pain go away.

HENRY ROJELIO, DAY SIX (CONTINUED)

The Mesa PD was a boxy, four-story building, all red brick, wheelchair
ramps and brown steel handrails, plopped among some older homes at
the edge of the downtown district. A desk officer paged the detectives.
Will Borden came out and escorted me inside a section marked
"Homicide." In their office I sidled over to the window. They had a
view of a parking lot full of police cruisers and clunky, unmarked
sedans. The latter were the more intimidating.

I tried to strike a relaxed attitude, to sound calm. Borden and May
probably found it amusing. I said, "No news on your missing nurse, I
suppose."

"No. Hasn't turned up, anyway," Will said. They looked at me like
they were reading a poster.

I said, "If you've got any unidentified bodies, you should know that
Robin had fake breasts." Their expression didn't change. I went on, "I
read about it in the paper. A woman's body found in a canal. Though
I guess that would be the Phoenix PD."

I looked from face to face. They showed me nothing. Finally Will
said, "Yeah. The papers are full of stuff like that. Happens all the
time." I nodded. I felt like I was there to be milked; information was
only going to move in one direction.

Ken said, "You're gonna sit for the polygraph?"

"Sure. I mean, there's no reason not to."

Will said, "Right. It'll help us all move along. You've never taken
a polygraph test before, have you?"

"No."

"Well, what we'll do is keep it nice and relaxed. You and Ken and I will go through all the questions here before you even meet the polygrapher. You know, so there aren't any surprises."

I knew it was not as friendly as he was painting it or we all wouldn't be sitting where we were. I nodded. Since the polygraph can measure only anxiety in the subject, I guessed they really just wanted to preload my stress level by showing me the mines I would have to step on. I just had to keep reminding myself I had nothing to lie about.

He went on. "We'll only ask questions with a yes-or-no answer. 'Is your name Malcolm Ishmail?' 'Are you a medical doctor?' 'Did you ever have sex with Robin Benoit?'"

I said, "Okay."

He flipped some pages on a yellow legal pad and began reading questions. Their list started with the usual identification and background data. He asked if I had ever stolen anything, and later whether I had ever driven a car after drinking alcohol. I thought, *Baseline. Most people will lie. They want to see what a lie looks like on their radar.* I decided I could afford to oblige them.

He moved to a yes/no recounting of what I'd already told them: "Did you go to Robin Benoit's house on the night before her meeting with Sally Marquam?" "Did you forget your jacket at her house?" "Did you phone her about it?"

To each of these I nodded.

He said, "You're going to have to speak up, when you're on the polygraph."

I said, "Uh-huh."

He read on: "Were you surprised by Miss Benoit's report to the Glory administrators?" "Were you angry?" Again, I nodded. "Had the two of you had an argument?" "Did you cut your hand in the Glory ER?" "Did it bleed in Robin's house?" "Did you cut your hand in Robin's house?" I shot a scowl at him but he waved his hand and read on.

He read questions about the details of Robin's physical makeup: height, weight, hair color, hairstyle. It got more interesting when he asked, "Was she particularly muscular?" "Did she have any bruises?"

"Was she bleeding anywhere?" He went into our sexual encounter: "Was there fellatio?" "Was there cunnilingus?" "Was there actual coitus?" "Did you use contraception?" "Condoms?" "Anything besides condoms?"

I started to frown. Something wasn't right. Robin was clearly used to sexual encounters—she had condoms and a can of sperm killer at the ready. Robin's toy box. It was not there when I had gone to her house. Though I hadn't thought of it at the time, the key in her night-stand drawer was gone, too. Surely she had taken her personal stash with her.

"You gotta pay attention," May said.

"Oh, sorry. I was thinking of something. Something missing." They looked at me. I said, "Robin left of her own accord."

"You think so."

"I know so. When I went to Robin's house. That next night. To pick up my jacket . . ." I paused. "Well, you should know first. The night at Robin's. She invited me for dinner. She wanted to talk over our ER disaster. We drank white wine. She said it should have been champagne, but she had a thing about bubbles. She made a fish stir-fry. She gave me a massage. We went to bed. I left without my jacket. I've told you this."

They nodded.

"I called her about the jacket. She said she would leave it on the couch for me. Told me where her house key was. I asked for a date. She kind of blew me off."

"Right."

"I told you I went out there that night. When she had gone home sick, but she wasn't home. The place was dark. I looked around. No jacket. I knocked some stuff off the kitchen counter. I broke a glass. I swept up the mess and put it in her trash. I looked around, like a guy who's seen too many movies, wondering if I could find any notes or anything that might explain what was going on. Where she was."

"And? You found something you didn't tell us about?"

"Nothing. Literally. Her clothes and some books and most of that shit was there. But her personal stash—that was gone, too. I'm sure of it. She had this wooden box. Said she got it in San Francisco. It was made to look like a pair of old books. Peeling paint and gold leaf on the edges. Really kind of cool. She got it off her bookshelf before we had sex. Had her condom stash in it, with spermicide. And a big wad of money. Said her father insisted on giving her money but her mother didn't approve so she got it in cash."

Ken began making notes. "Uh-huh."

"It was gone. It had to be." I was hanging my mouth open between sentences. "And it would be a very rare crime victim who could get home to retrieve her most personal belongings. So Robin left of her own volition."

Will said, "We'll see. Where did she keep the box?"

"It was on her bookcase in her bedroom. Left wall, from the bed, left of the window. Shelf at about eye level."

"You looked for it?"

"No. I mean I didn't search for it. But there was a blank spot in the row of books. I noticed it at the time, but didn't add it all up. And the key to the box was in her nightstand. I looked in that drawer for any papers. I found a blank sheet of hospital chart paper. There wasn't any key. I would have seen it."

"Why didn't you tell us this before?"

"I just didn't think of it. We were talking about all the other stuff. And he was making me nervous." I pointed to May.

Borden nodded. "You didn't take it? The box?"

"No."

"The key?"

"No."

"Because, you see, you could have taken it just as easily as she could have."

"Right, but I didn't." I pointed at his notepad. "Ask me about it when I'm wired up."

Borden started writing on his list of questions. "Okay, we'll ask you about that, too."

May said, "But it ain't gonna prove much. Any house thief could have taken it when he took her."

I said, "I suppose so."

Borden said, "It does narrow the thing down some, though, proof or no proof."

He finished reading the questions. When he got to "Did you ever hurt Robin Benoit?" "Did you hit Robin Benoit in the face?" and "Did you kill Robin Benoit?" I would have smiled at the bluntness, but the newspaper piece about the body in the morgue reminded me there was no room for humor, even the dark humor I was certain homicide detectives had in spades over doctors.

"Ready?" Will asked. I nodded. He said, "Let's go meet Carole." It sounded like a game show.

They walked me down a narrow hall to a windowless back room and introduced me to Carole, a thin strawberry blonde in the sand-colored uniform of the Department with an armload of stripes. "She's our local technical expert," Will said. She had a crooked smile and the smell of freshly smoked cigarettes. "Ken and I will leave you here."

Carole pointed me to a chair beside a metal desk. She said, "Take your shirt off and just relax now, dear." She wrapped two cables around my chest, one high, one low. She put a standard blood pressure cuff on my upper arm and inflated it until I could feel my pulse throbbing under it. She put my left index finger in a cup-shaped clip. "That's it, now." Where I sat I couldn't see the printout.

She read the same list, verbatim, absent all facial expression and most inflection in her voice. After each question I said "yes" or "no" as if my vindication depended on my enunciation. With each answer she scrawled something on the printout as it went by. I felt myself jerk to attention with the questions about stealing and driving drunk. I didn't really lie, I equivocated. She dutifully made her marks and absolutely nothing changed in her face or voice.

When she finished the list she unhooked me and ushered me to the lounge for a cup of coffee *en* styrofoam. She took the printout to the detectives, then sat in the lounge with me. She smoked.

My pager went off. It was Mary Ellen again. Carole nodded to a phone. "Just dial 9."

"You coming back to the hospital?" Mary Ellen asked.

"I wasn't going to. It's not really a happy place for me right now."

"I've got something for you."

"The love I've missed?"

"No. You've always had that. These are more mundane. Also more germane to your acute problems with a certain missing nurse."

"You always know how to tease a guy. I'll be there in . . ." I looked at Carole with a questioning look.

"I think you're about done," she said.

I said into the phone, "About half an hour."

A few minutes later Borden and May came back in to dismiss me. Will said, "Okay, guess you're all done, Dr. Ishmail. Thanks for coming out."

I looked from one to the other. "So, I'm cleared of, uh, suspicion?"

Their faces were impassive. Borden said, "We told you, there is no suspicion."

May said, "Before you go, though, a couple more things: a set of fingerprints and a blood sample."

I said, "Absolutely."

I found Mary Ellen at the nurses' station on the Pediatrics ward, bent over a chart, writing furiously, looking tired. And beautiful.

"What have you been up to?" I asked.

She turned to me and grinned. "Digging in the Biomed Library."

"Did I leave a trail?"

"Did you know your phone number is on the wall in the women's room?"

"It's your number, too."

"Yeah, I noticed that."

"Did it say I was a good time?" I said.

"No. I added that."

"You're a true friend. What were you doing at the library? Besides checking for phone numbers?"

"A literature search."

"Some really exciting form of diarrhea show up in clinic?"

"No, that was just plain old kid poop. No, after we talked I remembered something I'd seen on TV about nurses causing intentional harm."

"Do they do that?"

"It seems they do. At least in Indiana and Texas."

She handed me copies of two journal articles. The first report was from *The Journal of Southern Medicine*, titled "A Series of In-Clinic Seizures Found to Be Intentionally Induced with Lidocaine." It described an office nurse in Texas who apparently so enjoyed the titillation of emergency resuscitations, screaming sirens, and paramedics in jumpsuits that she repeatedly loaded children with intravenous lidocaine until they did what anyone does with sufficient lidocaine, they seized. There were seven such incidents before they figured her out. It said she was prosecuted for felony battery. Her name was withheld.

The second, from *The Journal of the American Medical Association*, was titled "A Nurse-Associated Cluster of Cardiac Arrests in a Medical ICU." It reported from an Indiana ICU a run of cardiac arrests, always associated with toxic potassium levels. The last two deaths also showed toxin digoxin levels. In-depth analysis showed they occurred only when two specific nurses were on shift together. The paper implied they were indiscriminate killers. Nothing had been proven, though, and both RNs had subsequently moved out of state.

I looked at my friend. She smiled and nodded. "Years ago on TV, I saw a piece about that same case from Texas. Only their version was it had more to do with her wanting to play the hero. I remember the idiot newsman pronouncing it 'lidd-o-kane,' and by the end of the piece it had become '*deadly* lidd-o-kane.' He said the kids were 'on the *brink* of death.' "

I half-laughed. I looked again at the second report. Something in it had caught my attention, as something at the edge of one's vision, moving.

"So anyway, I thought if you had something like this, to show the board in Glory, it's not exactly geometric proof, but it will paint a suggestive picture when you need it most."

I reached over and hugged her. "Can I buy you dinner?" I said.

"Maybe. We got two admissions supposedly getting here before five o'clock, and the nursery is suddenly overflowing. If we get things under control I'll page you."

"Is your team shaping up? Is Michelle taking form?"

She nodded at me. "She's coming along."

As Monty went off to her multiple charges I read through the articles again. It was a long shot to think Robin could have been an itinerant child-hurter, but I was living well outside the area of usual and customary occurrences.

I went to see Cynthia Blachly, my former Mom-away-from-Mom. When I poked my head in her door she said, "Oh my God, look who's back."

"Not really," I said. "Just passing through."

"Causing trouble?"

"Something like that. I do have a small favor to ask." She cocked her head at me. "You know anybody over at the Nursing Board?"

She chewed her lip. "No. I guess I don't. But Monica would."

"Who's Monica?"

"Monica Rouse. Across the hall in Human Resources. She talks to them all the time. C'mon."

The door across the hall said "Nursing Staff Services." Cynthia introduced me. She added, "Dr. Ishmail is—was—one of my 'boys.' He slipped in a little mess last year and he's on a break, but we're trying to get him back. He wanted to know if we knew anybody at the Nursing Board."

Monica gave a short laugh. "We got a regular *hot line*. We got nurses coming and going so fast around here I'm trying to get the board to just open up a branch office down the hall. Make my job a heck of a lot easier."

We all smiled. "Well, if you could . . . ," I said, looking from one to the other, "if you could call whoever you know best over there and ask them to peek at a file. Find out if this nurse ever worked in Indiana or Texas." I wrote out "Robin Benoit" on a notepad.

Monica keyed a number by memory. "Hey, Charlene. Monica. Can you pull a file real quick? On a Robin Benoit? . . . No, just a quick question. Look and see if there's any work history from Indiana or Texas. . . . Yeah. . . . No, I'll just hold." Monica covered the mouthpiece and said to Cynthia, "Charlene used to work with me over at the Arizona Medical Society. We both left when it got so crazy with that Medicare rules thing. . . ." A pause, then, into the receiver, "Okay. . . . Good. . . . You sure? . . . Okay. Thanks." She hung up.

Monica said, "Charlene says his record had nothing but New York and Arizona."

I blinked. "His?" I said.

"Uh-huh."

"You sure she said 'his'?"

"That's what she said."

My mind was at escape velocity: I tried not to look too shocked. As they watched me I listened to my brain arguing the possibilities: "I had sex with a man." "Not possible—not like that." "A former man." "Boy, that anatomy seemed God-given to me." "Where would that spermicide have gone?" "Transsexuals don't need contraception."

I said, "'His.' Did she have the right Robin Benoit?"

Monica gave me look. "Well, how many you got?"

That's the question, I thought. To her: "Did you . . . Did she . . . Is there a description? In the file?"

"Yeah. Usually a picture, too."

"I hate to be a pain, but is there any way you could call her back? Get the description? I mean, something is *really* haywire here."

She called Charlene again and got the details: Male. Six foot two, 195 pounds. Blonde, green eyes. Born 1966 in Bath, England. Et cetera.

Charlene added that this seemed to be a hot file—"A couple of cops were in here yesterday looking it over, too."

I forced a smile like I'd won a booby prize. I thanked them both. I promised Cynthia I'd come see her soon. Maybe bring her a bottle of wine. Maybe, with a lot of luck, be able to explain what was going on.

From a phone at a charting desk on the Orthopedics ward I called Will Borden, getting the same rasping "Homicide" solicitation and, "The detective is not in."

"Is Ken May there?"

"No, honey. They go everywhere together. They're both out."

"Could I leave a message?"

"Sure, honey."

"I'm hoping to find out what they really know about—"

"Who is this again?"

"Dr. Ishmail. I was just there a couple hours ago. They're looking for a nurse named—"

"Can you leave a number?"

"Sure." I gave her my pager number. I said, "They've been to the Nursing Board, I guess, so I'm hoping they can tell me what's next."

"You're at the Nursing Board?"

"Sure. Close enough. Tell them I called."

21

Figuring I'd try to clear my head with a workout before dinner, I headed down a back stairway in the 'Copa. There I ran into Gene Woods, my friend from Surgery. He said, "Eh-hey, it's the Prodigal again! Twice in one week. What are you up to, sneaking around here? You got something going with somebody around here I don't know about?"

"Geno, I'm pretty sure you know about every female within twenty miles of here."

"Yeah. That's the problem."

"What are you up to?"

"Going over to The Longhorn. Gordon Erickson has a new lady he wants me to drool over. Why don't you come along? Maybe she's got some *seesters*."

"He's bringing a date to The Longhorn?"

"Why not? It's better than a zoo. Doctors in their native habitat."

"I was hoping to hook up with Mary Ellen when she's free."

"You just keep hoping. For now, c'mon with me. You can call her from the bar. Tell her to join us. Even super-doctors have to eat."

The Longhorn was, as usual, smoky, noisy, dark, and beery. I paged Mary Ellen from the pay phone near the restrooms. A minute later it rang back. It was Michelle saying, "Dr. Montgomery can't come to the phone right now. She's doing a procedure." I knew this to mean Michelle had failed at the procedure and Monty had taken over. I said only, "Tell her we're at The Longhorn. Join us when she can."

Around the Oval Table and spilling into the nearby booths were interns and residents, inhaling chips and enchiladas, still talking with their mouths full about their patients' problems. Though entirely familiar, it was painful: I felt again like an interloper.

Worse, on that night I felt impotent. Henry's Care Conference, with all the major forces of society convened, had given a finality to his case. What I had wanted to say had been rendered irrelevant by my bad timing. Impotence makes me testy.

I rejoined Gene in one of the booths. He was sharing chips with Glenn Baba, a senior surgery resident, and a couple who looked like they were joined at the shoulder. I knew the male half of the couple: Gordon Erickson, an anesthesiology resident. Gordon introduced me to his date, a petite ball of *fuego Latino* named Angela. She was a PR specialist he'd met when she was interviewing around the OR for a promotional piece for the hospital.

The guys wanted to hear about life beyond the sleepless nights and near-constant call obligations of residency. I reminded them that, despite the immediate appeal of having a practice, even a half-assed one, I was working to get back *in*. Glenn offered to trade on the spot.

"Sounds good to me," I said, "let's just see what Hebert and Goodbout and the GME Committee have to say about it."

"Shit, Hebert would take you back in a second," Gene said. "He told me he wants to fire my ass just to make room for you, and I think he means it."

I smiled. I told them I was appealing my dismissal, but didn't expect a fair hearing.

Gene nodded at me and said to Glenn, "The dumb bastard managed to get his butt canned despite being the Old Man's favorite. Now that's talent." When I was "not renewed" I'd shared some of my distress with Gene over a few beers.

Glenn stared at me for an explanation. "I was accused—falsely—of stealing drugs from the hospital. That and the crime of trying too hard to improve patient care," I said.

"Shit. Your only crime was being criminally honest," Gene said.

I smiled. Thinking more of my Mimi issues than the drug accusations, I said, "Hard to figure honesty as a fault."

"Except about drugs. Half of all Americans use some kind of contraband, but none of them would admit to it."

"They'd get crucified," Glenn said.

"Precisely my point," Gene said. "Bucko here did just that. The Powers asked, he told the truth, they showed him the door."

"There was a lot more to it than that," I said. "For one thing, I never did cop to it."

"Yeah, but you danced around it. Didn't say no. What I'm saying is, there is no rationality about drugs. Always, always, always say no! Just say no. If they ask you if you have ever seen a marijuana cigarette, just say no."

"And how do you justify that?" I asked.

"Rationalize it, man, like everybody else. If you dance around drugs you're basically challenging them to fuck you. And they will. It's pure self-defense. They're looking for an excuse to kill you. Defend yourself."

I sighed. "I've always been a shitty liar."

He took a pull of his beer. He said, "It's an important life skill. Practice up."

We ordered dinner. They talked about the personal quirks of some of their Attendings. I was preoccupied. I stared at the various initials carved into the table. I didn't add much to the conversation.

Apropos of nothing, I said to Gordon, the nascent anesthesiologist, "You poison people professionally. If you wanted to . . . had some hideous reason, how would you kill an asthmatic?"

They all looked at me. Gordon said flatly, "Sux."

"Sux?"

"Succinylcholine."

"Depolarizing muscle relaxant," I recited. Miguel had refreshed me about it in the lab.

"Yeah."

"Why sux?"

"Works IM—" he turned to Angela, "intramuscular. A regular shot in the butt." She nodded.

"And in—what?—one, two minutes?—completely paralyzes the person?" I asked.

"About that. Dose dependent, of course."

"But it's short acting," Glenn said.

"Dose dependent," Gordie repeated. "A usual dose works in thirty to maybe a hundred and twenty seconds, lasts maybe ten to twenty minutes. Plenty long enough to get to a state of no brain oxygen, unconsciousness . . . death. Assuming the person—I almost said 'patient'—is only breathing ambient air, no supplemental O-two, he would probably die. With a larger dose you could almost guarantee it."

"How would you know if somebody got it?"

"With sux you get twitches all over, so-called 'fasiculations,' as they're paralyzed," he said. "It's a reliable sign. They jerk and jump."

"But I mean afterward. How could you test for it?"

"That's the beauty of it," he said. "You can't. A normal enzyme in blood breaks it down. Pseudo-cholinesterase. And the breakdown products, the succinyl part and the choline part, occur naturally throughout the body. Not traceable."

"The perfect murder weapon," Angela said.

"Well, not entirely. If the coroner suspects it, they can do an assay on a tissue sample from the injection site and pick up the parent compound, even in the small trace residuals likely to be left."

"But they have to be looking for it," Gene said.

"Yeah. And," he paused, "the guy's got to be dead."

"To get a tissue sample?"

"No, to stop the circulation. If the blood keeps flowing to the tissue area, all the sux gets pushed into the bloodstream soon enough and it *all* disappears."

A pause. "Seems you've given this some thought," I said.

Gordon smiled. "Anesthesia *is* a controlled poisoning."

"You hope so," Angela said. "I mean, you hope it's controlled."

Gordon smiled again. "That's why it's a whole specialty all by itself. We only get paid for bringin' 'em back alive."

He went on, "One of my Attendings, a short and very curvaceous Filipino woman who specializes in treating cancer pain—she can put a needle in places I never knew existed—carries in her purse a big syringe loaded with sux. She says if some asshole is going to rape her in the parking lot, he'd better be done in one to two minutes."

We laughed. "Wait a sec," Glenn said. "She's going to inject—

what?—five, ten cc's? IM? Before this hypothetical rapist can fend off a short woman with big tits and a syringe?"

"Well, it is an interesting defense weapon," he said.

"But I'm serious. What's the usual concentration?"

"Twenty milligrams per cc."

"So, say this is even a small rapist. Say he's a hundred and twenty-five pounds—sixty kilos."

Gordie nodded. "Okay."

"And what's the dose?" Glenn said.

"Four milligrams per kilogram."

"He's to get four per kilo? Two hundred and forty milligrams? Twelve cc's?"

Gordon smiled. I pictured his buxom Attending pushing a horse syringe into a combative rapist. "How big a needle she got?" I said.

"Never asked," Gordie said. "But now that you mention it, a fourteen would be best, unless you could find a twelve." He turned to Angie. "Remember that."

"Nobody's going to be raping me!" she said.

"Carry some sux and you can make sure of it."

"Maybe I'll try it out on you."

"You want me totally paralyzed?"

"Might be fun," she said, reaching up and taking him by the chin, turning him to look directly into her eyes.

Gordon started to say, "Naw, you'd have to do mouth-to-mou—" but was stopped when she covered his mouth with hers. The rest of us sat and watched, apparently rendered mute by the shower of stray pheromones not intended for us. Gordon put his arm around Angela and it seemed we should all be getting out of the way.

I wasn't through with pharmacology, though. "Aren't there any other concentrations of sux available?" I asked.

"Not premixed," he said idly. His focus on drugs was tenuous.

"What? A powder?"

"Yeah. 'Flo-Pack.' A thousand milligrams of the stuff in a little plastic squeeze bottle. We use it to mix up sux for continuous drips. You can run it continuously through short cases and have patients awake and moving right away at the end, it wears off so fast."

"A gram," I said mostly to myself. "How concentrated can you make it?"

"No idea," he said, his eyes regaining normal focus. "We usually put it in a five-hundred-cc bag so it's the same as the bottled stuff—twenty per. We also usually put in a couple cc's of blue dye and label the thing up and down the IV line so some bozo doesn't use it to start the IV in presurgery."

"That happens?" Angela asked.

"Well, at least once. That's how they got the idea for the blue stuff."

"They're fast learners," I said to Angela. To Gordon: "But there's no problem mixing them together? The sux and the blue dye?"

"Most things that will dissolve in an IV solution *are* compatible with one another."

I tried to picture the shapes of the molecules, bouncing around in solution, and imagine what might make them somehow cling together and inactivate each other.

"Okay," Gordie said, pulling his arm off of Angela's shoulders. "Greatest sux story ever. Supposedly—I mean these legends are never verifiable—supposedly an anesthesia resident at God's Own Hospital in Boston is by himself early one morning in the workroom, setting up a bunch of shit for a long day. And he's making up a sux drip. He's hurrying. He *bites* the cap off the little squeeze bottle, pulling on it, and—unintentionally—gives it a good squeeze. He realizes, to his own horror, he's just inhaled about half a gram of sux. Drops all the shit on the floor, runs and pulls the fire alarm, then grabs a laryngoscope and a breathing tube, lies down on the floor and sets these on the middle of his chest, praying someone will get there before it's too late."

We all grinned.

"What happened?" Angela asked.

"Doesn't matter," Gene said. "The story is about thinking under pressure."

"And being on the other end of the stick," Gordie said.

"But what did happen?" I asked.

"I dunno," he said. "Probably nothing. The sux molecule is very polar, so it probably isn't even absorbed."

"He probably could have just rinsed out his mouth," I said.

"Yeah. But I've always wondered," Gordon said, "how long would you lie there wondering?"

I smiled. Sitting in The Longhorn, knowing I would still be breathing ten minutes hence, I could afford to smile. Then, though, I imagined being the one lying still on a cold basement OR floor wondering how much longer I would be breathing on my own. I pictured a blue mixture running into me. But something was trying to get my attention again. The something that had been moving at the edge of my vision when I read Mary Ellen's reports of nefarious nurses.

It hit me—the moving piece—potassium and digoxin mixed in Indiana; sux and blue dye mixed in the Maricopa OR.

Sometimes I think there should be an annual awards ceremony, televised live from Hollywood, for those vacuous failures to perceive the obvious that reach epic proportions. I could make a fawning speech and get a little gold statuette. Maybe shaped like a vacuum cleaner—the "Hoovies."

I said to myself, *The epi syringe needs to be tested. For* second *drugs.* If a paralyzing drug had been mixed *with* epinephrine, in the dog model I'd still see only the epi effect. The dog was already paralyzed; she couldn't get *more* paralyzed.

I said to Gene, "I need to order a lab test."

He made a face. "Go phone it in."

"Nope. I wish I could." My mind was churning. I needed someone with a research account number to order a proper analysis on the contents of the syringe in my refrigerator. My only friend in such a high place was Dr. Richard Hebert.

I said to Gene, "You're on Trauma, aren't you? You got Dr. Hebert's pager number memorized?"

"Yeah, but I wouldn't be paging him right now."

"Why not?"

"He's hosting at that faculty thing over at Frost. It's that Grand Old Man in from Chicago, one of Hebert's old professors."

I frowned. I said, "I'll just have to go blend in."

On the way out, I ran into Mary Ellen, finally out of her white coat, hair down and inviting. "Gotta run," I said.

She looked me up and down. "So much for buying me dinner."

"I have to talk to the Old Man. Hebert's at a faculty shindig over at Frost," I told her.

"Hey, Tequila Breath," she said, "I'm sure whatever it is can wait. You're tired and probably half drunk. Don't be stupid."

"Too late."

"You might want to wait and be your old impressive self again."

"No, it can't wait. I'll have to be impressive enough as I am."

I kissed her on the head and left.

Outside Frost Lecture Hall was a placard announcing the Biannual Schaecher Memorial Lecture. Marie, Dr. Hebert's secretary, was sitting just outside the hall, listening through the open door, a stack of program handouts on her lap. The room was dark but for the projected image on the screen. The speaker was well under way.

"Is Dr. Hebert in there?" I whispered to her.

"Way up front."

I frowned. "Who is this guy?" I said, pointing to the podium.

"Franklin Weigand, MD, PhD," she whispered back, "a muckety-muck neurophysiologist."

I looked at the program. It said, "Practical Education in Neuro-physiology." I rolled my eyes. She smiled.

I crept in. As I cast about for a seat, several heads turned, bored faces seeking new stimuli. I sat next to a fleshy middle-aged woman I remembered as a dietary consultant I had met while rotating on Trauma. She smiled at me.

Projected on the screen was a daunting table of numbers and Greek letters. The title said, "Classes of Neurons." The professor was saying, with a Germanic accent, "This we also show, of course, to our students; you've all seen this many times. The type A fibers, the large diameter, myelinated, rapid-conducting fibers to muscle bundles; the type C nerve fibers, unmyelinated, much slower . . ."

I was sure I'd seen the chart up on the projector screen before, probably in medical school. It hadn't been very interesting then; it was less so now. But then, the subtleties of asthma weren't very interesting then and, I had to admit, were now perversely fascinating.

I said to myself, *Someday this knowledge could save a life*. It was something we used to say to each other with mock seriousness throughout second year. It had seemed that all lecturers in the long parade of specialists, from dermatologists to a research endocrinologist who hadn't treated a patient in fifteen years, had begun their talks with an explanation, usually statistical, of how much suffering their particular disease inflicted on humanity, the implication being that they were important and we had better pay attention. After a few months we all decided we had better become specialists, too, or we would inevitably kill someone because we had missed the wrong inflection in a lecture.

"Someone will die because I fell asleep in your lecture, sir," I remembered one of my friends offering up to the ceiling late one night in the donut shop. We all laughed, but partly in nervous fear.

Basic physiology. For six days I'd been thinking I'd missed something elegantly simple with Henry. Physiology is like that—when you know it cold it is elegant. And it can seem simple.

I closed my eyes. Maybe I'd been digging in the wrong end of human pathology: the cardiopulmonary. Maybe I needed to move up the body to the head.

I felt myself getting too comfortable in the chair and my eyelids getting heavy. I mentally shook myself awake. I needed to be analytic. Cover all the bases.

It was possible someone had put something in Robin's hands. If anyone were trying to hurt Henry, for whatever reason, it was almost a certainty I had the "weapon" in my refrigerator.

The GI tract was theoretically possible—the oral route, a favorite of centuries past. Not very glamorous. Not very effective, either. Very few poisons would have worked that fast, and the only oral poisons I could think of—like cyanide—produced a total metabolic disruption that would not have responded to any code on earth. Definitely not an oral poisoning.

I opened my eyes, glanced at Dr. Weigand's current slide, a high-powered microscope's view of a tangle of nerve endings, and decided I was better off with them closed.

How else can you give drugs? Under the tongue. Or nasally, or through the skin. There are only very few drugs that are absorbed via any of those routes, and they move slowly. None of those seemed possible.

The same would be true for the rectal route. Major problems with absorption, not to mention premature elimination. I pictured Robin giving a boy a poison suppository. It didn't fit. She's not the anal type, I thought. Definitely oral.

I realized I was falling asleep in a lecture again. With a belly full of Mexican soporifics, slouching in a padded lecture hall chair, it was probably inevitable. I didn't particularly care. It was a time-honored tradition among interns and residents as well as medical students.

Half asleep, I found Robin's oral tendencies far more compelling than neuro-physiology, practical or not. *Be analytical*, I told myself. *Maybe I enjoy the oral parts of lovemaking because the rest of my life is so fucking anal-retentive*, I thought with a smile.

I saw myself naked on her bed, gushing a smile just as I had during her fellatio. I kept on smiling and smiling as she arose and walked away, returning in a lab coat, though it was cut from yellow silk. She had it buttoned to the neck because there was nothing underneath. I tried to speak but couldn't—I was paralyzed. But she wasn't going to operate on me, just run tests.

Robin held up a tiny key. She fitted it to the edge of a book, which sprung open. She took a one-cc tuberculin syringe from it and held it to the light for a few seconds. Satisfied with its contents, she found the rubber injection port in my IV line and put the tiny needle through it. She slowly injected part of the syringe contents, then turned loose the roller clamp on the line to flush the drug in.

We could see the drug's advance toward me because there was a tiny air bubble, just large enough to fill the lumen of the IV line, moving toward me. I knew such a little bubble would not do me any damage—the capillary bed in my lungs would hold it until all the gas was absorbed—but its passing marked the moment the drug—whatever it was—entered me.

BANG!

I sat forward with a start. Someone had fired a gun.

My disorientation was overwhelming. On the stage, Professor Weigand was facing and pretending to fight one of the junior faculty, who was holding a small revolver in her hand and laughing in embarrassment.

I was breathing heavily. The woman next to me laid a hand on my arm and smiled.

"What the hell is this?" I whispered.

"That was a cap gun," she said.

"I hope so."

"He's demonstrating how the speed—or slowness—of neural transmission can limit one's actions."

"What?" I mumbled, still trying to regain full consciousness.

She shifted around to better lean into my ear. "He had the woman put the gun in his back and told her to pull the trigger as soon as he moved. Then he turned back to face her, fast as he could, and knocked the gun away from his back with his elbow. He says anybody with normal coordination can knock the gun away before the gunman can mentally process the sensory data of what's happening and send the neural message to the forearm to pull the trigger. Even, as he said, 'an old man.' "

"Every time?"

"So he says. Said he learned it from a karate master."

"Why, I guess this was practical," I said. "Any other hot tips I missed?"

"Go back to sleep," she whispered.

"Was I snoring?"

"Well, deep breathing anyway."

"Just kick me next time."

22

HENRY ROJELIO, DAY SIX (CONTINUED)

I did not go back to sleep in the lecture, though, nor even relax. I was troubled by something vague. It wasn't Dr. Weigand, even with a handgun. And it wasn't The Longhorn's dinner *plato*. Something in my dream.

The lights came up, signaling the end of Dr. Weigand's lecture. The applause was long; I suspect the faculty were impressed that anyone could make any part of neurophysiology entertaining. I joined, at its toil, the small rabble around the dais. Those ahead of me were anxious to shake hands with the eminence from Chicago. I only wanted Dr. Hebert but he was entrenched beside his guest.

As I waited my mind worked. I'd been dreaming about Robin in a lab coat. Odd. And then I remembered: the bubble. The bubble from the TB syringe. The dose of medication had come from the syringe and *then* the bubble. It didn't work that way. When you drew up a solution you tapped the bubble to the top and then expelled the air. Sometimes a little of the air stayed in the hub of the needle so that a bubble preceded the drug, but not the other way around. Not if you did it right.

I half closed my eyes in concentration. When Gordon and I had given the dog in the physiology lab the sample from the syringe, a bubble had come out of the needle. Of that I was certain. But that was not the first injection from that syringe. The first had been into Henry's forearm. And then a bubble.

"Holy shit," I mumbled to myself.

TB syringes were of such small diameter that an air bubble could easily occupy the entire lumen and act as an impermeable barrier between two different solutions, one on each side, both in the same syringe without intermixing. Surface tension in the fluid columns. Elementary physics.

It would have been so easy to do. First draw up about eight tenths of a cc of epinephrine, then a tiny air bubble, then highly concentrated succinylcholine. Give the kid the muscle relaxant, squeeze out the air, and all that's left is the epi. She just hadn't squeezed out all of the air. Some was hidden in the metal needle hub. She probably had just stopped the plunger at the 0.8 mark and not even looked. She was anxious.

I was anxious. I looked up to see Dr. Hebert with an amused smile, watching me talk to myself. He motioned for me to come closer. "Ishmail! Damnit. Someday you're gonna be invitin' me to these things, I hope." He turned to Professor Weigand. "This here is one of our—he *was* one of our better residents. He pissed off the wrong damn female. We gettin' him back, though." As I shook Dr. Weigand's hand I realized I did not need to talk to Dr. Hebert anymore. If the bubble separator worked, the contents of the syringe would be epi and only epi. Whatever had preceded it in the barrel of the syringe was long gone— into Henry.

Dr. Hebert said, "Ain't we, boah?"

I said, "Absolutely, sir. All my appeals are locked and loaded."

"Shit, son, fire at will."

I was dying to test my theory. I said, "I am, sir, I am."

Dr. Hebert said, "You needin' something again? How'd that project work out with Alphonse?"

"Fine. He was very helpful." I looked at the two men blankly. "I just wanted to say how much I enjoyed your lecture, Dr. Weigand."

Dr. Hebert gave me a cocked look. He said, "Ishmail. You nevah had no brown nose befoah. What kind of trouble you into?"

I grinned. "None, Dr. Hebert. I just thought of something I need to go do, though. Next time I see you I'll tell you all about it."

To find a tuberculin syringe I went directly to the Pediatrics ward, walking into the Procedure Room as if it were my home. Even at that late hour, with a UAMMB name badge dangling on my jacket I would be less than a face in the crowd to any of Maricopa's legitimate workers. If a nurse came into the Procedure Room, her most likely question would be, "Can I help you find something?" That would be the fastest way to get rid of me.

I ran through nearly a dozen drawers before finding the two basic items I needed: sterile water and a tuberculin syringe. I drew up half a cc of the water from a vial, then drew in a bit of air, then more water. As I moved the plunger back and forth, the bubble moved in unison with the two fluid columns. The bubble and its surface tension were a perfect barrier.

All well and good. But could I make a succinylcholine solution in the concentrated version?

I needed to steal a gram of dry sux. Paging the pharmacist and asking for it would have worked but certainly would have been an invitation for discovery and expulsion. Better to remain a bilge rat.

A back stairway I knew took me all the way down to the basement and landed me five gurney lengths from the doors to the OR suite. I adopted the half-dead mask of a resident and skulked past the main doors to the ones marked "Doctors (Male)." The combination to the locker room came to my hand without conscious thought. It probably hadn't been changed since the door was installed, and from the look of it, that had preceded my birth. For fun I thought about trying the combination to my old locker but rapidly figured the rightful owner, should clothes and wallet be hanging there, would not understand my nostalgic curiosity. I hung my jacket and clothing on the coatrack and got into full surgical garb. I pinned on my name badge in such a way that it would hang with the back side facing out—a common configuration—and took a rear hallway to the Anesthesia Prep Room, avoiding the control desk.

The Prep Room is actually little more than a supply room. No patient goes there, only anesthesiologists and their aides, usually just to fetch something, rarely to mix some concoction. I turned from cupboard to rack to shelves, mentally practicing my cover story. Eventually I found a six-foot-tall rolling rack of plastic drawers that housed all the anesthesia-related drugs. Each drawer was a different color and covered with printed labels, describing a roughly alphabetic distribution of their unique poisons. I crouched to the "S" drawer.

A male voice behind me said, "Whaddya need, Doc?"

Fortunately I was facing the drugs. I composed myself, turned, and drawled out, "Uh, succinylcholine . . . but in the one-gram thing. You know, to make a drip."

My helper was a pimple-faced young man with an angular mustache and thin goatee cut to resemble a can opener. Eager to be the source of knowledge for a bumbling surgery resident, he was all unquestioning help. "Oh, Doc, those are in the fridge, man." He yanked open the refrigerator behind him, retrieved two plastic squeeze bottles the size of 35-millimeter film cans, and flipped them to me one by one. He said, "Take two. They're cheap."

"Yeah. Thanks."

"Anything else?"

"Well, yes," I said. "One of the curved blades. What do they call them?"

"MacIntosh."

"Yeah. A Mac blade."

"What size?"

I looked blank.

"How old is the patient?"

"Um, thirty-nine."

"Adult. Take a three." He opened a drawer by the sink and handed me a laryngoscope blade.

"Thanks," I said, and strolled out as if I had real purpose. I took the first turn I could, then a second, ultimately looping back to the rear hallway. En route back to the locker room I slid the blade into one of the scrub sinks where I'd seen the anesthesiologists leave them after use.

I changed back into my clothes and hurried out of the OR suite. I ducked into one of the small "Staff Only" restrooms and locked the door. I peeled the protective shrink-wrap off one of the succinylcholine bottles but paused dumbly and stared before twisting off the funnel-shaped cap. I pictured the resident from Gordon's story who inhaled the contents of just such a squeeze bottle. He ultimately had been able to call for help. I was locked in a bathroom.

Being careful not to squeeze, I pointed it away from me and snapped off the cap. Nothing shocking happened. I pushed the cc of sterile water from the tuberculin syringe into the plastic bottle and swirled it around. The combined water and powder formed a thick white slurry reminiscent of a piña colada sans umbrella. I swirled it longer. The drug still did not dissolve.

Maybe time and heat would help. I drew into the syringe the entire slurry, dropped the capped syringe into the pocket of my jacket, and headed out to find a phone.

If you act like you own the place, most people will assume you do. I put my name badge on my jacket, went straight to the control desk on the surgery ward, picked up the phone, and asked the operator to page Gordon Erickson.

"This is Dr. Erickson." He sounded half asleep.

"Gordon. Hi. Malcolm Ishmail. Hope I didn't wake you."

"Nah. 'Ts okay."

"You alone?"

"No."

"Yeah. Sorry. But this is really critical. Like, saving-a-life critical. I need another consult."

"Yeah?"

"Succinylcholine. I need a little more info."

"You gonna kill somebody?"

"No. No way. But if somebody did get a load of sux, what else would you see? I mean, obviously he'd be temporarily paralyzed. But what else? Anything that might show up in a patient's chart? Side effects?"

He pondered, audibly. Something like "Ehhnnn." "Well, there's potassium. Sometimes people get a bump in their K that might show up in their labs. So you could check that. But usually it's pretty mild and you wouldn't even notice it. Sometimes, though, you can get a massive rise. People with muscular dystrophy or big, deep burns. Your intended doesn't have anything like that, does she?"

"No. And I don't have an 'intended.' Anything else?"

"It happens with some other nerve and muscle diseases. In fact, it's been reported in a lot of nerve and muscle diseases, but there isn't a clear pattern."

"So a bump in his K. What kind of numbers are we talking?"

"Depends. It can be big-time levels—seven, maybe eight. Nine. It's known to cause cardiac arrests, presumably from the sudden spike in the potassium."

"I'll check it. I know where to look. Anything else? I mean, I hate being desperate, but anything even suggestive. I've got to build a case, and impressions and possibilities seem to be what they go for. You know?"

He made the same "Ehhnnn" sound. "Myoglobin."

"Huh?"

"Sometimes in the hypercontractile state as the drug is taking effect—you know, like spasms—there's a shear injury to the sarcomeres—the muscle bundles. If it's severe enough some of 'em die. They spill proteins—myoglobin—into the bloodstream."

"But it would be gone after a couple of days, right?"

"Long gone."

"I'm sure no one checked a blood myoglobin level."

"Yeah, but that's what I was trying to figure out—something that would have shown up. Myoglobin gets filtered into the urine. If there's enough of it you get dark urine."

"Tea colored," I said, responding to some long-ago lecture I thought I had forgotten.

"Exactly. Just like rhabdomyolysis."

"Yeah."

"But even if it's not that severe, you might get some protein in the urine. If you did a urinalysis."

"I didn't order it. But they might have done one anyway. Urinalysis is still a basic admitting test."

"Yeah." A long pause. "I can't think of much else. And those aren't much to go with. They're pretty nonspecific."

"Yeah," I said, "there are about fifty causes each of protein in the urine and high potassium. But like I said, any evidence I can use, you know."

"Yeah." A pause. "So who do you think got sux that shouldn't have?"

"It's just a long shot. I can't really say, unless I can prove something."

"Well, good luck."

"Thanks, Gordon. I owe you."

Henry's chart was not to be found at the control desk of the PICU. I went down to his cubicle, again working to look tired and barely interested. His nurse, another woman I didn't recognize, eyed me. Her nametag said "Jeanie B." She was resetting the "volume-to-be-infused" on Henry's IV pumps. She looked at me only long enough to verify that I was only one of the pseudo-doctors expected to buzz around patients like flies around old meat.

Without looking up a second time, she said, "Are you by any chance from the neurologists?"

"Nope. Just, um, Pedes."

"Oh," she said. "I was just wondering because the neurologists apparently were going to do some tests in the morning but they didn't leave any orders. Like special meds or IVs or anything."

"They probably don't need anything special."

"Well, that's what I figured. I didn't think I'd page them, anyway," she said.

"How's he doing?" I asked. Anyone who's ever been an intern knows the bedside nurse can tell you more in fifteen seconds than the chart will in fifteen minutes.

"Same," she said.

"Stable?"

"Uh-huh."

I flipped out that day's bedside flow sheet. It's a chart centerfold—three continuous pages per twenty-four hours of minute-to-minute minutiae. His showed the bare minimum number of vital sign entries, all close to normal. He was off the life support drugs. His heart, lungs, liver, and kidneys had become boring.

"Waking up at all?" I asked.

"No, not quite waking up," she said.

"But what?" I asked, looking only at the flow sheet, trying to adopt the barely awake tone of the disinterested resident.

"But he's getting some reflexes back."

"What? Which ones?"

"Some cough, some breathing. When I suction him. Weak, but there."

Not brain-dead. Not alive. "Any gag? Corneals? Pupils?" I asked.

"I don't check all those," she said.

I walked around to Henry's right side. I pulled open one eyelid, then the other. His pupils were about half dilated and did not move with the change in light.

I needed more. "Got a penlight? Or an otoscope or anything?" Most med students compulsively carry around pocket penlights for such exams, but residents have generally become imperious enough to ask the nurses to find them one.

"There," she said, pointing at a common flashlight standing on its face.

"High tech," I said.

I repeated the exam, this time swinging the beam directly into each eye just after opening it. The pupils didn't change no matter how many times I moved the light.

I found a cotton-tipped swab and pulled off about half the cotton, twisting the trailing fibers into a long flame shape. I stroked each cornea as lightly as I could with the single cotton fiber. There was no response on the left, but there was a slight flinch on the right.

"Nothing," I said.

She was draining the urine bag. Apparently satisfied that I was only going to do a thorough and boring neuro exam, Jeanie left.

I knew how to do the bedside breathing test—disconnect the ventilator and wait to see if the patient makes any visible effort to breathe. There are certain preconditions that must be met, but I had seen in the flow sheet enough of Henry's data to know that was covered. The patient also should have lungs full of oxygen to keep it safe, but I accomplished that with a quarter turn of a single dial.

I waited through a dozen breaths, then disconnected the ventilator hoses from his breathing tube. The machine began squawking almost immediately, but a button on its face bought two minutes of silence. I stared, for the second time, at Henry Rojelio's chest and belly, waiting for any motion there to convince me he was breathing. This time, though, I was hoping for none.

Within about fifteen seconds his abdomen bulged upward. It was weak but real. He did it again after five more seconds, and again another five seconds after that. It wouldn't keep him alive, but it was breathing effort. Muscle effort prompted by nerve signals generated in the lowest part of the brain.

I reconnected the ventilator.

Taped to the wall above his bed were nearly a dozen photographs of Henry and his family. Optimism in the face of reality. Attempts to remind him who he had been, of who had loved him. His baby brother, in one particular shot, took the prize for the A-Number-One Heartbreak Look of the lot. Curly dark hair, entirely uncombed, berry-stained baggy T-shirt, still in a diaper. Looking straight up to the camera, eyes like big gooey chocolate drops, offering up to the photographer, presumably just for a lick, the half-eaten, just-beginning-to-drip prize of a strawberry ice cream cone.

Able only to stand and stare at Henry, I was not sure what I had come for. I recognized no piece of information there. No clues. No vital signs of interest. No look back at causation, no look forward to prognosis. I stood like a pillar of salt for a full minute.

Then I remembered my homework: I needed to recheck old lab values from Day One. I found Henry's chart on the bedside table. It was gaining weight like a newborn walrus. I took it back to the control desk.

Any time a patient is transferred from one hospital to another, photocopies of the most significant records from the transferring hospital are put into the new chart in the tabbed "Miscellaneous" section.

In this case, there were photocopies of my ER notes, the Code Sheet, Robin's nurse's notes, and the "Transfer Summary" I had dictated. I read Robin's notes carefully. There was nothing derogatory, nothing to suggest why she would later attack my care of Henry.

I found a page of lab tests, none of which had come back to me during Henry's code or even before the transfer—I checked the times. We had drawn one blood gas analysis during the code and one just prior to sending him out the door. The potassium during the code was 7.9. Decidedly abnormal. Into the range that can make hearts—patients' and doctors'—go pitter-pat, but might not. High enough to have possibly, unprovably, jimmied Henry's heart. But not diagnostic. It could have been the result of his shock state during the code. Cause and effect were not clear.

Two pages later I found a screening urinalysis. The row for protein was marked "3+," unequivocally a positive finding, highly suggestive but likewise not diagnostic of anything. That much muscle damage could have come from the jerking response to the electric shocks.

I flipped the pages, wondering where I could get the relevant ones photocopied before my Glory meeting. I thought of just absconding with the whole section of transfer notes. Nobody looks at them, anyway.

I had them all in one hand, ready to snap open the binder, but stopped as a nurse hurried past. I looked at the front page, pretending to be studying it. When I saw what it was I almost laughed out loud. It was a copy of the "Face Sheet" from Henry's ER visit. The Face Sheet is a printout from the hospital database of the patient's identifying data—name, address, birth date, social security number, religious preference, next of kin—and most important to the hospital, how the care is going to be paid for—responsible party, health insurance, etc. These come out of the printer in stacks of five, the lower four pages being pressure sensitive to pick up the printing from above. Because I had, at the time of seeing Henry, already pulled the top copy, on which I was required to enter the discharge diagnosis and my signature prior to letting Henry go, the Glory ER nurse had photocopied the next-lower page.

The copy showed clear evidence of its source having lain under other documents as folks wrote, their scratches and scrawls amplified by the wizardry of modern photocopying technology. I looked more closely. I recognized the handwriting. Squarely in the middle of the section for "Discharge Diagnoses," in Robin's looping style, was a cryptic set of notes, the code to which I readily recognized. There were the phone number for the Maricopa Pediatric ICU, Henry's full name, his date of birth, "asthma," "epi," and "CPR" with two exclamation points. Under those it said "Superstition Hwy," "60," "32 mi," "Tonto—Green," "R," and "two L forks."

My consciousness imploded.

It was Henry's "event." And directions to Mimi's canyon hideaway.

I closed Henry's chart. I stared. I quietly rose and left the Unit.

23

HENRY ROJELIO, DAY SIX (CONTINUED)

The only possible conclusion was easily reached, but, like a beginning medical student anxious to ascribe a fever to the exotic African parasite he has just read about, I kept trying to come up with an unobvious explanation. The implications of the one standing in front of me were horrifying. Robin had called Mimi Lyle. Sometime between Henry's arrival at the Glory ER and his departure for Maricopa. And Robin was going to the cabin in the canyon.

I was reeling.

Only now, years and miles away, does it make sense that I might have called Detectives Borden and May. At the time it never crossed my mind. Maybe my subconscious looked at how I had nothing to lose and did some cost-benefit analysis. If so, it was instantaneous, because once I was completely certain of the connection, I stopped processing at a rational level. I put on my jacket, walked to my car like a man late for a funeral, and drove to Miriam Lyle's condominium. It was, I suppose, an act of cold fury.

I pounded on her door and waited only a very impolite interval before pounding again. Behind the door she sounded only annoyed. "Who is it?"

I was hoping she would be scared. "Robin Benoit." There was silence. "That give you a chill, does it?"

"Malcolm?" I said nothing. She opened the door. I had not laid eyes on her in ten months. Her face seemed different. "What are you doing here?" she said. "Especially at this hour."

"I've been up to the Maricopa Pediatric Intensive Care Unit." She just stared. "I've been checking on our mutual friend, Henry Rojelio. Did you even know that was his name? Of course you did. Robin gave you the name when she called you from the ER. At least that's what her note shows." She said nothing. "Did Robin tell you she left a nice paper trail in the chart, with her directions to your canyon hideaway?"

She blinked. "I don't know what you're talking about."

"I believe you do. And I believe the police detectives in Mesa will want to talk to you. Would you like their number? Will Borden and Ken May. Will seems a nice kind of chap but Ken is a bit brutish. Probably has Parkinson's, though."

A silence.

"Did you know Henry is hanging in limbo? Have you been able to follow his case?"

She stared.

"I know how you did it. Or how you had Robin do it. A TB syringe with a dose of succinylcholine, a bubble, and a bit of epi. The perfect weapon."

She stepped aside and motioned for me to enter. She had on a terry-cloth robe and her hair was falling on her shoulders. She was not the lioness I remembered, stunning and powerful, deep red mane streaming, but grim-faced, harried, stiff, tired, more prey than hunter. I had the knowledge. I would have said I had the power, the control of the situation, but my instincts were on edge, saying otherwise. She said, "Sit down."

I sat but probably failed to hide my agitation.

"Coffee?" she said.

"No thanks."

"What is it you think I did?"

"I know what you did. Or what Robin did for you." I stared at her hard but she made no response. "The only thing I cannot figure out is why. What's the connection? Between you and her."

"Robin who?"

"Oh, cut it out. Robin Benoit. Actually, an ER nurse from California posing as Robin Benoit. It would seem the *real* Robin is an Englishman. The fake Robin was in a rented house out in Mesa I suspect you paid rent for. Had a wad of cash stuffed in a secret hiding place. Cozied up to me out in Glory. Picked out a ne'er-do-well asthmatic and shot him with succinylcholine instead of epinephrine to generate a disaster under my nose. Ringing any bells? On my watch. Blame me. Write a report that I can't handle an asthmatic much less an arrest. Get me fired, run out of town. Things turned to shit, though, didn't they? Probably way more than you planned."

She was impassive, even more rigid than before.

"Did you look up his potassium level? I mean the one from Glory? They were probably pretty normal by the time he got to Maricopa. But in Glory they were pretty high. It's funny, though, isn't it? We didn't get the lab results at the time. Sent the blood off but never saw the numbers, either. It happens, though. That's why we treat the patient, not the lab values.

"You didn't count on his funky little muscles, did you, Mimi? Got more that you wanted. All that potassium made his heart go a-titter. And all you'd wanted was a little apnea."

"You really should leave now."

I went on. "Your 'Robin' then laid out all kinds of bullshit, in writing mind you, about what a fuckup I seem to be. And we both know my position in the medical world is a bit precarious, also thanks to you."

Only silence.

"She left the epinephrine syringe—beautifully labeled and all— lying there for me to take. Not to worry about a chemical analysis. The sux was separated from real honest-to-God adrenaline by a simple air bubble. In a tiny syringe that's all it takes. I tried it. Surface tension, you know. 'Physics is everywhere,' my old professor used to say. But damn if Robin didn't leave the bubble in the hub of the needle. Saw it myself."

She leaned toward me and said, "You have no idea what you are talking about."

"Maybe you'd care to correct me."

She closed her eyes for a second, then took a deep breath. "Let me get some clothes on." She went into her bedroom.

"Hey," I called, "got Robin's dead body back there? I almost left that part out. The police are looking for the body, you know. They don't seem all that convinced the one they found in the canal is her. They asked me if she was bruised or bleeding the last time I saw her. And whether she was in any kind of trouble. You know, they ask an awful lot of questions."

"No," she answered, "no Robin. I know no Robin. But I will explain what you think you know." Her voice had a different timbre.

"I'm dying for an explanation. Really, I am."

There was an odd silence. I turned and looked back. She was standing in her bedroom door in jeans and a sweater, with light glaring from a bank of bulbs behind her. She had passed from frightened and haunted, through only a silhouetted change in physical attitude, to undeniably predatory. She said, "Stay very still." She was pointing directly at my face a moderately large black semiautomatic pistol, I guessed a nine millimeter. With less than ten feet separating us, I doubted she would miss. I did not move.

"You know I know very well how to use this. And here I am defending myself against a deranged former resident. Self-defense is still such a romantic notion, isn't it?"

"They would never believe you."

"Oh, don't forget, I am 'highly credible.' "

My skin burned.

"We're going for a drive," she said. "Your car." She waved the gun at the door.

I rose slowly and put both hands in my jacket pockets. The right came immediately to my ring of keys. The left found a long cylindrical thing I first took to be a pen. I almost pulled it out to check, but felt a flange in the middle and my brain turned over and fired up. It was a syringe full of succinylcholine.

With my hands still inside the pockets, I shook the right for her to hear the jangling keys. With the left I made a similar movement, feigning a child's insistence on doing something with both hands, turning the syringe around to an angle from which I could work the cap off the needle. I was working with only my two fingers and a thumbnail in the tightly confined arena of my pocket. The cap was agonizingly secure.

"Walk slowly," she said.

As soon as I was five feet out of her condominium, she said, "Stop." I turned back over my shoulder. She was locking her door. I stood still.

She got right up behind me. I waited. Just as I was envisioning the angle of her gun in my back, I felt the hard prod in my lower ribs. It pushed me forward. I had milliseconds to decide: I could have turned and fought there but with the cap still on the syringe I was unarmed. I hesitated and the moment was lost.

"Go," she said. I started forward and lost contact with her pistol. "Hands out of your pockets." I slid my right hand out slowly, still jangling the keys. In the left pocket the cap popped free of the needle.

"Both hands." I slowly withdrew my left hand, empty. "Keep your hands free." She stayed several feet behind me.

"Where are you parked?" she said.

"The usual visitor space." I took slow steps, visualizing the bare needle a few thin layers of clothing away from my flank. Once moving, I had lost sight of her. I could hear her behind me but could not have anticipated accurately her position.

We wound down a curving sidewalk and out to the open lot. Once to the driver's door of my car, I stopped, put my left hand in my jacket pocket, grasped the syringe, and waited for the feel of the gun in my back. It never came. "Unlock it and open it," she said. I did it. "Now go around and open the other side." I did that also. She was standing about ten feet behind the car.

"Now go around again. Quietly." I did so.

At that hour of the evening there were only scattered cars in the lot and none around mine. No cover. We were indeed alone together.

Certainly I felt stupid for having walked up to a trapped animal and asked her if she cared to bite my head off, but I felt the fearlessness, I thought, of a man with absolutely nothing in his life to lose.

She went slowly to the passenger side, all the while pointing the pistol, it seemed to me, quite accurately at my heart. When she was at the rear window she laid both hands on the car roof, leveling the gun at my head. "Get in slowly."

As I slowly ducked down she slid back from the car. As soon as my head dropped below the level of the roof, she darted back away from the car slightly, ducked down, and by the time I could turn to see her through the open door she was staring down the black barrel at me again.

"Well done," I said.

"Fuck you," she said. "Start the car. Slowly," she hissed. She slid into her seat beside me.

"Drive," she said. The gun in her right hand, braced against her lower chest, was pointing up just enough to prescribe a missile trajectory that would, barring divine intervention, pass through my right lung and the main branches of my right pulmonary artery, probably clip both upper chambers of my heart, and just might cream my descending aorta on the other side. I thought, *What a perfect time for her to figure out some three-dimensional anatomy.*

As I started the car I looked down at my left jacket pocket. It was gapping open just enough for me to see the tip of the plunger of the syringe lying there. Teasingly. *Deus ex machina, deus ex syrinx.* Out of reach and probably, when I envisioned the possible angle of attack, useless. A lunge to my right to push away the gun would lack leverage and probably accomplish nothing beyond adding my hand to the list of perforated body parts.

"Where to?" I croaked.

"Get on the Superstition. Then the highway up to Globe."

I drove. She watched me, she watched the road, she sometimes stared at the gun.

"Where'd you get the gun?" I asked.

"Shut up."

I waited several minutes, then reached down with my left hand to the side of the seat to adjust the seat back.

"Both hands on the wheel," she snapped loudly.

"I need to adjust the seat," I said. "I'm not exactly relaxed."

She leaned over and watched my hand. I slowly moved it around until I found the lever, then slid the seat up two notches. I put my hand back up on the wheel. She straightened up. I waited a minute, then reached down again, slowly, and under her stare moved the seat back down one notch. She looked up at a big green freeway sign zipping overhead. "Get over to the exit lane," she said.

"Haven't we been down this road before?" I asked. She said nothing. "Going to your friend's cabin?"

"Yes."

"Where Robin is waiting for us?"

"You'll never see her again."

"You don't know any Robin but you're pretty sure I will never see her again."

"Absolutely certain of it."

I looked at the black pistol, quivering only slightly with the vibration of the car at freeway speed. "What happened to Robin?"

"Robin has left the state. Safely."

"Well, I am glad for that. We were lovers, you know."

"Ha. You've always been such a terrible liar."

"Why? Didn't you hear?"

"I heard something about 'taking a specimen.' She got all panicky and wanted to see just how suspicious you were and got you drunk. Sucked you off and spit it onto the sheets. It wasn't part of the plan, but I think she made her weakness work for us. A little piece of you left at the scene of the crime."

I gave a slight nod. "Seems your new protégé is a better liar than I am," I said.

She glared at me.

"She fucked me," I said, stupidly proud.

She made her eyes slits and tightened both hands on the pistol grip. "You're living in lies," she said, the gun twitching slightly.

I took deep, slow breaths and watched the road. I thought, *Here, the truth might get you killed.* Better to back off that topic. I said, "What crime are you talking about?"

"Didn't you say you'd been questioned by homicide detectives? Why did you think they were interested in you?"

"You set this up to look like a murder."

"Let's see: Your girlfriend—at least there's your semen on her sheets—disappears shortly after you've been overheard making threatening comments and yelling at her at work. And then there's that blood in her house."

"But my cut wasn't bleeding. Didn't spill a drop."

"You're hilarious. A nurse can always get a couple tubes of blood. Throw it around, then wipe it up till it looks clean. It leaves plenty of traces. The police know how to find every invisible little corpuscle."

I bit my lips.

She went on: "I think my favorite part of the whole thing, though, was how easy it was to have Robin report what a bad doctor you are. Out of certain 'ethical compulsions.' A good nurse is like that." My skin burned again. She said, "Your plot against me has cost me a year without a promotion. My tenure is on hold. If it doesn't come through I'm as good as done with my career. And my career is what I have . . . left."

I thought, *Another topic to get me shot.*

"And where is Robin now?" I said. "Surely you didn't kill her."

"No. I didn't kill her."

"She's back in California?"

"Yes. Sure. California. If it's not Florida it must be California. Pick a state, Malcolm. She's safely there. You'll never see her again. She's gone forever."

"Then why am I going to your cabin?"

After a mile of silence she said, "A lonely desert cabin is the perfect place for a desperate man to choose for his suicide."

That was frighteningly true. My exoskeleton of calm was melting away. I had nothing to lose but my life, and the emotional component of seeing it pass away was beginning to well up. I fought to remain rational, to have the self-control not to cry or beg.

I needed to keep her talking. It would be good for both of us to be distracted. "Why would I kill myself?"

"Oh, Malcolm. You have so many reasons to hate your life."

She was alternately watching me and the road. We were ascending the plateau east of Phoenix, revisiting the bullet-riddled cacti and the bastard cotton farms, seeking the clean air and haunted dreams just this side of Globe. My left hand had edged down on the steering wheel. Mimi did not react. "Like what?"

"Your botched career. Your joke of a love life. Your botched asthma case. Lying there dying in the ICU."

I thought, *It's your case dying,* but kept it to myself. "How am I going to kill myself?"

"Actually you can have a choice. You can shoot up all the Demerol I have—and it's more than enough to put you out for good—or I will shoot you in the face from close range, then wrap your hand around the gun, then drop it. I recommend the first. It will be much more pleasant for both of us."

"So you took all that Demerol from the ICU."

"No, Malcolm, I just wrote a prescription. Much simpler."

"You have given this some thought, haven't you?"

"Just like I always told you, one needs contingency plans."

It was silent until she said, "Slow down." We passed a green highway sign. "Take the road to the right."

As we ground along the gravel toward the rutted trail, I said, "And won't the police think it odd that there is no vehicle outside the cabin? When the body is found? And the two sets of footprints . . ."

"Maybe you weren't paying attention when you were here before, but the wind in that canyon keeps all the sand and dust moving just about day and night. There won't be any footprints by the time the sun comes up."

"Am I going to write a suicide note?"

"Maybe. I'll think about it."

I began trying to think of ways to slip secret messages into a suicide note, but even if I could come up with some dandies they would not help me stay alive.

I slid my hand slowly off the steering wheel and into my lap. She made no response. "Actually my love life is wonderful."

"Just give up even trying to lie," she said. I began to edge my hand toward the pocket of my jacket, but she remembered her rules: "Both hands on the wheel," she spat.

I obeyed without thinking, gripping the wheel intently, wondering if I could hold up. I needed to keep talking. "Why are you so protective of Robin?" I asked.

"Watch the road and keep your hands high on the wheel."

"Why did Robin do it for you?"

She stared ahead.

Three miles of scrubby oaks and pines passed by as a procession of lost souls in the light of the moon.

Mimi seemed pensive, but then turned and glared at me. "She was willing to help me. You don't need to know anything more."

"Help you. By killing a boy."

"That was never the plan. You were right about that. When I told her my lover had turned on me, was out to destroy my career, destroy everything I'd ever been, ever wanted in the world, she wanted to hurt you. She would have killed you at first. I told her it would be sufficient to get you banished from medicine. Murderers we're not."

"Yet."

"I told you: contingency planning."

The full moon glowed high overhead. The sky at the horizon above us was a shimmering electric purple. By itself it might have seemed black, but the rim of the canyon was far darker. Even the darkness of night is relative.

"As for the car," she said, "it's only a five-mile walk to Globe. I've done it before. Any Boy Scout could do it in the dark. I'm sure a brain surgeon can handle it. Though I may drive out tonight and take a few days to get the car back here. I'll have weeks. Nobody will find your shriveled remains for months."

"Robin?"

"What?"

"You'll get Robin to drive the other car? It would be easier with a ride. And who else could you trust?"

"You're not listening. Robin is a long way from here and will never be back."

We bounced down the trail, wound around the final switchback, and rolled slowly through the cottonwoods. I pulled up to the cabin.

I switched off the ignition.

I set the brake.

I said, "I can't believe you would kill me over this."

"I don't have a choice. You want to tell the police I'm responsible for that boy in the ICU. Of course you could prove nothing, but even the investigation would be damaging. You brought this on yourself."

"You killed a boy to get me disgraced."

"You said he's not dead."

"No. Worse."

She sat silently, boring through me with a cold stare. Finally she said slowly, very quietly, "You. You were my lover. I took you into my life. I trusted you. With everything I knew about myself. You turned it against me."

I slowly straightened. "No, I did not. I tried to help you. You were hurting patients. People who could not know any better." Her face was hardening in front of me. "I tried to get you to get help. You wouldn't even talk about it."

"Get out."

I said, "You could still—"

"Get out!" she screamed.

I reached for the door latch. I opened the door. I swung my legs around. I slowly rose from my Datsun.

"Walk away ten steps and stop," she ordered.

I walked ten steps and stopped. I put my hands in my pockets. I turned to watch her.

She slowly and deliberately backed out of the passenger's side, keeping her pistol trained on the center of my vital organs. She walked cautiously toward me.

I waited.

She stopped five feet from me and laid a key on the gravel, then backed away.

I waited.

She said, "Pick it up. Slowly."

I stepped to the key, bent over, pinched it between my right thumb and forefinger, and slowly straightened up, holding the key before me as if it might explode. It glinted in the moonlight.

I slowly put my hand back in my pocket. I waited.

She said, "Go inside."

I turned around to face the door. I did not step forward.

I was wondering if my bowels or bladder would give out. Or if my heart would race away until I coded and dropped.

I heard slow crunching footsteps on the gravel behind me, drawing closer.

I didn't move, though it was as much from fear as any plan of action.

The footsteps ceased. Very close.

I felt a blunt prod in my mid-back.

I involuntarily arched away, stiffening.

The prod hit a second time.

I did not wait for a third. I slid my hands out of my pockets as fast as I could make my muscles obey and spun 180 degrees to my right, leading with my right elbow stuck out as a rotating hammer.

Her eyes saw. Her ears heard.

My flying right elbow hit her hand and the gun.

Her brain began to process. Mimi's motor cortex sent electro-chemical neural waves to her arm and wrist and hand, ordering them to contract the muscles to pull the trigger.

Simultaneously with my spin I brought the syringe in my left hand around and sideways as a dagger to Miriam Lyle's right thigh muscles. The needle easily passed between cotton threads, through Mimi's denim pants, and penetrated skin.

Nerves are slow. Mimi's arm was wheeling sideways as the electro-chemical waves made their way.

I squeezed on the syringe as the muscles in Mimi's forearm began shortening, pulling on the tendon to her hand, both squeezing the trigger and tightening her grip in anticipation of the explosion.

At the first penetration of her thigh skin, a few tiny subcellular structures, built to detect noxious events at the surface of the skin, sent electrochemical neural waves up their parent dendrites.

The gun went off.

When the neural waves were processed by the attached clump of nerve cells in her spinal cord, signals were sent within a tenth of a second to all the muscles of the lower spine, the hips and the legs, all the muscles needed to simultaneously pull back the offended leg and shift weight to the other, all without her brain's involvement. A simple protective animal reflex.

In the fraction of a second it took for the waves to pass up the nerves and the signals to be interpreted and the impulses sent to their muscles, my fingers emptied the syringe, most of it entering her quadriceps before her thigh jerked backwards.

The bullet flew up the canyon into the darkness.

The succinylcholine solution entered Mimi's quadriceps muscle, forming a tiny liquid pocket.

Wind resistance marginally slowed the bullet in its horizontal vector but gravity completely stopped it in its rising vector.

The liquid bubble in Mimi's muscle immediately began diffusing into the fluid spaces between muscle fibers.

The bullet accelerated back toward the ground.

The succinylcholine began moving from the interfiber space to her bloodstream.

Simultaneously with my left-handed stab I lunged for her gun with my right hand. The momentum I had imparted to her arm by hammering it away from my back kept it swinging in a circle, as if in a physics experiment, teasingly just out of my reach.

Mimi staggered backwards away from me, windmilled her arms, and regained her footing. She swung her gun back into the space between us and glared and seethed like a newly piqued bull in a Mexican ring.

The bullet found earth, probably striking a cottonwood tree or a rock or a coyote three or four miles away.

She would have killed me instantly had not her predicament flitted across her mind. She gulped and stared down the gunsight.

"Sux," I said.

I waited.

I held the syringe up to the moonlight. "I'd say you got at least half a gram."

She was audibly hyperventilating.

"You could kill me," I said. "It would be the last thing you ever did."

She raised the gun high and straight at my face and glowered and thought and pumped breath in and out of her lungs. The black pistol began to drift earthward.

"Malcolm," she said. "S-save m-m-m . . ."

Her hand opened like a flower in a time-lapse documentary. The gun dropped onto the sand.

She staggered again. She fell backwards onto her buttocks. She looked comical.

Her arms and legs were twitching. It looked like the muscles of her face were trying to dance off the bones, but her head turned and her face was in shadow in the shimmering half-light.

She fell over on her side and lay still.

I said, "You just quit breathing."

I stepped over to her and stood over her. I rubbed my face. I said, "You were going to kill me. You killed Henry. You were going to kill me."

I picked up the gun. I pointed it at Mimi. "The dead body. Killed in self-defense." My breath was seething. "So romantic."

I swung the gun straight up over our heads and fired. The slapping report echoed a half second later. I could see her immobile eyes staring up at me, open, reflecting the moon.

I fired again and again and again, empty casings raining on us both, crackling reports and muffled echoes flying out and back from all directions like so many bats, until the gun stopped responding to my finger on the trigger. The bullets flew over steep arcs, up and down, probably hitting only rocks or trees or coyotes on the canyon rim behind the house. I pulled the gun down and looked at it as if I'd never seen one before. The action had locked, open, hungry for more bullets. I pitched the pistol toward the cottonwoods.

I said, "You killed Henry. You can die, too. Your body, here, this— the gun, the casings—the evidence. The truth may come out yet."

I stepped over her to my car and got in. The keys were dangling in the ignition.

I closed my eyes, then opened them. I turned the key and the car fired up. I was going to get the sheriff.

I revved the engine to its loudest roar, then let it die down, then revved it again and again.

I shut off the car.

I went back to Mimi. I said, "I know you can hear me."

I bent and straightened her out into the position of a patient. Her eyes were wide open. "You can see me, too." I pushed shut each eyelid in turn. "Your corneas will dry out." The eyelids fell open again.

I was shivering.

I said, "Two minutes. It's been two minutes. They say it takes four minutes for the big pyramid cells at the top of your brain to start to die off. They need a lot of oxygen."

I knelt at her side.

"But those are the cells that count."

I tilted her head back a bit, as if to do rescue breathing.

I said, "But I don't need to tell you that. Should I breathe for you? Should I save your life?"

I squeezed her nose shut with my left hand, pressed my mouth fully around hers and blew my used breath into her lungs.

I said, "Should I tease you? One breath every minute or so? Drag out your unconsciousness. A prolonged death. Like Henry."

I gave her another breath. "Too cruel?"

I gave her another breath. "Are you listening? I think I'll tell you all about Henry. His pain."

I gave her another breath. "I bet Henry felt like you do right now."

Her eyes were startlingly bright pools of reflected moonlight, but quiet and lifeless as a rain puddle after a storm.

I gave Mimi two more breaths. I laid two fingers on her throat. Her pulse was over 160. "I wonder if desperate breathlessness will be an epiphany for you."

I picked up the pace of the breathing. "I wonder if Henry even knew he was dying. He was so used to breathlessness. Maybe it didn't bother him as much."

Three more breaths. "Of course then his heart went shitty. He surely was unconscious by then."

A breath. "Did you know this is the morning? The apnea challenge. All the bedside tests."

A breath. "His EEG is bad, but not brain-dead."

A breath. "His cortex has already started to atrophy."

A breath. "If he can make a breathing motion he will go to a home for the not-quite-dead."

A breath. "Purgatory on earth."

A breath. "His mother wants him back the way he was."

A breath. "Like *that* is still on the list."

A breath. "His stepfather wants a big lawsuit so he can feel important."

A breath. "His lawyer wants forty percent of the settlement."

A breath. "That, no doubt, will happen."

A breath. "His priest wants Jesus to come down off the cross and make a call."

A breath. "That, no doubt, will not happen."

A breath. "His brothers and sisters want their mommy back."

I stopped talking. I stared up at the night sky. The white of the moon looked like quicksilver on fire, though its canyons and craters stoically refused to melt. The stars to be seen above the other wall were few because of the aura of King Moon, but the stalwarts present seemed to crackle, not twinkle.

I said, "They want their mommy back," then did only rescue breathing. The physical work involved began to warm me up. My adrenal glands backed down off their own red-line output. I quit shivering. Mimi's pulse came down to around 125, then 100. I had apparently gotten her carbon dioxide level below the panic line.

"My knees are killing me," I told her. I gave two quick breaths and dragged her off the gravel path into the sand and feathery grasses.

There I continued breathing another twenty minutes. I had nothing else to say. To her. Henry—Henry I needed to talk to.

Mimi's eyelids twitched. She blinked. I gave another breath. Her belly twitched as if she had hiccups. "You're recovering," I said. I gave more breaths. She began spastic intermittent jerks of her arms and legs, faint and weak at first but quickly building to a comic fugue. As I bent to her to give another breath I felt her exhale against my cheek. She had pulled a breath on her own.

I waited. I watched her face. She inhaled, exhaled. It was shallow but real. Her mouth was moving. She inhaled again.

I stood and stretched.

I rubbed my knees.

I got into my car and drove away.

24

HENRY ROJELIO, DAY SEVEN

My descent to Phoenix was semiconscious; staring; blinking at the few oncoming headlights. I replayed my fight with Mimi as if it were a continuous loop, endlessly repeating itself, never changing. I was intellectually certain of every detail and nuance but never viscerally convinced it had really happened, that it had not all been another bad dream.

The driving time let me face the vision of Henry and his family I had acquired while speaking my broken monologue to Mimi. Henry was the primary unfortunate in our Passion Play. Had I gone straight to the detectives, Mimi Lyle might have been apprehended, evidence intact, but more important to me was the chance to make a partial fix.

I drove to Maricopa and pulled my car into the exact parking spot I had left only hours earlier.

5:02 A.M. Henry, Day 7. I knew the med students and interns would start showing up at bedsides in an hour or so, silently and sleepily blinking through charts and flow sheets, cribbing notes on file cards, hoping to have at hand whatever minutiae their attendings might ask for. I would easily move beneath notice in such a crowd of zombies.

I was surprisingly unafraid, and not the slightest bit uncertain. But I envisioned my hands or my lips trembling. Responding to the epinephrine pouring from my adrenals and giving me up as a man with something to hide. The body's epinephrine system is not tuned for deceptions.

Politicians, I had read, sometimes used Inderal to slow their systems down before public appearances; Richard Nixon used it to stop his upper lip from sweating.

I had a little time to kill; why not get some along with my other necessaries? I figured I needed ten or twenty milligrams. I slouched toward the ER.

At the edge of the mercury vapor light pool provided for ambulance crews, I nonchalantly checked my pocket. I still had the second gram of sux.

Were it a Saturday night I could count on a carnival quality in the Maricopa ER—clowns and hawkers and lost children all milling about in search of something intangible. But even on those besotted nights, by 3:00 or 4:00 A.M. of the Sunday morning, after the bars have closed and the drunks have finished driving into trees and shooting, stabbing, and beating on each other, it is often eerily quiet. On this boring workday at 5:00 A.M. then, it might be altogether empty and not a good time for minor larceny.

The code on the digital keypad controlling the "Staff Only" door to the Emergency Department was easy to remember—9-1-1-9-1-1. The heavy steel door opened itself with a lethargic electric whir. I mumbled, "Alacazam." Instead of a hoard of gold and jewels I was instantly slapped in the face by the escaping stench of vomitus. A Hispanic voice shouted, "Careful, Doc!" The floor in front of me was a lake of stomach contents. An arm of the lake trailed into the exam room just off to the right. A pillar of the Maricopa wee hours, Teresita, a 250-pound ER aide, was chugging toward me with a mop and bucket at her usual frenetic pace. Someone retched long and hard in the exam room, then began a muffled sob.

"Sita," I said, "what's goin' on?"

"This one?" she replied, with a head tilt in the direction of the crying patient. "OD. They give her Narcan, she puke." Teresita shrugged and began mopping.

"Mother*fuckers!*" the patient screamed. A female voice.

The ER was lively after all. I need not have worried. "Ruined a good high, eh?" I said as I went around the puddle. Through the door, I could see the woman was shivering in a grimy jogging suit, huddled against the wall just inside the door. She was staring at me, her face practically imploding in a pained contortion. I was frozen for a second, virtually in mid-step. I stared back. Her face seemed to soften a bit as she mentally wrote me off, then she closed her eyes. I tried for a second to imagine narcotic withdrawal. She spat on the floor, wiped her mouth with the black and brown sleeve of her otherwise red sweatshirt, then spat again.

Around a corner from Sita was the central station, entirely vacant. In a little room behind the Com Desk—the radio and computer links to the city—are all the drugs and supplies. I ducked in and found in the alphabetized drug cabinet two 10-milligram Inderal pills, popped them and drank from my hand under the sink spigot. I checked my watch—5:15. The Inderal would kick in in about twenty minutes.

In a drawer under the med cabinet I grabbed a syringe and needle and an amp of sterile water and slipped them into my pocket.

When I emerged I found another old friend, Alva Leon, the charge nurse on nights, staring at the grease-pencil control board. Nothing was written in for the cursing woman's room.

"What's in Ten?" I asked.

"Dr. Malcolm! Hey, I thought you disappear off the earth." She gave me a big hug. "In Ten? Just got her. Nice little lady had too much of the heroin. Medics gave her Narcan, then hit every bump in the road getting her here. Kind of like roller coaster. They probably take the corners extra quick, too. She makes a mess." I said nothing. Alva finally looked at me. "Why? You step in it?"

"Almost." Alva went back to staring at the control board. "Actually, I was wondering if you needed orders on her or anything. Didn't seem like anyone had gotten to her yet."

"Cooney is on his sweet little way. He doing a plastic surgery repair of forearm in Center Stage. Take forever with those little teeny-tiny sutures no one can see."

"The guy's an artist."

"Yes, he think so. Patient is dirtball."

I gave her a hard look. "Careful. You never know who may hear you."

"Well, he is. The laceration go right through the boobs on his tattoo of naked lady and Cooney decided it would be fun to give *her* anatomic repair."

"At five in the morning."

"At five in the morning," she echoed. "What kind of orders you have in mind?"

"Well, I don't know," I said, "the usual kind of withdrawal stuff. Some IV fluids, if you can find a vein. Librium. Something for nausea."

"But I didn't think you could write orders here anymore."

"Oh, I can write them," I said, "the question is whether the nurses who work for the hospital will honor them." She nodded a small laugh. "Actually, it occurred to me that right now what would do her more good than anything would be a cup of water to rinse her mouth out."

"You're a nice man," she said.

"Now, don't start spreading that around, Alva. Everybody's going to want a drink of water."

"I'll get her some water. But Cooney will kill me if I give her Librium."

I scanned the control board. One old man with a headache waiting on Cooney and one older man waiting on Redway Cab for a ride out of there. Probably sobering up and unhappy about it.

On the Com Desk was a wooden box holding the paper records, arranged with paper clips and awaiting transit to Medical Records, of every patient seen in the ER that shift. Usually it makes good reading.

Underneath two toddler brothers with diarrhea was a guy with a scorpion sting to his scrotum, then a woman who had started to kill herself by running her car's motor in the closed garage, but panicked when the nausea set in. A couple of lacerations, an old lady with a broken hip, a thirty-two-year-old cocaine shooter with an apparent heart attack. And two more headaches.

Alva returned and looked at me suspiciously.

"When does the helicopter go for donuts?" I said.

She grinned. "Whenever they want. You want them to get your breakfast?"

I stood and stretched. "Nah. I think I should go get some sleep. But you gotta tell me how a man gets a scorpion sting on his scrotum."

"He uses kitchen sink for bathing after his job. He keeps a piece of water hose in under the sink, uses that for rinsing. Last night he plugs hose to faucet and flushes out little scorpion. It stings him on the way to the floor, then he step on it, too. His foot not stung, though."

"Ouch."

"Yes, ouch. Very big and painful."

"I'm sure. Hope Cooney gave him some good drugs."

"Only the best."

I said my goodbyes and shuffled out.

The OD woman had lain down on the exam table and folded her arms over her chest. She was staring at the ceiling.

I turned left just short of the exit, ducking down a hallway. In a men's room stall I mixed the gram of sux in the sterile water and drew it into the syringe.

In an intensive care unit the light never changes and the doors never lock, just like Las Vegas casinos. I wandered in, trying to look sleepy. I spun the chart rack like a kid kicking the merry-go-round in spite of his vertigo. The slot for Henry's chart was empty.

I went to his cubicle. He was alone. His chart was on the bedside stand. I went and bent over it, pretending to study the lab result printouts and the vital-sign flow sheets and the nurses' neuro checks, all the time scanning around to see who was to be watching him. A nurse popped her head in. She was one of the legion of hospital folk I had seen many times in the cafeteria and the elevators but never had reason to speak to. I didn't know her name. If I had run into her in the shoe department at Goldwater's, I'd have had the vague sense that I was supposed to know who she was, but didn't.

I looked up but said nothing. She said, "If you need anything, I'll try to help. I'm just covering Jeanie while she's on break." She nodded at Henry. "He's been just rock steady, I guess."

"Yeah, that's what I see. I'm just making some notes." She nodded and left.

I began to repeat my neuro exam. I peeled back the sheet covering Henry and crossed his right leg over his left, then tucked my left arm under the right knee, lifting about two inches. Karate-chopping the patellar ligament will usually elicit a good reflex if one is there to be had.

I walked around to the other side of the bed and I recrossed

Henry's legs the other way. While knocking on his left patella I scanned the various IVs to see which was his "maintenance" line—the one sure to go on running all day unchanged. The only choice was his hyper-al—his milky IV feeding. The bag was still half full—enough to run at least until late afternoon. The bag would not be changed out—no intern on earth would write the day's full page of hyper-al orders, specifying in detail every nutrient and mineral, *before* determining brain death.

I looked over my shoulder. I knew doing so would appear suspicious, should anyone actually be watching, but I couldn't help it. I took the syringe from my jacket pocket and pulled the needle cover. I put the full gram of succinylcholine through the latex nipple into Henry's IV feeding bag and gave the bag a couple of squeezes to mix it in. I spoke quietly: "You can rest now, Henry. Sleep well. If you're going to some kind of other life, I hope you get to leave behind the scars from this go-round. I hope we all do. I hope all of you is straight and strong and happy on the other side." I started to leave. At the door to his cubicle I turned back. "And Henry, if it works out, come back and let me know."

I looked at the pictures of his family. I recapped the needle and put the syringe back deep in my pocket. I left, nodding my thanks to the nurse two cubicles away.

When I made it home it struck me as odd that nothing had changed. Logically there was no reason for things to be different, but I did not expect logic to hold.

Mary Ellen was up, drying her hair, already dressed for the hospital.

"You got early rounds, still?" I asked.

"Uh-huh. Where have you been?"

I grunted. "Had to see a man about a horse." She took that to mean I was getting laid. "You remember a case you told me about two years ago?" I said. "Eight- or ten-year-old girl you got into a fight over. You wanted to take her off the ventilator?"

She stared at me for a few seconds. I said, "Brain-stem infarcts. All locked in . . ."

"Gawd. Nancy Madsen."

"Yeah. That sounds familiar."

"Malc, why bring up Nancy at six in the morning?"

"I need some clinical history for an important case," I said.

"But you're not working," she said.

"Don't get technical. I've been thinking about Henry."

"What do you want to know about Nancy?"

"She was the one with the brain-stem strokes."

"Right."

"Not brain-dead."

"No. Worse. At best—or worst—we predicted she would have been awake and completely unable to talk, breathe on her own, or move a finger. Unable even to blink. Imprisoned in her own skull. I wanted to take her off the ventilator. Her respiratory failure was so severe her heart would have quit in about two minutes."

"But they didn't let you do it."

"No. And her lungs got better, but her brainstem didn't."

"Yeah, I remember. I used to see them all touring around the hospital. Broke your heart."

She nodded.

I hesitated. "Do you ever wish you had done anything differently?"

"If there had been anything to do differently, I would have done it."

"When you told me about the girl, we talked about the tragedy of our insufficiency. Somebody doesn't quite die and we hand her back to the family to drag around. Make them carry the weight of a medical failure."

"When someone dies you can cry and grieve and get over it and then get on with life—you know, have an actual life—or you can a carry around a formerly human albatross and live in an unending disaster."

I said, "Funny how the best and worst outcomes are indistinguishable at these extremes."

"It proves the universe is spherical."

"God may not play dice, but He's got a warped sense of humor."

She nodded.

"There was something you used to say in those kinds of cases. A summary statement."

"'Her disaster is *over*?'"

"Yeah, that's it."

"I say that all the time in the ICU," she said.

I nodded. "The patient's disaster is over. We should stop spreading it around." After a minute I said, "But you didn't know."

"Know? Know, like for sure? An absolute?"

"Yeah."

"Malcolm, you know there are no absolutes. In her case they wanted to wait to see if the brain would miraculously recover, and when it didn't it was too late. The family was stuck with the result." She was putting on her jacket and heading for the door. "Swelling goes down. You know how it works."

"Yeah. But it's good to review."

"You're a doctor. They didn't put those two little letters at the end of your name just because they wanted you to pass out antibiotics for colds and sore throats. Sometimes you have to make decisions in the land between what you know and what you can prove. It's where we live. You do it to help people."

I nodded and smiled at her. I said, "I know."

She nodded at me, closed the door, and left.

25

Hooker, two censuses ago, was a town of 10,300 souls. Like many such anachronistic towns, it is slowly wasting. Last census it was at 9,858.

The brochure from the Chamber of Commerce has a glossy picture of Herefords grazing on gently undulating pastures, with a windmill, Nebraska's favorite cliché, just this side of the horizon. Also a picture of two prepubescent boys gleefully holding up a stringer of undersized bluegills, and a picture of a father and son (presumably) ambling into a sunset, shotguns over shoulders, carrying a dead pheasant. If your town lacks demonstrable culture, has a monolithic and disappearing economic base, a shrinking population, and nothing on any restaurant menu more exotic than Chicken Kiev, deep-fried straight from the freezer, you have to go with what you got: fishing, hunting, simplicity, and cows. The tag line on the brochure is one I see everywhere here, even on the license plates: "Nebraska. The Good Life."

Thank God—and Dad—I had a license here.

When I lost my residency I didn't give up and run. I entered an appeal at Maricopa, citing the obvious issues. I also applied to seven other surgery residencies, in California, Oregon, and Utah. I stayed in the town house with Mary Ellen, though I had squandered part of our friendship. I picked up work in ERs like Glory while I awaited my fate.

When Mimi Lyle got me flushed out of Arizona, I thought I was merely taking an extended trip home to my folks. I wasn't running away, only hoping to reconnoiter. I needed work. I found Western Acute. I talked often to Adrienne. Mom cooked meals. Dad had strokes. I stayed.

At the end of two years my appeals had run aground in Arizona. Each of the residencies—initially seemingly so happy to find me a spot—had sequentially decided I was unworthy. I could easily imagine the facial expressions when they got the copies of the file from the Arizona board.

By then, luckily, I found I really did like ERs. Through experience and study and asking "dumb" questions, I was sufficiently up to speed to feel adequate. By now, it seems, I am adept.

It was obviously convenient for Western to book me here in Hooker, but I asked Adrienne to keep me moving; half my time has been splattered at Western Acute's various ERs around Nebraska and Kansas and South Dakota and Colorado. All in towns like Hooker—they're everywhere—"nice quiet little ERs where nothing ever happens."

I make enough to live on and even save a little. I've been able to pick up some of the things that naturally got away from me moving from school to school—photography, fishing, hunting, skiing.

At least once a month I get junk-mail job offers. "Exciting mid-sized city in America's Heartland, 45 minutes from a major university . . ." I called on a few of them. Theirs is a unique code; "three hours from the heart of Colorado skiing" means it's in Kansas, and the "three hours" assumes you own a rocket sled.

Adrienne told me when she pitches Hooker to any of her other charges, naturally she tells them it's "a quiet little ER where nothing ever happens." We laughed conspiratorially.

Just a few days ago, right here in Hooker, an anorectic dopehead with jailhouse tattoos pulled up with his two little kids in the back of the station wagon. One of the Wattle brothers I'd spent much of junior high school avoiding. He said he thought they needed antibiotics and he would take 'em on home. He was partly right.

The admitting nurse went out to the car, took one look at the blisters running from their feet up to a very cleanly demarcated line around their lower chests, realized they'd been forcibly dipped into very hot water, and called me for approval to send them straight to Lincoln to the Burn Center. We were standing, I knew, beside the perpetrator. I said in my best simple-country-doctor aw-shucks drawl that we oughta bring 'em on in and get 'em some IV fluids going. The look I gave the nurse said this was not negotiable.

The burns were forty-eight hours old. Both children—ages two and three—were massively infected, fevered, and dehydrated, bordering on shock. Dad said the kids splashed the hot water on each other while the tub was filling and he was called away to the phone. They all say that. We summoned the transport helicopter and the police.

ER work is mainly swollen ankles, twisted knees, bellyaches and backaches, coughs and anxieties. Lots of anxieties. It is surprising how often saying "You don't have anything that needs surgery today" or "Your pain almost certainly is not cancer" will melt the anxiety off faces.

Occasionally there's the life-threatening to keep your adrenal glands in shape. About once a year I save someone's life. Mostly, though, it's triage—sorting out the incoming. The well I send on their way and the sick I send to someone else, but it's not a trivial role.

It was never what I had in mind, though.

Which makes this new job in the Othello clinic intriguing. I've now done five consecutive Wednesdays there, and it's beginning to click. Annie Parrott is teaching me her routines for age-specific screening tests, what to tell people about vitamins C and E, and which smoking cessation programs sometimes get some traction with the locals.

The Henry Rojelio debacle came in the middle of Mary Ellen's third and final year of residency. That was about the time she admitted to herself she was an acuity junky: We had talked about it before I ever met Henry Rojelio. She did not want what many pediatricians want—a "general practice for children"—an office full of kids of all ages, colors, sizes, and degrees of wellness. Mary Ellen wanted the sick ones. She wanted a daily fight with Death even if losses were guaranteed.

Such a commitment is akin to religious vows. Most ICUs put an intensivist "on" for a week at a time. While on, your life is not your own. You can spend hour upon hour with a single child, doing bedside exams and procedures, checking esoteric lab values and adjusting your orders until your pen runs dry, explaining to parents and grandparents the limits of knowledge about the workings of the body and summoning whatever ghost of philosophy you like best to describe the whims of fate, then pronounce the child dead.

You maintain a veneer of professional detachment and melt down at home. You cannot do children's intensive care if you don't take it entirely seriously, but you can't survive if you take it too seriously. You live by finding balance, though the fulcrum is ever moving with the caseload and the caseload is unpredictable.

Then you get a week off to try to be normal.

I asked her if she knew what inside her made her want that kind of practice.

She said, "Does it matter?"

"Of course not," I said. "Regardless, they'll be lucky to have you. You'll be God's gift."

She applied for and got a fellowship in Pediatric Critical Care—children's ICU medicine—in San Francisco. From there she took a position as a staff intensivist at the Children's Hospital of Colorado in Denver. Two years later she was made the Director back at Maricopa.

Mary Ellen Montgomery is as good as they get. I know this by bits and pieces of intelligence from the little contact we had, from what I have heard from my other remaining friends in the area, and because I know Mary Ellen could not do it any other way.

She lives alone in a ranch-style house on the slope of Camelback Mountain in Scottsdale. She has never married, surviving on work and a long-distance affair with an architect in Portland.

HENRY, DAY SEVEN (CONTINUED)

The Rest.

After saying my final goodbyes to Henry Rojelio, I was a bedraggled mix of sorrow and agitation. With the help of the Inderal, I had managed to hide my state from Mary Ellen. After she left for work I tried to sleep, but only lay and watched the streaks of sunlight creep down the west wall.

I wanted to call Will Borden promptly at 8:00, tell him I had some puzzle pieces for him. But I pictured sitting before Borden and May, bouncing on my chair, laying out my tale, my theories, my explanations, with the real corpse over in the Maricopa PICU, lying still, but not yet dead, at least by the universal definition, as Mary Ellen's team did their tests, blissfully ignorant of my addition to Henry's IV nutrition. It was unlikely the detectives would pick up on something I did or said and drop everything and run over and stop the process, but I didn't trust myself to leave out exactly the right parts of the story.

So I had to wait. The town house felt like a cage.

Just before noon Mary Ellen called to let me know it was over.

I called Detective Borden. I told him I had some answers. I said, "You know, I guess, that Robin is a man." I told him about my phone call to Charlene through Cynthia and Monica.

He laughed. "Yeah. We know. Come on out. We'll go through it all when you get here."

I went for a long run, took a slow shower, and made myself sit down for lunch—table, chair, place mat, napkin, silverware, the whole bit. I put on dressy pants and shoes. I got my envelope with its adrenaline syringe from the refrigerator. I drove to Mesa, slower than usual. The Salt was receding.

I made myself walk and talk slowly, too. Will got me coffee. He and Ken looked surprisingly fresh. Another day at the office.

Borden handed me copies of the Board of Nursing file, then sat on the front of his chair, leaning on his knees, face close in. I stared at the blotchy xerox of the photo in the file; it looked like a broad, ruddy, grinning man with light hair and thin eyebrows. Will said, "An Englishman. Born in Bath, moved here eleven years ago. My guess is he was seeking the, shall we say, freer lifestyle of the 'confirmed bachelor' here in the U.S."

"Dead?"

"Two years ago. Cause of death listed as Kaposi's sarcoma. Along with a secondary diagnosis of some kind of cystic pneumonia."

"Pneumocystis pneumonia."

"Yeah, sounds right."

"AIDS."

"Yeah, that's what I figured." He shifted in his chair to an upright posture. "Basic, unglamorous police legwork fills in a lot of blanks. The morning after we met you at your condo, we went knocking at the

State Nursing Board. The photo and description pretty much speak for themselves. License lapsed about eighteen months ago, no response to renewal notices. Then it was renewed. No big deal. New address, new phone number. About three months ago. All back fees and penalties paid with a cashier's check."

"Not traceable."

"Not traceable."

May added, "I went over to the County Clerk's Office. Death certificate on file, dated, signed, et cetera, et cetera."

I nodded as I pictured Mimi, daughter of law enforcement, cooking up this, surely her most spectacular "cover story."

"You knew this when I was here for the polygraph."

They nodded.

"Why didn't you tell me?"

Ken said, "We're here to get information. Not give it."

"Okay," I said. "Here's the answer." I rubbed my eyes. I reminded myself to talk slowly and take pauses. Silences wouldn't kill me. "I don't know who she was. But I know why she did it." I felt them looking at me harder.

I explained in detail my affair with Professor Lyle, my attempts to have her professional deficiencies dealt with, my failed residency. I detailed her apparent campaign of revenge, right down to the bubble as a barrier, handing them the syringe of epinephrine as I did. They listened. Halfway through it Detective May started scribbling notes. They put on gloves before picking up the syringe. "It's only got epinephrine in it." I explained my "bioassay" in the dog lab.

"You put half the evidence into a dog?"

"Uh-huh."

Will said to his partner, "I told you doctors think they know everything." Ken nodded. "You doctors may know a lot, but you don't know shit about criminal evidence."

I nodded ruefully. "It seemed pretty important to know what was in the syringe. And it wasn't really a criminal case. Yet."

They smiled. Ken asked, "Couldn't the bubble have come into the syringe after it was used on Henry?"

"Well, it's possible. In theory," I said. "But in reality it's almost impossible. As it gets handled the incidental pressures that might move the plunger are always pushing it in, not pulling it out."

He said, "Mmmm. Not exactly something you could use in court."

I nodded. "There's more, though," I said. I explained exactly where in Henry's chart they could find a sample of "Robin's" handwriting and directions to a certain mountain hideaway. Ken wrote it down. I gave them every detail of our drive up toward Globe, the adobe cabin, Mimi's landmarks to find it, our confrontation, my ultimate escape, and where the bullet casings had fallen.

They listened, but didn't look excited. Ken scribbled some notes and rubbed his eyes. He repeated back to me for clarification the landmarks. "We'll be checking it out."

Borden said, "You said your 'Robin' drove an old Camaro?"

"Yeah."

"Black?"

"I thought it was dark blue, but I only saw it the one night."

"Because they found a black Camaro in the Salt River last night. Few miles out west of Tempe. Somebody saw the roof sticking out of the water. The river's falling. Not much in it but mud. No papers. The plates, though, are registered to Robin Benoit." He paused. "There was a leather jacket in the backseat."

I stared at him. "My jacket?" I said.

"So it would seem. There were some notes from the Glory Hospital in the pocket. It's in our evidence room," Ken said.

"Caked with mud, but there's still traces of blood smeared on it," Will added. "Whoever your 'Robin' is, she's very good at disappearing. No one who knew her has been able to give us a clue. Nothing from her phone bills or bank records, either. Just a chain of the normal type stuff that abruptly stopped five days ago. Though it was a really thin chain. Hardly any calls. No long distance. Not but about twenty-five checks written since the account was opened. And no final withdrawal, no forwarding address, no nothing."

We sat and stared at each other.

I said, "Seems they thought of everything."

May said, "Except the Nursing Board file."

I looked from face to face. "So let me guess what got you to knock on my door so fast. I mean, she hadn't been gone long when you guys paid me a visit."

"No, she hadn't," Borden said, "but the doc in the ER said you were fighting. Said it sounded like you were threatening her. The nurse said you wanted directions to her house."

"I wouldn't have hurt her."

"Maybe not. But they don't know that. And then 'Robin's' neighbors hear crashes and swearing from her house, and write down the license plate of a Datsun that came and went in the night."

I gave him a rueful smile.

Will smiled back. "I told you, when someone is reported missing we send a uniformed officer to the door. If there is no answer we gain entry, maybe break out a small window—they're cheaper to repair than door jambs—then look around. In this case the Uniform didn't find anything at first, but he thinks he's a hotshot so he looks all around and finds blood under the bathroom sink. We went back with Forensics. They found traces of broken glass on the kitchen floor and traces of blood all over the kitchen and bathroom."

Ken said, "The semen and spermicidal jelly on the sheets were good, too."

I nodded again. "But no 'toy box.' " I said.

"No. Whoever this phony 'Robin' is, she took her cash and contraceptives and left everything else there, even the money in her checking account. All to let suspicion fall on you."

"So who's the floater?" I asked.

"Don't know yet." A pause. "Like I said, those show up from time to time."

"Are the breasts made of silicone?"

Will smiled. "No."

"Not her," I said.

"We didn't think so." A pause. "And the victim?" Borden asked. "The kid? Where is he?"

"In the morgue at Maricopa. He died today."

He sighed. "I'm sorry."

I said, "Yes. It's really a tragedy. At least it's over, though."

After a few seconds I said, "I don't want to sound stupid, but all this is pretty important to my future. It seems there's been a murder. Is there any . . . Do you see any way there could be a case against Dr. Lyle?"

They looked at each other silently. After a few blinks, Ken May said to his partner, "You know, if we can find some evidence in the canyon—the gun and casings—we can tell the DA we're getting the syringe analyzed. . . ."

Will said to me, "Sure, we'll go look in the canyon. We'll get the notes from the kid's chart. We could go ask around the airport about our 'Robin,' but we don't even have a picture of her. And we'll go knock on Dr. Lyle's door and see if she's dumb enough to say the wrong thing." He turned to Ken. "I'm going to say right here I am not looking forward to going to the DA for a warrant. With what we got now we can't even call it a homicide. His death certificate probably says 'asthma.' All we have is the word of this ex-doctor who got trashed by his professor and now he thinks she's out to get him." He turned to me: "No disrespect intended, Dr. Ishmail."

"DA might laugh us off the force," Ken said.

Will said, "And if the DA can't or won't get us a warrant, we'll have to be real polite to Dr. Lyle. Even if we do get one I'm going to bet she's done a lot of housecleaning by the time we get there. There won't be a thing that would lead us to 'Nurse Robin.' So we'll do all the leg-work, sure, but I'm betting it comes to a big goose egg. We're not going to be able to do much unless we find 'Robin.' There's a lot of room to hide in this country and you can bet the Mesa PD ain't going to be looking door-to-door."

"But if I had left Dr. Lyle there to die?"

He thought for a few seconds. "Well, that would have made it all different, yes. We would have had to prove you did or didn't plot to kill her. That would have been interesting, but I suspect the evidence would have backed you up. We would have been proving your version of the events. With the physical findings at the scene, the note in the chart, an automatic search warrant, and a condo she had not been able to 'clean up,' we might have found 'Robin.' I think the picture would probably have been at least filled out enough to clear you."

May said, "And your not doing mouth-to-mouth resuscitation—

not saving her—would not have been the same as killing her. In a self-defense situation there's nothing says you have to go back and try to save the dying."

A few weeks after Henry's death, I called Detective Borden to see if they had uncovered anything that might help my case. Will described their search for the canyon with the adobe cabin. It took two days to find it. The day I told them about my "shoot-out" with Dr. Lyle, they asked a county deputy from Globe to go check it out. That night he reported back he couldn't find it. The first landmark I gave them was the large green sign saying "Tonto National Forest." Turns out there were several.

The next day they called an assistant ranger from the National Forest district office to help. He couldn't get away until the day after that. They drove up and together found the right set of ruts and trailed down to the cabin. The assistant ranger said, "Shit, I remember hearing there was an old adobe down in here, but they told me it burnt down."

Naturally there was no sign anyone had been there for a long, long time. No tracks, no gun, no bullet casings. Only wind.

Detective Borden said, "You know, Doctor, in your world, sometimes the patient dies. In ours, sometimes the bad guys get away."

My reinstatement hearing at Providence of Glory Hospital actually went better than predicted. Sally Marquam and her Executive Committee had their private powwow over a catered dinner, then invited me in to tell my side of the Henry happenings.

Of course, the key witness against me, "Robin," was not there. That was not the plus it might have been, though, since everyone there had heard the rumor that I had been suspected of killing her. I had no choice but full disclosure.

I handed out folders with a written synopsis of the events: Henry's code and resuscitation, how "Robin" had done it, the evidence that "Robin" wasn't Robin, and finally who had been behind it. I attached as appendices copies of the text material I had found at the Biomed Library and the journal articles about nefarious nurses. Last I included, as much for flavor as argument, photocopies of the cover page of the police file, replete with the file number. Unfortunately it was labeled "Missing Person," not "Homicide." While they were reading I picked at the food they gave me.

Mr. Schteichen, the CEO, maintained a look of incredulity through the whole thing. When they had all closed their folders, after a good long silence, he said, "I must say, Dr. Ishmail, I admire your chutzpah in trotting out this whole . . . tale." He said it with a note of condescension. I took it to mean *adios*. The next day I began looking for work in Nebraska.

Two days later I got the call from Sally Marquam. Instead of dismissal, though, it was a conditional reinstatement. She said Dr. Cunningham had argued vehemently that his fellow physician be treated as innocent until proven guilty. He apparently bullied the others into agreement. I could not tell from Ms. Marquam's telling whether Dr. Cunningham truly believed my version of the events or perhaps had some other reason for keeping me around. Maybe as "Staff Raconteur."

So I worked at Glory for another month. Then the administration signed an exclusive contract with the ER group that covered all of Tucson. I applied with them but they wanted nothing to do with me, answering politely that they had all their own folks lined up. I was left with hard-won clinical privileges at a hospital where a convenient business arrangement had me locked out.

My displacement was not quite complete, though. To this day I am licensed by the State of Arizona to practice within her borders as a physician and surgeon. For years I got to come back at intervals to meet with lawyers.

All of us expected a malpractice suit, so when I was served with the summons it was almost a relief. I expected a certain unity among the lawyers for my insurance company and those for the hospital, but it soon became clear I was seeing war dances done quietly with blandly painted wooden masks.

I soon figured out the interpretation of the dance: First, I was just a sideshow. All the lawyers knew, especially Ted Priestly, that juries are far likelier to stick it to a faceless hospital than a struggling young doctor.

Second, when Priestly and his team found out about the open police file, albeit a thin one, the hospital, as the employer of the putative criminal, looked like easy pickings. The hospital's best defense, though, was the lack of any evidence of anything. Their strategy, then, was to wait, forever if possible.

I thought my side should settle up cheap while the lawyers were focused on other prey and get on with life, but my insurance people, too, wanted to wait. An administrator friend explained to me why: They like the interest they earn on money they keep in reserve for big potential payouts—money they would otherwise have to refund to their policyholders under an agreement with the state medical association. As long as this wrongful death suit was open, they would be justified in keeping $2 million—the upper limit of my policy—in their very own FHA-backed home mortgage fund.

My lawyer, too, said that settling the matter would be crazy: First, he reminded me, I had not done a thing wrong. The claim against me had absolutely no merit and should be energetically defended. Second, there was relative advantage in uncertainty: I was better off in the job market with an unsettled claim hanging out there than a history of having lost a case, even if we got out cheap.

For added flavor we had, snooping around the edges, the reporter from the *Arizona Republic* who had written the original story about Henry's ER event. Not surprisingly he had been watching the public filings for Henry's name. As soon as the suit was filed he began calling everyone involved, even me. He got a chorus of "No comment." When the judge heard about it he issued a gag order, citing to the attorneys assembled before him the potential for a "firestorm of innuendo" and making it clear any leaks would mean fines and jail time.

All the reporter could generate was a back-page filler that the story "first broken by this newspaper" had come to legal action, that So-and-So had said "No comment," So-and-So had said "No comment," and the proceedings had been sealed by the judge. Since he didn't know why they had been sealed, he could not generate even a whiff of legitimate implication. It was boring reading.

So no one was in any rush.

Except Daniel Mendoza and Ted Priestly. They wanted money, and waiting for an unspecified number of years had no appeal. The hospital people said they were happy to wait for the imaginary criminal to be brought forward. Compromise was inevitable. Ultimately the two parties negotiated a $1.1 million settlement from the hospital's reserves.

My lawyers refused all settlement offers, though, doubting Mr. Priestly would ever take us to court when his key witness would be entirely unavailable to testify and could be shown to have used the name and license of a dead male nurse—Robin Benoit. So we waited, stone-faced. Soon enough the Court got fed up with inactivity and told the Priestly side to fish or cut bait: They dropped the claim. Hard to think of it as vindication, but better than any of the real-world alternatives.

Feeling somewhat immune and maybe a bit cocky, I called the *Republic* reporter. I asked him how he had first heard about Henry's case. He said, "Somebody phoned in a tip. Happens all the time. Anonymously. Didn't leave a name but she said she was a nurse and appalled by what she'd seen. I started asking around. Why? Any idea who it might have been?"

Once in a while, Adrienne gets a call from a tiny-town Marcus Welby who needs a one-or two-week break and has to pay for imported coverage. Being mobile and licensed over millions of acres of grassland, I seem to qualify. Last month I went for nine days to Cedar Knoll, Colorado, population 910.

I told this one to Adrienne but I'm not certain she quite felt the jaws of the trap.

As an intern, I did six weeks of obstetrics and gynecology. At Maricopa that meant I saw just about everything there was to see—high risk, low risk, smiling faces and streaming tears. I learned that birth is a wondrous, beautiful, happy process—until, abruptly, it's not. Everyone involved—Mom, Dad, grandmas, grandpas, techs, nurses, and docs—is smiling away, thinking everything is groovy and then—Bam!—big trouble. Lots of yelling, running, bleeding, turning blue, brain damage, and death. Nothing like it.

The worst are the total surprises, of course. Everyone is planning on a christening but ends up at a funeral. But some of the disasters are at least partly predictable. Infection and prematurity, of course. Diabetic moms, hypertensive moms. Really small or really big babies. Placentas awry. Twins are bad, triplets are worse. Anything more than that is a freak show. In the human uterus more are less.

From that rotation I give you the Kletts. They had wanted kids for years. Already in their mid-thirties, they finally managed to conceive triplets, reportedly with no pharmaceutical aid. So blessed, she did everything right. Never smoked. Made every clinic appointment and took her vitamins.

Kept the faith even when her husband went away to prison—his offense I did not ask about.

Through some miracle, she carried those three fetuses to thirty-seven weeks—term. She was scheduled for a cesarean section within days.

But she got a funny feeling. It was a Saturday night. She came in to be checked. The Chief Resident, who had been following her in clinic, came in from home and saw her himself. Carlos Alvarez. A polished individual, a Spaniard by birth, well dressed, articulate, and as near as I could tell, undisputedly knowledgeable. He examined her by hand, by stethoscope, and by ultrasound. All three babies looked perfect, swimming around in their allotted amniotic fluid, hearts strong, regular, not too fast, not too slow. Then, for no reason other than "good measure," they put Mrs. Klett on a monitor for two hours—not a single contraction. Dr. Alvarez explained everything to her and her mother, then sent the five of them home.

When she came back at nine o'clock the next morning, all three babies were dead. Cause unknown.

Mr. Klett did not arrive until 1:00 P.M. It had taken our social worker the intervening four hours to get him a one-day release from state prison. It was clear the authorities wanted him back very soon and he would not otherwise be visiting for some years yet.

An anesthesiology resident got her snockered beyond meaningful consciousness and we induced labor. Mr. Klett stood with his wife through three stillbirths, crying and clenching his teeth.

The dad wanted nothing to do with Dr. Alvarez, that "slick-talking taco bender," so it fell to me to sit with them for thirty minutes and try to help them understand that we doctors don't understand some things that are very important to some people. And to try to deflate Mr. Klett's need for vengeance. And to stare back at them blankly when they asked me how they were ever going to have children, especially with him still tucked away.

This particular memory strongly colors for me any high-risk OB encounters.

The Marcus Welby of Cedar Knoll, whose practice I was covering, must surely be as lonely as he is anachronistic. The only doctor for miles. He bought the local hospital to keep it open. Sold his house. Lives in a double-wide mobile home. Altruism and community commitment are not in question.

My second morning in clinic I did a prenatal check on a twenty-two-year-old. All smiles. Only three and a half months along. First pregnancy. But two strikes against her: High blood pressure needing medication even before she got pregnant. That's high risk. Twins. Also high risk. In combination about as high risk as an early pregnancy can be.

The thing about high blood pressure in pregnancy is it leads to inadequate blood flow to the fetuses, and they grow poorly and tend to curl up their toes and die under stress. Stress like labor and delivery or even getting big. Or, late in the pregnancy, blood pressure can shoot up suddenly and cause big ugly strokes in young mothers.

The thing about twins is they compete for blood flow. They can be chronically stressed and ready to die. They are usually premature arrivals simply because the uterus is overstretched and good and ready to empty itself once it reaches a certain size. Then, if the grown-ups involved even attempt vaginal delivery, the first may come out okay, then the second gets locked into a bad angle while its placenta is leaving the building. If the uterus clamps down, the baby is stuck; if it relaxes, Mom hemorrhages like an outgoing tide.

If you cannot do a C-section on five minutes' notice, you have no business attempting twins. If you don't have someone ready to resuscitate two preemies, you have no business doing twins. I knew this town of nine hundred could not muster a C-section in thirty minutes, nor probably two hours, since there was no anesthetist available. And no one to tend to preemies if the good doctor was doing the section. I don't think there was lack of desire but surely there was a lack of modern resources.

It was all I could do to smile back at the young mother-to-be. I measured her uterus, checked her weight gain, checked her blood pressure, made sure she was taking her blood pressure pills and her iron and vitamins, told her alcohol or tobacco would kill her babies, patted her shoulder, and sent her out.

I dictated a lengthy chart note describing how I thought her management should go. I tried to drop huge hints that the woman and her future babies deserved to see a specialist.

Just as I hung up the dictation microphone the office nurse came in. I asked her if she thought there was any chance the doctor might possibly consider referring this smiling victim of circumstance on down the road to, say, at least an obstetrician if not a high-risk pregnancy specialist.

The nurse's reply is still a classic of revealing—perfectly—the unintended. She said emphatically, "Oh, no! Doctor is really looking forward to this. He hasn't delivered twins in years!"

So that was my moral dilemma for the day. Should I have called back the hopeful girl and told her to find her way out of the 1930s and avoid a stroke or a baby with cerebral palsy or both? Or should I respect the doctor-patient relationship that I had only stumbled upon, an interloper, wet behind the ears, carrying assurance of neither success nor failure, only gross estimates of probabilities? Like betting a life on the turn of a card.

Or three lives.

"High risk."

Since my aborted residency I have promised myself I would stop taking these things so seriously. But they pop up like corpses in horror movies.

Retelling, though, is reliving, and reliving is, in some small ways, getting to revise.

Two weeks ago, after my Wednesday in Othello, I came home and dug through old boxes until I found my bear's face belt buckle. I took it to a Western clothing store in Ogallala the next weekend and bought an expensive hand-tooled belt for it to cinch around me. Been wearing it ever since. It reminds me to ponder—even to articulate to myself at times—a possible connection to the spiritual. To things Larger.

Last week I made an offer on twenty-nine acres along the Dismal River, thirteen miles out of town. A place I used to go for catfish as a kid. "Dismal" is an unfair name. Sure it's muddy, but so is every other river in the state. The entire riverbank is covered by mature cottonwood trees, four of the biggest dead a few years from beaverkill. They house redheaded woodpeckers. There are morel mushrooms nearly every spring, wood ducks in the summer, and pheasants in the fall. In the winter there are bald eagles. I love it out there.

The acreage is mostly bottomland, prone to floods about every fifteen years or so, but there is an old dike running through the middle. The weed canes and grass are over eight feet tall in the open areas on the upland side of the dike. Best of all, there's a small hillock at the northwest corner, sparsely covered with little cedar trees and a couple of juvenile cottonwoods. That is the area where the morels show up. There is a spot just beyond there, between trees, where I want to build a small house, if I can get the permits. From the front rooms I'll be able to see the river. Maybe Mom and I can get Dad to come sit there.

I couldn't leave, anyway. Dad fell again a couple weeks ago. Mom saw the whole thing this time. She swears he was just trying to go too fast and tripped. She wants him home. I'd be an ogre to argue again for a nursing home.

So with him on her hands she deserves whatever help I can muster. Which means Hooker will be home. Moving to Maine or Oregon or Tahiti is out of the question, for now.

Only since the second stroke have I realized how much they are part of the heart and soul of Hooker. People come to see Dad at least once a week. Old friends in from the ranches and patients from down the street. They bring food and plants and cookies and wine. The

guests and Mom talk. I guess he listens. I think I saw him smile once,
but it could have been a reflex.

Seeing Mary Ellen again, after these years of oblivion, brought a tide
of feelings from their supposed retirement. We'd been the best of
friends. We had been through all flavor of romantic choices together.
She knew my weaknesses.

She had seen me pass up a guiltless but cheap encounter with an
RN only because she was married—however unhappily—but take to a
sex-for-sex's-sake hookup with a fast-food manager I met at a party.
She knew the desperado's rules of engagement most of us used: Cheap
sex would not hurt anyone if the consenting adults had identical and
appropriately low expectations. And it might help.

Still, there had been no one like Mimi Lyle.

At first I gave Mary Ellen no clues because it didn't come up. We
were never ones to tap the other on the shoulder and say "Guess who
I'm fucking." Mimi, of course, quickly convinced me of the necessity—
on her part more than mine—for absolute silence, even on the radar
screens of half-formed suspicion. After Monty and Mimi had their toe-
to-toe in the PICU, I thought Mimi might best remain my little secret.
After my epic debauch with Madame Lyle in front of the fireplace in
the canyon, I did not think I was completely outside Mary Ellen's capacity for respect, but the hole I was in was pretty deep.

When I learned of Miriam Lyle's operating inabilities, or more
importantly, her refusal to act in her patients' interests, it seemed that
anyone who had ever been on Mimi's side must surely burn in hell.

When I was not renewed in the residency I told Monty a skeleton
version of the flap over Mimi's inabilities. I left out sex and drugs. She
could not believe that was sufficient to get me fired. I held out my own
incredulity. She knew I was hiding something. But my hemming and
hawing had become a habit.

When Henry Rojelio fell into my lap and I lost my paltry job in
Glory, things swirled quickly out of control, but I mustered a passable
lie for Mary Ellen; lying is easiest done to those who trust you. I told
Mary Ellen the Glory Hospital had hung me out to dry when the story

hit the press. All along I had good intentions for a full disclosure some night over dinner, but I never came through.

My passive acceptance of stasis on the plains became a passive choice. One I denied, for years, having made. Living away from Mary Ellen, working my itinerant's jobs, schtooping Cheryl on the every-third-month plan and whomever else might understand and accept and in some cases welcome emotional distance as the foremost aspect of my character, it was easiest to pretend Mary Ellen did not want to talk to me.

But what I'd thought was hell turned out to be purgatory: Mary Ellen called three months ago to tell me about a message. The message was a reprieve, not by its contents, by its point of delivery.

Mary Ellen's call came on a Monday morning. I'd just gotten home from a sixty-hour shift in a quiet little ER where, truly, nothing happened. Boring days and fitful nights in a saggy bed. I had read a mediocre spy novel and watched two baseball games. After shifts like that I feel like skiing for ten hours straight or running a marathon. That particular Monday, though, it was 104 degrees with 75 percent humidity, so neither seemed likely. When she called I was looking at baseline torpor with intermittent periods of ennui, ruined only by the need to mow the lawn at my rented house.

Mary Ellen said my mother had given her my number. She told me there was a message for me on her answering machine. She said the caller had asked that she relay it on to me without listening to all of it. The caller said to tell me it was from "Robin."

The small dorsal hairs on my neck stood up. I probably gasped. Here was one last shot at vindication. I said nothing.

Mary Ellen said, "Who's Robin?"

After a pause I said, "Robin is dead."

There was a long pause. I wasn't picturing Robin; I was seeing Mary Ellen's face.

She said, "Do you want me to mail you the tape?"

I thought. I said, "No." There was a pause. "Keep it there. I'll be there by tomorrow night."

It was summer; the days were long. I got to Mary Ellen's just before sunset the following night. She seemed guardedly happy to see me. I was barely out of the car when she came to me, threw her arms around me, and kissed my cheek. I was as emotionally stiff as a sixth grader.

"The message awaits," she said. "Though I'm hoping you'll be able to speak to me at some point."

"Mary Ellen." I looked at her. "I don't know what I can say."

She looked at me. "What's it been? Three years since our last conversation?"

"About that."

"How have you been?"

I smiled. "Stable."

She smiled.

Mary Ellen sat me in her den.

"I think I'd like a drink," I said. She brought Scotch, studying me.

"I guess you'll want to listen to it alone. I'll be in the kitchen." She left and shut the door.

The tape held a lightning bolt. An electric voice from the past, *vox ex machina*, though not a *deus ex machina*. Not my ticket out of limbo. It was evidence of the inadmissible sort—just like an unsigned letter, it could not be verified. No one would be coming forth to testify. There are no witnesses, only we perpetrators.

Hello, Dr. Montgomery. This is actually a message for a friend of yours, Malcolm Ishmail. I tried to get his address or phone number from the Medical Board in Phoenix, but it was like they never heard of him. So I asked for yours. I figure you two should be married by now, so, well, anyway, if you could get this message to him, somehow . . . And maybe he should just hear it himself, if you don't mind. I'm sorry but there just isn't any other way.

Just tell him it's from Robin.

[A pause.]

Malcolm. It's me, Robin, or I should say, the woman you knew as Robin. I guess you figured out I wasn't really Robin Benoit, him being dead and all. And you can figure of course that I can't use my real name. I really wish . . . [A pause.]

Your old friend, Dr. Lyle, told me things would go different. God, was she wrong. She told me it was a super-short-acting drug, the resuscitation would go okay and the kid would be fine, but that we—she—the report! . . . [Her voice was trembling.] . . . the report I was going to file would be damaging enough to you to get you out of the state, maybe out of medicine, probably for good.

She . . . she said you were a bad doctor. You had bungled surgical cases, and lied and hurt people. She told me you had tried to destroy her reputation. She said you were out to get her because she had reported you and gotten you fired from the residency.

Oh, I hated you so much. At first. You never knew that, did you? When I heard what you had said and written. But ever since the boy totally coded in the ER, I wanted to explain to you that I never meant to hurt him, really. I wouldn't have done that. If I had known.

Mimi . . . Dr. Lyle . . . is my mother.

You must think I'm so evil. That's why I called. I've come to realize some things about my mother. She's not the saint I thought she was.

I'm getting married, Malcolm. That's what got me thinking about all of this again. We want to have kids . . . [She was sniffling.] Once in a while, I remember what I did. I have nightmares. Awful . . . [A stuttering deep sigh.]

I have to make up what I can. I thought about trying to see you, or writing you, to try to, I don't know, tell you I never meant to really hurt that boy like that. But I have to be completely untraceable.

Mom may have problems, as a doctor. But I know she is really good. She has done so much good for so many people. You must not have seen. All the good things. You never saw that. How could you have said those things? About her? [Her voice trailed off.]

I never knew her when I was a kid. My dad's parents raised me. They were always sort of vague about my mother, told me she was sort of . . . gone . . . like off in the wilderness, I imagined, doing these really great things to help people. Like a missionary in Africa.

When I was in nursing school, though, she wrote to me, then we finally met. It was so great. To finally know my mother and see that she really was doing great things for people.

She told me she was pregnant when she left my dad. She told me she left him 'cuz he beat her. And why, when I came along, she had to give me to Dad's parents to raise. She had nothing for a little girl.

She said her career was her life. Like it was her baby, you know, for some women.

You know she didn't even know that the real Robin was a man until those detectives came to question her? Afterward she called me to tell me to be extra careful. She told me she rechecked the obituary from the paper and it just talked about a nurse, never used a "he" or "she." The obit writer probably didn't know either. [A laugh.]

And she said you told her we had sex but she knew you were lying. I think even the idea of it makes her blow a gasket, if that's any kind of consolation to you. [Another pause.] Maybe that's why I did it.

Mom—Mee-em . . . [A deep breath.]

Don't try to find me. You can't. I left Arizona right after you yelled at me in the ER. That was all part of the plan. I've never been back. You can understand, I'm sure, why I need to be someone else. I have a pretty good life, now. I gave up nursing after all that. I'm selling real estate. What a laugh, huh?

Henry wasn't really much of a . . . he didn't have a life ahead of him, from everything I read about and heard about. But that doesn't change what we did. Nothing would make that okay.

And I didn't know, even when I did it, what to believe about you. When I worked with you I had a hard time believing you were so awful. You seemed like a good doctor. You did a good job and cared about people.

But I did it anyway. To you and to Henry. I went through with it because it was all I could do. And then it all . . . it all fell apart. . . . [She was crying again.] And I could see that.

Mimi said she couldn't wait forever for a crisis to show up in that little ER when we were both on shift. She said we could make our own without hurting anybody. I mean, it wasn't even supposed to be a full-CPR code, it was just supposed to be respiratory. He was going to quit breathing, you wouldn't believe it, you'd take a little extra time, but you would breathe for him until he could do it on his own again. Then I would write up all the little things you had missed or waited too long over, and they'd pull your license. Mimi said in a crisis everybody can be second-guessed. She called it the "basis of the whole malpractice industry."

You picked up the epinephrine syringe like she thought you would, but . . . God, it all went to shit!

And I had done it. I needed to know what you knew. Mom told me not to worry, but God, I was so freaked. I thought I could feel you out, so to speak, over dinner. Then, it seemed you kind of liked me, so I figured I might as well make it all really confusing, buy time to go ahead with the report to the hospital, like Mom wanted. She had the money. She came up with the plan to get me out of town. "To lay down the cover," she called it. It was too late to do anything else.

[She sniffled and gulped.] Malcolm, all I wanted to say . . . to say was, I hope you're happy. Somehow. I am sorry for what I helped do—what I did to you. I am . . . way . . . sorrier . . . for what happened to the boy, but I wouldn't know where to begin to apologize. . . .

I am so sorry. [Deep sniffles.]

But, all in all, I guess Mimi got her way with you, didn't she? [Sniffling. Clicks.]

Coming from the den, I must have looked to Mary Ellen—correctly—like someone who had heard a ghost. She said, "Robin isn't dead after all?"

"I think I need to talk to the police." I didn't explain.
She bit her lip.

She kindly put me up for the night in her guest room. Claiming exhaustion from the drive I said little.

The next morning I called Will Borden. I said I had something I thought he'd be interested in. He said to come on out to Mesa.

I asked him if he knew any good lawyers.

He laughed. He said he still didn't think I needed one, but he rattled off a few names.

That was the morning I shared my story with Gerry deLee. With his reassurances—incomplete as they were—fresh in my ears, I drove to Mesa. I took the tape to Detective Borden, though I know what he would say. Ken May was gone—retired on disability. I walked into Will's office bearing the cassette like a crumbling map to secret treasure.

He said the file was, of course, still open.

We got coffee and he pulled a tape player from the evidence room. He nodded all the way through the message, but after it was finished shook his head. "I don't doubt a word of it, but it's just more file filler. Without a real live 'Robin' we're just talking to ourselves."

As expected.

Will Borden said he knew, at least, that Mimi Lyle and her daughter, aka Robin Benoit, had committed murder.

He said he knew he could not prove it.

I nodded. "It's where we live."

Outside the Mesa PD, I thought about driving straight home to Stasis on the Plains.

Something—gravity—pulled me to Maricopa first.

It occurred to me to try the doctors' parking lot again but I was drawn to a slot marked "Visitor." It felt better.

I went up to Dr. Hebert's office. Marie didn't recognize me, but when Dr. Hebert heard my name in the anteroom he called out, "Gawddamn, Ishmail! They ain't kilt you?" He was genuinely glad to see me. I told him about my stasis in Nebraska. He said, "You oughta be applyin' again. You surely done your penance." I told him it really wasn't that bad.

He said he was sorry he hadn't been able to help more. I told him he'd helped tremendously. I asked him if Dr. Lyle was still at Maricopa. He said, "Still here? Shit, she's a frikkin' full pro-fuckin'-fessor.

Still puttin' out her version of the Show. Lyin' still, about why her patients are dyin'. And ain't nobody askin' no questions anymore. I think that woman is half voodoo, son."

I went back downstairs, bound only for my car and home on the plains. I was going to page Mary Ellen, tell her I was truly sorry, but I would not be sticking around, that I'd gotten old and stuck in certain habits and that I'd definitely call someday. My own ongoing lie.

But I stopped in the Lobby of the Seething Masses. It had been redecorated with a massive mural depicting the various peoples who had successively elbowed their way into the Valley of the Sun. The faces in the painting were intended to be ethnic generalizations, but to me they looked familiar. I thought I saw Henry Rojelio's baby brother in there.

I looked around the lobby. The real live versions were bustling or creeping through, some bringing candy and cards and balloons to the ones they loved, some struggling with casts and walkers, all trusting that we'd be good enough when they needed us.

There, in the Lobby of the Seething Masses, across from the mural, I saw a new glass case with the names and office numbers of all the faculty. Miriam Lyle, MD, Professor of Neurological Surgery, was on the top floor. There, in silent defiance of Professor Lyle's flowering career, I changed course. I chose to lose no more.

I paged Mary Ellen to see when she would be home for dinner.

Instead of driving with my head down, I went to the grocery and got the best food I knew how to cook.

When Mary Ellen got home I put a hot meal in front of her. I saw the magic smile I had given up. I told her I was sorry. Then I explained every detail, starting with the first time I made Mimi laugh.

She said, "I'm glad you're back."

I found amazing the size of the hole I had cut in my life by keeping Mary Ellen away.

I came home to Nebraska then and went back to work, different.

Robin's message, by virtue of her sending it through Mary Ellen Montgomery, achieved her intended result: It made me happier. For what she did to me, I forgave her. Henry's forgiveness or that from his family would, for now, remain beyond any of us.

Now, having retold, I have relived. If one is blessed he may get a reprieve. I called Mary Ellen yesterday and invited her to come visit. I offered the usual suspect excuses: I said my folks hadn't seen her since medical school graduation. I said she needed a break from her work. I gave her a glowing preview of the wildlife at the Dismal River.

But I ended with "I'd really like to see you."

She said, "Yes. I'd like that."

One final thing: Yesterday after my eight hours in the Othello clinic I nearly cried to the sky before driving home. One of Dad's old patients, a seventyish man with mild diabetes and an overgrown prostate, came in to see me. That is, his wife drove him twenty-seven miles to see me. She told me the names of two other people who were going to be doing the same thing. People I knew only vaguely as living in Hooker. They were having their records sent from Dad's old office to the clinic in Othello. He said they're going to be seeing me from now on.

They want me to be their doctor.

ENDNOTE

Every patient story, except those of Henry Rojelio, Keith Coles, and Susan McKenzie, is drawn from the case histories of the author.